ALCHEMY AND A CUP OF TEA

THE TOMES AND TEA SERIES

rebecca thorne

ALCHEMY AND A CUP OF TEA

A COZY FANTASY BREWED WITH MAGIC AND ROMANCE

BRAMBLE

TOR PUBLISHING GROUP / NEW YORK

This is a work of fiction. All of the characters, organizations, and events portrayed in this novel are either products of the author's imagination or are used fictitiously.

ALCHEMY AND A CUP OF TEA

Map by Rebecca Thorne
Chapter ornaments by Amphi
Tip-in illustration by Perci Chen

A Bramble Book
Published by Tom Doherty Associates / Tor Publishing Group
120 Broadway
New York, NY 10271

www.torpublishinggroup.com

Bramble™ is a trademark of Macmillan Publishing Group, LLC.

The Library of Congress Cataloging-in-Publication Data is available upon request.

ISBN 978-1-250-33327-8 (trade paperback)
ISBN 978-1-250-33328-5 (ebook)

Our books may be purchased in bulk for promotional, educational,
or business use. Please contact your local bookseller or the Macmillan Corporate
and Premium Sales Department at 1-800-221-7945, extension 5442, or
by email at MacmillanSpecialMarkets@macmillan.com.

First Edition: 2025

Printed in China

0 9 8 7 6 5 4 3 2 1

To all the publishing professionals who deal with my terrible sense of humor and impulsive nature—for without their guidance, I would have enthusiastically titled this book *Fuck It, Let's Try Coffee*.

THE REALM

DRAGON COUNTRY

TAWNEY

KYARON

THE QUEENDOM

VELLIA

THE CAPITAL

NATILAU

ERCON

LEONOL

1

Reyna

Kidnapping a queen in the middle of her own palace was bold. In a past life, Reyna might have admired the careful planning and sheer audacity of such an operation. Mapping the Grand Palace's hidden passageways, bribing her officials to look away, timing it *just right* to exit the Capital with an unconscious sovereign after the alarm had been raised.

Reyna missed all of that, for obvious reasons, but she'd thwarted enough royal abductions to surmise how this one must have gone.

It would be bold indeed . . . with any other sovereign. However, Reyna *wasn't* any other sovereign. Reyna was a tea maker, a bookseller, a former guard to a tyrant queen, and spouse to the Realm's most powerful mage. Reyna's comrades included councilmembers, scholars, lords, pirates, spies, and the dragons themselves.

Which made *this* kidnapping downright stupid.

Reyna almost felt bad for them.

Almost.

They'd kept her blindfolded, which was . . . an attempt at proper kidnapping procedure, at least. It also meant she was purposefully obstinate as her captors manhandled her off a wagon. It was covered with a burlap tarp, and she tangled herself in it. When they finally wrenched it off her, she made every attempt to trip, collapse on them, feel for weapons and the like.

A few daggers, a sword. Nothing she could swipe with her hands tied, but good to know.

"Still woozy?" one of the captors jeered, jerking her upright.

Reyna didn't deign to respond to that. Instead, she assessed what she could of her surroundings. They were likely in the western Queendom, judging by the arid winter climate. The air smelled of dirt and dry grass. The wagon's wheels had bumped along an increasingly uneven road, which implied they'd left any congested travel routes and had arrived somewhere long abandoned.

"Hurry up. This way," another of them grunted.

The first one released her, pushing her forward.

All right, then.

Reyna tripped over a nonexistent stone. The ground hit her hard, scuffing her knee, sending pain through her shoulder, but it worked. One of them hissed indignation. "Don't *damage* the goods. Get her up!"

Reyna pushed to her feet, making a show of staggering upright—which, to be fair, was mildly difficult with her wrists tied behind her back. She finally allowed a bit of a smile to show. "Perhaps removing the blindfold would make this an easier process?"

"Nice try." The first captor scoffed.

"You're hardly hiding anything." Her tone was reasonable, almost friendly. "Judging by the light, it's early morning. Blue locke loses its efficacy after a half a day, so we must be fairly close to the Capital. Considering the dirt and rocks, and the fact that the air is clearly thinner, I'm guessing we're at one of the watchtowers on the western border?"

A sharp intake of air, and another captor whispered, "How did she know that?"

Reyna tilted her head. "My point is, the blindfold isn't accomplishing what you think. If you want me uninjured, you can haul me inside better without it."

A quick exchange by her captors, and finally one of them ripped it off. The morning sun was bright, blinding, and Reyna squinted past watery eyes. Sure enough, a squat watchtower, decaying from centuries of disuse, loomed before her.

"Inside, queenie."

"Your wish is my command," Reyna replied, her eyes cutting across the grounds. Five people patrolling—potentially six if one was covering the back of the watchtower. Six additional captors stood armed to the teeth, watching as she was hauled toward the door. Another one urged the donkey and wagon toward a squat hill, where a few pine trees offered coverage from above. Which implied, at least subtly, that they were anticipating overhead surveillance.

Not unwise, considering Kianthe was about to be livid.

Still, this was such an odd mix of preventative tactics and utter lack of protocol. She'd have hidden the wagon, but *never* unmasked a prisoner. Honestly, it was an embarrassment that tactic worked.

The two men leading her inside made fourteen so far. Most of them waited outside; the stone hallway she was shoved into was tight, narrow, which meant her captors had to stand in front of and behind her. When it opened into a wider hallway, she counted two more women standing guard.

So, sixteen captors. More than she expected, but not so many she was in real trouble.

Not if she played this right, anyway.

"Bit different from your fancy palace, hmm?" the lead captor drawled. His grip on her arm was rough, and his backup flanked her left.

Reyna's steps were measured, and she held her chin high. The confident posture was a ruse; after the blue locke, her head pounded and her body felt weak. But revealing that could mean a world of difference later.

"I only assumed the throne two seasons ago," Reyna replied. "To the contrary, this is far more familiar terrain."

And it was. This watchtower was one of many that used to

guard the borders between the Queendom and Shepara. It was a relic from a time when war could erupt at any moment, and the centuries had eaten at its hasty construction. The place was crumbling, the crevices of its stone walls speckled with moss, the ceiling open to the elements in some areas. The main building was flat and winding, intended to protect the guards inside with tight passages and few windows. The actual watchtower would be large and open, but it was deeper into the building.

A curious choice for a captive . . . especially a royal one. Considering her country now had excellent relations with Shepara, this hideout put her squarely between two very motivated governments.

How many armies would Kianthe bring to rescue her?

A smile flitted across Reyna's lips at the thought. Her moonstone—a spelled connection between her and her wife, no matter the distance—was inert now. Most likely, Kianthe was grudgingly pulling herself awake to open their bookshop. She might already be coordinating with Matild to stock the morning's pastries. Word of Reyna's kidnapping wouldn't have reached Tawney yet . . . and Gods forbid when it did.

Another tight hallway forced them to move single file—and again, they chose one captor in front, one behind. Another amateur move; she'd have kept a prisoner in front of her and a weapon out, just in case he tried anything. Her sword had been removed, but they missed at least three knives while she was unconscious.

"Are you rebels to the new regime?" Reyna tilted her head. "Sympathetic to Tilaine? You must know that her half sister is running our new parliament."

"We should have gagged her instead," the captor in front drawled.

The one behind her forcibly pushed her forward.

Hmm. Reyna swallowed her next statement, assessing his tone. It didn't seem frustrated at the Queendom's recent coup—she could pin *that* sentiment instantly, although dissenters were fewer and fewer in number after two seasons of a calmer rule.

Not frustrated, no. He sounded . . . disinterested.

So, this wasn't personal to him. Then it was all for a payout? She'd assumed they were united by some common ideal, but if these men were merely hired muscle, that simplified things. Those propelled by coin were those who'd flee at the first sign of conflict—and she had every intention of introducing said conflict, after such a rude end to last night.

They arrived at the exact kind of cell Reyna expected: a windowless stone room with only a door of lattice metal—studded with rusting rivets—for company. The floor was wood, but the layer of grime that coated every other surface was surprisingly absent over the worn grain—perhaps they'd cleaned for her? That level of decorum was absent now, of course. They tossed her inside, the metal door squealing like a pig as they wrenched it shut. The hinges probably hadn't seen oil in a century.

A clean floor and decaying cell door. What a curious combination.

Reyna sat upright, feigning disdain. Her white shirt—embroidered in gold, intended for a regal appearance after a day in court—was smeared in dirt from the journey, and her meticulous bun had started to come loose. With her back to the stone wall, her fingers expertly located the sheath sewn into the hem of her pants. The thin, sharp knife was meant for this exact purpose, and she used it to slice her restraints.

Oblivious, her captors locked the lattice door with a huge, ancient key, peering at her through the metal bars. "Get comfortable," the lead captor said. "As comfortable as a queen can on the floor, anyway. You'll be here for a while, *Your Excellency.*"

At his side, his comrade laughed.

Reyna squinted at him. She'd been more concerned with counting men and assessing floor plans before this, but now he had her full attention. "Do I know you?"

Both men stiffened. The one she had addressed scrubbed his short beard, blue eyes glinting. "You don't. I never met a queen afore last night." His voice was dark, but his hand drifted to the short, wicked sword at his hip.

A sword that clearly hadn't been sharpened, cleaned, or oiled in years. It wasn't even sheathed, just secured in a leather loop at his belt. She'd have been more intimidated by Matild wielding a fire poker.

Reyna kept her newly free hands hidden, coiling up the rope and resheathing the thin knife, just in case. She made the motion look like she was searching for a comfortable spot on the wooden floor. "No, I remember you. You came to New Leaf for an assignment. In Tawney." He flinched, and her lips quirked upward. "It was last winter—do you remember? Our shop hand offered you the envelope, but I was wiping tables near the front door."

Bandits rarely came to their shop anymore, but Reyna always made a point of memorizing their faces. The Realm's main bandit encampment was on the northwestern tip of Shepara, nestled in a mountain range wedged between the ocean and the Northern Bay. Ceasing their operations hadn't been a priority, but if someone was telling these men to kidnap royalty, perhaps she and Kianthe should address them properly.

"Wha—" He cut himself off, grabbing his comrade's shoulder and twisting him forcefully away from Reyna. His fervent whispers were laughably audible. "You said she was a *queen,* not working for the boss!"

"She *is* a queen," the other hissed. "We stole her from the Grand fucking Palace. Don't be a moron."

"I ain't losing my job over this—"

"This *is* our job. Handed to us *from* the boss, remember? Big fancy request from someone 'important.'" The air quotes were as mocking as a physical hand gesture could get. He huffed in frustration. "He must know who we took."

Reyna leaned against the cell's back wall, swallowing a yawn. One would think being unconscious all night would mean she was well-rested now, but blue locke only ensured a ruthless headache, not fulfilling sleep. The aftereffects of the flower's extract lingered in her body, adding an irritating heaviness to her limbs.

"If I may," she inserted. "I *am* a queen. You did take the right person. But you clearly weren't informed that the boss himself helped us stage the recent coup. We overthrew Tilaine to gain freedom of movement within the Queendom."

The one thing Tilaine had done well was quell the bandit threats. They were still afraid to travel within the country . . . hence the secretive "assignments" Reyna doled out at New Leaf Tomes and Tea.

The lead captor tightened his grip on his cohort's shoulder, his blue eyes promising murder. The smaller man shoved him off and grumbled a curse. "We'll get this sorted. Stay put." He kicked the rusted metal framework of her cell door and laughed at his own joke.

She shrugged. "I'll be thrilled to know what you find." Her tone implied the exact opposite, and she rolled one of her shoulders to loosen her muscles. "And when you realize you've riled an entire country by kidnapping their queen—thereby making an enemy for every bandit in the Realm—feel free to release me. I'm happy to negotiate."

A pained whine echoed from the lead kidnapper's throat, and he towed his friend away from the cell, through a door to Reyna's right. It slammed shut behind them, and silence echoed in their wake.

Reyna chuckled, easing to the floor yet again. With her hands free, she fixed her bun, retying the twine swiftly to get her hair out of her eyes. She was reaching for her set of lockpicks when her moonstone positively *burned* against her throat. With a yelp, she wrenched the hot stone off her neck, glaring at it.

Kianthe was awake.

"Yes, yes," she murmured, mostly to fill space. The heat died quickly, a flare that passed with a breath, and in the resulting calm she tapped a response that resonated across the country. *I'm fine.*

Communication through their moonstones was limited, but they'd had plenty of practice developing a language through it. Kianthe tapped a question: *Hurt?*

No, Reyna replied. She strained to remember the code they'd only needed once before. A swirl of her hand, accentuated with two vicious taps. *Kidnapped.*

Because her partner was Kianthe, they had also developed a code for: *No shit.*

Reyna swallowed a laugh, tapped three simple times. *I love you.*

Safe?

Mostly.

A pause, where Reyna could almost imagine Kianthe drawing calming breaths, soothing a panicked heart. She'd made immense strides with her anxiety over the years, but it was a continuous process, something that required practice each time stress arose. Apparently, Reyna was doing her part today to reaffirm Kianthe's emotional growth.

"How very kind of me," Reyna said, lips quirking in amusement.

Of course, Kianthe couldn't hear that. But after several long moments, the mage tapped a reply on her moonstone: *On our way. I love you.*

Reyna sent a simple warmth back through their connection, something that felt like a kiss over her heart. As the moonstone went inert, Reyna shook her head.

She changed her mind; these kidnappers weren't bold. Just stupid.

After a bit of contemplation, Reyna left her lockpicks stowed. The lock was ancient—something she could pick almost as quickly as if she held the key. But it wasn't the *lock* that kept her contained. The bigger issue was that once she opened the cell door, the squealing hinges would alert the entire watchtower. At that point, she'd be committed to an escape, and she wasn't at her physical best right now.

Well, that, and curiosity had won out. Reyna wanted to know more about her captors . . . and this mysterious, "important" person who thought it was a good idea to kidnap her.

She settled back into the cell, examining her surroundings instead.

Why was the floor so clean?

She ran a finger along the wood, squinting at her calloused skin. There should still be dirt in here. The Queendom was mostly sand and dirt, with craggy mountains along the western edge that hid several working mines. Dust was a way of life.

But this cell, they'd *cleaned*. How courteous.

Reyna paced the edges, scuffing the wooden planks with her boot. One floorboard near the back wall was loose, so she knelt beside it, running her fingers along the seam. A divot in the wood caught her forefinger, and she pried it up with ease.

Underneath, painted on the dirt, was a rust-colored line.

A circle of blood.

The response was swift and vicious. Reyna's entire body tensed, her heart literally skipping a beat. Her skin felt both hot and far too cold, and the image of a pristine stone basement slammed into her mind. Almost a year ago, now. Sheparan architecture of archways and pillars, a narrow staircase, and a circular entry that led to their prize: an underground repository showcasing a pair of stolen dragon eggs. With Arlon's end in sight, Reyna had set one foot on the entry's floor—and electrifying agony seized her muscles and consumed her senses.

Kianthe had screamed.

Her baby griffon had screeched.

And on its heels was a silence so encompassing, Reyna thought she'd never hear anything else.

Slowly, the present slid into focus again, and old memories faded. Reyna became aware that she'd scrambled to the far wall, that she was hugging the stone as if she could escape the alchemy circle with sheer willpower. Sweat prickled her forehead, trailed down her temples, and she clenched her hands into fists.

This was ridiculous. She wasn't dead yet. Whatever this sigil was meant to do, it wasn't anything as ruthless as that one below Diarn Arlon's library. Alchemy was a magic based in sacrifice, versed in causing pain—but it had other uses, too.

Knowing that didn't calm her nerves.

Another tap came from the moonstone. It must have reported

her distress, her fear, because Kianthe was insistently prodding her for more information. *Hurt? Hurt?*

No, Reyna tapped back. *Okay.*

A pause.

A long pause.

Okay, Kianthe agreed.

Yet again, Reyna could read between her lines. She could imagine her wife narrowing her eyes, muttering, "*Liar.*" If she were home, Kianthe would have already handed her a steaming mug of tea, pressed a kiss to her forehead, and tucked a heavy wool blanket around her shoulders—and then faced the threat in Reyna's stead.

Reyna desperately wanted to be with Kianthe instead of here.

I love you, she tapped. The presence of alchemy meant this wasn't an amusing adventure now. If an alchemist was involved, things could get deadly . . . fast. Reyna was capable, powerful in her own right, but she wasn't an alchemist, or a mage, or a dragon. She had no counter to this kind of force.

Stay calm. Reyna drew five long breaths, the same practice Kianthe used when she was too anxious to function. She tapped her thumb to each of her fingers, letting the subtle pressure ground her. She hadn't been hurt yet—and alchemical circles could do a lot of things. What she needed was more information.

She slid the wooden plank back into position, hiding the fact that she'd discovered the sigil. But with it, everything had changed; her information-gathering period was over. Reyna reached for her lockpicks—and then the heavy door thudded open. Her captors strode into the room, led now by a lithe woman with a scathing expression.

Well, shit.

Reyna relaxed her posture. Any physical sign of her earlier panic was gone, and she was back to acting. The picture of ease. Alchemy didn't change the fact that three potentially hostile bandits were the more immediate threat.

If they noticed that she'd untied her restraints, none of them commented on it. Likely their minds were on other things now.

"They said you worked with the boss," the woman said. Her voice was low, tight, and cruel.

Reyna inclined her head, seizing power through silence.

When it was apparent she wasn't going to reply, the woman jerked a head at the cell door. One of the men scowled, stepping forward to unlock it.

"Come with us." The woman crossed her arms.

Reyna smiled, equally cold. "Gladly."

Showtime.

2

Kianthe

"You didn't have to join me," Kianthe called over the wind.

She cast a sideways glance at Venne, her wife's lead Queens-guard and oldest friend. Considering they were flying quite high over the desolate land of the western Queendom, Venne did not look happy. In fact, he looked vaguely sick.

Thank the Stone of Seeing that Reyna handled flight better than him.

Kianthe continued, casually: "Not that you aren't stellar company. Not that I'm *not* glad Reyna made up with you, then chose you to be her primary bodyguard and all that. I mean, this is great. Me, the Realm's most powerful mage, effecting a daring rescuing of my endangered wife, the queen . . . with you in tow. It's almost romantic."

Almost.

Visk, Kianthe's griffon, was watching the ground with rapt attention, following fresh wagon-wheel tracks along a dirt road. His feathery wings beat rhythmically, then spread wide, coasting when he found an updraft. Every so often, Visk would glance at his daughter, Ponder—Reyna's beloved griffon—to check that they were on course.

Mounted on Ponder's back, Venne gritted his teeth, his eyes

stalwartly locked on the horizon line. "We're not here for romance. We're here to make sure the *queen* is safe."

If Kianthe were a kinder soul, this would be the time to inform Venne that Reyna was, indeed, safe. If she were feeling benevolent, she'd lift the moonstone pendant from the folds of her shirt and inform him that she'd already spoken to her wife—in a manner of speaking.

But once upon a time, Venne had broken into their bookshop and threatened her friends. Once upon a time, he'd been madly in love with Reyna. *Once upon a time,* he'd been an absolute nuisance.

That was a year and a half ago. Reyna had forgiven him. Kianthe had too, just to make her wife happy. For the most part, they coexisted well, a truce formed under the mutual goal of protecting Reyna.

But sometimes, Kianthe couldn't avoid messing with him. Especially when he said things like "You may be the Arcandor, the Mage of Ages . . . but I'm the lead Queensguard. Her Excellency's safety is my responsibility."

"You did a great job." Kianthe's tone was wry.

Venne's face colored. "I alerted the palace immediately. I sent the messenger hawk to summon you. I rallied the whole of the Queensguard to follow us."

At the mention, Kianthe twisted to look behind them, toward the Grand Palace—which was now a speck in the distance. They'd left the Queensguard's thundering horses behind, but Visk and Ponder were flying low enough to guide the army west. A cloud of dust was the only indicator that dozens of Queensguard were hot on their trail.

Venne involuntarily followed her gaze—then caught a glimpse of the ground and groaned miserably.

"Gods, we're high." He cleared his throat, eyes yet again locking on the horizon. A pause, as if he was rallying himself. "Arcandor . . . I *am* sorry. If something happens to her—" He cut himself off, grimacing.

Well, now Kianthe just felt bad.

"She'll be fine. I know you did your best." Realistically, Kianthe pitied the Queensguard charged with Reyna's safety. Her wife wasn't built to be royalty, pampered and protected inside palace walls. She was built to be a warrior . . . which made her an absolute menace to her staff.

Venne's tone darkened. "My *best* wasn't good enough. I shouldn't have let her out of my sight; there's a protocol for that. But I thought it was *fine,* because Reyna insisted on one permanent guard, not two. Her exact words were, 'Come on, Venne. I'm the other guard.'" His voice climbed an octave to imitate her.

Fondness welled in Kianthe's chest. Stars and Stone, she loved her wife. She couldn't keep the amusement out of her tone. "Well, she *is* the other guard, in every practical manner of speaking."

"Except when someone kidnaps her in *plain fucking sight,*" Venne snapped. "She's not a Queensguard anymore. She's our Gods-damned sovereign. Her safety is paramount. We have *procedures—*"

Kianthe snorted, started laughing, forced herself to stop, then exploded again at his deepening scowl. "You know what you should do?" She wheezed past her laughter. "Why don't you write up a report, *really* fine-tune the details of your complaint, and submit it to Reyna for assessment? Oooh. Maybe during her morning sword drills! I'd love to see that fight."

Venne huffed. "Aren't you worried?"

Yes. *Of course* Kianthe was worried. But worrying in the past meant she succumbed to panic. It meant her heart pounded and her chest tightened and she couldn't stop shaking. It meant the idea of eating—often for *days*—was wholly unappealing. It meant she didn't sleep, even after things were arguably fine.

Kianthe was worried. But she just didn't have time for that response anymore. Reyna deserved so much better.

"She'll be fine," Kianthe reiterated, partly to her own mind. "Look alive; I think we're getting close."

They were nearing the western edge of the Queendom, soaring over craggy rocks and stubby mountains. The only plants were smatterings of dormant grass and the occasional pinyon pine. Even in the middle of winter, the sun was bright and warm, which helped at this altitude.

Ponder slowed, her body language shifting. She'd shed her rebellious attitude—mostly—in favor of being a proper griffon mount. It meant that even though Venne was a terrible passenger, gripping her feathers too hard and gasping at every updraft, she was clearly trying *very hard* not to throw him. Ponder's eagle eyes scanned the distance, centering on a wooden structure. It looked like a . . . clock tower? Or a bell tower. Some kind of tower, surely.

Visk whistled softly for Kianthe's benefit.

They'd found her.

"Here we go. Brace yourself," Kianthe told Venne, and bent over Visk as the griffon slid into a fast dive. Griffons loved circling the skies, but nothing was quite as exhilarating as when they sighted prey. She was convinced they were the fastest creatures alive when they entered free fall.

"What do you—" Venne's query cut off into a strangled cry somewhere behind her. Kianthe risked a glance to make sure he hadn't fallen off Ponder when she dove. It appeared to be a near thing, but he was still clinging to her back.

For his benefit, Ponder shifted into a slower descent. She didn't seem happy about it.

Visk landed on a nearby cliff, far enough away that they could examine the stronghold without being seen. Definitely a tower—just not a clock or bell one. It was an old watchtower, right along the Sheparan border. Kianthe dismounted, stretching her arms above her head. Every moment they neared Reyna, she felt calmer; even now, she could count the people patrolling, and there were hardly enough to scare her.

This wouldn't take long at all.

Ponder landed lithely beside her father. Venne slid off the young griffon's back instantly. He staggered a bit, unsteady from the flight, but drew a relieved breath at hard ground beneath his feet.

Ponder ruffled her feathers, lion's tail swishing. For a moment, Kianthe thought she was going to nip Venne's ear—a painful experience—but she clearly thought better of it. Instead, the young griffon offered a full-bodied huff, flew to a nearby rock, and preened her crumpled feathers.

"Thank the Gods that's over," Venne muttered. He'd been told about the inefficacies of the Gods, how the pantheon was crafted by the old regime to control its citizens, but old habits died hard for some. Even Reyna still swore to them when she was swept up in conversation.

"Sure," Kianthe said. "I'll do my best to keep you on the ground from here on out."

Venne adjusted the sword at his hip, shot her an exasperated look, and crept to the edge of the crag. He squinted down the hill at the watchtower. "What's our plan?"

Kianthe stepped alongside him, but didn't bother crouching. She *wanted* the kidnappers to see her coming. Her magic swelled in her chest, bright and yellow. There weren't many ley lines in the Queendom, but they'd found the one that trailed between the Capital and Wellia. The Stone of Seeing pulsed from the distant walls of the Magicary as she checked her reserves.

Preparing for battle.

"Arcandor? Your plan?"

"Hey, you're the one with procedures."

Venne snorted quietly. "And somehow, I doubt you'll follow them anyway. My first step would be to identify how many guards there are."

Easy enough. Kianthe pressed a hand to the ground. Instantly, the earth itself leapt to her attention. The very *air* inside the watchtower reported back. Seventeen breathing bodies. One of them was Reyna.

The rest . . . well.

"Four patrolling the perimeter, and twelve inside." Kianthe mounted Visk again. He was a handsome griffon, even by normal standards—larger than most, with stunning colors of tawny brown, like that of a golden eagle. He spread his wings, ready to fly on her command. Kianthe petted him absently. "A tower like that will have a trapdoor on the roof. You handle the ground patrol, and I'll capture everyone else."

Venne hesitated. "At the risk of sounding ridiculous . . . ah, can you handle twelve of them alone?"

Cute. Kianthe grinned. "If I know my wife, I won't be alone. Wait for my signal, okay?"

"What's your signal?"

Kianthe, the Arcandor, the Mage of Ages, winked. "Oh, you'll know it." With a nudge, mage and griffon took off again.

As they approached, Kianthe twisted clouds out of the condensation in the air. They formed a heavy fog that settled over the watchtower—and it happened so fast that shouts of alarm echoed from the ground.

Venne must have mounted Ponder again—brave of him—because almost immediately, the cries were cut off one by one. In just a few moments, only silence remained.

Regardless of what she thought of Venne, he *was* good at his job.

With the outside secure, Kianthe directed Visk to the roof. As expected, a heavy trapdoor was set into the stone. Kianthe wrenched it open with a twist of magic, then told Visk, "Stay alert. We may need a fast escape."

Visk folded his wings, lowering his head like a lion stalking prey.

"Good boy." She scratched under his beak, then crept down the staircase. As she moved, her fingers trailed the wall, and the stone echoed in response. A picture of wispy yellow formed in her mind: a gathering of people in the base of the watchtower, far below her feet.

All of the captors, it looked like.

And Reyna.

Kianthe frowned. The closed-off passageway ended, opening instead into a large room. The wooden staircase continued, spiraling along the wall to a floor several stories below. Once she stepped out there, she'd be exposed. Cautiously, she summoned fire to her fingertips, ready to ignite if necessary.

But at that moment, laughter boomed.

"—chasing this boar—"

"Oh, here we go."

"You did not!" Reyna's voice filtered through the din. She sounded amused, perfectly delighted. "With your *bare hands*?"

"He had a knife!"

"A tiny knife. It was mostly with my bare hands." When another roar of laughter erupted, the man speaking interjected indignantly, "It *was*! I cornered it and wrestled it to the ground—"

Another voice said, "You were nearly impaled, and the only reason you got that thing to the ground is because it crashed into a flower cart—"

"Oh, shut up!"

Kianthe peeked around the stone wall, leaning over the railing to see the scene below. The base of the watchtower was clearly meant as a main gathering space, crammed with tables and a hearth that vented along the western wall. A huge crowd had gathered around Reyna, holding mugs of wine and beer. On a nearby table was a spread of meat and cheeses.

Their weapons were forgotten.

"I'll be damned," Kianthe whispered, snickering. That took Reyna . . . what? Half a day?

Magnificent.

The center of attention, the new sovereign of the Queendom clapped the man's shoulder. "That's still incredible." She held a glass, but didn't seem to have consumed its contents. At some point, they'd given her back her sword, a stunning gem of meteoric steel—which only told Kianthe they were the worst kidnappers *ever*.

Well, Reyna clearly had this handled. High above them, Kianthe settled into a seated position. Her legs dangled over the staircase's edge, and she draped across the railing to watch

Reyna dazzle the folks who'd held her hostage. The best kind of show, in Kianthe's opinion.

"That boar had been terrorizing an entire village, and you killed it." Reyna's voice was silken, saturated with praise. "With a tiny knife or with your bare hands, it's still extraordinary. Does the boss know about this? He must be impressed."

The boss? Kianthe's brow furrowed. Bandits, then.

"Maybe you'll put in a good word." The man puffed his chest.

Reyna waved a hand, gesturing to a willowy woman beside her. "Maybe we should, huh?"

The bandit woman snorted. Based on her body language, she was clearly the leader here. "A good word for *this* crowd? They couldn't even get you out of the palace without sounding a city-wide alarm."

"Well." Reyna shrugged good-naturedly. "That's tough to do without magic, considering the Queensguard rotations." A pause. "I honestly expected you'd have alchemists here. Or maybe an elemental mage. Someone to get you straight through the stone walls."

"No elemental mage would kidnap the Arcandor's wife." The woman heaved a sigh, as if they'd asked *many* of them. Kianthe didn't know whether to be impressed or annoyed. "We did have an alchemist on staff. But once we had you in the cart, they flew off. Which was fine, mind; we had things well under control."

One of the men nearby snorted. "'Under control.' Our prisoner is drinking with us."

"Listen." The willowy bandit stiffened in offense. "I'm not messing with the boss's favorite."

Reyna smiled, lifting her mug to her lips.

This was all well and good, but Kianthe was starting to feel a bit left out. She drummed her fingers on the worn wood and called, "I'll give you this: your stories aren't a total . . . boar." Her voice echoed in the large room.

Everyone craned to look at her: the Arcandor, the Mage of Ages, with her feet dangling over a staircase's edge, her chin resting on the wooden railing. Reyna alone didn't seem surprised. In fact, amusement flashed across her features. "Hello, love. I'd like to introduce you to the finest set of bandits east of the Nacean River."

"Not in the whole Realm?" One pouted.

"Well, west of the Nacean includes the boss himself." Reyna raised a questioning eyebrow. The bandit pressed his lips together and swallowed any retort, and she hummed acceptance. "Everyone, this is my wife, the Arcandor."

"*Fuck.*" The bandit woman set her glass of wine on a nearby table, pushing to her feet. Her tone was cautious. "Look, we didn't know, okay?"

"Know what?" Kianthe asked innocently.

"Know she and the boss had a deal." The woman gripped her sword with white knuckles. Taking her cue, a few others reached for their own weapons—but none of them looked eager to pick a fight with the Mage of Ages.

Smart.

Reyna stood, dusting herself off. She was physically unharmed, which allowed an edge of tension to ease from Kianthe's shoulders. "The leader of the Realm's bandits made a mistake. He told them to kidnap a queen, but . . . well. It's possible something was lost in translation." Now her tone assumed a curious lilt, and she addressed the bandit leader. "Are you positive you weren't supposed to kidnap the *old* queen? We had to drop her in the Roiling Islands, but that might make for an equally daring abduction, considering the pirates down there."

The woman wrinkled her nose. "Please. We're not *that* stupid. We were supposed to bring you, Queen Reyna, to this watchtower."

"And then what?"

The bandit leader rubbed her neck, glancing at her comrades. "Ah, then we wait for orders."

"Hmm. I am beginning to suspect *I'm* the one issuing that order." Now Reyna patted her hand earnestly. "Thank you for the wine. Your hospitality truly has been phenomenal, and your kidnapping skills are second to none."

The woman lifted her chin. "Well, thank you."

Reyna began picking her way out of the crowd.

The woman watched in bemusement, and then seemed to realize what was happening. "Hang on. I can't let you leave yet. We're waiting on orders from—"

"Someone 'important,' correct?" Reyna chuckled, gesturing at Kianthe overhead. "Well, if it isn't me, then I'm betting it's the Arcandor. Who's more important than the Mage of Ages?"

It was fun, watching her work. Kianthe waggled a few fingers. "Yes, hello. I am awfully important, and your boss is definitely trying to get in my good graces. This is a solid first step—the amicable release of my wife."

It took everything she had to say that with a straight face.

"But—why would he want us to kidnap you in the first place?" The bandit leader frowned. Slowly, the ruse was ending. "This doesn't make sense."

"Unless you were always supposed to feed and release me. Trap me in a cell for a day or so, and then stage a 'rescue' and return me home. Then you, the bandit populace, can prove you're turning over new leaves by winning the favor of the Queendom's new royal." Reyna winked. "It's honestly a brilliant scheme on his part."

"That is pretty good," one of the bandits grunted.

"Yeah, that makes sense," another chimed.

Reyna clapped the leader's shoulder. "Stay here and enjoy your meal. I'll check that cell for any personal belongings and say farewell on my way out." She headed for an innocuous door on the northern edge of the room, near the base of the staircase.

"Uh . . ." The bandit leader bit her lip. "Okay. Sure."

Kianthe pushed to her feet, strolling down the stairs to meet Reyna. As she moved, Kianthe squinted at the bandits. Doubt flickered on several of their faces. A few shifted uneasily as Reyna reunited with her partner.

Grifting was all well and good, but Kianthe didn't want

swords at their backs if the bandit leader finally grew wise. She tried one more ruse: "Actually, you know what? To do this right, you lot should head east and report to the Grand Palace. Reyna can offer you formal pardons. A public display of gratitude."

Now a couple of the bandits recoiled. One exclaimed, "We can't report to the Grand Palace! We'll be arrested."

"Damn right," a voice said from the second entrance, and Venne stepped into the room. His sword was already bloody, his outfit torn, but he narrowed his eyes. "Everyone here is charged with abducting Her Excellency, the venerated Queen Reyna of the Queendom. You will be hanged for your crimes."

Well, that went a little far.

It shattered any illusion Reyna had created. Panic surged, and the bandits scrambled for their weapons. Glasses of wine and tankards of beer clattered to the floor. Before anyone could start an honest fight, Kianthe magically wrenched up the dirt floor and trapped them all at the knees.

There. That felt better. Ignoring their shouts and screams, she strolled to Venne and Reyna, her tone dry. "Nice job."

"Venne. That was hardly protocol." Reyna shook her head.

Venne abandoned assessing the bandits to gasp indignantly. "I'm sorry. I must have misheard, Your Excellency. *You* want to talk protocol?"

Reyna crossed her arms, teasing now. "Such a tone with your new queen."

Venne wasn't amused. He massaged his forehead. "Don't even start. Not after you were kidnapped under my watch. What the hell happened, Reyna?"

"I—" Reyna's cheeks colored. "They snuck up behind me and knocked me out. Blue locke. It was an amateur mistake."

"I'll say," Venne grumbled.

Kianthe folded her arms. "'We're so happy you're safe, Your Excellency.' 'We can't imagine how we'd survive without you, Your Excellency.' 'Let me know how else I can help, Your Excellency.'"

Now Venne's face flushed. He cleared his throat and shifted his weight. "Ah, yes. All of that, too."

Reyna snorted, but moved on quickly. "I'm glad you're here, Key. You need to see this." She flicked two fingers, leaving the bandits trapped as she led them down a nearly hidden staircase. Clearly, she'd already mapped the entire watchtower . . . somehow.

Not that Kianthe expected anything less.

As they walked, Kianthe injected, "And here I thought I'd get a nice, romantic reunion."

"I saw you three days ago, dearest."

"And then you were kidnapped." At Reyna's unimpressed glance, Kianthe coughed. "But it's fine. I'll be romantic some other time." They lapsed into silence, and Kianthe took that time to assess her wife's physical well-being. But aside from the bags under Reyna's eyes—bags that never really went away, even before Reyna became queen—she looked fine.

It helped to see, anyway.

Venne covered their backs, watching for more bandits, his sword ready.

A few more steps, and they reached a wooden door. It opened easily, revealing a small room with a single cell. Before they could step for it, Reyna sighed and spun on her heel. Since Kianthe was already stepping forward, it brought her right into Reyna's space, their faces close, their noses almost touching. Reyna had that intense look in her eyes, the one that cut off any of Kianthe's retorts.

Reyna's fingers intertwined with Kianthe's. "I'm sorry, dearest. I'm a little distracted. Thank you for saving me. It's actually quite romantic." Reyna's free hand wound behind Kianthe's neck, and she pulled her in for a kiss.

The world went blissfully blank, and all that mattered was Reyna's lips on hers. Kianthe sighed against her wife, the final knot inside her chest unwinding. She was okay. Safe. Everything was fine.

Reyna pulled away too soon, searched Kianthe's eyes, then gave her another gentle peck on the lips. "You're going to want to see this, though." And with those murmured words, she stepped into the room and opened the lattice metal door of the cell. Kianthe moved to step inside the cell, mildly dazed, but Reyna stopped her from crossing the threshold. "Don't go inside. Just lift the floorboards for me."

Huh. Kianthe raised an eyebrow and twisted her hand, her magic pulling the floorboards away from the dirt.

Instantly, an alchemy circle revealed itself—but it wasn't like any Kianthe had seen. Most circles used the same symbols, the same language, with varying qualifiers to achieve results. This circle *seemed* similar to the alchemy she'd examined before . . . but the longer she looked, the less comprehensible it became. It was like trying to grasp a language she'd learned in a dream.

"Alchemy, in the cell where they kept your wife?" Venne frowned. "I thought you were on good terms with the Alchemicor, Kianthe."

"I am," she whispered.

"Alchemists hardly report to the Alchemicor, any more than Kianthe has mages reporting to her." Reyna lifted her chin, reciting a well-discussed line. "Their titles equate to power, not responsibility. If I'm not mistaken, a rogue alchemist could have easily done this with no knowledge on the Alchemicor's part."

It was wholly accurate. Kianthe should be proud that Reyna had learned so much about magic users in the Realm.

Instead, she was struggling to take deep breaths. Panic welled in her voice. All her meditation, her soothing exercises, were suddenly useless. "Rain, what'd it do to you?" Unbidden flashes of last year, of the stone room beneath Arlon's library, slid into Kianthe's mind. Reyna's body arching under magical electrocution, the *thump* as she crumpled to the stone floor. Her body had been so still.

She'd almost died.

It was bad enough Reyna had been kidnapped from the Grand Palace, but an *alchemical sigil* beneath her cell was terrifying. Kianthe's words sounded distant. "A-Are you okay? Did they hurt you?"

It wasn't often that the Arcandor went on a rampage, but

Kianthe could feel herself edging there. But something wasn't sitting right.

What was this circle meant to *accomplish*?

Kianthe was so focused on its implications that she didn't feel Reyna stepping closer, not until her wife's hand ghosted along her arm. "Love, I'm fine." Reyna pressed a kiss to her lips. It was a quick reassurance, but it worked to calm Kianthe's pounding heart. Her voice was soft. "It alarmed me as well. But I promise, I feel perfectly normal. I don't think it had a chance to activate before they pulled me out of the cell."

"That's weird, too," Kianthe said petulantly. Alchemy usually activated when someone entered the circle, but *could* be delayed for the right trigger. If that was the case here . . . what was the trigger?

Reyna set her jaw. "I agree. But I'm not prepared to test it further."

Damn right. Kianthe stepped away from the cell. "Can you memorize this?"

Reyna chuckled. "I'm good, but I doubt my memory is *that* reliable." And she rifled through the leather bag at Kianthe's hip, sifting past linen bags of seeds and soil for her prize: a sheet of parchment and a stick of charcoal. A quick check, a few strokes of the charcoal, and she'd drawn a perfect image of the circle. In an alchemist's hands—and with the proper sacrifice—it'd be dangerous, but in hers the symbol was inert.

Reyna tucked the parchment in her pocket. The moment that was done, Kianthe shifted the earth of the cell, churning the blood circle into dirt until only fresh earth remained. Another wave of magic, and the wooden planks realigned themselves over the new ground. Messy, but it finished the job.

"Good riddance," she said.

Venne cleared his throat. "Your Excellency, are we following protocol after this kidnapping? The Queensguard are on their way; it shouldn't be long."

Reyna sighed. "It's been a tiring ordeal, and I have no desire to be poked and prodded by the palace doctors. Take the bandits to the Capital, and speak to Tessalyn about options for rehabilitation. In the meantime, we really should see Feo."

Their resident alchemy expert. Kianthe nodded absently, still staring at the cell's floor.

Venne saluted. "Yes, ma'am."

Reyna squeezed his arm. "Thanks for coming, Venne. I'm sure it was a long night."

"Just . . . two guards next time, all right?" Venne heaved a sigh and nodded to Kianthe. "Enjoy the flight. Send a messenger hawk to let us know you're back in Tawney."

"Yes, Mother," Kianthe couldn't resist saying.

Venne tossed up his hands and stomped up the staircase. Reyna's laughter followed.

3

Reyna

A year and a half ago, Reyna and Kianthe decided to abandon their lives and relocate to a small, icy town that straddled the borders of the Queendom, Shepara, and dragon country. Back then, they'd questioned if it would ever become home.

Now, Reyna wondered how she ever doubted it.

This high up, Tawney positively glimmered: an oasis of warmth nestled between huge meadows of snow. Southwest of the town, a pine forest and some even more distant mountains interrupted the plains. The town itself had been built in the shadow of a small escarpment, which offered a clear marker between human territory and the dragons' domain. The eastern half of Tawney sat unused and burnt, a charred reminder of the town's tumultuous history with the dragons—turmoil caused by the theft of three dragon eggs, only resolved by Kianthe and Reyna last year.

Still, the lively half of the town was stunning from the sky. Reyna stroked Ponder's feathers as she craned over the griffon to get a better view. "Gods, remind me not to stay at the Capital for so long next time. Kidnapping aside, the Grand Palace's never-ending stone corridors are only riveting for a time. This is much better."

"Still struggling to cut 'Gods' out of your vocabulary, huh?"

Kianthe grinned. She was mounted on Visk, as always, and although the griffons flew in close formation, she had to raise her voice to be heard.

Reyna rolled her eyes. "Try cutting out the word 'Stone' and see how *you* fare. After a lifetime, it isn't so easy."

"And what would you replace it with? *Dragons Bless?*" Kianthe snorted. "After dealing with two baby dragon menaces, I'm hardly inspired."

"My point precisely. It sounds ridiculous. The Gods don't exist, but the dragons know my beliefs. That's what matters."

As if on cue, two little specks soared over the rim from dragon country, and a pair of deep-throated roars echoed across the plains. In response, Ponder screeched, dipping in excitement before surging even with Visk again. She twisted her head to silently plead with Reyna, her golden eye unblinking, a kid asking to go play.

"Speaking of two baby dragon menaces," Kianthe muttered.

"Oh, hush," Reyna teased. She patted Ponder's neck, smoothing the feathers Venne had crumpled. The flight from the watchtower had been rather enlightening, and the pair agreed that Venne was no longer allowed on a griffon's back.

It was best for everyone.

"Care to catch me?" Reyna asked, eyes alight.

Kianthe nudged Visk with her boot, and the older griffon chittered. "I feel like there are safer ways to practice this."

"You never know what might happen in an emergency." Over Tawney, Pill Bug and Gold Coin had surged into the sky, and Ponder was clearly itching to meet them. The baby dragons had become her best friends. Despite her duties as a full-grown mount, the griffon was still young, and she deserved a break after today.

"*I* think you got a taste of free fall on our wedding day, and now you crave it." Kianthe rolled her eyes, nudging Visk into position. The older griffon slowed, chittering exasperation, and dropped a bit to make the catch easier.

Reyna gave Ponder a swift hug around the neck and murmured, "Have fun, darling." The griffon chirped fondly, wings tilting to catch a frigid updraft. Reyna tightened her scarf around her neck, tossed her sword back to Kianthe—who definitely had to manipulate the air to catch it seamlessly.

Then Reyna cheerfully said, "Perhaps. Or maybe I just like . . . falling . . . for you," and tipped sideways off her mount.

"Funny," Kianthe drawled, but it was swallowed by the rushing wind.

Reyna's breath was sucked dry, leaving her gasping and giggling with exhilaration. It only took a gentle twist of her body to turn parallel to the ground, and then she had control—or some guise of it, anyway. With a laugh, she swam through the air, arms spread wide . . . and for a blessed moment it was like she was truly *flying*.

Dazzling. Incredible. She understood completely why Kianthe had no problem falling, and often chose this route. Even without magic to manipulate the winds, there was something so freeing about free fall.

Reyna laughed delightedly, the wind stealing her amusement. *Freeing free fall.* For some reason, that was hysterical to her right now.

In far too short a time, Visk drew even with her, keeping pace as she plummeted toward the earth. On his back, Kianthe looked almost bored. "Finished yet, dear? The ground is awfully close."

"I am a busy queen with intensive duties," Reyna gasped, then laughed again at the absurdity of this moment. "I have the weight of a country on my shoulders. This might be the only chance I get to unwind."

"Unwind . . . or un-wind?" Kianthe smirked.

"Both," Reyna replied breathlessly. It was absolutely freezing. She needed a better cloak if she'd make a habit of this.

"Hmm. Well, you can always unwind with sword practice." Kianthe hefted her wedding present, the sword made of meteor metal.

Intense emotion bubbled from her throat, and she tilted toward Visk. "I think I love you."

"What a relief." Kianthe yanked her onto Visk's back. Seamlessly, the griffon eased open his wings and tilted them into an upward curve, avoiding the ground with plenty of time to spare. Far ahead, Ponder was already flitting with her dragons, playing a similar game of aerial pursuit. Resting on the rim, barely visible as night settled over the horizon, an adult dragon—the perpetual babysitter—lazily observed its charges.

All was well.

Reyna hugged Kianthe's back as Visk angled toward their barn. Her surge of affection lingered, and she pressed a kiss under Kianthe's wild hair, at the base of her neck. Her wife shivered at the warm touch, which only made Reyna smile wider.

"Thank you for finding me, Key."

"I mean, last time you rescued *me* from an abduction, you came with an army. I came with Venne." Kianthe paused, the weighted moment before she spouted a truly awful pun. "It was quite an ad-Venne-ture."

Right on cue. Reyna snorted, burying her nose in Kianthe's hair. It always smelled vaguely like soil and cloves, and it had become synonymous with "safety" to Reyna. "Well, it's a good thing you brought him, because now we don't have to worry about the messy leftovers. The Queensguard will process those bandits, and my entire evening can be devoted to you and a warm cup of tea."

"And just for clarification's sake, how is he going to *process* them?" A heavy pause. "I know you won't actually hang them, but—"

"*Key*, come on." Reyna pushed her shoulder. Part of her was a little hurt that Kianthe felt the need to clarify.

"Sorry, sorry! I trust you. I just . . . don't know about the Queensguard these days." Kianthe ducked her head.

It was a valid concern. Reyna had killed many under Tilaine's rule . . . and in the prior regime, a hanging absolutely *would* have been the bandits' fate. She pushed her initial flare of emotion aside and answered logically: "If you trust me, you'll trust my Queensguard—they answer to my command. I didn't lie,

dear. Tessalyn and I have been working on a rehabilitation program. I think they'll be excellent candidates to test it."

"Sorry." Kianthe's cheeks colored, and she stared pointedly
ahead. "I think I forget how fast you changed policy around the
Queendom. I should have known better."

Reyna nuzzled her nose into Kianthe's hair. "Like it or not,
you've become my moral compass. Every decision I make now, I
think to myself: *Would Kianthe approve of this?* It's reduced our
public hangings by ninety-seven percent."

"Wait, what about the other three percent?"

It was fun to mess with her, sometimes. Reyna feigned dis-
interest, infusing a casual tone into her voice. "Oh, you know."

Kianthe snorted. "Maybe you're the menace."

"That is wholly possible."

Visk tilted his wings, subtly adjusting his flight pattern as they
approached New Leaf. A crowd had gathered, Reyna noted, people
milling in front of the shop even as long shadows cast the entire
street in darkness. A few shouts as people pointed to the griffon overhead, holding their hats as his wings beat up dirt. Visk
screeched, touching down in the clear area they'd hastily offered
for him.

And then, the shouting started.

"Queen Reyna. The Arcandor!"

"They're here. What do I do with my hands?"

"*Stars above,* they're on the griffon and everything—"

"You serve a stunning cup of tea, Queen Reyna!"

It blended into a cacophony that had Reyna's head spinning.
She took her sword from Kianthe and dismounted Visk, ever
aware that her cheeks were likely flushed from the cold, that her
bun was less than proper.

So, this was still going on. She exchanged an exasperated
look with her wife. "So . . ."

Kianthe hopped off Visk, plastering a very fake smile on her
face. Her words were low, nearly inaudible. "Yep. The first snowfall did not, in fact, deter them."

"Wonderful." Reyna offered a slight wave to the crowd. They

were keeping their distance because of Visk, but it was a near thing. "And they're—"

"*All* over the town. You got it. Flee while you can, buddy." Kianthe patted Visk's flank and stepped back, allowing him space to leap into the air again. He wasted no time—human matters like an oversaturation of tourists meant little to a griffon, and Visk's mate would be waiting for him in the mountains west of town.

Reyna sighed, massaging her forehead. She offered the crowds a gracious bow and raised her voice to "royal decree" levels. "We greatly appreciate your patronage here at New Leaf. However, the shop closes at nightfall—"

"Nightfall happens so *early* in the winter," one tourist complained. "We came all this way to have a cup of tea."

Kianthe's eye twitched, and heat radiated from her hands. Reyna swiftly stepped in front of the mage, cutting off any hasty actions. Her voice shifted again, this time settling on the authoritative Queensguard tone—the one that said: *leave, or I'll make you.* "The shop is closed for tonight. If you'd like a cup of tea, we'll be here in the morning."

"Promise?" another piped up. "I want an autograph!"

Gods and dragons and everything in between. Reyna laughed good-naturedly and followed Kianthe inside the barn—but the moment she shut the doors behind them, her composure vanished. She drew the curtains, speaking with desperation. "They're really getting bad, aren't they?"

"It's insufferable. Took me ages to get them outside without stealing our mugs," Gossley, their shop hand, said from behind the counter. "Welcome back, Miss Reyna. Sorry about your kidnapping."

"As far as kidnappings go, it was rather mild," Reyna replied. She locked the door with finality, casting a bare glance at Kianthe as her wife staggered farther into the shop, dropping onto one of the armchairs by the hearth.

Gossley wiped his hands on a cloth. "Did, ah . . . did you have to kill anyone?" His eyes dropped to her sword. Once upon a time, the teenager would have been eager for that, but now he'd settled into a life as a blacksmith apprentice, managing their shop on the side. The glamour of adventure had long since worn off.

Kianthe snorted. "If Reyna has to kill someone, I wouldn't classify it as 'mild.'"

"I might." Reyna wove through the bookshop's tables, reveling in the privacy. It was warm and cheerful, the hearth blazing day and night this time of year. Overhead, ever-flames drifted between the ivy-covered rafters, offering a cozy ambience. The plants were thriving, a common occurrence in the home of an elemental mage.

But there were signs of distress from these new patrons. The bookshelves were barren, tomes snatched up before a new shipment could arrive. The rugs were worn, the furniture stained. Even Gossley looked harried, his clothes rumpled and bags under his eyes. Reyna paused at one of their wooden tables, running her finger over a new divot. It looked like someone had dug their spoon into the wood.

Sadness settled into her bones, and she glanced again at the barn doors. "I never thought I'd regret hosting so many folks."

"You're telling me." Kianthe settled into the armchair, then grimaced as she brushed crumbs off the armrest. Her eyes drifted shut. "Gosling, you heading home?"

Their shop hand nodded, stretching his arms over his head. "Yeah. Can I leave through the back?"

The one spot they guarded carefully was the back garden—a private oasis for them alone. It made for a safe getaway from the tourists, many of whom hadn't bothered exploring Tawney's nooks and crannies . . . partially thanks to the wall of earth Kianthe had erected in the alleys on either side of their barn.

"You never have to ask, Gossley," Reyna said.

"I always will. Welcome home, Queen Reyna." He grinned at her, then untied his apron and strolled for the back door. It closed behind him, and they were alone.

The hearth crackled. Eventually, Kianthe's breathing evened

out. She wasn't asleep, not yet, but it was a near thing. Someone—
Matild, most likely—had delivered dinner: fresh bread and soup
in a ceramic container. It was still steaming, so they must have
just missed her.

Reyna drew a slow, calming breath. Good to be home, indeed. "I think I'll draw a bath. Want to join me, love?"

"Mmm. Not tonight." Kianthe offered a half-hearted wave.
"I'll wash down later. Might grab something to eat. You want to
read tonight, or something else?"

"I'd love to talk." Reyna paused, chest warm. Even after
years, it still embarrassed her to admit it, but she was trying to
say these things out loud: "I missed you."

It was such a simple thing, missing the company of her wife.
But it woke Kianthe right up. She pushed off the chair, strode
across the room, and swept Reyna into a glorious hug. She even
spun her around, a gentle twist that had Reyna laughing again.
Kianthe pressed a firm kiss to her lips, then another, and traced
her cheek.

"I don't think I ever stop missing you, Rain."

Moments like this made Reyna wonder how she got so lucky.

She flushed like a teenager in love, which only made Kianthe smirk. Realizing her wife was about to become insufferable,
Reyna pushed her away, composing herself with a few quick
breaths. "Make me some tea? The chamomile mint blend, perhaps?"

"Are you set on that? I grew something special in my greenhouse, and I've been saving the result for you." Kianthe grinned.

"Ah. Well, that's fine too." Prickling with happiness, Reyna
ducked into the washroom.

They had piped water in Tawney, a luxury Reyna still appreciated, but living with Kianthe had further benefits. An ever-
flame warmed the pipe as it pumped water, which meant her
baths in New Leaf were somehow more luxurious than inside
the Grand Palace.

She didn't need a full staff and high-end upgrades. She just
needed her wife.

As Reyna stripped, she found the folded parchment with the copied alchemy sigil. It cut through her elation instantly, and she set the parchment well away from the water—careful to protect the charcoal image so nothing was distorted. Eyes locked on the symbol, she propped her sword by the door, absently unlacing her boots. Concern slid through her veins.

She felt fine, but . . . what if she wasn't?

What if this symbol had poisoned her somehow?

Alchemy was an odd magic, something she didn't fully understand. "Built in sacrifice," Feo always said. There seemed to be an alchemical circle for *everything,* which meant Reyna had no idea what its limitations were.

It was unnerving.

Reyna sighed and made a conscious decision to focus on other things. No use fretting until Feo—diarn of Tawney, councilmember of Shepara, and their resident alchemy expert—could examine the sigil. Until then, she sank into her bath and luxuriated in the warm water against her skin. A cloth was draped over the tub, and she rolled it into a pillow for her neck.

At her side, the roses in the vase beside the bath unfurled. It happened gently, like a morning stretch, and their soft fragrance drifted over her. Reyna's lips tilted into a relaxed smile. Even when they were apart, Kianthe found ways to show her love.

"You're quite beautiful," she told the roses, because Kianthe told her once that plants adored compliments. She never used to be like this, but watching their leaves lift—as if proud to be admired—made her wish she'd talked to flowers all her life.

Or maybe that was just the effects of an elemental mage.

She contented herself with listening to Kianthe puttering around their storage room, listening to the boiling water of her copper kettle, listening to the gentle clink of silverware as Kianthe set a table for them. But Reyna didn't rush; this was the longest moment she'd had undisturbed in weeks.

Most of her days were spent in meetings at the Grand Palace, determining policies and holding court, or bustling around their bookshop serving customers. But for now, the world was still, and her mind settled as she admired small things like the ever-flames flickering overhead and the lovely hues of the roses' petals.

Good to be home.

When she finally emerged from her bath, she slid into a silk nightshirt and a warm fleece robe, then padded into the barn proper. The ever-flame had dimmed on Kianthe's command, softening the light, but it was still comfortably warm. The street outside had quieted for the evening, and Kianthe lit two of the candles at their smallest table.

"This is lovely, Key," Reyna said softly.

Kianthe pressed a mug in her hands. "Well, I thought you'd be in the Capital until the half-moon. I'll take advantage of the extra time."

"You even saved my mug." This one was Reyna's favorite—an experiment in a collection they'd commissioned from the local ceramicist. It had vertical streaks that caused the glaze to drip like orange flames, but the color faded into a deep, nighttime blue near the rim. On the handle was a tiny divot for her thumb, and turquoise blue pooled there like a calm glacier lake.

"I had Gossley stash it in back once we realized some were missing. Losing it would be quite the . . . traves-tea."

Reyna had her nose to the mug, savoring the scent of the tea, but the pun made her snort. Hot water flicked her nose, and she recoiled with another laugh. "Clever. Maybe one of your best."

Kianthe basked in the praise. "Thank you, thank you." She led Reyna to the table, and Reyna took another careful whiff of the herbal blend. Kianthe, meanwhile, steepled her fingers over the table, amusement tilting her features as she watched her wife puzzle through the conundrum.

"Blackberry leaves, rose petals, and . . . honeybush tea?" The tisane was sweet, almost buttery, but nothing overwhelming. In fact, its beauty lay in its subtle flavor. Reyna sipped it, quirking an eyebrow. "Were you experimenting?"

"I got bored. Thought this one was pretty good. Feel free to correct me." Kianthe shifted a bit, looking sheepish. They both knew *her* specialty was books, and *Reyna's* was tea—but a certain amount of crossover was expected.

Reyna drew another sip. "It's wonderful. Perfect for a cold winter night."

"Well, we're in Tawney near the Mid-Winter Celebration. I think we have that covered." But pride swept into Kianthe's voice, and she took a sip from her own mug—a treasured piece fired in purple glaze flecked with white, like stars.

"Cheers," Reyna said, and clinked their mugs together.

The night passed with amicable conversation and excellent company, and much later, they fell into bed together—exhausted, but utterly content.

4

Kianthe

The next morning dawned far too early, and of course Reyna rose with the sun, which was downright disgusting.

Kianthe grumbled, fumbling for the covers as her wife pulled open the drapes. She muttered against a pillow, "Rain, you haven't rested since you were kidnapped. Sleep in. The customers can wait."

"Considering the recent influx of tourists who visit this town *specifically* for New Leaf's tea and ambience, I doubt that. Besides, I feel fine," Reyna replied, buttoning a white blouse. The ridiculous thing was, she *did* look perfectly refreshed. Kianthe was secretly convinced Reyna had suffered sleep loss for so many years that her body forgot what it was like to be well-rested.

Kianthe's body hadn't. Exhaustion weighed on her like a winter blanket, and she groaned, flipping onto her stomach to bury her nose between their pillows. "Well, *I'm* sleeping in." If Reyna could understand her petulant, muffled words, it'd be a miracle.

But her wife just smoothed Kianthe's hair and pressed a stupid, gentle kiss to the back of her head. It'd be sweet, except she followed up with, "Don't be too long, dearest. We're meeting Feo at noon."

Feo. The alchemical sigil. That swept the dust from Kianthe's mind, and she turned her head to watch Reyna slide into her boots. She left her sword propped by the door, but that was fairly typical when she opened the shop. Kianthe clawed her gnarled thoughts into some semblance of order. "Does *Feo* know that we're seeing them at noon?"

"Considering I haven't told them, I'd be shocked if they did." Reyna's voice was light, tinged in amusement. "But I'm confident they'll admit us. They can't ignore a good mystery." And she swept from the room, humming softly as she eased the door closed.

It was far too bright with the curtains open, but Kianthe dozed for a bit longer. When she awoke properly, it was to the overly loud chatter of tourists, the clinking of mugs and silverware, the soft laughter of folks perusing books.

There was a time when Reyna was worried about paying bills with their income, which seemed laughable now. No, these days, Kianthe would take far less coin if it meant more peace.

Cursing the newspapers and traveling bards who kept *telling* people about Tawney, Kianthe hauled herself out of bed and fumbled into her clothes. While Reyna always presented herself properly, the epitome of a regal queen even when serving the general public, Kianthe didn't give two shits about looking nice. She staggered into the shop with knotted hair and her cloak hanging off one shoulder, smacking her lips as she tried to identify the taste on her teeth.

Did blackberry leaves linger this long? Gross.

Preoccupied, she almost missed the swell of enthusiasm as Reyna pressed a kiss to her cheek. The patrons chittered like birds, admiring the way Queen Reyna doted on her wife, and look how sweet they both were, and didn't they make the most gorgeous couple in the Realm?

Kianthe stared blearily, then rolled her eyes and turned her back to the shop, sagging against the countertop as Reyna flitted to her copper kettle. "What happened to our friends? You know, the people who *live here*?"

"Sigmund and Nurt stopped by to say hello—but they're the only ones who managed. No seating when we're swarmed first thing in the morning." Reyna pressed her lips together, absently sorting through the apothecary drawers of tea leaves. "I'm planning to visit Wylan after Feo. We might need to summon Tessalyn here to discuss city planning."

"City?" Kianthe wrinkled her nose. "This is a town. A cute, quaint, *quiet* town." She raised her voice for the last word, but the tourists were unfazed. A few of them even chimed agreement, gushing about what a cute town Tawney was, and how they'd definitely have to make this visit a regular occurrence.

Irritation seeped into Kianthe's chest, even as she grudgingly took the mug Reyna pushed her way. A strong black tea. Good call for a morning like this. She listened to the chatter, and when it became unbearable, she lowered her voice and asked, "Reyna? Do you think we . . . ruined . . . Tawney?"

"No," Reyna replied swiftly. "I think we saved lives by quelling the dragon attacks, and then the rest of the Realm realized it's a lovely place to live."

"It's unbearably cold half the year and frigid for the rest of it," Kianthe deadpanned.

Reyna lifted her chin, determination settling over her features. "We didn't ruin anything. We built a nice place, and people want to visit." She drew a short breath. "And because we are also considerate neighbors, we'll coordinate with the necessary lords and diarns to ensure this town isn't overrun. All right?"

"Sure," Kianthe replied, but only because Reyna had her *don't push me* face on. Clearly this was affecting her more than she wanted anyone to know.

Kianthe filed that away for later.

"Gossley enlisted his girlfriend to come help today. Once they get here, we can leave." Reyna's tone turned contemplative, and she waved as Janice, one of the town's bakers, strolled through the door. "I'd like to see Matild and Tarly before we find Feo."

Kianthe watched Janice pause, assess the crowds, and hastily backtrack. To be fair, Janice and their next-door neighbor, Sasua, were good friends . . . but it still hurt that she wouldn't brave the tourists to come say hello.

Whatever. Today, they had bigger issues. *Alchemy* issues.

"Anytime you want to go, just let me know," Kianthe replied, raking a hand through her hair. She moved behind the counter as a young couple approached. "Considering yesterday, it feels wrong to keep serving folks as normal."

"We have many jobs, love."

The couple arrived at the counter, cast them hasty glances, and then bent over a menu. They squinted at the script pinned to a portable, leather-wrapped board, but the woman murmured to her partner, "Holy hells, that's really Queen Reyna." Then, quiet enough that she clearly thought she could get away with it: "Well, good. Queens *should* be serving us."

Considering her Sheparan accent, that was pretty ironic. Kianthe bristled, but Reyna merely set a hand on her forearm. "Welcome to New Leaf. Let me know when you're ready to order." Somehow, Reyna's voice was calm and level, allowing the woman to truly believe her comment had gone unnoticed.

It was a courtesy Kianthe wouldn't have offered, but whatever.

She needed some air. Kianthe stepped aside, shouldering a damp rag. "Mmm. Feel free to handle your adoring fans, love. I'm going to wipe some tables." If any emptied long enough to be cleaned, that was.

"Thanks," Reyna said, and only Kianthe could detect the sarcasm in her tone.

The one good thing about a crowd was that it made the day pass quickly. Kianthe wiped tables, tidied the bookshelves, swept crumbs, answered questions, and before she could blink, Reyna was tapping her shoulder. Kel—Gossley's girlfriend and the carpenter's daughter—had confidently set up shop behind the counter, and Gossley was working on crowd management as more people streamed through the front doors.

"Will they be okay?" Kianthe didn't think *she'd* be okay, left alone with this growing crowd.

Reyna chuckled. "Considering they've run this shop together almost as often as we have, I suspect they'll be fine." With a wave at the gaping crowds, she led Kianthe out the front. They always had little tables set up outside, surrounded by flowers and potted plants, but the rise in demand had called for more seating. Now, their front patio extended into the road, and horses had started treading through the dead grass of the meadow across the street instead.

The crowds thinned as they entered the town proper, but only a little. Several of their friends were relaxing in the town square. The inn was bustling already—every room had been booked all season—and someone had already lit the bonfire in the center of town for another day of warmth.

Kianthe stoked the flames with a hand, waving at the two kids chopping firewood. They wiped their foreheads, leaning on their axes as they waved back.

The only good thing about these increased crowds was increased revenue. Several merchants had set up stands in the town square, forming an almost impromptu market. Patol, their beekeeper, offered Reyna a slice of bread topped with honey as they approached. "For you, *Queen* Reyna." He grinned, making a show of it.

A few tourists clearly took note, but kept their distance.

How clever. Kianthe rolled her eyes. "I'm famous too, you know."

"Certainly, Arcandor." Patol raised his voice at her title, too.

Reyna chuckled, took a bite, then offered half to Kianthe. The honey was sweet—creamed into a buttery consistency that spread evenly over the warm bread.

Kianthe hadn't realized how hungry she was before now. "Is this the summer stock?"

"It certainly isn't a winter one! Bees are dormant now; it'll be a while before I'm able to restock." Patol gestured at the jars in front of him. "If I keep selling a 'little taste of Tawney,' I'll be able to take the rest of winter off!"

Kianthe snorted. "However will you fill your time?"

"Might play a board game. Is Cocoa & Capitalism still banned in New Leaf?"

"Yes," they both replied.

Patol heaved a sigh. "Shame. It really grew on me."

"That's because you won the last three games." Kianthe didn't bother hiding her bitterness. The moment she'd relinquished her position as the Manager of Revenue was the moment she'd started losing. It wasn't nearly as fun when she was in the lower half of incomes . . . and by the end of the game, everyone except the Manager and the bankers were.

Matild swore that could change, but they'd done enough runs that Kianthe doubted it.

Reyna craned her neck to examine the clinic behind them. "Is Matild in?"

"Yeah. Some kid tripped running around the inn this morning." Patol sounded wholly unsympathetic about that. "That was *after* Hansen told his parents to wrangle him—twice. Kids outside Tawney must be raised different."

"It's not just the kids," Kianthe groused.

"Careful, love. You're starting to sound like you're six decades older." Reyna nudged her wife, then told Patol, "Set a jar aside for us, all right? We'll be back for it."

"Anything for you, Your Excellency." His tone was teasing, and he plucked a jar from his dwindling lineup to wrap in paper and twine. The moment they stepped away from the stand, tourists flooded it, and Patol was all smiles.

As they stepped away, Reyna breathed a relieved sigh. "Perhaps someday, I won't flinch at that title, especially when it's spoken by our friends."

Kianthe could sympathize. "For the first few years as the Arcandor, all I wanted was to be normal again. But the hype dies down, trust me. You're shiny and new right now—you just need some time to settle into the role."

"Mmm." Reyna was clearly unconvinced. She rapped on the wooden door of the clinic, then eased it open.

Kianthe followed, shutting the door behind her and shedding her cloak in the sudden warmth. Contrary to the chaos of New Leaf, the clinic was pristine and nearly empty—a welcome change. A boy sat on the edge of one bed, his head wrapped in clean white bandaging, kicking his legs and looking very bored.

Matild was in the middle of telling the boy's father off: "—your son run around the inn on such a busy morning. It's disrespectful, and frankly dangerous." The midwife waggled a finger at the man, who actually looked abashed.

Reyna cleared her throat.

Matild glanced their way, heaved a relieved sigh, and shooed the boy off the bed. She caught his shoulder before he could sprint for the door, and her tone somehow became *more* stern. "No running. I mean it."

The boy nodded meekly, and she handed him a stick of hardened taffy. He squealed in delight, sucking on it. Matild's eyes swiveled to the father, and her gaze darkened. "None for you. You don't deserve it."

"Ouch," Kianthe drawled, leaning against the front counter beside the window. It was covered in parchment, spread across the wood with no semblance of order. The handwritten script across the pages included things like: *Headache remedy, room 12. Pregnancy supplements, room 7.* Orders from the inn, maybe? Her clinic might be physically empty, but Matild was clearly just as busy.

As the father and boy exited, Kianthe asked, "What about me? Do I deserve a piece of candy?"

Matild swiveled on them, quirking one eyebrow. "Did you stop any natural disasters today?"

"Did *he*?" Kianthe jerked a thumb at the boy as he sprinted past the window. His father jogged after him, face painted in exasperation.

Matild massaged her brow, sweeping behind the counter as she parsed through the orders. "I haven't been this busy since I worked in the palace. I really thought the first good snowstorm would dampen their enthusiasm for Tawney, but they just keep coming. And folks on vacation are *morons*."

"Has there been a town meeting?" Reyna frowned, one hand resting on her sword. Sometimes she left New Leaf without it, but it was rare—and after the kidnapping, Kianthe couldn't blame her for keeping it close. "Lord Wylan should—"

"We've had four since you left." Matild plucked out an order form stained with tea, squinted at her own handwriting, and muttered, "Wolfsbane. Great." Then she strode to a row of cabinets near the back of the clinic and swept the doors open, whispering under her breath as she surveyed the labeled jars.

"Four?" Reyna balked. "I wasn't informed."

Now Matild paused, glancing over her shoulder. "I think Wylan is embarrassed. He wants to report *good* news, and right now Tawney doesn't have much of that. But I'm far less concerned about my public image—if you can get these people off my doorstep and lighten my workload, I'd kiss your feet, *Your Excellency.*"

The title was spoken with mild amusement, and Matild punctuated it with a wink.

"Kinky," Kianthe couldn't resist saying.

"Oh, Gods." Reyna scrubbed her face.

Matild tucked three jars under her arm, grabbed a fourth as an afterthought, and spread them across a counter adjacent to the row of beds. She uncorked a bottle of sickly brown leaves and tugged out a few. "How was your kidnapping, by the way?"

"Does everyone know about that?" Reyna muttered, her cheeks tinging pink. "They used blue locke. There was nothing I could have done."

"She was captured by low-level bandits," Kianthe inserted gleefully.

Matild smirked. "The same bandits who think you run a secret operation out of New Leaf? That bright bunch?"

Reyna looked like she wanted to melt into the floor. She smoothed her shirt, fighting for composure. Her mouth opened, closed again. It was a rare moment when Reyna was actually speechless.

Matild paused in her work to lean against the counter, arms crossed, clearly waiting for the excuse.

"Never mind." Reyna heaved a sigh.

Kianthe almost felt bad for the prodding. She slid around the counter, casually opening drawers to peek inside for the hardened taffy. "Don't worry, Matild. She isn't losing her touch. By the time I got there, she was having lunch with them."

"Well, they *are* colleagues." Matild's words dripped sarcasm.

Even Reyna laughed at that.

Matild pushed away from the counter and swept Reyna into a welcoming hug. "Either way, we're happy you're back. Using hawks to deliver messages was a smart move; Kianthe was able to fly south much faster than if a Queensguard came by horseback." Now Matild pulled away, lifting one of Reyna's arms, then the other. "Injuries?"

"Just my pride," Reyna said drily.

Kianthe snorted, choked on her own spit, and dissolved into a coughing fit. Reyna and Matild watched, unimpressed, although Reyna's lips quirked ever so slightly. Matild rolled her eyes. "That's what you get for trying to find my candy."

"Second drawer on the left, love. Behind the quills."

Matild slapped Reyna's shoulder. "Now I need a new hiding spot." A shout from the town square caught her attention, and the midwife glanced at the crowds outside. Her eyes drifted back to the stack of orders on her desk. "Work awaits." She sounded weary.

"How'd you handle this volume in the Grand Palace?" Kianthe asked, unwrapping a piece of taffy with barely contained glee.

"Bigger facilities and more staff. But so far, I haven't seen any medical professionals coming to visit, which means it's just me." Matild began grinding the dried leaves in a stone mortar, her wrist moving with practiced motion.

Reyna tilted her head. "I'm certain we can attract more folks—"

"We don't need *more* folks. We need fewer." Matild pointed the pestle at Reyna. "You may want to visit Wylan. At the last town meeting, the general consensus was 'make the town unlivable so they leave,' and for some reason he's entertaining it."

The candy was getting chewy—it was flavored with raspberry

extract, and stuck to Kianthe's teeth as she chewed. Her lips smacked, and her words were muffled. "I mean, that worked in Lathe. But it was probably because of the bandit attacks."

"We'll visit Wylan," Reyna said with a grimace.

"Good. Never thought I'd *miss* waking up to dragon fire." Matild uncapped another jar and scooped a spoonful of thick black syrup, adding it to a second bowl. "Good luck, guys. Put the candy back, Kianthe—they're for the kids, not you."

"Aww." Kianthe swallowed the lump of taffy, then glumly returned the two extra pieces she'd swiped. Reyna shook her head, a fond smile on her lips as they headed back into the cold.

5

Reyna

"I thought Feo was our priority," Kianthe said as they climbed the staircase to Lord Wylan's estate.

Considering Tawney straddled two countries' borders, its governance was often called into question. The Queendom had taken the liberty of establishing an impressive mansion on the north end of town, nestled against the rim—a clear show of power that felt ridiculous now that Reyna was queen.

Granted, Diarn Feo, the Sheparan leader in Tawney, had every opportunity to bolster their own estate. And yet, they hardly altered their little compound, instead choosing to spend more and more time here . . . with Lord Wylan.

Which was why Reyna replied with confidence, "I have a feeling we'll find them both. Save everyone some time."

"You think Feo's sleeping over now?"

"Feo was 'sleeping over' two seasons ago. Now, I think they've moved in."

Kianthe's grin grew wicked. "Well. That's one way to muscle into Queendom territory."

"Darling, please." But Reyna was laughing too. She lifted the knocker on the front door, admiring the detail of the dragon head bolted to the wood, and counted internally. After forty-six, she gave up, because clearly Ralund was off-duty today.

A shame. The butler would never leave guests on the stoop this long. Reyna had to rap three more times, enough that when Kianthe offered, "I can just magic the door open," Reyna actually considered it.

But finally, someone inside shouted, "I'm coming, I'm *coming*." The words were acidic, barely audible through the heavy wood and stone. If someone could channel irritation into the action of opening a door, Feo—half-dressed and bleary-eyed—managed it.

"*What?*"

A sly smile crossed Reyna's lips, and she folded her arms. "Councilmember. What a surprise to see you here."

"And so early in the morning," Kianthe drawled, even though it was nearing noon.

Rather than sink into the embarrassment of being caught, Feo lifted their chin, eyes flashing, and owned it. "I am the diarn of Tawney, and an esteemed member of the Sheparan council. It's only natural I'd visit the local lord on occasion."

"What a familiar excuse," Reyna mused, sliding her arm through Kianthe's, her light brown eyes never leaving Feo's. "Darling, didn't you used to say it was a matter of 'international politics' to befriend a right-hand guard of Queen Tilaine?"

"If I remember correctly, we moved past 'befriending' at a shocking speed." Kianthe rocked on her heels, clearly relishing this. "I expected you'd court someone more formally than this, Feo. When are you two going to make things official?"

"We are not—" Feo cut themself off, raising their hands as if they wanted to strangle Kianthe. When the mage's grin widened, Feo instead smoothed their shirt—buttoned unevenly, Reyna noted—and clenched their jaw. "You want to make things official? Make an appointment." And they slammed the front door shut.

Kianthe and Reyna exchanged an amused glance. Reyna casually tapped the knocker against its brass plate again.

Feo wrenched open the door a second time. "Go *away*."

"Is the lord of the house home?" Reyna asked mildly. "I'm afraid his queen requires his presence. It's a matter of urgency."

Kianthe's shoulders shook with mirth.

Feo glowered at them. "You've got to be joking."

"As an esteemed member of the Sheparan council, it might reflect poorly on our alliance if you interfered in Queendom affairs." Reyna should stop, but this was far too much fun. She kept her expression stern, as if Feo didn't regularly attend game night at the bookstore, as if Reyna didn't take tea with Lord Wylan every few days.

"You're a menace," the diarn muttered, and stepped aside to admit them.

"I was about to pull magical rank next." Kianthe patted Feo's shoulder as she strolled past.

That made Feo scoff, even as they stepped around Reyna to take the lead. Their familiarity with the labyrinthine hallways of the mansion was more telling than the state of their clothes. Feo spoke over their shoulder: "I'm an alchemist, not an elemental mage. And after the Magicary banished me, I hardly give a rat's ass about rank."

"So, if the Alchemicor arrived at your doorstep, you wouldn't let him in either?" Kianthe asked, offering half-hearted glances at the oil portraits of Wylan's family that framed the hall. Reyna almost laughed; if Ralund were here, they'd have stopped at each one, paying respects to the lord's lineage before meeting Wylan. Instead, they walked past fast enough that Kianthe's fingers could barely brush the smooth marble of a pedestal displaying a small dragon statue.

"The *Alchemicor* only makes an appearance in the Magicary every half decade to defend his title in that farce of a tournament. I hardly expect him to interrupt our morning." With a growl, Feo shoved open the door to the study. "Wait here. I'll get Wylan."

"*Lord* Wylan. In the Queendom, it's polite to use a lord's title unless you're . . . well, more than friends." Reyna smiled amicably as she strolled into the massive room.

Feo looked like they were contemplating every single life choice. They scrubbed their face and slammed the door. Their stomping footsteps echoed, then faded, leaving Kianthe and Reyna in silence. The pair glanced at each other, then burst out laughing.

"That was my favorite '*but I'm royalty*' argument yet," Kianthe wheezed, bending over her knees.

Still chuckling, Reyna strode to the armchair beside the study's hearth. Without Ralund here today, no one had prepared tea, but a covered plate of scones had been left from the night before. She lifted the glass covering and chose one, taking a bite. "It's hardly a lie. But . . . I'll admit that was fun."

"Pulling rank on Feo is *always* fun." Kianthe immediately stepped to the bookcases lining the room. The study had two levels, with the upper one framed with a balcony overlooking the main floor. Both had shelves framing the walls, but upstairs acted more as a museum, preserving artifacts from Tawney's history. The drapes had already been opened—or perhaps they'd never been drawn—so the study was bright and welcoming.

Kianthe, of course, only ever cared about the bookcases. "Do you think Wylan's going to stock my book in here? I wonder if they're even going to distribute beyond Wellia . . . ?"

"I'm sure we can hand him a copy, if not. What a change of pace—offering him a book instead of stealing his supply."

Kianthe gasped. "It's not stealing. We have an arrangement."

"Mmm. An arrangement that you could collect a tome every visit, as a way to convince Tilaine you were good friends with Lord Wylan. It hardly applies now that she's off the throne." Reyna took another bite of her scone, watching her wife with amusement. "And yet, here you are. Acting as if we don't own an entire bookshop."

Kianthe cleared her throat. "He has vintage copies. Rare stock."

"I'm sure." Reyna finished the scone, then moseyed to the table that held an ornate kettle, four mugs, and several blends of tea. She'd prepared them herself, and now she sifted through the linen bags. "Light the kettle for me, dear?"

"Huh? Oh, sure." Kianthe flicked a finger, and across the room, a small flame ignited beneath the circular heating rack.

While the water heated, Reyna scooped a tiny spoonful of honey, then placed a blend of lavender rose into the mug. "We should check that your book will be stocked at—"

The study's doors opened again, and this time Lord Wylan strode inside. Unlike his Sheparan counterpart, Wylan was composed, dressed formally in a tailored shirt, a red jacket embroidered with gold, and dark slacks. He swept into a deep bow, addressing Reyna first. "Your Excellency. What a pleasant surprise." Then he turned to Kianthe. "Arcandor. Stealing more of my books?"

"Why is this suddenly such a problem?" Kianthe demanded, almost petulant. "We had a deal. Six per visit."

Reyna rolled her eyes.

"One, was the deal," Wylan replied with a touch of exasperation. "I know your shelves are bare at New Leaf, but many of these tomes are from my family collection." His eyes shifted to Reyna as Kianthe grudgingly replaced the book she'd chosen. "Queen Reyna, please. I would be more than happy to serve you."

Reyna lifted one brow, pouring hot water from the kettle. "If I can't steep my own herbal blends, our tea shop will have a problem."

Diarn Feo strolled in behind Wylan. Their appearance was less unkempt—their shirt had been fixed, their hair combed—but their annoyed expression remained. They dropped onto the couch. "Come now, *Your Excellency*. You insisted this is a formal visit. I figured there'd be protocol for the queen visiting a lord in the Queendom."

"Why is there a protocol for everything?" Kianthe asked.

"There is indeeed. It requires all Sheparan dignitaries to vacate while we discuss Queendom matters." Reyna ignored her wife, tilting her head at the councilmember. "Is that your preference?"

Feo scowled, waving a dismissive hand. "If it's about those damned tourists, that's absolutely my preference. Let the influx of visitors be *your* problem."

Guilt prickled in Reyna's chest. Something about confirming

the problem with Feo, who wasn't fazed by much, made that a bigger problem—and it would seem she and Kianthe were the crux of it. Reyna shifted her weight, pulling out two more mugs and choosing herbal blends for the lord and diarn. "Well, that brings me to matter one. Wylan, can you summarize the town meetings?"

"Of course." He closed the study doors. Considering his manor was typically empty, it was more of a formality than anything. "Speaking frankly? They've been a fucking mess, Your Excellency."

Reyna nearly spilled the hot water. Of course, based on what she'd seen, that report was hardly a surprise. There was no *easy* solution to a town scaling this rapidly. Still, she'd been secretly hoping they'd uncovered one.

Wylan unbuttoned and removed his formal jacket, hanging it by the door. He took the proffered mug from her, and Reyna noted the stress lines along his face. Hmm. Things were worse than she thought.

Wylan spoke wearily. "We should be grateful that attendance is so high, but everyone has an opinion at these meetings. So far, they range from 'let it be' to 'provoke the dragons into attacking again.' Feo and I are doing our best, but there doesn't seem to be a decent option here. We concluded our last meeting after midnight with nothing actionable to show."

Reyna wanted Queendom lords to run their towns as they saw fit . . . but this was getting out of hand. When the first tourists started appearing after the wedding, Reyna clung to the argument that two people *couldn't* be responsible for visitors flooding a town. Especially a town so far north, so inhospitable in climate. But the internal debate fell to shambles when she saw the crowds outside New Leaf yesterday.

"The townsfolk are trying to make the town 'unlivable,'" Kianthe said. She'd settled on the floor by the hearth, as usual, and was flipping through a thick tome. When Wylan raised an eyebrow, she hastened to say, "I'm not stealing it. I'm just reading."

"What a change in pace," Wylan drawled.

Kianthe snorted, but pressed on. "Matild said that word: 'un-livable.' Is that true?"

Feo avoided their gazes. Wylan pinched his brow, heaving a sigh. "That is where the last town hall meeting landed, yes. Some folks thought that if Tawneans weren't so nice, if the town wasn't as welcoming, we'd develop a different kind of reputation."

That idea hurt Reyna's soul. "Come on, Wylan. You can't be entertaining that. We visited this town and were *charmed* by the locals. Why is it fair that we shut the gate behind us—or worse, foster a darker culture within our own town limits?"

She adored that her neighbors had become friends. She loved helping them when times were tough, knowing that she could rely on them for the same. After leaving the comradery of the Queensguard, Tawney gave her a similar kinship. It was *home* for a reason.

"I won't let them ruin the town," Wylan promised. "But we are reaching a tipping point here. At first, the influx with our local economy seemed like a blessing . . . but everyone's at their limits dealing with these crowds."

Feo leaned against the armrest, sniffing the tea Reyna had made as if it might be poisoned. "Tessalyn wrote and suggested a limited number of tourists per day. A ticket system where only a specific number of folks can enjoy the town at a time. It sounds tedious, but if we hold that line for a while, we might be able to convince visitors this town isn't worth it."

"Have we tried telling them all to go home?" Kianthe drawled.

"Believe it or not, we did." Wylan settled beside Feo on the couch, drawing a deep swig of his tea. "The nice ones listened and moved on. The rude, disruptive ones were left. It wasn't a perfect system."

Reyna grimaced. "I'll contact Tessalyn again, and we'll brainstorm other ways to fix it. I do appreciate your dedication to the problem."

Now Wylan offered her a tight smile. "Tawney is my home, too. We'll find a solution; don't worry." A pause, and his lips spread wider. "Speaking of worry, how was your kidnapping? Awfully short stint with those bandits, hmm?"

How had this information spread *so* fast? The rumor mill in Tawney was alive and well, it would seem. Reyna's cheeks heated. "It was fine. Thank you for asking."

"How *did* second-rate bandits overwhelm you?" Feo was clearly still bitter at their morning interruption, and now gleefully poked at an obvious wound.

"They had an alchemist." Kianthe closed the book with a resolute *thump.*

That stopped any humor. Feo had been nearby during Reyna's *last* run-in with alchemy—and Reyna knew they'd lent their talents to Dreggs's alchemists, undoing the damage of Arlon's nearly murderous security system. Their demeanor shifted instantly, and they leaned forward in their chair. "Were you hurt?"

Their protective tone warmed her heart. Despite Feo's posturing, they did care about their friends. They just had a hard time showing it externally—which could get them into trouble sometimes.

Reyna shook her head. "They used blue locke to render me unconscious, so apart from a headache, I felt fine. But hidden beneath my cell, I uncovered this alchemical circle." She tugged out the parchment, careful not to smudge the charcoal as she passed it to Wylan.

Feo craned over Wylan's shoulder as he held it up for examination. But Wylan had no ties to the Magicary, so after a brief study, he tried to hand the parchment to Feo.

Except Feo wouldn't take it.

How curious.

Kianthe noticed too. She set the book in her lap, instead paying rapt attention to this analysis. "What's the problem, Feo? Afraid you'll activate something if you touch it?"

"Even I can't activate alchemy without a sacrifice," Feo retorted. They still didn't reach for the parchment. "But—this sigil shouldn't exist. The base circle is fine, but the extra symbols here and here . . . they're like another language."

"I thought you said alchemy wasn't a language." Wylan's tone was teasing, as if he was prodding the diarn into an age-old argument.

Feo set down their mug, finally taking the parchment. They braced themself, almost like they expected a true ramification for holding that symbol. It sent a shock of fear through Reyna's chest.

How dangerous a position had she *been* in?

Luckily, nothing happened. Feo squinted at the circle. "Alchemy uses symbols in specific combinations to channel magic, and in that way, it can be learned—*similar* to a new language. But true languages have syntax, accents, and adaptations. The written form of alchemy can be streamlined with extensive experimentation, but it's just perfecting what we already know."

"So . . . you have a base alphabet, and are finding new combinations of letters. New words, almost." Wylan elbowed them.

"It's not the same, Wy," Feo retorted.

Kianthe and Reyna exchanged delighted looks.

Feo seemed to realize their slip, and a subtle flush appeared over their ears and neck. They dropped the parchment to the table beside them, stubbornly picking up their mug. "I don't know what this was intended to do. It shares patterns with the circle we found below that church—the one that extracted magic from the dragon eggs. But Reyna doesn't *have* magic, so maybe that's why it remained inert. Or maybe it wouldn't work at all. This combination of symbols really shouldn't exist."

Kianthe winced, leaning back on her palms, ankles crossed on the plush carpet. "Then it was meant to drain magic?"

"I just said, I have no idea," Feo reiterated. "Researching a sigil like this would take time. It shares *similarities* with that circle, but it isn't the same. Everything beyond noting that comparison is conjecture."

Kianthe rolled her eyes. "You must have been so much fun in the Magicary."

Feo sniffed. "I won't pretend to be an expert if I don't *know* something. That's a rule you could follow, Kianthe."

Reyna was still puzzling through the sigil. "Perhaps they were anticipating my rescue?" Her brows furrowed, and she glanced at Kianthe. "Kidnapping you would be dangerous. Maybe I seemed like a safer bet. It's possible I was bait."

"Someone smart enough to create new alchemy symbols can't be stupid enough to think you're *easier* to kidnap." Kianthe rolled her eyes.

"Well, I was two nights ago." It was embarrassing, especially when Wylan hid a smile, so Reyna pushed ahead. "Perhaps it's time to interrogate those bandits again. Or maybe we should revisit the watchtower and see if we missed other clues."

Feo coughed pointedly.

Reyna cast a glance at them. They were still examining the parchment, their mug resting in their lap, forgotten.

"Unless you have another idea, Feo?"

"Well, I'm sure you're aware that the Alchemicor hides in the Vardian Mountains for years at a time. No one can find him."

Kianthe scoffed. "No shit. He's impossible to contact. That's why we're asking for your help instead."

"As flattered as I am, my alchemy use has been limited since coming to Tawney."

"You created an alchemy circle that cleared an *avalanche* last year. You literally beat me to it." Considering she boasted about being the Realm's most powerful mage, there was an undeniable note of pride in Kianthe's voice when she talked about Feo's magical ability.

If Reyna had to take a guess, that stemmed from Feo being exiled from the Magicary, and having to perfect their alchemy alone. Before the Stone of Seeing chose her to be the Mage of Ages, Kianthe said she'd been losing touch with the elements. She probably saw more in common with Feo than the alchemist realized.

Feo flushed with her praise, waving the words away. "The point is, if anyone would know about these new symbols, it's the Alchemicor. And it's been so long since you've visited the Magicary, Kianthe, I bet you forgot this year is the Mid-Winter Alchemical Showdown."

"No fucking way," Kianthe exclaimed, straightening. "It's been five years already?"

Wylan and Reyna exchanged a glance. Wylan drummed his fingers against his mug, amused. "Do you want to ask, or should I?"

Reyna gestured for him to proceed.

"What, pray tell, is the *Mid-Winter Alchemical Showdown*?" Wylan's voice was dry.

Kianthe pushed to her feet, suddenly animated. "Only the best festival *ever*. Imagine every mage in the Realm converging in the Magicary for several days of celebration. There's food and shops and competitions and—"

"My dear, what's the purpose of it?" Reyna prodded.

Kianthe huffed. "To choose the next Alchemicor, obviously. Alchemy isn't like elemental magic. The Stone of Seeing chooses its main conduit—currently, me—and divvies out leftover elemental magic to mages of its choice. They receive a set amount of power, so their fates are predetermined. But alchemy is a *learned* skill. Study and practice enough, and any mage can be a great alchemist."

"Don't be fooled. It's still considered second-tier to elemental magic," Feo drawled. The words were spoken as fact, albeit with a sour undertone. "These symbols channel our magic, but blood sacrifices are our power source. It isn't a *good* thing to be a 'great' alchemist. Not to most."

"Hence why I'm a public figure, but the Alchemicor is a recluse." Kianthe seemed to realize how that sounded, because she hastened to clarify, "But he's a nice guy. A bit quirky." Now she spun back to Reyna, eyes alight. "Still, the Alchemical Showdown is a great time. It's a chance for the current Alchemicor to be dethroned, if someone demonstrates more ability."

Reyna was still caught on the "sacrifice" part. She knew how alchemy worked, but this contest was new—disturbing—

information. "Hold on. Every five years, the Magicary condones killing animals for a silly competition?"

Kianthe raised an eyebrow at her tone. "Livestock. The same things we eat for dinner every night. Nothing is wasted."

"That's why the event is hosted over the Mid-Winter Celebration," Feo supplied. "The Sheparan council has an agreement with the Magicary. We pause all culling of our own food supply for half a moon's cycle, to allow the alchemists to take that magic for the festival. Afterward, the mages prepare the food and ship it across Shepara for the holiday. It's a desired vacation for most of our butchers and cooks."

It made a certain kind of sense. News of *that* deal certainly hadn't reached the Queendom, or Tilaine would have had a fit that she'd been excluded. There was utility in claiming magic from a sacrifice that would happen anyway.

Feo shrugged, handing the parchment back to Reyna. They held it between their thumb and forefinger, as if it might shock them. "Point is, that's all I can offer. Take it to the Alchemicor and see if he knows who created it."

"Perhaps you should come?" Reyna crossed her legs, leaning forward. The sigil in her hands represented a mystery now, and it sent a thrill through her veins. She hadn't had a good mystery since the missing dragon eggs—and Feo had been her research companion through that. "You know more about alchemy than we do. And frankly, I trust you more than some ruthless recluse."

"The Alchemicor," Kianthe laughed. "*Ruthless.*"

"His magic centers around blood sacrifice, dear," Reyna said.

Kianthe wiped tears from her eyes. "You haven't met him. But she's right, Feo. If you show up with us, the Magicary can't ban your entry. You should come. Maybe try for the Alchemicor's position this time."

Feo drained the last of their tea, pushing to their feet. "After all those mages have done? Please, Kianthe. The high-mage of the Magicary owes me an apology, and until she offers that, I won't set foot on their grounds."

That seemed entirely fair, in Reyna's opinion. "We'll miss you, then."

Feo was already heading for the door. "Sure, sure."

Kianthe, meanwhile, slid onto the armrest of Reyna's chair, one arm draped over her shoulders. "I won't miss you that much, Feo! Because you know what this means, Rain? A romantic retreat for us." She paused, then amended, "Well, romance, plus alchemists dueling out their differences while we eat ourselves silly."

"You know the way to my heart," Reyna deadpanned.

Kianthe winked. "Always."

To the Magicary, then.

6

Kianthe

The most direct route to the Magicary crossed the Vardian mountain range—and a small section of dragon country. Considering that dragon magic in excess still made Kianthe queasy, they opted to fly over the foothills instead.

Of course, their southern route didn't seem to help much. Half a day into the flight, Kianthe's stomach was churning and she felt generally miserable. She slumped over Visk and muttered, "Either I ate something bad, or I'm a lot more susceptible to dragon magic than I thought."

Nestled on Ponder, Reyna tsked sympathetically and cast a glance over her shoulder. It was a cloudy winter day, and this high up, the wind was cutting. She had to tug down her scarf to respond. "It's probably our entourage."

"Our what?" Kianthe frowned.

"Pill Bug and Gold Coin have been following us for half a day, and I'm pretty sure a couple adult dragons are following *them*."

Kianthe blanched, twisting on Visk to squint at the clouds behind them. It took some concentration, but she could barely make out four leathery wingtips flitting through the clouds. The baby dragons were clearly making a game of this hide-and-seek. Now that she was paying attention, she noticed that Ponder wasn't being subtle either; the griffon kept craning her head, struggling to fly straight while she scoped out the area behind them.

Two massive shapes loomed in the clouds beyond the baby dragons. They looked ominous from this angle, huge and silent, like an impending storm. Even though they were on good terms with the dragons now, it still sent a shiver up Kianthe's spine.

Or maybe that was the cold.

"Ugh. No wonder." Kianthe turned a scrutinizing gaze on Ponder. "Pondie. Did you tell them to come?"

Reyna's griffon chirped, an innocent *Who, me?*

Visk heaved a whole-body sigh, shaking himself like he wanted no part in this nonsense. Kianthe tucked a few stray strands of hair into her hood, grumbling, "Unbelievable. They're going to ruin the festival." Her stomach flipped, and she swallowed a groan. "Or my favorite cloak."

"She misses her friends." Reyna patted Ponder's neck. "I'd have said something sooner, but I didn't realize you could feel their magic from here. Stay put, love. I'll turn them around." And with a click of her tongue, she angled Ponder back toward the dragons.

Visk slowed in a leisurely circle, giving Kianthe a perfect view as Ponder flitted up to the pair of young dragons. For a moment, they chased each other through the clouds, but then Reyna whistled sharply and Ponder straightened, ignoring her friends with an artificial air of self-importance. If a griffon could be smug, Ponder embodied it, especially as she casually soared toward the two huge dragons lurking in the clouds.

Some conversation happened. Kianthe still didn't understand it. No one could speak to the dragons—humans didn't have the throats or the tongues for their language, and vice versa. Kianthe had managed a semblance of communication with them using magic, sliding images through a specialized link. It was incredibly unpleasant, but got the job done.

Now that Reyna had forsaken her Gods and embraced the dragons, she seemed to have free access to speak her mind. They understood her just fine, apparently, and it was earning her a reputation.

Well, *another* reputation, anyway.

After several moments, one big dragon snorted, the sound echoing through the clouds. The other roared, and the baby dragons instantly stopped playing with the clouds. Pill Bug raced toward its babysitters, and Gold Coin paused to nip at Ponder's wings before following.

Ponder screeched goodbye, and easily angled back toward her father and Kianthe.

Kianthe felt better with every passing breath, gaining distance from the adults. She leaned back on Visk, smirking slightly as the pair of griffons continued on. "You're just embracing the Dragon Queen thing, aren't you?"

"Dragon Queen?" Reyna wrinkled her nose. "The dragons hardly have a queen. Those two lost a bet. They wanted to tire Pill Bug and Gold Coin so the rest of their shift would be easy." Now she cast a sideways glance at Kianthe. "They *were* interested to know that their magic makes you sick. Apparently, no elemental mage told them that before."

"Only the Arcandor could establish a link with them anyway," Kianthe muttered. "And we were probably all too busy puking onto the snow."

"Charming." Reyna offered a smug smile.

"You're enjoying this." Kianthe hunched into her cloak, summoning an ever-flame to warm her chest.

Reyna righted her scarf, and her next response was muffled. "Of course not, love. I take no pleasure in your misery." And yet, a vein of pride was obvious in her tone. Kianthe could understand—Reyna had lived her life in the shadow of a queen, viewing herself as nothing more than a royal's sword. It must be a pleasant change to have stand-out skills that made her special.

Kianthe smiled privately. Reyna deserved that.

The Magicary was a circular city nestled in an unforgiving mountain range. They reached it well after sunset, when the moon shone bright and the forest was dark enough to be an ocean. Despite its remote positioning, griffons flitted overhead, and the entire city pulsed with music and laughter.

"Considering none of you drink, mages really know how to party," Reyna remarked.

Kianthe snorted. "No, *some* mages know how to party—and they only come back for this event. The ones who live here full-time are boring as shit." Still, she cast a quick glance at Reyna, her heart pulsing with anticipation. "You've never been here before, right? Not with Tilaine or anything?"

"Considering the Queendom doesn't have mages, she had no reason to visit—and it rankled her every day that no personal invitation appeared in a steward's hand." Reyna paused, doubt coloring her tone. "I hope I'm welcomed. I would hate to intrude, but . . . it's exciting, the thought of seeing where you were raised. Other than Jallin, I mean."

"I'm excited too." Was Kianthe talking too fast? Her nerves thrummed, which was silly. It hardly mattered what Reyna thought of the Magicary, in a logical sense. Kianthe rarely went back unless it was to check with the Stone of Seeing in person. Otherwise, her life with Reyna was separate from this place.

But as they circled overhead, as Reyna craned over Ponder's back to gape at the huge circular city, pride warmed Kianthe from the inside out. Because this *was* her childhood. She was born in Jallin, but the Magicary shaped who she became.

And now that they were married, *and* Reyna was a visiting royal, none of those stuffy mages could argue her presence.

"So . . . are the buildings underground?" Reyna's voice was hesitant.

Well, that tracked. From an aerial view, the Magicary looked like a wheel. The fortresslike walls were thick, but the center was an open courtyard. Roads cut through the middle like spokes, separating huge wedges of open land used for training and magic practice. In the very center was a curved dome, glimmering with the red hue of alchemical magic.

Kianthe thought it was impressive, especially from above—but it didn't look much like a city.

"Sort of. It extends down and into the mountains," Kianthe answered, nudging Visk over the high walls to show just how tall the fortress was. From here, it looked like a cylinder stuck into a mountainside. "It's ten stories deep; the courtyard is just the top two. And there are caverns even below that and into the mountainside."

"Incredible," Reyna breathed.

The single road to the Magicary was illuminated by everflames, millions of tiny balls that lit the treacherous mountain path. Merchants needed an elemental mage just to traverse it, but dozens were doing so now, even at this late hour. Huge carts pulled by oxen and mules caught Kianthe's attention, and she grinned. "Tomorrow, the festival will be in full swing. We allow anyone to bring their wares into the Magicary and set up booths. I spend so much money."

Reyna raised an eyebrow, leaning over Ponder.

Kianthe backtracked. "Ah, *spent* so much money. I was young."

"I'm not sure age has anything to do with it," Reyna teased.

The road climbed to a huge gate in the courtyard, high enough that the rest of the building fell to steep cliffs on either side. On the parapet overhead, someone cupped their hands and shouted, "Arcandor approaching!"

A cheer swelled from inside.

Reyna grinned. "Wow. You really are famous."

A flush crept over Kianthe's cheeks, and she suddenly felt too warm. "It's just my magic. The Stone gets more generous when I'm around. The Magicary was built over multiple converging ley lines, but when *I'm* here, it's . . ." She paused, considering. "Well, I imagine it's how you feel when you get drunk."

"Aren't there children in the Magicary?"

"There isn't an age limit on magic use, Rain." Now a wicked smile parted Kianthe's lips. "I used to love when the old Arcandor visited. Kept all the bullies busy and left the library wide open."

"So, what I'm hearing is that even when you *could* get drunk, you chose to hide in a dark library with a book instead." Reyna's voice was so fond it made Kianthe warm for another reason. Being here with her made this entire experience better.

Especially considering how isolating it had been before.

Visk chirped, guiding Ponder over the wide wall of the Magicary. He watched the griffons circling overhead, but he dutifully touched down just inside the open metal gate. Ponder followed suit, shaking her feathers, eyes wide and eager. Reyna dismounted, tying off her sword as a couple mages nearby whistled at Ponder.

"The Arcandor's *wife* has a griffon, too?" one of the mages complained. "I've been waiting six years. That's so unfair."

"Shut up. She's going to hear you!" They were barely teenagers, and the lanky one waved nervously.

Kianthe rolled her eyes, but Reyna waved back. Visk and Ponder took off again, angling toward the rocky outcroppings of the mountaintops above the Magicary. Reyna watched them leave, then told the kids, "If it makes you feel better, my griffon is Visk's daughter."

"That won't make them feel better," Kianthe said.

"Oh."

Kianthe laughed, looping her arm through Reyna's. "Come on. There's so much to see." She towed Reyna farther inside the Magicary.

The massive courtyard was like another world. The training areas were barren, arenas waiting for elemental command or alchemy sigils, which meant the true competition hadn't yet begun. But the roads were brimming with stalls, so everyone was warming up for the endeavor. Ever-flames drifted like fireflies, casting the entire area in a warm glow, and magic was as prevalent as breathing.

A mage slapped his hands together and pulled a seed into a beautiful bulb of flowers, then handed it to his partner. The other man laughed, wrapping his own hand under the bulb. From his fingers, moss crawled over the roots, encompassing them in damp warmth. He handed it back to the first mage, then pressed a kiss to his lips.

Another gaggle of students passed, goofing off between the carts. Several had tankards of something—cider, perhaps—and one yelped as another shoved her, spilling the drink into the dirt. She gasped indignantly, and from her feet, the earth shifted to capture her offender's ankles.

That display of magic almost captured Reyna, too, but she sidestepped with ease. "Where can we get some of that?" She pointed at the cider.

"Over there," a third student said.

"Sorry," the other two gasped between bursts of laughter, sprinting away.

"Normally, they're asleep by now." Kianthe pulled Reyna close—partly for enjoyment, partly because an alchemist nearby was experimenting with magical fireworks, and they didn't seem entirely stable. "But this festival shakes everything up. Come on. We'll need to find—"

Someone behind them cleared his throat. "Well, well. If it isn't the Mage of Ages herself, come to grace us with her presence at last."

Kianthe glanced over her shoulder, quirking an eyebrow. "Ah, Harold. I should have guessed you'd be the first to find us. You missed our wedding, you know."

"We knew you married well before that wedding. The Stone of Seeing pulsed, and every mage nearby felt it. Seemed like a waste of a trip to attend the union ceremony after the fact—especially considering your ulterior motives." Harold appraised Reyna, his tone begrudging. "Congratulations, Queen Reyna."

"Thank you, Master Harold."

The fake title seemed to pacify him a bit, and he swelled self-importantly. "Yes, well. High-Mage Polana wants to see you, Kianthe."

"High-Mage?" Kianthe balked. "They made that crone *high-mage*?"

That made Harold swallow a laugh, one that straddled the line between horrified and righteous. "If you wanted to prevent that, you could have responded to our summons and voted for me instead. The endorsement of the Arcandor would have tipped the scales, but alas." He lifted his chin, his tone bitterly smug. "Now you get to pay respects to *her* instead."

"Lucky us," Kianthe grumbled. "We're getting cider first."

Tankards in hand, they followed Harold into the belly of the Magicary. It was clearly a long, agonizing journey for Harold, since Kianthe had no qualms about pausing every few feet to tell Reyna stories or explain the architecture. And once she realized it, Kianthe *really* leaned into her tour, just to piss him off.

"This is the nook where I'd hide from my roommate and her friends. I swear, they were like a pack of wolves. But I fit right back here—well, it's tight now, but I was smaller then—and it hid the light of my ever-flame so I could read."

Several more steps, then:

"Ah, Rain, duck in here. See how far down that fountain drains? Natural mountain spring—the original mages really tried to unite the Magicary with its surroundings. Go on. Take a sip!"

And a little farther:

"That hallway leads to the best part of the Magicary: the tertiary library. You'd think the *primary* library is the best, but it's a well-guarded secret that this one is better stocked. I'll take you there tomorrow; we'll have a blast."

Harold looked like he wanted to scream. "Arcandor, if you *please.*"

Kianthe crossed her arms. "I didn't ask for a summons. And Her Excellency requested a formal tour of the Magicary. Are you going to deny the ruler of the Queendom when relations with her country are so tenuous?" A dramatic pause. "What would High-Mage Polana think?"

At her side, Reyna laughed out loud. She pressed a swift kiss to Kianthe's lips, then squeezed her arm. In the ever-flame, her ivory cheeks were tinged from their walk, and she looked absolutely beautiful. "I'm savoring this, dear, but perhaps there's a better time. I'd personally love to meet the Magicary's leader."

"The high-mage isn't our leader. It's just a stuffy title the mages here fight over because it makes them feel important."

Harold scoffed. "The high-mage coordinates all education within the Magicary."

"Sure. But I'm not a student." Kianthe examined her nails. "Ergo, her command over any adult mage is tenuous at best. Which is something I can't wait to remind her of."

Harold tossed up his hands and led them down a grand hallway, pausing at a set of impressive double doors. The floor was wood, and plants grew between the boards. A tiny stream burbled alongside them, vanishing into a crevice in the rock walls. While Reyna admired that—it was cute how she marveled at the architecture of the Magicary—Harold rapped on the door twice.

"Enter," a stern voice called.

Polana.

Nothing was cute anymore. Sweat prickled on the back of Kianthe's neck. "Fuck. I hate this part."

Harold smirked. "Remember this next time there's a vote. I would be delighted to receive your endorsement." And he tugged open the door, standing aside to admit them.

7

Reyna

The Magicary was an absolute wonder, a marvel of nature and human engineering. She'd expected a big, round building . . . but no artist rendering did this place justice. It was a veritable fortress in theory . . . and a luxurious nature retreat in practice.

Polana's office was no exception: the floor itself was a natural spring, the ceiling a living cavern. A wooden path had been built to a circular floor in the room's center, but even that was framed with tropical plants more fitting for Leonol than the icy Vardian Mountains. Ever-flame flitted between the stalactites, and the water seemed to glow blue when it rippled.

Despite the room's wondrous appearance, the woman at the desk rather commonly reminded Reyna of her aunt. While her uncle trained future Queensguard, her aunt used to handle the logistics of supplying an entire army. She found little joy in anything but numbers and efficiency.

When she died, even her funeral wishes had been meticulously planned.

This woman had the same unamused expression, the same meticulously clean desk, the same scathing tone. Instead of glowering at Reyna, however, she had her gaze set on Harold. "Master Harold. You were not part of the invitation. You may leave."

It wasn't a suggestion. The high-mage narrowed her eyes, which were an almost unnaturally light blue and set deep in her wrinkled skin, and waited.

Kianthe rolled her eyes. "Witch."

"Excuse me, Arcandor? Speak up, if you have something to say." Polana's voice was harsh.

"Oh, sorry." Kianthe cupped her hands around her mouth, raising her voice so it echoed across the cavern. "I said that you're a witch!"

Reyna barely refrained from smacking her forehead. "*Key.*"

"What? She is." Kianthe crossed her arms. "Congratulations on the promotion, High-Mage. Allow me to introduce my wife, Her Excellency Queen Reyna, newest sovereign of the Queendom. To be honest, Polana, we're only here to see the Alchemicor and watch a few duels, and then we'll be on our way."

Polana frowned, lips pursed. "Don't be ridiculous. Surely, you're here because of my summons."

Kianthe cast a questioning glance at Reyna, who shrugged subtly. As far as she was aware, no letters or messengers from Polana had reached Tawney. Although she supposed it was possible they just missed its arrival.

Kianthe easily refocused on what was important. "I *am* ridiculous. Oh, and I don't respond to your summonses."

High-Mage Polana pushed to her feet, the movement slow and weighted. With intention, she paced around her desk. Her posture was rigid, her eyes glimmering like ice as they slid right over Kianthe—almost as if she hadn't spoken at all.

"Harold. Did I not dismiss you?"

He mock-bowed—an overstated gesture that would have resulted in his beheading, had he tried it in Tilaine's old court—but dutifully left. Narrowing her eyes, Polana waved a hand and the wood slammed shut.

Which meant they were trapped now.

Reyna wasn't afraid, not this close to Kianthe, not with her own unique skillset in combat and protection. But any fool could see Polana was hostile, whether she overtly tried something or not. Reyna's hand drifted to her sword's hilt, palm resting on the pommel.

Kianthe saw it too. She bristled. "You're as rude as ever, I see."

"And you're as childish as I remember. I'd hoped immense magical power and the favor of the blessed Stone would age you, but alas." Polana stepped closer to Reyna, examining her with a disdainful scowl. "*Queen* Reyna. Yes, I heard all about your little coup. Quite clever, marrying the Arcandor to gain a position of power yourself."

Her disapproving tone sent old habits screaming back into Reyna's mind, habits of forced reverence and mindless compliance. On the heels of that was irrational anger, because Reyna *wasn't* a Queensguard anymore. She was a sovereign, and would be treated as such.

The fact was, Polana held no more power over *her* than she did over Kianthe.

That let Reyna relax into an easy stance.

Kianthe, meanwhile, shared none of her wife's composure. Her hands actually ignited, and she took a threatening step forward. "Say that again, *High-Mage*."

The disdain in Polana's expression was irritating. "Mmm. Impulsive as ever. It's shocking you haven't drowned someone in a tidal wave yet." Polana lifted her chin, daring Kianthe to attack. Daring her to prove the point.

For all that Reyna wasn't intimidated by Polana, she *was* irritated at that statement. Kianthe was impulsive, and sometimes even childish, but never when it mattered. When push came to shove, the jokes fell away to reveal a strong, capable, caring woman.

Her wife didn't need defending . . . but sometimes Reyna couldn't stop herself.

She stepped forward, her tone shedding all politeness. "Think what you will about me. But what's shocking, High-Mage, is that the Magicary's top representative would treat the Stone of Seeing's chosen as common filth."

Polana's eyes widened, and she spat, "Excuse me—"

"I don't excuse rudeness toward my wife." Now Reyna *tsk*ed.

"Every leader knows it's best to present a unified front, and solve spats in private. Your attitude makes it shockingly obvious who truly holds the power here . . . and who is posturing with a bad attitude and grandiose displays."

A deep chuckle echoed from farther within the cavern, cutting off Polana's reply.

Against the cavern wall, a glowing red circle flashed and faded, and a wiry man strode through the rock itself. Well, "strode" implied suave confidence. In actuality, he stepped instantly into knee-deep water, slid on a rock and nearly impaled himself on a stalagmite, then had to ease around the would-be murder weapon into the pond proper. All the while he kept his arms lifted, as if it might save the lower half of his well-worn cloak.

"Sorry I'm late," he called, still laughing. "Stars above. Your wife has a bite, Kianthe."

He hauled himself onto the wooden platform in the room's center, dripping all over Polana's plush crimson rug—a shade the older woman's weathered skin was starting to match. He flicked a piece of algae back into the water, then noticed the tropical plant he'd smooshed climbing up here. With a nervous laugh, he said "No one saw that" to the two elemental mages and carefully smoothed the leaves.

It didn't work. Kianthe heaved an exasperated sigh and flicked a finger at the plant. Instantly, its broken stems knitted back together, and red flowers bloomed across it. With that done, Kianthe gestured between them. "Al, this is Reyna, sovereign of the Queendom. Reyna, Al."

"Al . . . the Alchemicor." Reyna took a guess.

"Albert Chemicor, at your service," he said, bowing low. He was only a little younger than Polana, but he moved with a spry fervor. She wasn't surprised when he gently took her hand and kissed the back of it.

Reyna must have misheard. "Your full name is Albert Chemicor?"

But Kianthe and Polana seemed to have one thing in

common—their mutual exasperation for the esteemed alche-mist before them.

Polana scowled and swept behind her desk again, silent.

Kianthe, meanwhile, shook Albert's hand. "Albert changed his name, decades ago." He was still dripping, so she waved a hand, tugging the water from the fabric of his clothes and balling it. For a moment, it looked like she might chuck the ball at Polana's head, but instead she let it slide back into the pond. "And before you say that's ridiculous, you should know that I've already hunted down the paperwork, and it was truly, honestly legal."

"I wasn't even the Alchemicor at the time!" Al chimed with a full-bodied laugh. "I just believe destinies can change if you *really* want it. You're a perfect example of that, Your Excellency. How's life as a royal treating you?"

"It was fine until recently," Reyna said, her eyes cutting to Po-lana. She wasn't about to ask for help about the alchemical sigil with the high-mage lurking on the edge of their conversation.

Kianthe seemed to realize it and swooped in. "Polana, we're only here for Albert. Did you need something specific, or were you just hoping to smack us with your broomstick?"

"That's a Magicary burn," Al whispered to Reyna. "Before we partnered with the griffons, mages tried to spell different objects to achieve flight. The stupidest of them thought broom-sticks were the way to go. Imagine that!"

Reyna swallowed a laugh. "I pieced together the context. Thank you, Albert."

Polana set her jaw, ignoring them both. "This is absurd. There was a reason for the summons, Arcandor. I expected *you,* of all people, would know that the Stone of Seeing is fading in power. Your selfish decision to remain apart from the Magicary is directly impacting our deity, the blessed source of our power."

That made everyone pause. Kianthe physically stiffened, and Reyna could almost *see* her tapping into her magical reservoir, following it back to the Stone of Seeing. She'd explained her magic once as being like glowing golden threads, all linked to a single, brilliant sun.

The way her frown deepened wasn't encouraging.

"The Stone is losing power?" Reyna asked, gently.

Kianthe brushed her arm—a touch that said, *Not now*—and held Polana's gaze. "I'll check on the Stone. In the meantime, prepare my suite and clear the mages out of the Stone of Seeing's chamber."

"Good." Polana narrowed her eyes. "I will escort—"

"You won't get *near* the Stone," Kianthe hissed, and her tone was vitriolic enough to make Polana flinch. As the mouthpiece of their god, Kianthe was the real authority—and her humor was utterly gone.

It shouldn't have been sexy, but it was. Just a little.

"A mage of my power—" Polana tried again.

Kianthe strode to her desk, and the magic crackling off her was powerful enough to ripple the pond, antagonize the plants, sweep their very breaths away. "You wanted an Arcandor? You've got one. *I* will handle this. *You* will stay in this miserable office and try not to traumatize our vulnerable youth with pathetic power displays. Do you understand, High-Mage Polana?"

"Oooh," Al whispered. He fidgeted, checking his pockets. "I have a sigil somewhere to steal some popped corn. Smaller version of the teleportation spell I used getting in here. Should I grab you some, Reyna?"

Reyna couldn't tell if he was serious.

"Don't bother with popped corn. We aren't staying." Kianthe glared at Polana. "Well?"

"I . . . will await your response." It seemed to physically pain Polana to speak the words.

Kianthe patted the desk, her fingers leaving scorch marks in the wood. "Good. Have a miserable day, High-Mage." And with a wave, she gestured for Reyna and Al to follow her.

Albert didn't take the cue, not until they were almost in the hall, but then he said, "Ah, yes! Me! Until next time, Polly. We'll have tea." He jogged after them, and the doors swung shut with finality.

Kianthe didn't stop moving, not until they'd rounded six

corners. Every time they passed a student or adult mage, they'd identify either Kianthe or Albert and chitter like crows or stop and bow. It was oddly exciting, watching people fawn over Kianthe. But then again, the Mage of Ages was in her element inside the Magicary—literally.

They finally paused in an empty hallway. At some point, they'd left the mountain's interior passageways and returned to the circular building, because along this wall was a gentle curve of windows. It was too dark to see much through the glass, but based on the gradient of black from the stars overhead, it'd be a long fall into the valley below.

"Now?" Reyna asked.

"Almost." Kianthe squeezed her arm, expression pained, and glanced again at Albert. The Alchemicor straightened under her gaze, seeming pleased to be along for this ride. Kianthe puffed a sigh. "I'm going to need a favor, Al. This will keep me busy—but we came here for a different reason. Reyna was kidnapped a few days ago, and they put this sigil under her cell."

With the Stone's safety called into question, Reyna had almost forgotten. She patted her pockets, tugged out the folded parchment, and handed it over.

"Think you can decipher its purpose? Feo—ah, Fylo, you remember them?—well, they couldn't figure it out. Said you might know."

"Fylo! Of course. How are they?" Al chuckled, squinting at the sigil. "I heard they were banished for questioning the scripture. See, this is why it's easier to be an alchemist. There's no question of deities or religious practice. Just the spells we cast, and the conundrum of how to power them."

"Al. Focus." Considering her own personality, Kianthe didn't see the irony in that statement.

Reyna chuckled, but her humor faded as Albert took a closer look at the sigil, tracing the lines. She'd been trapped in a cell with this unknown sigil not long ago, but the memory had faded as Tawney's tourists and their Magicary visit took priority. Now, that fear slid right back down her spine.

After careful assessment, Albert rubbed his brow. "I *do* think I've seen this before, but damned if I can remember where. Decades just slip by, you know?" He laughed good-naturedly. "Let me check some things in the libraries and get back to you in a couple days. You're fine enjoying the festivities?"

"Ah, yes, I'm sure we can stay occupied while you explore it." Reyna forced a smile.

Kianthe deflated. "Apparently, *I'm* going to be working with the Stone."

"Key. I can keep myself busy. Do what you need." Reyna traced her arm, the light pressure offering added reassurance. Kianthe nodded, and Reyna addressed Albert: "Thank you for your help . . . and your cheerful attitude. I must admit, I'm not fond of the high-mage."

"No one's fond of her. She breathes more fire than a dragon." Al strolled around them, waving the parchment between two fingers. "I'll be in touch, Kianthe. Good luck with your Stone!" Al stepped lightly down the hallway, singing under his breath.

Kianthe didn't even wait for him to vanish around the corner before she started in the opposite direction. "They give the Arcandor and Alchemicor designated suites in the Magicary. You'll like mine. It's a lot bigger than my old dormitory. Big windows. Lots of plants and comfy furniture."

But the words had lost their spark. Any enthusiasm she had to give Reyna the "guided tour" was gone. Reyna followed silently as Kianthe led her up several staircases, through the labyrinth to an innocuous door on the Magicary's northern side. The door unlocked with a whisper of magic, not a key, and she swung it open with ease.

Reyna followed her inside. For a space built with stone, towering ceilings, and dramatic buttresses, it was somehow quite cozy. A linen couch framed by two leather armchairs faced a rounded bank of windows. No fewer than six knitted blankets and two furs draped over the bed, the couch, and the chairs. Plants of every kind offered punches of green, with ivy cascading between the stone blocks and flowering trees growing from the floor.

A huge hearth occupied the corner. Upon closer inspection, there wasn't a chimney—just an inset stone square with a heavy mantel. Then again, the roaring fire was another ever-flame, so there wasn't smoke to vent.

It was just similar enough to both New Leaf Tomes and Tea *and* the Grand Palace that Reyna instantly felt at home. A pair of bookcases even lined the far corner—had Kianthe requested those, or did the previous Arcandor use them too?

It took some concentration to return to the most important topic of the day.

"Now?" Reyna asked again, crossing her arms.

Kianthe closed the door behind them, locked it with a wave, and told the metal, "No one else gets in. Got it?"

She must have been satisfied with the lock's response, because she staggered to the bed and fell onto the plush mattress. "Yeah," she mumbled into the blanket. "Now."

"Tell me how you're feeling." Reyna eased onto the bed beside her, carding a hand through her hair.

"Pretty fucking shitty. Polana was right. The Stone has been weakening, and I didn't even *notice*."

"Surely, it would have summoned you if it were truly in danger?" Reyna frowned, her fingers stilling against Kianthe's scalp. "Perhaps the festivities mean more people are drawing on its power. It might be an isolated event."

Kianthe twisted her head to look at Reyna. "It doesn't work like that. More mages mean *more* magic. The Stone should be at the peak of its power over the festival. I'm going to have to commune with it tomorrow—which means I won't be able to entertain you." The disappointment in her voice was obvious.

Reyna laughed fondly. "Oh, love. This is far more important, and that's okay. You have a job to do, same as me."

A pause. Kianthe stared at Reyna. Her voice was quiet, almost timid. "Am I the only one who's starting to feel like we couldn't escape our lives after all?"

Considering Reyna had voiced that exact concern two seasons ago, the question took her breath away. She swallowed hard, thinking of their growing list of responsibilities, thinking of the paradise they'd created in Tawney and how even that, somehow, had soured over time.

Life was change. She knew that.

But a dark part of her soul wondered why all of these intensive roles were *their* responsibility. Why did Kianthe have to be the Arcandor? Why did Reyna agree to be queen?

Why couldn't they just be two people in love, basking in the glow of a life they'd chosen?

Run away with me, Kianthe had said, perched together with Reyna beneath a pinyon pine. *You like tea. I like books. Care to open a shop and forget the world exists?*

They forgot the world. But the world didn't forget them.

Reyna pressed a kiss to Kianthe's forehead. "It's okay. We'll figure this out, just like everything else. Things that seem impossible in the dead of night are often simple in daylight. Maybe we should get some sleep, love."

Kianthe pushed to her elbows. "You didn't answer my question."

It took more bravery than Reyna realized.

"Yes," Reyna said, and anguish cracked her voice. She cleared her throat, forced a smile. "I'm scared we can't escape our lives forever. And I'm not sure where that leaves us." They would always be married, and they weren't strangers to long distance within their relationship. But the bookshop? Tawney? Those were bigger questions.

And Reyna wasn't loving the answer solidifying in her mind.

But her partner looked miserable, so Reyna reiterated: "Bed. Everything looks better in the morning."

"Looks bed-ter?" Kianthe said half-heartedly.

Reyna rolled her eyes and pressed a kiss to Kianthe's forehead. "Yes, dear."

They went to bed, but Reyna didn't sleep for a long, long time.

8

Kianthe

Kianthe remembered the first time she ever saw the Stone of Seeing.

She'd been seven, maybe eight, and the Arcandor himself escorted her class into the depths of the Magicary. She recalled the old man only in fleeting glimpses—a graying beard, a kind smile—as he chatted about the life of an elemental mage, and what services they might offer the Realm after they were educated.

"Most mages will find a home in a new town, but some return to their families and establish a business. Upon graduation, you're free to go where you choose! Some mages roam the Realm, offering their help where they can." The Arcandor glanced over them, a coy smile on his face. "I know one mage who sailed as far as the Roiling Islands, hoping to calm the rapids."

"Did he?" one of the kids asked, eyes wide.

"No, they did not." The Arcandor chuckled. "There are forces in this world even more powerful than myself, or the strongest elemental mage besides."

The kid clamped his mouth shut. Kianthe snickered, then covered her mouth when the teacher shot her a warning look.

The Arcandor led them down another winding staircase, his old voice echoing off the walls. "Elemental mages can help with many things once they find their home. You may pull fresh groundwater for towns without access to it. Or perhaps you'll magically enhance the soil to ensure a bountiful harvest." He paused at the base of the staircase, facing them dramatically: "Or . . . you could be a mage on the grand Nacean River, pulling sailboats up and down the shoreline!"

Boring, Kianthe thought. *I'll never do that.*

They arrived at a short hallway that ended in a wall, in front of which stood a huge stone disc painted with gold markings. It was grandiose, bigger than even the Arcandor, and it quieted any murmurs.

Even the children could sense the magic beyond.

"But remember . . . none of those feats would be possible without what lies beyond this door," the Mage of Ages said, gesturing at the circular door. "All our magic, all our abilities— they derive from the Stone of Seeing."

Kianthe couldn't see him over the heads of her classmates, but she craned anyway, jaw unhinged as he effortlessly waved a hand. On his cue, the stone disc rolled into a channel in the adjacent wall, revealing a quiet inner chamber. It was tough to see from here, but it looked like another garden. A short path led to a stone pedestal, on which sat . . . a rock.

Kianthe hadn't actually thought it would be a rock. She'd assumed "Stone" meant like . . . a statue or something. But nope. Mages actually worshiped a rock.

She suddenly felt very, very embarrassed for her teachers.

It was obvious this shrine was meant to be impressive: "*ethereal,*" one of the older students had said when he heard where they were going. He'd been pretty self-important about it, too, chest puffed like he was better than them, just because he'd visited a fancy rock first. Maybe it *was* ethereal. The cavern was illuminated by glowing crystals, dust glimmering in the soft light, luscious vegetation skirting the edges. The mound in the center was covered in a carpet of grass, and wildflowers surged at the pedestal's base.

But to Kianthe, it was still just a rock.

The Arcandor beamed. "Do you feel the magic of our blessed Stone? It's saying hello."

Their teacher, a young woman with an odd love of chickens, dabbed her eyes. Several of Kianthe's classmates gasped. A few held out their arms, like they'd been coated in glitter or . . . or Stone spit. Gross.

Kianthe didn't feel anything. Magic was tenuous at best to her, this fleeting thing she could sometimes grasp but mostly just made her feel like she'd peed herself. She examined her arms anyway, but they looked the same. Her skin was that light clay color, as always.

Maybe the Stone of Seeing was broken.

The Arcandor's voice hushed. "One at a time, children. It's important that you know what we revere. The Stone gifted all of you with a hint of magic, but only devout worship will allow your powers to grow."

Kianthe frowned. That didn't make sense. She raised a hand.

Her teacher bit her lower lip. "Ah, Kianthe. Can it wait?"

"Nonsense. Let them ask questions." The Mage of Ages chuckled, peering over the other students to see Kianthe properly. Everyone's eyes were on her now, and she was solidly regretting this decision. A few of her meaner classmates sneered.

"She's a bit precocious," her teacher warned.

Kianthe had definitely heard that word before. No one had bothered to explain what it meant, so she always assumed it was a compliment, something like "precious." They sounded similar enough.

Encouraged, Kianthe plowed forward: "If worship is enough, why can't alchemists do elemental magic?"

A discerning silence fell over the room. Their teacher shifted uneasily, clearly unwilling to tackle that with the Arcandor in the room. A few of her classmates snickered, muttering about how ridiculous that question was—but none of them could answer it, Kianthe noted.

The Arcandor contemplated her, then replied steadily, "All mages begin with elemental magic. But over time, the Stone gauges your competency—and decides whether to continue supplying you with magic. Alchemists are mages who were . . . ah, *passed over* by the Stone, but still wish to achieve great things."

"So, alchemy means we *failed*?" one classmate asked, panic in his voice.

"My dad is an alchemist," a second said.

The Arcandor hastened to cut them off before chaos descended. "Alchemy is a valid form of magic, but it's separate from the Stone of Seeing."

"I'm confused," Kianthe said.

The Arcandor raised his hands, forcing a smile now. "The Stone has bequeathed all of you with elemental magic, and here at the Magicary, we progress with your studies until that is no longer true. At that moment, *if* you lose touch with the elements, an alternative will be made available: alchemical studies."

That barely helped. Kianthe's brow furrowed, and she raised her hand again. "Where's *their* Stone of Seeing? The alchemists."

Now the Arcandor shifted, clearly uncomfortable. "There is only one Stone of Seeing. Alchemists cannot borrow its power."

"Do they use ley lines?" Kianthe pressed.

"No."

Why couldn't adults just *answer* a question? Kianthe huffed in irritation. "So, how do they cast a spell—"

"That's quite enough, Kianthe," her teacher chimed, cheeks coloring. "Alchemy is a topic for a later time, if it surfaces at all. Until then, we will pay homage to our blessed Stone."

And that was that.

Kianthe jolted awake, disoriented by memories of the past. It took several moments to realize she wasn't a child preparing for class, several more to recognize the Mage of Ages's suite inside the Magicary. At her side, Reyna breathed rhythmically, sound asleep. Kianthe swallowed a groan and rubbed her eyes with the heels of her palms.

By the Stone, it was *early.*

She lay in bed for a long moment, prodding out into the mountain with her magic. Deep in the Magicary's depths, the Stone of Seeing answered, pulsing a response. It was about the same strength as yesterday, so whatever was affecting it, it was a slow decline. That was comforting, at least. Still, now that the Stone had her attention, it pulsed again, begging her to visit.

Fine. *Fine.* Burden her with sour memories and pry her out of bed at the ass-crack of dawn. Duty awaits . . . or whatever.

Kianthe rolled out of bed, doing her best to stay quiet. Of course, Reyna was impossible to sneak away from. She pried open her eyes and mumbled, "Did someone die?"

Because *that* was the only reason Kianthe beat her out of bed. The mage snorted. "No, love."

Reyna pushed upright, blinking blearily. Her hair was messy, and she was so stinking cute that Kianthe almost hopped back into bed for morning snuggles. The horizon was soft pink, but the mountains surrounding the Magicary cast dramatic shadows over the windows. It cast her in a golden hue. Stunning.

But Kianthe was abruptly returned to her duties when Reyna asked, far more coherently, "Is the Stone of Seeing in danger?"

Ugh. No morning snuggles today.

"No changes in the Stone or my magic since last night." Kianthe wrapped her cloak over her shoulders; for some reason, the cold was even more miserable in the early mornings. As she dressed—which was tough to do around a cloak—an idea dawned. She might not have time to show Reyna around, but maybe she could keep her wife entertained somehow.

Reyna was preoccupied glimpsing the morning sunrise through the windows. For anyone visiting, the Magicary *was* a stunning locale. Even a childhood inside its walls didn't quell the admiration Kianthe felt for the view of sharp mountains and cascading forests.

Kianthe retrieved a few note cards from a nearby desk, wetting her quill with ink to scribble some things. She cast a glance at Reyna, feeling more awake now—but it wasn't like Reyna could find these locations herself.

No, Kianthe would have to enlist help. She waved the note cards to dry the ink and tucked them into her cloak, righting it over her shoulders. Then she stepped back to the bed and pressed a gentle kiss to Reyna's forehead. "Stay here, love. Sleep in for once. I'll be back."

The deadpan look Reyna offered made Kianthe laugh out loud. "Sleep in?" her wife repeated.

"Come on, Rain. One of us has to be coherent tonight." Her teasing lilt softened the request. "Live vicariously for me?"

Reyna wrinkled her nose. "Your idea of living vicariously through me is me sleeping in?"

"Obviously. Besides, I have something grandiose planned, but it won't be ready for a few hours. Wait here for my signal, okay?"

"Your signal? What, pray tell, is that?"

"You'll know it when you see it!" Kianthe winked, blew a kiss, and strolled out the door. It eased closed behind her, and Kianthe sternly told the metal lock, "You let her in or out whenever she wants, okay? Pretend she's me."

The lock swelled with yellow magic. It was, after all, the *Arcandor's* lock, which meant it had a more important job than any other door in this hallway. Maybe in the whole Realm.

Kianthe chuckled and left it to brag.

She passed Allayan in the hallway, Harold's counterpart from the dragon magic disaster a year and a half ago. The mage stopped short and seemed genuinely shocked when Kianthe greeted them. They swept into a hasty bow. "Ah, Arcandor! I heard you were visiting. What a pleasant surprise."

Unlike the other mages, Allayan sounded like they actually meant it.

Kianthe grinned. "Allayan. You're perfect."

"Excuse me?"

"I need your help." Kianthe swept out the note cards she'd

written and pulled the mage into a two-person huddle, one that gained attention the longer she whispered her scheme. Allayan's expression grew increasingly more concerned, but they nodded as if they understood and forced a hesitant smile at the end.

"I . . . ah, would love to spend a day with Reyna."

"And read the note cards." Kianthe pushed them into Allayan's hands. "But don't read them. Some of them are a bit raunchy."

The mage paled further, and it took them a moment to muster some forced positivity. "Yes. Of course. Anything you need, Kianthe."

Kianthe clapped their shoulder, then winced as the Stone of Seeing pulsed again, demanding her attention. "Ah, great, because I have to go. Enjoy the day, Allayan! Should be fun."

"So, so fun," Allayan said, with a tiny hint of sarcasm.

They'd have fun. Reyna was *always* fun. They just wouldn't realize *how much* until they started Kianthe's guided tour. With an eager wave and a new bounce in her step, Kianthe strolled for a staircase to visit the Stone of Seeing.

She retraced the steps she'd taken as a child, but now people hastened out of her way and gaped at her back. It made her feel powerful, important. Once upon a time, the Arcandor had been that smiling old man. Now it was just her, and she couldn't emphasize enough what a terrible choice that was.

She told the Stone that every time she visited, too, but it never seemed to care.

Not that a rock—even an admittedly fancy, highly magical one—cared about much.

Two mages were inside the Stone of Seeing's chamber when she arrived, tending the garden that blossomed around its regal pedestal. They bowed when she stepped inside, allowing her unbridled access. "We'll be in the hallway if you need our magic," one said, her voice far too chipper this early in the morning.

Between the ley lines converging under the Magicary and the Stone's physical presence, there'd be a *much* bigger problem if

Kianthe needed these mages' magic, too. But she kept that to herself, smiling and waving instead. "Sure, sure. Thank you."

"Let us know if you need anything," the other mage echoed, and together they stepped into the adjacent room and commanded the huge stone disc to roll back over the doorway, trapping her inside. It was a little ridiculous that they even bothered—the magic it took to move the disc was immense for a normal mage. For Kianthe, though, it was as easy as breathing.

She stood in the entryway of the chamber, squinting at the Stone of Seeing.

Still just a rock.

And yet, when Kianthe said, "Long time, no see," the Stone swelled with welcoming magic. It embraced her in a hug almost as warm and loving as one from Reyna. The moment she felt it, relief came fast on its heels, and Kianthe realized she'd been terrified all night that the Stone would hate her for ignoring it so long.

But that was silly. Her magic *was* the Stone, and the Stone was her magic. It couldn't hate her any more than a human hated their beating heart.

The Stone was silent as she hiked up the mound, stepping around wildflowers to reach the pedestal. Overhead, the crystals glowed brightly, mirroring daytime inside the cavern. Everything was alive here, and magic spread through her with such intensity that she could barely recall how feeble it had felt over her first visit as a child.

"*Hopeless,*" Polana had said to Kianthe years later, scowling down her straight nose as Kianthe, barely twelve, struggled to freeze a puddle into ice. "*I suspect that the best you'll ever accomplish is minor alchemy. Resign yourself to that fate.*"

Kianthe *had* resigned herself to that fate. The Stone clearly missed that message.

"I saw Polana last night. You know they made that crone high-mage?" She snorted. "What a terrible idea."

The Stone of Seeing was a meteor, and a fairly small one at that.

Its metallic surface was pockmarked and rough. Kianthe bet it would fit inside a sack of flour, but probably not a pillowcase.

She wrote that into a research paper once, and her teacher had not been pleased.

The Stone pulsed again, quieter now. Nudging her into more conversation.

"I don't know. Seeing her made me feel like a child again. Do you remember me back then, before the last Arcandor died? That sad, lonely kid who crammed into hideaways and read because I couldn't do magic." Kianthe paused, pinching the bridge of her nose. "Do you *know* how many nights I spent praying to you, hoping you'd fix me? Why was I struggling when my classmates were moving mountains?"

The Stone stayed silent.

"Okay, they weren't moving mountains. Not literally. That's a bit advanced for kids. But honestly, this?" She gestured to herself, implying the immense magic inside her internal reservoir. "I was ready to swear you off. I was going to abandon *all* magic—even alchemy—and just go home. And the day I packed a bag, the old Arcandor died."

The Stone seemed to glow, but it was weaker than normal. A better Arcandor would have noticed this sooner. A *proper* Mage of Ages would have flown here the second the Stone's power faltered.

Kianthe pressed a hand to the Stone, closing her eyes. Her voice was small, now. "I'm grateful, don't get me wrong. Your magic gave me *everything*. A place in the world. A best friend. A partner. A home." Kianthe choked, clenching her eyes shut. "Whatever you need, I'm here. I didn't understand back then, and I'm still confused about some things . . . but I see enough. You do care for all of us, in your own way."

There shouldn't be a breeze so far underground, but one appeared anyway, ruffling her hair almost fondly. Even the flowers seemed to hug her ankles.

"Yeah, yeah." Kianthe chuckled. "I missed you too. I'll try to visit more."

The Stone settled in satisfaction, like a big sigh around her. She rested her forehead on its lumpy surface, closing her eyes, letting her magic intertwine with its source. It twisted with the Stone, spiraling deep into the earth itself.

Or, it should have. Something was blocking it.

"Ah," Kianthe muttered. "There's the problem."

The Stone pulsed again, fading far too fast. It was like the silent cries of a dying animal, and she fucking hated it. The Stone was always bright, almost blinding, and offered its magic freely to its mages. Seeing it like this was . . . difficult.

Kianthe patted it reassuringly. "I'll fix this." Amusement tilted her voice. "You just sit around. Look pretty. All that good stuff." With a smirk, she strolled to the exit of the shrine. The stone disc rolled away at her command, and the mages outside straightened in attention.

"Will the Stone of Seeing recover, oh great Arcandor?" one asked.

Kianthe hadn't heard "oh great" at the start of her title in a while. Well, she'd heard the words "Oh, *great*" when she strolled into some rooms, but that always had a different connotation.

"Arcandor?" the other mage asked.

Right. Kianthe cleared her throat, assumed an authoritative tone. "Everything will be fine. Now, if you'll excuse me—" and she crossed the outer chamber, strolling for the staircase.

"Isn't she going to fix the Stone?" the younger mage whispered.

"Don't question her process," the older one replied, but even he sounded doubtful.

Her process. Right. Kianthe climbed the staircase and hoped she could figure out that process . . . and fast.

9

Reyna

Kianthe left, told her to *sleep in,* and locked the door in her wake.

Reyna dropped back onto the pillows, contemplating what it'd be like to just . . . go back to bed. After all, no one could need her in the Magicary—most people probably didn't even know she was here.

Besides, this bed was so, so comfortable. There was a strong chance that when Kianthe became Arcandor, she went wild with requisition orders, because whatever stuffed this mattress *must* be spelled. Add in the fact that there were no fewer than six pillows surrounding her, and even if she didn't sleep again, Reyna certainly wasn't moving. If she were a griffon, she'd certainly call this a nest.

Reyna tugged the heavy wool comforter over her shoulders, settling so deep that only her nose and eyes were exposed to the crisp air. The ever-flame crackled in the hearth, and otherwise it was peacefully silent. Through heavy eyelids, Reyna watched griffons soar past the windows, playing with a few smaller birds.

Mmm. Maybe a bit more rest wouldn't hurt.

When she awoke next, it was to a gentle rap on the door. The sun was higher now, illuminating the entire room in a warm golden glow. Snow on the distant mountains shimmered with it. A redspar was perched on her windowsill, chirping cheerfully.

Another knock at the door, and a tentative "Your Excellency?" came muffled through the wood.

It made Reyna feel like she was back at the Grand Palace, which filled her with exasperation. There, she'd open the door to three servants and two ladies-in-waiting, each with a very specific job to prepare her for a day in court. Before, it had seemed so reasonable for a queen. Now that she *was* the queen, it was ridiculous.

But she wasn't at the Grand Palace—she was at the Magicary, and surely mages wouldn't bother preparing the Arcandor for the day. Curious, Reyna hauled herself out of bed, slid into some plush slippers Kianthe had left nearby, and wrapped herself in a robe. She briefly checked her appearance in the mirror, tied her hair into a well-practiced bun, and strode for the door.

On the other side was Allayan.

Reyna blinked, taken aback. The one mage she recognized and knew by name—which meant Kianthe must have sent them. "Ah, good morning."

"Do you remember me?" They seemed uncertain, rubbing their arm. "I came to Tawney with Harold, back when Kianthe was sick with dragon magic. You weren't queen then, but—well, I'm happy to default to your proper title."

It was ironic, since Allayan claimed no title at all. They were apparently a powerful mage, far more capable than Harold, but with none of the adjoining arrogance.

Reyna smiled warmly. "Please, Allayan. I remember you. No title needed; I'm just glad to see a familiar face. Would you like to come in?"

"If that's all right?" On her nod of approval, Allayan stepped tentatively into her space. They stood just inside the entry, rocking on their heels. It was awkward.

To break the tension, Reyna kept a conversation. "Kianthe sent you, I presume?" She pulled the bed's comforter over the pillows. It was a half-hearted attempt at making the room presentable, but in her defense, she wasn't expecting to entertain first thing in the morning.

"Well, I wouldn't miss an opportunity to say hello regardless." Allayan offered a crooked grin. "Even before Kianthe approached me, I figured you might need some decompression after your time with Harold. I'm happy to offer my services."

Reyna swept into the washroom, leaving the door open a crack so she could change clothes while maintaining conversation. "Services?"

"Even mages get lost in this place. The last thing we need is the ruler of the Queendom vanishing in the confines of the Magicary. Imagine the outrage." Allayan sounded amused. Furniture creaked, as if they'd settled into a chair while they waited. "Kianthe wants you to have a proper tour, so I have a list of places to show you—and, ah, note cards."

Reyna tied her sword to her belt, then retrieved a washcloth. There wasn't piped water here—mages, and all—but water streamed down one of the natural stone walls, glistening in the morning light. She tentatively pressed the cloth to it, pleased when it soaked in fresh mountain spring water. It was chilly, a welcome contrast to the warmth of the room, and woke her up nicely.

"What kind of note cards?" she asked.

"I was instructed not to read them until we reached the coordinating location."

"You didn't take a peek?"

Allayan sucked in air. "The *Arcandor* told me not to look. I would never betray that trust."

Reyna chuckled. "You're a good soul, Allayan." She checked her hair, nodded in satisfaction, and stepped back into the main room. "I'm ready when you are. Where's our first stop?"

"The grand banquet hall," Allayan said, taking the lead with confidence. Behind her, the door locked automatically, so whatever Kianthe had spelled into the metal apparently stuck.

They descended farther into the mountain, pausing in another cavern. This one made Polana's office seem *small,* towering at least four stories with a curved ceiling covered in stalactites. In the space's center was a huge stone column, something Allayan pointed to with pride. "That column is made entirely of mineral deposits from the water. It took thousands of years to form."

"Oh, wow." Reyna squinted at the column. It was a light sand color, hued with shades of red, black, and brown. Ever-flame drifted around it, highlighting certain features in the unusual stone. Her eyes followed it to the ground level, tracing tables of mages eating and joking. There, she noticed a second column shoved in the cavern's dark recesses. "That one, too?"

Allayan rolled their eyes, derision in their voice. "*That* was the Class of '232's attempt at mimicking a natural formation. We keep it as a reminder of how elemental magic can mirror, but never beat, nature itself."

"It's, ah . . . lumpy." She meant it as a compliment, but winced at how it came out.

Allayan snorted. "It is that."

They descended a curved staircase and joined the buffet line. Reyna picked up a plate and admired the vast spread of food, but Allayan had tugged out a hand-ripped sheet of parchment instead. It was small, with Kianthe's writing scribbled on it. "Ah, the Arcandor has a message for you here. 'I know you'll want to go for the egg-soaked toast, but trust me, it's trash.'"

At that, the staff member serving said egg-soaked toast stiffened. He looked distraught, and his voice was strangled. "The Arcandor *said* that?"

Reyna might kill Kianthe today. She hastened to reassure him. "No, no! It's an inside joke with my wife. The toast looks delicious." And she held out her plate for a slice. He beamed, making a show of plating it for her, and gestured down the line. "Try the cornflakes with milk, too. They're a great complement."

Allayan cleared their throat, flipping Kianthe's card around. "'And walk right past the cornflakes. They taste like bark.'"

The staff member by the cornflakes let out a sob.

"Maybe next time, you let me read the card *before* we get into line," Reyna told Allayan, and forced a polite smile as she retrieved a huge bowl of cornflakes, too. They took seats far, far from the buffet line—and after tasting her haul, she had to admit Kianthe was right. The egg-soaked toast was gooey inside, clearly not cooked enough, and the cornflakes started out too crispy and wound up soggy.

Reyna went back for a few eggs, but fervently reassured the kitchen staff that she adored everything she'd tried.

Later, she'd need to have a lecture with Kianthe about manners, because *Gods.*

"Where to next?" Reyna asked as they left the dining hall. After breakfast, she always felt alert and eager, ready to move. Normally, she'd be on their back patio doing sword drills by now, or bustling around New Leaf serving customers.

But Allayan cheerfully replied, "The primary library," and led her down a massive interior hall to a set of double doors. Walking this path felt like she was meandering through a forest—likely because of the towering pine trees they'd encouraged to grow here. Lantern bugs flitted between the needles, and a few redspars chirped as they passed underneath.

"A library," Reyna said. "After a light breakfast, I always prefer a bit of exercise—"

"Oh, this will be exercise." Allayan sounded far too eager. They pushed open the double doors into a space easily as large as the dining hall.

Reyna's jaw dropped. How big *was* the Magicary? Kianthe said it went deep into the mountain, but even that felt like an understatement the more she walked around.

More importantly, what the *hells* kind of library was this? Reyna had been expecting something mild and easily digestible: a few stories, dozens of bookcases, maybe some tables for studying, some artifacts on display throughout.

Instead, they'd left one forest and entered another. The room was tall and circular, with deciduous trees stretching the entire height. A huge hole in the ceiling offered natural light, shining in sunbeams toward the earthen floor. The trees were so big that they'd carved bookshelves right into them, and each trunk was labeled with a different genre. The leaves were only now starting to turn, and they washed the room in hues of gold, yellow, and red.

"Welcome," Allayan said, sweeping their arms out, "to the primary library!"

"Shhh," one of the librarian mages hissed.

"Sorry," Allayan murmured, and led Reyna farther into the space. They kept their voice low, even as they toured the forest. "The only way to reach the higher shelves is with elemental magic, so most of the alchemy reference books are in the secondary library."

Reyna spun in a slow circle as they walked, dazzled by the towering trees. The buzzing of bees and chirping of birds created a gentle ambience. "If I may ask . . . why is it a forest?"

"Why wouldn't it be a forest?" Allayan asked, perplexed.

Well, okay then. Kianthe's desire for plants all over New Leaf suddenly made vivid sense. Reyna cleared her throat. "I, ah, figured it'd be too late in the season for the leaves to still be changing."

"It's warmer in here. These trees lag a little as a result." Allayan gestured through the crimson leaves of a sugar maple, at the circular opening high above them. "We get fresh air through that, but we're still mostly underground."

"They survive with magic instead of sunlight, then?" Reyna pressed a hand to the worn bark of another tree. This one was labeled BOTANY. Maybe Reyna was imagining it, but the tree itself seemed proud of the fact that she'd examined *its* books. She paid attention to how the leaves moved around mages now, and this tree perked up when it caught her attention.

Allayan patted it too. "Doing a great job," they reassured the tree. Then they cleared their throat and answered, "This close to the Stone of Seeing, plants don't need much to thrive. It's actually a rather rude awakening for most elemental mages when they leave the Magicary."

Reyna could imagine. Growing up in the Queendom, she'd never had much of a green thumb. To this day, the only plants she could keep alive were the ever-plants spelled by Kianthe—

ones that probably used magic similar to what this library required to survive.

Huh. It added newfound respect for her wife's spells.

They ventured deeper until they found a tree in the very back. Despite clear attempts to hide it, the towering oak had attracted a huge crowd. Students and educators alike were perusing its titles, using magic to lift the ground beneath their feet so they could snag a well-worn book from the top shelves. Although some of the mages here seemed ashamed to be browsing, several were engaged in animated conversation.

Highly explicit, very inappropriate conversation, Reyna noted with amusement.

Allayan flipped to another note card. "'Tell Reyna it isn't just the romance tree. It's the *sexy* romance tree.'" They sounded vaguely miserable to be reading that aloud, but it sent Reyna into a fit of laughter.

Of course her wife would send her to a library just to see the sexy romance tree.

They left shortly after, and Allayan took a pause to detour to their own workspace. "I'm a full-time Magicary mage," they explained. "There's nowhere else in the Realm I'd rather live, although it is nice to visit other places. I enjoyed seeing Tawney."

"We appreciated you and Harold coming," Reyna replied honestly. "Kianthe, especially."

"Holding dragon magic must have been excruciating for her." Allayan shuddered.

The staircase they were cresting opened to a greenhouse, of sorts. The far wall was a bank of windows, warmed by actual fires. She could tell by the unpredictable way they moved, as if they were pleased to be alive and eager to consume.

"Ever-flame doesn't put out enough heat," Allayan explained when he saw her looking. "We use real fires here." He gestured her farther inside.

It was a tree nursery, but the trees here weren't like anything she'd ever seen. She caught a few glimpses of lime and citron trees around the outer edge, but the ones in the middle were taller, with flat bark and dense leaves.

"I specialize in cross-germination," Allayan explained. "Most citrus trees grow on the southwestern side of Shepara, so you probably haven't seen many of them."

"We have limes," Reyna replied. "Imported, I believe."

"Right. Well." Allayan squinted through the leaves of one of the trees, then flicked a finger. A fruit fell, and they caught it with surprising ease. It was about the size of their palm, and they tossed it to Reyna. She snatched it with one hand, examining it.

Bright yellow. Its rind felt like the rind of a lime, or maybe a grapefruit, but she'd never smelled anything quite like this.

"We call it a lemon. I bred a lime and citron tree, just to see what would happen—and these started forming. So far, they're a hit in the Magicary's kitchen." They grinned, leading her to a table covered in equipment. It reminded Reyna of Matild's clinic, except that the beakers and test tubes held seeds instead of healing tonics. They reclaimed the lemon and sliced it with a large knife, revealing yellow flesh. "Suck on it. It's safe."

Reyna smelled it, then sucked some of the juice. Instantly, her face puckered, and she grimaced. "Ah, it's quite sour."

"It is, isn't it? Like a lime, but so much worse." Allayan laughed boldly.

"How do you, um, breed . . . trees?" She took another tentative suck of the lemon. Now that she was prepared, its taste wasn't unpleasant. Actually, she could probably sweeten it nicely in some kind of baked treat.

Allayan's eyes alighted, even as they led her back out of the nursery. "Oh, it's a very complex process, but actually has its roots in nature. Get it? Roots?" No wonder they got along with Kianthe. Allayan chuckled at the pun, then launched into a long explanatory speech that made Reyna's mind spin.

Their next stop was the tertiary library, and Allayan paused at the doors, flipping through their note cards. "'This is the best library. You'll see why.' And there are a few cards she's marked private, just for you." Allayan handed those over, then glanced out the nearby window at the sunlight. "I'll let you explore this one alone. Just tell the librarian when you're ready to leave, and she'll send for me."

Reyna quirked an eyebrow, but dutifully slid the door open and stepped inside alone.

This library was tiny, maybe double the size of Lord Wylan's own study. Its walls were cut stone, not natural caverns like almost everywhere else. In fact, it almost reminded her of New Leaf—with a roaring hearth, comfy armchairs, and bookcases galore. A couple chandeliers glimmered overhead, and the room smelled of cinnamon.

"You must be Reyna," the librarian said. She was an elderly mage with half-rimmed glasses and a kind smile. "The Arcandor requested I rope off the back room for you. I've called up our best local blends of tisane, and the kitchen baked blueberry muffins."

It touched Reyna's soul. She smiled, feeling warm all over, and glanced again around the small room. There were a few other people reading in the corners, and one particularly isolated teenage mage was hunched between huge stacks of books.

Kianthe had said this was her favorite library, and Reyna instantly understood why. Compared to the hustle of the primary one, this place was a veritable oasis.

"Thank you," Reyna said earnestly, and stepped to the back room. Its entrance was a stone archway, roped off with a sign that said RESERVED. Inside was a small desk and a . . . chair, she guessed? It didn't look like any chair she'd ever seen—instead of legs and a back, it was just a huge round sack covered in furs. Candles blazed around it, and a stack of books awaited her. On the desk, a teakettle was set over a gentle flame, ready for use.

Reyna left her sword by the archway and steeped a cup of tea. After a moment's contemplation, she picked a simple black today, sweetened with sugar and a touch of milk. Finally, she set the mug down and eased into the sack chair. It was *shockingly* comfortable. The filling gave more support than down did, but she couldn't quite tell what it was.

Heavenly, she decided, holding her mug against her chest and savoring the warmth.

The window beside the chair was huge and low, offering a pristine view of the immense mountain landscape. This library was on a lower floor, which meant she could also see a tall waterfall cascading between the pine trees. It crashed into a nearby river, which swept down the mountains. Up close, it'd be fearsome terrain . . . but from this distance, it was merely awe-inspiring.

Reyna sipped the tea and opened the first of Kianthe's notes.

I found this place when I was eight, and never wanted to leave. This room is my inspiration for New Leaf, the reason I dreamed of opening a bookshop. I fantasized about everything we've created in the exact chair you're sitting in. It's filled with beans, by the way.

Reyna ran her fingers over the thick furs, feeling the beans trapped in the soft fabric. Huh. She wouldn't have expected it'd be so comfortable. She flipped to the next note, filled with fond admiration for her wife.

I used to think a cozy environment was the only thing that could capture this feeling, the one you must have right now. Reyna turned the page over, eyes skimming Kianthe's next thought: *But I feel like this whenever we're together. It's nice to know that's all I ever need.*

"Oh," Reyna murmured, clutching her mug a little closer to her chest. She flipped to the last note.

This library only has fiction, and I picked a selection I think you'll enjoy. Have a wonderful day, my love. See you tonight.

Tears pricked Reyna's eyes, and she drew a shaking breath. These moments were fewer and farther between now that they were married and established, but every once in a while, Kianthe would remind her that their initial, butterfly romance was alive and well.

Reyna basked in it, tucking the notes close to her chest, and chose a book.

Time for a relaxing vacation day.

10

Kianthe

Find whatever was hurting the Stone of Seeing—that was Kianthe's plan.

As plans went, it was frustratingly vague. She climbed the staircase away from the two mages tending the Stone's inner chamber, mostly for privacy. Once she was out of view and certain they wouldn't follow, she plopped down on the steps with a heavy sigh.

"Something's hurting the Stone. Except not physically—which means it's magical. Not encouraging in a city full of mages . . ." Kianthe pressed her lips together, wrinkling her nose in thought.

Well, what would know the goings-on of the city better than the city itself?

Kianthe pressed a hand to the smooth stone wall at her left and asked the limestone, "What's weird?"

Her magic slid into the stone blocks, which came to life with ancient excitement. No one *ever* let it talk. A mage near the courtyard was practicing a drilling technique that was, frankly, embarrassing. A child mage had just discovered she could turn rocks into sand, which felt awkward—the sand didn't want to be underneath her fingernails, but whatever. Oh, and someone had *burned* it? The limestone was pretty miffed about that.

"Someone burned you?" Kianthe repeated in disbelief. "Where?"

Below was the general answer. Limestone was notoriously bad at giving directions.

Welp. Thus began the *least* fun scavenger hunt *ever.*

Kianthe tracked the Stone of Seeing's cavern and systematically hit each level beneath it, exploring classrooms and research labs and libraries and an empty kitchen in her effort to locate . . . whatever burned the limestone. All the while, the Stone of Seeing pulsed encouragement, which was nice at first but grew more frustrating as the day progressed.

"You know, my wife is reading a *very* inappropriate book right now," Kianthe muttered to the Stone. "That means nothing to you, but it's pretty damn important to me. Are you sure you can't muscle through this?"

Somewhere far overhead, the Stone sent a shock wave of disapproval through their magical connection. Kianthe flinched as her insides flipped disconcertingly. "Okay, okay, *fine.* Just a suggestion."

A pair of students passing her stared like she'd lost her mind.

Kianthe waved them along. "Official Arcandorly business." Then she very confidently stepped into a washroom.

It was nearing dinner before Kianthe realized one of the classrooms had a secret storage space. Her stomach was twisting in hunger and she was feeling vaguely shaky as a result, but the Stone was insistent, and she wasn't about to remind her deity that humans needed to do things like eat or sleep.

Not a fifth time, anyway.

With a grumble, she paced the length of the wall. This classroom had the strongest sense of wrongness, a pervasive feeling that she couldn't ignore. And considering she'd checked everywhere above and below it, this was her final stop tonight. She communed with the limestone again, only to have it confirm that it was *still* being burned, and that was *quite unpleasant,* and couldn't she do *something* to—

Kianthe removed her hand and grumbled, "Stone bless,

there's a reason most mages can't understand you. We'd all lose our sanity otherwise." She turned back to the classroom, squinting at it from every angle. There wasn't anything off here . . . but perhaps there was a room she couldn't physically see. The Magicary was full of odd passageways, considering mages could simply burrow through walls when they desired.

Counting steps, she paced. Thirty-seven steps. Holding that number in mind, Kianthe moved into the hallway and paced again. Forty-three steps. Which meant the classroom was shorter than the hallway.

So, clearly, she was missing something.

Well. The night wasn't getting any younger. Kianthe paused at the area where she suspected a secret room, gripped the limestone blocks, and wrenched a seam in the stone. It yelped, startled, but she pulled it farther apart, magically creating a crack up the wall that shuddered into a crevice she could squeeze through.

The limestone had *plenty* to say about that, and it all boiled down to *expected as much from the students, but from the Arcandor herself, such a brazen display of uncouth magic, how absurd, absolutely ridiculous—*

"Yes, yes, I get it," Kianthe grumbled. "I'll put it back; just *give* me a minute, will you?"

To emphasize her words, the Stone of Seeing pulsed warning. Abruptly, the limestone of the Magicary fell silent.

About time.

The crevice had revealed a tiny room, which sent a rush of excitement through her veins. She respected her duty to the Stone—but this had become *such* a slog, simply because she'd rather be reading with Reyna. And yet, discovering secret rooms in the Magicary made her feel like a sleuth, straight from the books on their shelves back home.

Humming theme song music to herself, Kianthe slipped through the crevice. It was dark—*really* dark—on the other side, and icy cold with stale air. She coughed, waved a hand in front of her nose to dissipate the musty scent, and cast a spell for a few ever-flames. They drifted upward, lazy as ever, but their flickering light illuminated the space.

Hmm. Nothing terribly exciting. The tiny room looked like it had been a storage space at one point, but someone had walled it off—likely through incompetence, considering there really wasn't a reason to block this off. Ancient texts and decaying scrolls lined the dusted shelves, and what looked like an old mop was braced against the back wall.

So, storage room *and* janitorial space.

She stepped farther into the room, examining every corner— and the Stone *screamed* at her. A shock of power sliced down her spine, and Kianthe yelped and leapt backward, slamming into the crevice. Behind her shoulder, the hallway was empty, which was apparently good, since there was no reason for anyone else to have the *living daylights* scared out of them.

Kianthe craned her neck upward to glare at the Stone. "What the hells was—"

She cut herself off.

On the ceiling of the storage room was a rusted sigil.

It had been painted in blood, now dried and brown. There was no telling how long it had been up there. She thought about asking the limestone, but time passed differently for earth, so it likely wouldn't have an answer. But the alchemy sigil still had power, since even the ever-flame she spelled avoided it, flitting to the corners of the storage room instead.

Kianthe immediately recognized this circle. Reyna had sketched the same one on a piece of parchment back at the watchtower.

"Fuck," Kianthe breathed. "Okay. Don't step under the circle. Got it."

The Stone throbbed, as if it was physically aching after that power display. She tugged magic from the ley lines, sending it into their deity, soothing its wounds. But her mind was racing with possibilities.

Feo had said it might be a draining spell, something to displace magic. Or steal magic? It seemed probable, considering some alchemist had painted the same sigil *right below* their venerated Stone of Seeing.

Siphoning elemental magic? For what purpose?

It hardly mattered. An alchemist had attacked the Stone—which was essentially an act of treason.

Or war.

She had to deal with this, quickly. Thoughts of Reyna fled from her mind as Kianthe became the Arcandor, the Mage of Ages. Every mage in the Magicary and beyond felt her threatening swell of magic as she reached for the ceiling and crushed the stone—and the sigil—into dust.

Heavy limestone crashed around her, but every piece conveniently swerved mid-fall, piling at her feet and saving her from nasty injuries. Simultaneously, the Stone of Seeing flashed back to full vibrancy, its magic brightening like a burning sun. The ley lines converging under the Magicary surged into the Stone.

She'd spent so long in Tawney, the land of little ley line, that she'd almost forgotten what it was like to be *so* close to the Stone of Seeing at full power. That was probably a big reason why she hadn't realized it was suffering until Polana said something.

Now, it filled her with vivacious energy—which only fueled something darker: fury.

Above her, a couple students from the classroom overhead peeked into the hole, squinting through the settling dust. Alchemists, or budding ones. One's eyes widened. "Arcandor! Do you need help?"

She'd had enough help from alchemists for the moment. "Did you know about this?" The words were spoken with all the power of the Stone of Seeing itself, reverberating through her teeth like a promise.

Or a curse.

"Know that the floor was about to collapse? N-No," the other alchemist stammered. He was maybe fourteen, and he trembled from head to toe. "Are you okay? Or—or did you cause that? Do you want us to call someone?"

They were just kids.

She couldn't be furious at alchemists for existing, just because one had shown malicious intent. It snuffed her anger, and she pinched her brow instead. "No. It's fine. Thanks for checking. You may want to back up, okay?"

They did, and she lifted the stone back into place, magically realigning the ceiling so it wouldn't be a hazard to the upstairs classroom. Through the reconstruction, she left any pieces of the bloody sigil discarded in the decrepit storage room. The circle was broken; it wouldn't harm anything now.

But it led to a bigger problem.

She left the storage room, sealing it off again. Then, against her internal desires, Kianthe stormed straight to the high-mage.

Polana was leaving her office for the evening. When Kianthe stormed up to her, she raised one eyebrow, her posture dismissive. "The Mage of Ages, the hero of the day. Everyone in the Magicary greatly appreciates that you've done your singular duty and replenished our blessed Stone." Her voice was brittle, and she waved a hand to close her office behind her. The wooden doors slid shut, the locks slamming into place.

Singular duty? That was laughable. Facing her tone, it wasn't difficult to summon the anger Kianthe previously held. "That's not why I'm here."

"In my opinion, that is the only reason we have to talk." Polana offered a terse smile and tried to step around her. "If you'll excuse me."

"Ah, ah." Kianthe flicked a finger, and the floorboards lifted into a wall, preventing her from passing. The stream from Polana's office saw the opportunity and began flowing through the newly created divide, resulting in a tiny river between them. Rapids formed as Kianthe said, icily, "I've done my magical duty. *You're* failing in yours."

"I beg your pardon?" Polana's eyes flashed.

"I found an alchemical sigil beneath the Stone of Seeing. Something clearly meant to drain its power from a distance."

Kianthe watched her expression closely. She didn't *really*

think Polana was responsible—they were both elemental mages, not alchemists, and she knew for a fact Polana revered the Stone more than Kianthe herself. But the high-mage's entire job was to monitor the Magicary, and supervise education and magic practice within its walls. Which meant if Polana hadn't known about this sigil, she truly had failed.

There was something satisfying about the myriad of emotions crossing her face. It was less satisfying when Polana settled on fury, her leathery skin tinging crimson. "*What?* An alchemist in *my* Magicary tried to harm the Stone?"

Kianthe had the same reaction—and she tempered it far quicker. Because the fact was, they had no idea who'd created and implemented the circle, much less what their intentions were. The Stone regained power when she destroyed the circle, so it clearly *was* draining it somehow. Beyond that . . .

It was supposition at best.

And yet, it instantly became apparent that Kianthe had given the high-mage a piece of dangerous information.

"I should have known. Alchemists should be *exiled.* All of them. It's dark magic, and it has no place near our venerated Stone of Seeing."

Such vitriol. Kianthe bristled, thinking of Feo and Albert and everyone crowding the upstairs courtyard. "That's bullshit. Alchemy has always been taught here. It's never been a problem before."

"It's been a problem for decades. I seem to be the only one who will address it." Polana narrowed her ice-blue eyes. "Alchemists are unnatural. You probably have no idea how many animals we slaughter to 'educate' our discarded youth."

"Those animals are sent straight to the kitchens. We should be thanking alchemists for saving us a step," Kianthe snapped.

Polana barked a rasping laugh. "We send them farther than the kitchens, Arcandor, because there's *too many to eat.* They are a blight on society, and because they are sent into the world with Magicary endorsement, no one thinks twice.

I, for one, will not allow the Magicary to remain sullied with blood."

Polana spat on the floorboards, then wrenched the path back into place with surprising force. Kianthe sometimes forgot that *Polana* was probably the strongest mage in the Magicary—after her, at least. She would have to be, to wrench the elements out of the Mage of Ages's grasp.

It didn't come without a toll. Polana wiped sweat off her forehead, her jaw set. "Move aside, Arcandor. It's time I handle our internal affairs."

Kianthe nearly laughed out loud. She held her ground, and around her, the air sparked with magic. "Absolutely not. What are you going to do? Forcibly eject a thousand alchemists during the Alchemical Showdown?"

"If I must. Today will be the last day alchemists are welcome here."

Stone and Stars, she was *insane*. Kianthe narrowed her eyes, humor gone. "It was one circle, and I destroyed it. That doesn't mean—"

"One circle that nearly destroyed our Stone's power. Without it, we are *nothing*." Polana's voice dropped to a hiss. She'd never sounded more like a snake. "You, of all people, should know that."

She really wasn't going to back down from this. Kianthe knew Feo was right, that alchemists were second-class citizens in the Magicary and beyond. Everyone wanted the Stone's blessing, and losing it meant a mage was lesser by default.

This was still so fucking ironic. There had been so many days where Polana watched Kianthe cling to what little elemental magic she had left, where she'd scoff and snarl, *Alchemy will be your only option, girl.* Kianthe just thought she was playing favorites, back then. But if Polana felt this way about alchemists, or any mage who didn't hold a candle to her own power . . . well, she had no place in a school.

She had no business being a mage.

Kianthe's voice was flat. "I see." She stretched, the movement cold and calculated. "It has become abundantly clear that you are a danger to yourself, all alchemists, and likely any elemental mage inside this Magicary. With that in mind, I give my hearty and formal endorsement that Master Harold replace you as high-mage. You're finished, Polana."

Polana looked ready to murder. She actually started smoking, trembling like the ground before an earthquake. "You cannot usurp me."

"Oh, that's for the Zenith Mages to decide. And considering the obsession you *so clearly have* against alchemists, I doubt they're going to argue. You know that half of them are alchemists themselves." Kianthe rolled her shoulders, bracing for a fight. Her dark eyes smoldered. "You were supposed to be a teacher. Encouraging, educating. Instead, you ridiculed me, disparaged me, and scorned me. Once upon a time, you held power over my future—but now, the tides have turned."

Polana's breath came in short trembles. Her words were tight with fury. "You *never* should have become the Mage of Ages. *I* was the most competent mage of the time. You were a child."

Ahh, there it was. Jealousy, rearing its ugly head years after Kianthe thought the world had moved on.

It was a scary thing, how some people acted when they felt they were owed something.

"Thank the Stone itself that you didn't receive my power, because the Realm would be a lot worse." A breeze kicked up in the hallway, and the stream on either side of them thrashed. Deep in the heart of the Magicary, the Stone of Seeing swelled in violent power, reinforcing Kianthe's words. "One last chance, Polana. Will you accept your retirement, or do I need to physically remove you before you start a civil war?"

A long, tense moment passed between them. The stream actually started freezing in spots, crackling as the ice broke apart.

Finally, Polana set her jaw. "There's no need. I quit. Whatever happens next is on *you*, Arcandor." She finally stepped past Kianthe, striding down the hallway.

Kianthe let her go—but only because she could physically feel the Stone of Seeing reclaiming some of her magic. A fight with the Mage of Ages would end very, very poorly for one of them, and Polana knew it.

Still, this wasn't over. Reyna would have to wait.

She needed to find Albert and Harold, fast.

11

Reyna

The Alchemical Showdown was heating up, despite the freezing mountain temperatures. Reyna perched in the stands of one of the arenas, swallowing a rush of excitement as one alchemist flattened the other with a gust of wind. Watching these fights, Reyna had learned quickly that although these weren't elemental mages, their alchemical circles were inspired by the elements anyway.

These two were a particularly competent blend of alchemy and elements. Flying rocks, twisting windstorms, and combat like she'd never seen it. When Kianthe fought, she moved *with* the elements. It was the difference of a griffon taking flight versus a child leaping into the air with a board tied to each arm.

But these alchemists were somehow still flying.

Reyna leaned forward in her seat, trying and failing to hide her interest.

"Told you this would be the best arena," Allayan said cheerfully, stuffing their face with fried bread covered in ground sugar. "There's a growing subset of alchemists who are convinced the best path is studying the elements, developing sigils that can mirror nature. It's . . . intriguing. If not a bit derivative." They ripped off a coil of bread, offering it to Reyna. "Bite?"

"No, thank you," she said, grimacing as one of the alchemists smacked the ground, and a giant fist emerged from the rock. It was crude at best, and she snorted. "I somehow doubt this will become any preferred form of magic."

"Well, it's flashy. Alchemy is quiet at best, cruel at worst." Now Allayan gestured at the other arenas, where the "battles" were less duels, more like contests of skill. Rather than attacking their opponent, alchemists lined up and drew mirrored circles meant to accomplish dozens of things. Slowing time, countering gravity, swallowing substance. But all of that was boring to watch, especially when only another alchemist could judge its power.

Reyna glanced back at the duel at the exact moment that one of the alchemists lifted the other in the air by the ankles. The tornado-like windstorm ruffled Reyna's hair, forcing her to secure the embroidered "Alchemy Rules" hat she'd bought for Kianthe—and had somehow been convinced to wear in the meantime.

"Match," one of the educators called. The other alchemist dropped to the dirt, and the victor strode forward, clapping his chest with pride. Cheers erupted from the mages watching, although a few of the elemental ones were laughing outright.

Allayan pushed to their feet, dusting their pants free of sugar. "What are you thinking next? Perhaps we can mosey the shops? I bet you'd enjoy the tea stands. We get vendors from all across the Realm."

Reyna's gut twisted in guilt. "I—think I'd prefer to return to the room. It doesn't feel right to enjoy this without Kianthe."

Allayan shrugged. "She'll probably be done soon. The Stone of Seeing is back to normal; we all felt it. I bet she's just wrapping things up with . . ." Allayan trailed off, squinting at the arena. "Ah, with—the high-mage . . . Sorry, that's Kianthe, isn't it?"

Reyna followed their gaze. Sure enough, her wife had stepped into the emptying arena. She stomped the ground, and the earth rose to lift her high above everyone, enough to see and be seen by anyone in the courtyard. With another twist of magic, the air amplified her voice.

"Attention, mages of the Magicary. Attention. This announcement is to inform you all that the previous high-mage, Polana, is retiring, effective immediately. She will be escorted from the Magicary . . . permanently. Don't attempt to speak with her on her way out—it'd be a terrible experience for everyone involved."

"Uh-oh," Reyna muttered.

Kianthe looked exhausted, irate, and frustrated. She ignored the perplexed murmurs of the crowds, pausing for only a moment to draw breath. "As the Mage of Ages, my endorsement will ensure a replacement succeeds in the judgment panel of Zenith Mages. With everyone as my witness, I formally recommend that Master Harold be Polana's replacement."

"Uh . . ." Allayan grimaced. "Harold? Really?"

"Even you have to admit, that's still an improvement," Reyna pointed out.

Allayan couldn't argue that.

"Congratulations, High-Mage Harold." Kianthe clapped her hands again, and the sound echoed the same as her voice. "That's it. Enjoy the festivities."

The platform she'd created sank back into the ground. Kianthe hopped off it before it melted into sand, and a swirl of wind eased her down. Reyna hopped off the stands and followed her into the road, slipping through the crowd with ease.

It was far harder for Allayan, who was quickly swallowed in the masses. "I'll catch up," he called, before vanishing between gaggles of students. Reyna briefly contemplated going back to retrieve him—but ultimately, this was more important.

"Key," Reyna said, catching her wife's arm.

"Rain." Kianthe sounded utterly relieved. She had heavy bags under her eyes, and her muscles were tight. "Sorry about that. Had to cut off any authority before Polana made a very rash decision." She scrubbed her face, then glanced hopefully over

Reyna's shoulder. "Is Allayan going to get me some fried bread? I'm starving."

Reyna searched her face. "What's going on, Kianthe? Polana didn't seem like the type to just . . . retire."

"She's a lunatic, is what she is," Kianthe groused. "I found that same alchemical circle below the Stone of Seeing—a siphoning circle, draining its magic. When I told her, she flipped. Said we needed to—" Kianthe realized the crowds around them, paused, and tugged Reyna to a quiet corner between two stalls. Her voice was nearly inaudible now. "—to *expel* all alchemists. All of them, to keep them from 'sullying' our magic. It was purity bullshit."

"Gods." Reyna covered her mouth. "All of that happened while I read books and watched the duels?"

"Yeah. But it's over now. Harold is an asshole, but at least he's sensible." Kianthe slumped against Reyna, pressing a kiss to the curve of her neck. Her voice was petulant. "I want food and a warm bed."

Reyna smiled fondly, patting her cheek. "We can get that. Whatever you'd like, love." She looped her arm through Kianthe's, led her back into the crowds of mages. As they walked to the fried-bread stand, Reyna's tone dropped. "I don't mean to imply anything, but . . . have we considered Albert is behind these sigils? If Feo didn't understand them, their creator must be a powerful alchemist."

Kianthe didn't look convinced. "Here's the thing about the Alchemicor, though. He might not even *be* the strongest alchemist. He's just the one who showed up for these duels." Now she shrugged. "You remember when Feo created circles to heal dragon burns after the last attack, back when we first built New Leaf? Healing alchemy isn't a thing, but they did it anyway. Matild told me later those circles were active and functioning within a few hours. That means Feo created a new kind of alchemy *overnight*."

"I didn't realize. I was fairly distracted that evening, what with your heroics." Reyna raised an eyebrow.

Kianthe snorted, waving that off. "I got better. Look, the point is, if Feo deigned to be here, they'd win any duel they joined. But they've never bothered to fight for the title, because then they'd be forced to mingle with the hoi polloi."

"Well, they *were* exiled. I can see why they wouldn't bother." Reyna chuckled.

"My point stands. Feo might not be unique. There are a lot of alchemists around the Realm. The ones sailing with Dreggs's pirate crew are very competent. I'm sure the council employs several, and I bet there are more in the Leonolan university."

Reyna hated that thought—that there might be more alchemists experimenting across the Realm, that whoever was behind these draining circles could be a complete unknown.

They arrived at the fried-bread stand as she mulled that over. Kianthe patted her pockets. "I, ah, left my coin in the room."

Reyna snorted, fishing for her bag of coins. "The Arcandor doesn't eat for free?"

"Damn. I wish."

They spent the evening catching up in one of the empty vendor stands, sharing fried bread and hot apple cider and playing a game Kianthe dubbed Who'd Date Whom? It involved picking mages from the crowds and surmising reasons why they would—or wouldn't—be together.

Allayan joined them halfway through one round, and blinked as Reyna said, "She's way too gorgeous to be with *him*. Come on."

"He's a powerful mage. I can feel it from here." Kianthe grinned, taking a swig of cider. "Ah, hot. *Hot.*"

"Power means nothing."

"Well, looks aren't everything."

Allayan cleared their throat. "Ah, am I interrupting?"

"Oh shit, you totally are. Quick, Reyna. Put your clothes back on." With a little bit of food, Kianthe was back to her old self. Reyna was happy she felt better, but they'd have to find a *real* dinner here soon. Not sugar and bread, but vegetables and protein.

Reyna was enjoying the night for now, though.

Allayan snorted, then covered it with a cough. "Apologies, Arcandor. The Alchemicor has requested an audience. He's waiting in the dining hall."

"Convenient," Reyna said, smiling. "Protein and vegetables."

"I'll have you know, bread is a perfectly suitable dinner."

Reyna squeezed her wife's arm. "Sure, love. And when you're starving at midnight, I'll remember you said that." She pulled Kianthe upright and they left the festivities, heading into the belly of the Magicary once again.

Harold intercepted them before they'd made it very far. He positively glowed. "Well, well, Arcandor. Polana pissed you off enough that you ousted her?" He laughed outright, slapping his leg. "That's so satisfying."

"Congratulations on your promotion," Reyna said, offering a smile. Harold had been nice to help Kianthe after the dragon magic fiasco, but she hadn't loved his personality then, and she was less impressed now. Since he was fun to heckle, she added smoothly, "I look forward to seeing how you attempt to incorporate Queendom citizens into your curriculum. I think you'll find many willing to worship the Stone of Seeing now that the Gods have been disproven."

She didn't actually expect Queendom citizens to find elemental magic all of a sudden—but if worship was truly the path to it, it was possible. And as queen, she didn't want to discount any possibility.

Harold's eyes widened. "Um—y-yes, of course."

"And I have another job for you, *High-Mage*." Kianthe laid the title on thick, grinning as Harold swelled.

"Anything, Arcandor."

That was a dangerous thing to offer her wife. Kianthe grinned wider. "Excellent. Polana is a traitor to our ideals, and needs to be exiled. I need you to personally escort her far, far from here. Drop her on a beach or something."

Harold balked. "You want *me* to get Polana—one of the most powerful elemental mages—out of the Magicary?"

"You're powerful too," Kianthe reminded him. "Get Allayan to help if needed."

Allayan pressed their lips together. "Polana has been a scourge on our education system for years. I'd be happy to lend my expertise."

That seemed to make Harold fumble. "No, no. I'm high-mage. I'll do it. *Of course,* for the benefit of the Magicary, I will exile her." Harold pulled his shoulders back, jaw set in determi-nation. He didn't sound fully convinced that it'd work, but he sure looked like he'd try.

Reyna gave him mental points for that, at least.

"Excellent. You're off to a fantastic start." Kianthe handed him the sugar-coated paper that held her fried bread. He took it, clearly taken aback, then seemed to realize in the next breath that she'd literally handed him trash.

"Um—"

"Thanks, Harold. Congratulations!" Kianthe waved, yet again following Allayan into the Magicary. Harold remained at the top of the steps, holding the crumpled, sticky paper with two fingers. He looked utterly baffled, and Reyna suppressed a chuckle as they rounded the corner.

The dining hall was mostly empty. Food still lined the buffet tables, but the staff serving it had left. They were likely upstairs helping with the Showdown. But it left them a great deal of pri-vacy *and* plenty of options for dinner, so Reyna was pleased.

"Ah, Arcandor! Over here!" Albert waved fervently, as if they couldn't see him. Considering he was the only person on that half of the dining hall, it was almost comical.

Reyna separated to get Kianthe a plate of food: elk medal-lions topped with sour cream and a hearty stack of potatoes and carrots. Allayan was heading back up the curved staircase when she returned, and they offered a smile. "I'll leave you three alone. I had a nice time today, Reyna. Feel free to visit anytime."

"I'd love that," Reyna replied earnestly. She shook their hand, balancing their food in the other. "Thank you for everything. Do me a favor and send me some lemons, okay? I bet I can create some great recipes with them."

"That'd be amazing!" Allayan grinned.

They left, and Reyna joined Kianthe at a long, rectangular table. Across from them, Albert was doodling something on a new sheet of parchment. "—here are meant to contain the power, and this circle directs it. But *this*—" He tapped the page with emphasis, careful to avoid touching the circle itself. "This is where it's directing it *to*. Normally it's a storage sigil, or something that represents an object or person. Here, it's blank."

"Blank," Kianthe repeated. "How is that possible?"

Reyna slid her the plate, pressed a fork into her hand, and then squinted at the parchment. "So, it's taking power, but not directing it anywhere?"

Al snapped his fingers. "Exactly. That's why this symbol shouldn't exist. It's incomplete. But from a distance, it's really hard to know that, especially with these qualifiers here . . . and here." He pointed at two other squiggly lines on the top and bottom of the page.

It'd take a lifetime of study to truly comprehend this, even with Albert simplifying things. Reyna sorely wished Feo were here to verify. While Kianthe took a bite, chewing in contemplation, Reyna scrutinized the Alchemicor. Analyzing his body language, his facial expressions, his tone of voice. Checking for inconsistencies.

She'd identified more than one would-be assassin through a simple conversation.

"Why would this be beneath my cell, then? I don't have magic." Reyna tilted her head.

But whatever she was hoping to find on Al, she came up empty. His enthusiasm was catching, and he was frowning at the sigil just like Kianthe. "I *know*! That's what's so strange. You had a run-in with the dragons, so my best guess is that someone took that 'Dragon Queen' title a bit too literally. It's possible once you entered the circle, utterly magic-less, they realized their mistake."

"Who is *they*, Albert?" Kianthe's voice was sharp. "Because this alchemist has Magicary access, which raises concerns about alchemical mages existing alongside the Stone of Seeing at *all*. I won't be as alarmist as Polana, but we need to find this alchemist."

Albert nodded vigorously, his tone darkening. "Absolutely, we do. Trust me, Arcandor. After I reclaim my title, it's the top of my priority list."

"You're waiting half a week?" Reyna asked.

"Well, if I leave in the middle of the Showdown, I forfeit my title—and any authority that comes with it." Albert grimaced, staring again at the sigil. "However, if the Stone of Seeing was threatened, there's no telling what might happen next. If you feel strongly about it, I can forgo the duels. It's likely time someone else claims my title anyway."

Kianthe waved a hand, her mouth full of carrots. "That kind of disruption would only complicate things now. I can handle an investigation; all I need from you is a lead. You get regular updates on your alchemists, right? Or at least hear rumors about any powerful ones setting up shop?" Her tone dipped into pleading, which told Reyna she had no idea if that was true.

It struck the Alchemicor like a lightning bolt. He straightened immediately, slamming his hand on the table. For a moment, the sigil he'd touched glowed, but he yelped at the contact and quickly tore up the circle. "Shit, sorry. Got excited, and still have a bit of chicken blood on my fingers." With a half-hearted laugh, he flashed his thumb, then wiped it on a handkerchief.

"Did it burn?" Kianthe asked curiously.

"Not burn. Pins and needles." He shook his hand out, scowling at the paper. "Nasty circle. Anyway, I might have a lead. Have you heard of Winterhaven? That cute town east of here, near dragon country?"

Kianthe groaned, swallowing her food. Except it was too big

a bite, so she choked it down while they waited politely. Finally, she coughed. "Dragon country? How close? I'm so sick of feeling sick."

"You get sick from dragon magic?" Albert drummed his fingers on the table, contemplative now. "Actually, I might have a spell for that. I was working on a barrier to stop alchemy, but it might work on dragon magic too. On a smaller scale, I bet I could twist it to keep you from absorbing any by accident."

Kianthe perked up. "Yes, please."

"Hang on. They named the town *Winterhaven*?" Reyna deadpanned. She thought she knew most major towns in the Realm, but that was . . . a ridiculous name.

Kianthe chuckled. "It's always decked out for the Mid-Winter Celebration. That's why."

"They've expanded their brand. Now it offers year-round winter festivities," Albert confirmed, nearly bouncing in his seat. "Daily tree-lighting ceremonies. Gifts galore. Nightly bonfires with live music. It's growing fast, too! Listed on all the same travel articles as your hometown."

Kianthe and Reyna exchanged glances, and Reyna could practically read her wife's thoughts. *A town growing like Tawney? Maybe we can find out how they're countering the population boom.*

Reyna didn't want to get her hopes up—if there was an easy solution to their plight, someone in town would have solved it already—but that hope persisted. She forced herself to focus on why they were actually *here*.

"How does Winterhaven relate to a rogue alchemist?" Reyna was still assessing Albert, but her suspicions were dying fast.

Albert sighed, massaging his temples. His enthusiasm for the town seemed to be dampened significantly by the weight of responsibility. "I received a report that some 'terrible alchemists' have constructed a workspace in a mountain north of town. Apparently, they're stealing goats and chickens. Some sheep. It's very poor etiquette, if I'm being honest."

"No shit." Kianthe snorted, dipping the last of her elk medallions in the sour cream. "What makes you think they're capable of . . . well, this? Creating a new kind of alchemy?"

"They stole a horse, apparently." Albert's lips thinned. "A horse is a big sacrifice."

The words settled over Kianthe and Reyna like an ominous blanket. They exchanged glances, and Kianthe heaved a sigh. "Well, then. I hope you enjoyed the Magicary, Rain, because it looks like we're heading east."

12

Kianthe

If Tawney was considered "quaint," this place was *sickeningly* sweet.

Even from the air, it was exactly what Kianthe would picture as a beautiful, Mid-Winter village. She thought they'd found it when they first arrived in Tawney, but the dragons burning half the town wasn't very picturesque. Then, traveling the Nacean last year led them to Lathe and Koll, both adorable towns in their own right, even if their architecture was disjointed and their streets felt lived-in.

Nothing compared to Winterhaven. Every house was constructed with wood stained the same dark shade, adorned with frosted windows and trimmed with carvings of snowflakes. Each wooden shingle was covered with the perfect amount of snow. The mountains surrounding the town presented a dramatic backdrop that almost looked fake. And to top it off, the *people* were overly pleasant. They waved as Visk and Ponder soared overhead, just as welcoming as could be.

"This place is . . ." Reyna hesitated, letting the wind steal her words.

"Weird," Kianthe finished loudly, grateful Visk had enough altitude that the villagers couldn't hear.

"I was going to say 'inauthentic,' but yes. You're right." Reyna's cheeks were pink from the cold. It had been a shorter flight to Winterhaven, which was roughly halfway between the Magicary and Tawney. Of course, that flight had been directly into the Vardian Mountains, which did put them very close to dragon country.

Still, Kianthe wasn't feeling sick yet, so the alchemy circle Albert drew for her remained in her pocket.

"What are you thinking?" Reyna called as Ponder circled the picturesque pine forest that encompassed the town. The townsfolk had decorated the trees along the path leading north. A painted sign cheerfully warned, HERE BE DRAGON COUNTRY!, coupled with a little image of a person swallowed by dragon fire.

Kianthe swallowed something that was half laughter, half groaning. "Oh, this is going to be *great*. Let's go to the inn, I guess. I wouldn't mind a bite before we fly north."

"Same," Reyna replied, and they landed near the town. She scratched under Ponder's chin, pressed a kiss to her beak. "Have fun, Pondie. Please don't antagonize the dragons—they might not be as nice as the ones back home."

"Don't let her get eaten," Kianthe told Visk, and she wished she were joking.

Visk chittered, clearly irate that Kianthe had to *clarify* that.

She held up her hands. "Don't look at me, sir. You're the one who let her befriend the only two kids in dragon country. She might think they're *all* like that."

Ponder screeched indignantly, and Reyna gently petted her wing. "Dearest, she's right. You don't have the best record."

With a full-bodied huff, Ponder spread her wings and took to the skies. Visk nipped Kianthe's shirt, then followed. They vanished over one of the lower, snowcapped mountains.

Reyna chuckled. "She's not going to forgive us for that."

"Teenagers." Kianthe waved a hand. "Let's go get lunch."

They'd set exactly two feet in Winterhaven before they were greeted by an *actual* welcoming committee. A curvy young woman dressed in red and white pinned a poinsettia to Reyna's cloak, and a child tugged on Kianthe's shirt. When she knelt to see what the kid wanted, the little boy beckoned her closer, then draped a crown of cranberries over Kianthe's hair and laughed gleefully.

An older woman—who was either a kindly grandmother or a complete sham—spread her arms wide. "Welcome, travelers, to Winterhaven, where it's the Mid-Winter Celebration all year round."

"But—it *is* the Mid-Winter Celebration this week," Reyna said, suspicion lacing her voice.

The older woman laughed brightly, as if that was the funniest joke. "You're right! This is our busiest time of the year. But we still take the time to greet everyone—we recognize it's difficult to reach our little village, and we're so grateful for your patronage."

Kianthe cleared her throat, feeling a bit awkward. "Well, we flew here. Pretty easy for us."

"Mages! Wonderful. You'll have to let us know what you think of our forest. Our trees are one of the prettiest parts of town." The grandma lady gestured at the spruce trees that lined their main road. Each seemed strategically placed, which Kianthe had to admit *was* impressive. Either an elemental mage lived here, or they'd built this town with a greater plan in mind.

The grandmother ushered them down the main street, then told the young woman and child, "To the south side, quickly! Talat said there's another carriage coming."

"Ah!" The boy squeaked and took off. The young woman, who might be his older sister, waved cheerfully at Kianthe and Reyna and followed at a swift pace.

Reyna touched the soft petals of the poinsettia pinned to her cloak. "So, you're . . . a town of never-ending winter?" Her tone was flat, and a bit suspicious.

"Not *just* winter," the grandmother chimed, beckoning them toward the local inn. "We embody everything cozy and wonderful about the holidays. The warmth, the family, the laughter, the music. We import wine from the Nacean River, and the juiciest boar meat from the plains near Jallin. We have two of the finest chefs from Wellia, and even some delicacies from the Queendom." Now she winked at Reyna. "I hear your accent, dear. You'll have to tell me how we've done with the nut rolls."

Reyna perked up. "You have nut rolls?"

Kianthe's mouth was already watering. Apparently she was hungrier than she'd thought—and if their nut rolls were anything like Reyna's, she might skip the boar entirely.

"Indeed. Everything is available once you book a room."

They stopped at a large building in the center of town. It was the only structure made from asymmetrically cut stone, fitted in a puzzle-like pattern with wood beam accents. The roof sloped dramatically, and bundles of holly hung from the eaves. A plaque dangling from a metal rod boasted the inn's name: WINTERHAV-INN.

An inn in Winterhaven. The Winterhav-inn.

Kianthe snorted, and snot *actually* bubbled out of her nose. "Shit," she yelped, and swiftly buried her face into the sleeve of her cloak. The grandmother had politely turned away, a ghost of a smile on her face, but Reyna offered no such reprieve. She folded her arms, her voice deadpan.

"Are you quite finished, love?"

Snot smeared her cloak, and she wiped it with her other sleeve so it'd absorb into the woolen fabric. "Come on. You have to admit the name is funny."

Reyna's eyes were bright, wholly amused, even as her tone remained level. "And somehow, your reaction was funnier."

"I'd be embarrassed, but you chose this."

Reyna moved as though she wanted to take Kianthe's arm—then remembered the snot and lightly patted her shoulder instead. "That I did. No regrets." With a wink, she strolled into the inn. Kianthe followed, and the grandmother lady entered last.

"Everyone! Welcome our newest visitors—mages from the Magicary!"

The inn's tavern was absolutely *packed,* and a cheer exploded from the crowds. Half of them seemed drunk already. Children sprinted past tables pressed so close together that it was a miracle they managed at all. There were so many bodies it should be sweltering in here, but they'd opened every window and the frigid mountain breeze kept things oddly comfortable.

"I'm actually not a mage," Reyna said to the woman.

"No. She's the queen," Kianthe added, just to brag.

The grandmother pulled up short. "The *queen*? Queen Reyna? Royalty, visiting our humble abode?" With a warm laugh, she muscled through the crowd, clearing a path to a tiny counter in back. A man dressed in formal shirt, vest, and slacks, with a poinsettia tucked in his chest pocket, offered a well-practiced smile and opened his mouth.

The woman cut him off, clearly thrilled. "This is the *queen*, Nolan. The new ruler of the Queendom herself, come to experience our festivities over Mid-Winter."

The man's smile fell, replaced with panic. "Th-The queen? Oh, Stars. My lady—wait, no, it's Your Excellency, isn't it?" He took a step back, then a step forward, as if he couldn't figure out where to be. He drew a short breath, then replied in a calmer voice, "It's an honor, Your Excellency. How may I serve you?"

The grandmother patted Reyna's hand, smiled at Kianthe, and left with a final "Enjoy the town, dears."

"Thank you for your time," Reyna called after her. With a sigh, she turned back to the inn's owner. "We're here on business, actually. We'll just need a room and lunch."

"A room." Nolan clenched his eyes shut, then pivoted, muttering as he examined the board bolted to the wall behind him. The board had maybe thirty bronze hooks, each labeled with a tiny metal plaque stamped with a room number. Very organized affair, compared to Tawney's inn.

Problem was, only two hooks had keys. He hesitated between them, then chose one. "We're nearly booked, regretfully. I can try to persuade a couple to vacate our grand suite? They're on their honeymoon, but with the right incentive, I'm positive I can—"

"Oh, Gods, no." Reyna gently took the key dangling off his

fingers. "I was a Queensguard before last year, so even a *bed* is a luxury when I'm traveling. Trust me, Nolan. My tastes aren't so refined."

He relaxed so visibly that Kianthe felt bad for causing this problem at all. "She's right. We usually just camp outside, but this place seemed so . . . cute . . . that we had to stop." It wasn't a compliment. The townsfolk seemed nice, but everything here felt a bit too fake for Kianthe.

Nolan cleared his throat. "Well, if that's the case, I think you'll find this room accommodating. It overlooks our town square, so you'll have a private view of the tree-lighting ceremony tonight. And tomorrow. However long you wish to stay, really."

"A whole ceremony every single night?" Reyna quirked an eyebrow. "That sounds tiring."

For a brief moment, exhaustion flickered in Nolan's face. In the next breath, it was replaced with a bright smile. "Nonsense. Because of our schedule, we attract tourists year-round, and we're so happy to host." His tone dropped, an afterthought. "It's, ah . . . it's better than the alternative. We're so remote that it's tough to convince merchants to make deliveries in the winter otherwise."

It sounded eerily similar to their issue on the Nacean River last year. Kianthe had naively assumed the council was distributing Arlon's food reserves appropriately, but clearly some towns were left behind.

"Isn't there a diarn assigned to this region?" Kianthe frowned.

"You just met her. Diarn Yalinda. Without her intervention . . . well, let's just say that Winterhaven wouldn't be any kind of attraction, unless people like ghost towns." Now Nolan paused, tilting his head. "Huh. Ghost town. I bet we could work with that too." He absently scribbled a note onto a sheet of nearby parchment.

Reyna slid a few damins across the counter—she always kept both Sheparan and Queendom coin on hand—to pay for their room. It was good; Kianthe wasn't the best candidate for holding their money.

Nolan took the cue, sweeping the coins away. "Ah, apologies. Thank you for your patronage to Winterhaven, Queen Reyna. And, um—"

"Kianthe. The Arcandor," Kianthe supplied.

Nolan's face paled. "Th-The Arcandor. Right." His eyes flicked to the key as if he might try to grab it out of their hands, force an occupied suite on them instead.

Reyna noticed and tucked it into her shirt pocket. "We'll be back for lunch." And she towed Kianthe away from the counter, down a hallway to a staircase tucked in the corner. As they climbed to their room, she said, "Dearest, not everyone *has* to know our true titles. Sometimes, it frazzles people."

"I wanted them frazzled." Kianthe shrugged. "I doubt he'd have let his guard drop like that otherwise. While you have lunch, I think I'll speak with Diarn Yalinda."

"I don't expect anything problematic is happening here." Reyna paused at a door on the third floor, checked the number stamped into the key, and unlocked their room. "They're folks trying to survive."

"They don't seem *happy*. Or rather, they're *too* happy. Like they're being forced to act every day of their lives. It's unsettling."

The room was small, but arguably cozy. It had every element of a quaint time—a soft bed, a nice hearth, a little table to eat breakfast at, and a wide window that was eye level with the top of a towering spruce. But everything was crammed too close together, almost like they were trying to achieve every *single* element of a cozy evening.

The result was claustrophobic. Kianthe dropped her knapsack on the bed and suppressed a shudder.

Reyna slid out of her cloak, her voice grim. "If the alternative is a dying town, I can understand why they'd think acting is preferable."

If things were that bad, Yalinda should have come to the council. Kianthe swallowed the retort, scrubbing her face. "I know we have a goal here, but . . . give me some time to speak with Yalinda. Have a drink. I'll be back before you know it."

"If you say so." Reyna caught her arm, pressing a kiss to her lips. "Just remember, Key. Some problems don't have easy solutions." And the warning in her voice lingered—a clear parallel to the changes in Tawney.

Kianthe forced a smile and left the tiny room.

Diarn Yalinda had rejoined the welcoming committee on the southern side of town, and they were indeed greeting a carriage. The sun was bright overhead as the couple and their two children disembarked, all wearing big smiles. They received the poinsettia pin, the cranberry strands, and the children were gifted tiny wooden toys that, frankly, made Kianthe a bit jealous.

Yalinda noticed her and seamlessly separated from the group. The cobblestone pathway was lined with potted plants and winter flowers decorated with glass adornments, and it was easy enough to find some privacy behind one of the larger ones. The diarn offered a sly smile. "So, a mage, traveling with Queen Reyna. That would make you the Mage of Ages."

"It would," Kianthe agreed, crossing her arms. "We need to talk."

"As expected. You're here about the alchemists north of us, aren't you?" Yalinda pressed her half-moon spectacles farther up her nose, then patted Kianthe's hand. "I figured the Magicary would send the Alchemicor, but I'm pleased to see this issue went straight to the top. We've had quite an issue with disappearing livestock."

Kianthe extracted herself. "I'm here about your citizens, Diarn Yalinda."

That took the elderly woman by surprise. She glanced around

the main street, eyebrows raised. "My citizens? Is something wrong?"

"Everyone we've met seems . . . overly enthusiastic. It's creepy."

For a long moment, Yalinda didn't respond. Then, when she'd parsed through what Kianthe said, her full-bodied laugh echoed across the square. "I should have expected the Arcandor would be unfamiliar with the hospitality industry."

"I run a bookshop and teahouse in Tawney," Kianthe said stiffly.

Yalinda's eyes were cunning. Gone was the grandmotherly persona, replaced with something far more befitting of a Sheparan diarn. "Well, I manage sixteen similar businesses, and advise the owners of thirty more. You only recently heard of Winterhaven, haven't you? Last few years, perhaps?"

Kianthe shifted, feeling uncomfortable now. "Or more recently, yeah."

"A decade ago, this town was named Loarl. The children were thin, the businesses empty. They can't grow their own food here. No room between the mountains, unforgiving seasons, you know how it goes. Worse, the roads to town were so treacherous that merchants didn't bother delivering. Too little profit for an abundance of risk, especially if they're unfamiliar with the terrain." Yalinda chuckled, although the sound lacked humor. "Something had to be done. I took their one selling point and twisted it into something that would entice the Realm to bother."

That . . . was actually brilliant. Considering there weren't many towns in the eastern half of the Vardian Mountains, Kianthe had never taken steps to meet the diarn here. She'd assumed any supervisory figure would be more private, less cunning, but Yalinda took her by complete surprise.

If Arlon had tried half as hard to save his dying towns, Kianthe wouldn't have needed to replace him last year.

The mage relaxed, stuffing her hands in her pockets and

rocking back on her heels. "That makes sense." An awkward pause. "Sorry for any negative assumptions. It just felt . . . a little forced. I wanted to make sure people are happy here."

"I care about my citizens greatly, Arcandor." Yalinda fixed a crooked ornament on one of the little potted pines. "There's a magic in the holidays, and few places are as lovely as Winterhaven. We promise a vacation to remember . . . and that allows the locals to survive in the same town where their ancestors made memories. Anyone is free to move—I've offered relocation assistance within my region—but most love it here too much."

Kianthe surveyed the couple looping arm in arm, watching their children run up the cobblestone street with their new toys. And she couldn't deny that the moment the tourists turned away, the young woman and little boy exchanged a pleased high five—clearly satisfied with a job well done.

"That's admirable, Diarn Yalinda."

"I appreciate your endorsement." The old woman smirked. "Now, about those alchemists."

Back to business.

13

Reyna

The moment Reyna stepped into the inn's tavern, Nolan was there to greet her. He'd changed into a fancier jacket, one with gold embroidery and an even bigger poinsettia pinned to the lapel. With a broad smile, he swept into a bow. "Right this way, Your Excellency."

"I don't require special treatment, Nolan. Any table is fine."

"I was in the midst of preparing exactly that, but someone else insisted you join his table." Nolan nodded at a figure sitting alone in one of the inn's turrets, a rounded space framed with windows, candles, and wooden accents.

Alarm prickled along Reyna's arm. She couldn't quite see the man's face from here. "Ah, *who,* exactly?" There were far too many civilians nearby to safely unsheathe her sword, but her fingers slid to the dagger strapped to her forearm, hidden under her long sleeve.

"He said his name is Locke," Nolan replied, suddenly nervous. "He seemed to know you—but of course, I shouldn't have presumed. Shall I send him away, Your Excellency?"

Reyna relaxed. "No, of course not. Locke is a good friend." With a wave, she stepped toward the table.

Locke, the Queendom's former spymaster, leaned back in his chair as she took the seat beside him. His telltale uniform was gone, replaced instead with a bright red shirt embroidered with white flowers, and pants *far* too tight for anything professional.

"Retirement is looking well on you," Reyna drawled.

"And royalty looks terrible on you," he replied, taking a swig of his beer. When he worked at the Grand Palace under Tilaine and her mother, Locke was known for a shadowy appearance, a stern attitude, a swift blade to end conversations. With foam in his mustache and laugh lines around his eyes, he looked amusingly unthreatening. "Is that shirt stained, Reyna? Tell me it's not blood."

It was a fair question. Reyna glanced at the fabric, then chuckled. "Ah, no. Jam from this morning's breakfast. Thank you for pointing it out."

"Thank *you* for representing our homeland with dignity and grace." Locke's eyes sparkled at the joke. "Nolan, she'll have what I'm having. And bring me another, if you please."

The innkeeper waited for Reyna to nod confirmation before he bowed and vanished into the crowd. A clamor of laughter arose from one of the other tables, and in the corner, a bard had lifted his lute and begun to sing. A few tables nearby joined his tune, singing raucously to a popular Mid-Winter jingle.

It made Reyna feel invisible and safe. She relaxed into her chair, assessing Tilaine's right hand. "What brings you to Winterhaven?"

"The missus wanted a vacation. Figured it was the least I owed her, after all those years apart." Locke raised his tankard in cheers. "She's browsing the shops now, and I'd rather not see how much she spends. For your comfort, this"—he gestured between the two of them, implying their meeting—"wasn't planned. I usually track your movement, but last I heard, you were at the Magicary."

"You track my movement? Still?" Reyna quirked an eyebrow, although she wasn't surprised.

"Oh, I track a good number of things. Knowledge is power, after all." Locke smirked, leaning over the table. "How was your kidnapping, Your Excellency? Are you finally rethinking Venne as your right-hand Queensguard?"

Reyna rolled her eyes, although her face warmed. Did everyone know about that by now? She shouldn't be embarrassed—but it was a little embarrassing. Locke had probably never been kidnapped.

"I'm rethinking allowing *your* retirement."

"There are plenty of spymasters who can replace me. I sent you a recommendation list last season."

"And I will continue to ignore it. I'm attempting to be less like Tilaine." Bitterness swelled in her tone, and she gratefully accepted the tankard a server brought her. She pushed Locke's new beer toward him, waited until the woman left, and took a swig. The drink was bitter, yet with a tinge of sweetness she wasn't expecting.

Her face said a lot, she was sure.

Locke laughed and took his own swig. "They brew it with spruce needles." He belched, lips closed to stifle the sound, one fist against his chest. It was a display Tilaine would never have allowed—a display that made Reyna relax even further. "Local specialty, only available in Winterhaven."

"Clever," Reyna replied. They drank in silence for a moment before she dared to ask, "Since I have you here, and you're clearly still paying attention . . . what, ah, what *is* the general consensus on my rule?"

Do I need to be worried was her internal thought. She thought people were settling into the idea of her as a sovereign, but the kidnapping had shaken that mindset.

Locke shrugged. "That you're absent more than you are present. But that isn't necessarily a bad thing."

"No?" Guilt colored Reyna's voice, as she thought of all those nights she stole away in New Leaf with Kianthe.

"No." Locke set his tankard down, drumming his fingers on the wooden table. Behind him, a group of carolers had taken position in the town square and were attracting a crowd. Their soft music was barely audible through the tavern's windows.

The ex-spymaster massaged his chin. "You're an enigma, and that makes you dangerous to any dissenters. They don't know your capabilities, so most aren't willing to rile anything up."

A familiar prickle of determination settled in Reyna's chest. "Well, if they did make a display of it, I'd have a swift and fair response."

"Exactly, and that's why you haven't had any real public dissent *or* assassination attempts. If there's one avenue folks aren't pleased with, it's the dissolution of the Queendom's single ruling religion. But true devouts were a declining trend well before your reign, so most people seem relieved that they have a choice, not angry that you've turned from the Gods."

That was . . . optimistic, she supposed. She wasn't expecting to be welcomed with open arms, but the lack of rioting in the streets had emboldened her into thinking she was a good substitute for Tilaine.

Of course, a part of her always doubted that. She wasn't royalty. Her title was stolen, not given. Even if she stopped Tilaine's rampage, there wasn't any question—in Reyna's own mind, at least—that she was a temporary replacement at best.

"Otherwise, the rest of the Realm is adjusting. It's going to take time. The good news is that no one realized we dropped Tilaine in the Roiling Islands, so any true loyalists can't *find* her to reinstate her." Locke leaned back in his chair, admiring the carolers for a moment. "And the motivation to try is fading fast, at least with the radicals I'm watching."

Reyna traced the rim of her mug with a finger, wishing she felt more confident with this news. She *was* a better fit for her country—she agreed with that. But things would have been easier if Queen Eren's other daughter had interest in the throne instead.

But the silence dragged, so she said, "That was a thorough report. You're terrible at retirement."

Locke snorted. "A network like mine doesn't stop reporting in because I left the Grand Palace." A drop of beer had spilled when she pushed his second tankard over, and he dabbed it with his sleeve. "And before you feel the need to ask, my official answer will always be: *never*."

"I see. And what was the question?" She already knew he was finished being spymaster in any official capacity, and after the career he'd had, she couldn't blame him.

So, he genuinely surprised her when he replied, mildly amused, "How long before it's appropriate for you to step down as queen. The answer is never." Locke waved another server over. "Ah, yes, sorry to bother you. We'd love two bowls of boar stew. She hasn't eaten yet, and her wife will be here soon."

The server nodded, flitting back into the crowds.

Reyna didn't do much to hide her scowl, or her stiff tone. "I'm not a sovereign for life, Locke. I was never meant to stay in power forever."

The old spymaster patted her hand, almost sympathetic. "What you want is irrelevant now, and deep down, you know it. I'll reiterate what we told you last spring: blood doesn't make a sovereign. Peaceful relations between the Realm's countries have never been stronger. Queendom citizens across the Realm are reporting more widespread acceptance, less derision. That's because of *you*."

"It's because of Tessalyn and her new parliament."

"None of that would be possible without a queen willing to step aside."

"You're telling me not to step aside," Reyna replied, frustrated.

Locke's gaze was stern, a glimmer of his old personality flitting back into the conversation. "I'm telling you that because of your *willingness* to step aside, you're making positive change. I'll inform you with absolute confidence that if you leave in five years, or ten, or twenty, someone will see that power vacuum and steal it. And they won't be as kind."

He'd been in the business of international politics longer than Reyna had been alive. She had no doubt he was speaking from experience, and that his information was accurate. When the spymaster made a recommendation, only fools failed to listen.

She hated it . . . but she trusted him too much to ignore his words.

"Perhaps," she said grudgingly.

"Never lose that side of you, Reyna." Locke smiled warmly, and raised his tankard to cheers. "Your mother would be very proud."

"Liar," Reyna replied, and clinked her mug to his.

They chatted for a little while longer about everything and nothing—catching up more on personal affairs than political ones. The stew was starting to cool when Kianthe strode into the tavern, dusting her cloak. She took a seat beside Reyna, nodded at Locke, did a double take, and groaned.

"Oh, great. We're kind of in the middle of something, Locke."

"And I'm in the middle of a vacation." Locke shrugged. "A happy coincidence, I assure you."

Kianthe narrowed her eyes. "I'm not assured. Coincidences don't happen when your spies are involved."

"He's retired." Reyna smirked.

"Is he?" Kianthe's eyes never left Locke's, which was fairly sexy to watch. Considering his spies were the main threat for years under Tilaine's reign, Kianthe had no love for the man. And her protective nature made Reyna warm through and through.

Locke's lips tilted upward. "Always a pleasure, Arcandor." He pushed away his empty tankard, glancing around the inn. "I'm afraid I have to leave; there's my ladylove now."

Reyna glanced over her shoulder, but with the ever-growing crowd of tourists, it was impossible to tell who he'd gestured at. "Who is she? Can we meet her?"

"Mmm. No. I'll leave you with the bill, Your Excellency. Have a lovely evening, you two." With a wink, he strode away, vanishing into a crowd of folks moving toward the staircase. As far as Reyna could tell, he didn't join any woman in particular, but there were a gaggle of them, so it was truly impossible to tell.

Which was by design, Reyna was certain.

"He didn't bother you, did he? No upcoming world events

I should know about?" Kianthe pulled the third bowl of stew closer, digging in with a nearby spoon. "Thanks for this. I'm famished." It came out *flamshd,* considering her mouth was already full of food.

"I think he's truly on vacation," Reyna said with a hint of amusement. Her grin grew. "But thank you—you know, for scaring him off. His updates on our friends across the Realm made him *terrible* company." Sarcasm dripped from the statement.

Kianthe snorted. "Oops. What's happening with everyone?"

"Bobbie bought a ring . . . last season. Apparently, it's still in her bedside drawer."

"Oh, sure. But he's totally out of the spying business." Kianthe shot a glare where he'd disappeared, as if she was confident he'd still see it. She jammed another spoonful of shredded boar meat into her mouth, then grudgingly said, "This is damn good stew. What else?"

Reyna ticked off another finger. "Serina has repurposed her pirate crew to make emergency runs during inclement weather. Resupplying towns like—" She paused, gesturing at the inn. "—well, like this. In the Southern Seas, a new contender tried to claim part of Dreggs's fleet, but he didn't make it very far. And apparently your parents have listed the farm for sale."

That made Kianthe blanch. "Really? They're heading north after all?"

"Mmm. Bought a property in Koll, right beside Fauston's parents." Reyna watched for her reaction, but after the wedding, any prior exasperation or anger about her parents was gone. They exchanged semi-regular letters, and this was the final confirmation that her parents had accepted her path and moved on with their own.

Kianthe sounded satisfied—even a bit pleased. "Well, good for them. I'll have to swing south and visit the farm before it's gone."

Reyna was thinking the same thing. "Locke expects the sale will take a while to finalize. How about this spring? Weather should be lovely, and it'll give us some time to ensure Tawney won't be . . . ah, overrun." A pause. "Did you find anything out about Winterhaven?"

"Only that Diarn Yalinda is very good at her job." Kianthe scraped the last bit of stew off the bottom of her bowl, sucking on her spoon. "They had the opposite problem of Tawney: no visitors at all. I'm not sure their solution will help us much."

Reyna glanced around the bustling tavern, contemplating that. They had more tourists here than she'd seen in Tawney, and while the inn was crowded and the streets had healthy traffic, it didn't feel . . . crammed. There was a certain order to how they funneled everyone: the greeting party to set the tone, a direct lead to the local inn, a set process for obtaining a room, clear-cut activities that kept visitors occupied and out of local areas.

Trouble was, Kianthe had a point. There was no guarantee any of that would work in Tawney, and they didn't have the same kind of start-to-finish attraction as Winterhaven. Folks didn't visit for a specific experience, a specific celebration, and then leave. They were browsing the *humanity* of Tawney, hunting for a slice of happiness and friendship in their chaotic lives.

"Well," Reyna sighed. "At least we can help with their missing-poultry problem."

Kianthe drank deeply from a tankard of water. She looked refreshed, ready to dive into the afternoon day. "Yep. Diarn Yalinda expected nothing less. But she did promise a prime seat at the tree-lighting ceremony tonight if we're back in time."

"Lovely." Reyna chuckled, following Kianthe out the inn's front door. "Let's confront some alchemists, then."

14

Kianthe

The flight to the mountains north of Winterhaven was fucking *freezing*.

At some point, Kianthe reasoned, she should be *used* to the cold. But even with Visk's warmth beneath her, even with a heavy cloak, scarf, and a tiny ball of ever-flame clutched to her chest, she was still shivering. It had started to snow, and evening darkness arrived far too early for her preference. What had begun as a routine canvassing of the region became steadily less methodical as nighttime slid over the landscape.

And worse, the farther north they flew, the sicker she felt.

"Dragons," she groaned, clenching her eyes shut. "Rain, if this is what happens to Pill Bug and Gold Coin when they get older, I'm going to have a problem in Tawney."

"If they cause this kind of issue, we'll just send them home. Ponder can play there just as easily as they play above New Leaf." Reyna's tone was sympathetic, even as she ducked her head against the pelting snow. Her words were almost lost in the wind. "What happened to the Alchemicor's sigil? The one that stops you from absorbing dragon magic?"

Kianthe had forgotten about that. Now she hunched over Visk, fumbling in her pocket with numb fingers. "How do I activate it?"

"Press it against your skin, I believe? He already infused it with a sacrifice."

Thank the Stone she'd been listening to his instructions before they left the Magicary. Stomach roiling, Kianthe pulled up her arm and desperately pressed the square of parchment against her skin.

She wasn't expecting it to *burn*. It flared, singeing skin, making her gasp. But that wasn't the end. The pain doubled, then quadrupled, and she was left biting her tongue hard enough to bleed, hunching over Visk as her whole body overheated. At first, her thoughts were a litany of *oh Stone, oh Stars, make it stop make it STOP*—and then coherent thought ceased in favor of numbing *pain*.

The ever-flame vanished, but she barely noticed and certainly didn't care. Kianthe was dimly aware of herself hunching over Visk, trembling, his hot feathers against her sweating skin, a distant screeching, someone shouting.

And after Kianthe genuinely thought she might die, the agony faded into blessed calm.

"—nthe! Key!" Reyna's voice sounded much closer now. Kianthe blinked blearily, realizing they'd landed on a stone outcropping over the forest. She'd been utterly unaware of their descent. Sweat dried on her forehead as she lifted her hand from her forearm. The parchment had burned away, leaving an alchemical circle seared on her skin.

It took her mind several breaths to catch up to what happened, and several more to form actual words in response.

"Th-That bastard," she hissed.

Reyna had leapt off Ponder, and lifted Kianthe's chin to hold her gaze. "Are you okay? What in the five hells happened?" Her eyes dropped to the circle, and she tentatively ran her fingers over it. The charcoal smeared off, revealing a reddened scar.

Like she was cattle, branded without warning.

"Key, I may murder a very powerful alchemist." Her voice trembled, and she didn't sound like she was joking.

"Get in line," Kianthe muttered, scrubbing her face. The remnant of pain was there, but fading fast as her energy returned. As an afterthought, she tested her magic, but her reservoir was still there, bright and happy and yellow. She twisted the air around them—and sighed when a breeze leapt to her command.

Just a random-ass branding, then. Great.

"Are you okay?" Reyna helped her off Visk's back. Her griffon shifted his weight nervously, nipping her scarf in question. At his side, nearly crawling over her father's wing, Ponder was watching her too.

She waved at the griffons, gripping Reyna's shoulder for balance. "I'm fine. Bit shaky, but I'll be okay."

"Your magic?" Reyna clearly had the same line of thought.

Kianthe fished into her knapsack for a seed, tossed it on the ground, and stomped beside it. A spruce sapling sprouted on the outcropping, unnaturally fast and absolutely perfect. Now that the pain was vanishing, she realized she didn't just feel fine.

She felt fantastic.

"Everything's okay. Al should have *warned* me about the 'physical searing of my skin' bullshit, but—" Wonder tinged Kianthe's voice. "It worked. I don't feel the dragon magic at all."

"He *should* have warned you." Reyna's voice was still dark with murderous intent. She drew a deep sigh, hunching against the wind. "I'll ride with you on Visk, okay? Just in case." She slid onto the older griffon with practiced ease, offering a hand for Kianthe to join her . . . in front, Kianthe noticed wryly, as if Reyna didn't trust the mage wouldn't tip off at the first strong wind.

Although honestly, fair. Kianthe hopped onto Visk's back, pleased when Reyna's arms snuck around her waist.

She was warm, a comforting presence against Kianthe's back. Now that Ponder was old enough to ride, Kianthe hadn't realized she'd missed this kind of contact on their travels.

Visk checked that they were settled, then chirped at Ponder and leapt off the outcropping. His daughter dutifully followed behind, and they continued their flight north.

"Don't use alchemy again," Reyna said, resting her chin on Kianthe's shoulder.

"Trust me, love, I'm not an alchemist. I was ready to leave the Magicary altogether before the Stone chose me." Kianthe ran her fingers over the new mark on her arm, breathed a sigh. "If I knew it'd scar, I'd have hid it better."

Reyna peered around Kianthe, her fingers tracing it again. "Maybe it'll fade. Or vanish once its power runs out."

"Mmm. Maybe. I'll ask Albert about it."

"After *I* speak with him." Her tone promised that wouldn't be a pleasant conversation.

Kianthe chuckled. They flew in silence for a few more moments, and she ventured to say, "I missed this. It's really nice to fly together now that Ponder is old enough, but . . . well, I got used to holding on to you."

Reyna's arms tightened around her waist. "Me too." She pressed a kiss to Kianthe's neck, just below her hairline.

It was so romantic, Kianthe almost forgot they had a *reason* to be up here.

Reyna didn't. As they rounded the next mountain, she leaned over Visk's flank and pointed. "There! A cave."

Kianthe startled. "Oh, right."

Night was so encompassing that the moon was their only light, and the snow pelting them made visibility terrible. It took several concentrated moments of squinting just to *see* the cave Reyna mentioned, but once she did, Kianthe noticed a tiny lantern flickering on a post beside it. "Well, someone's home."

She nudged Visk, who began a slow descent into the nearby trees. Ponder landed hard in a nearby spruce, knocking pine cones off the tree as she adjusted her hold on the branches, chittering softly. Visk chirped at her, and she clamped her beak shut, spreading her wings to drift reluctantly to the ground.

She was normally so active, so animated, that Kianthe sometimes forgot Ponder was an apex predator. Her approach was silent, and she'd shifted easily into hunting mode, mirroring her father's behavior perfectly.

Kianthe helped her wife dismount, speaking softly. "Okay. My magic can counter alchemy when we see the circles in advance, but we'll need to approach with caution. There's clearly a lot we don't know about these alchemists."

"Such as whether or not they're actually *behind* the draining spells," Reyna said. "So far all we have is supposition. And after your arm, I'm not inclined to believe Albert's word without evidence."

Kianthe paused. That was a good point. She tugged her scarf down a little further—it was warmer in the cover of the trees, but she was still wet and icy. The snow crunched under their feet, and she told it silently to *hush*. "Yeah, that's true. We'll just . . . see what they say. No reason to be hostile."

Reyna shrugged, unsheathing her sword. The dark steel of the meteorite made her blade almost invisible in the cover of night. "No reason to be stupid, either. You should approach from the front. I'll follow behind and provide support if needed."

Immediately, Kianthe flashed back to Diarn Arlon's library, the night Reyna almost died. She shuddered, feeling the blood drain from her face. "Don't take this the wrong way, Rain, but I'm *highly* uncomfortable with you walking through a hostile alchemist's lair alone."

At their side, Ponder shifted her weight as if she was already bored of this discussion. She prowled away, silent on the snow, wings folded as she hunted for something in the trees. Visk chittered softly, but she'd caught the trail of something and was clearly determined to find it.

Probably a rodent. Or a very unfortunate rabbit.

"Trust me, Key. I have no intention of stepping in another circle." Reyna rested the sword's blade in the snowdrift. "In the Queensguard, we'd rarely show our hand all at once. But if you'd prefer to play this another way, I can approach with you. Whatever you'd like."

That made Kianthe feel safe, even in this remote forest, even approaching a very *un*safe situation. There was something wonderful about having a partner she could rely on—someone who tackled problems and still paused to ensure she was comfortable.

Kianthe stepped closer, pulling Reyna into a hug. Her wife

grunted at the force of it, blade brushing the snow as she hugged back with one hand. Kianthe buried her nose in Reyna's scarf and said, "Have I mentioned that you look sexy as *hells* with that sword?"

"Have I mentioned this sword is sexy as hells, all on its own?" Reyna offered a sly smile.

Before she could respond, a screech echoed.

A *griffon's* screech.

The snow swallowed the bulk of the sound, but it was still piercing. Kianthe and Reyna leapt apart, spinning for the source. "That was Ponder," Kianthe exclaimed, heart pounding. Where was she? She'd prowled into the forest, but where?

"Visk—" Reyna started, but the older griffon had already taken to the skies, disappearing into the growing snowstorm. When Ponder didn't make another sound, Reyna set her jaw. "The alchemists." And with barely a glance to ensure Kianthe was following, Reyna angled for the cave. She moved cautiously, eyes on the ground for dangerous circles, but her graceful steps promised pain.

No one hurt Ponder without a swift, vicious response.

Kianthe followed, pulling her magic. Visibility was low, but the forest paid attention. A quick hand on one of the trunks connected her to their leaves and roots, and finally to their metaphorical hearts.

Good news was, trees loved to gossip.

Dragon, they whispered through rustling pine needles, the creaking of trunks in the wind. *There's a dragon.*

"Uh, Rain—" Kianthe started, but her partner had vanished into the snow.

Shit.

Kianthe left the trees, sprinting after Reyna. Her partner was waiting for her to catch up, scanning their surroundings. The moment Kianthe rejoined her, Reyna strode past the last row of trees. A short path carved up the mountainside, leading to the cave, and Reyna assessed, then started up, determination on her features—

—and Ponder landed in front of them.

Kianthe yelped, startled, but Reyna just lowered her sword. "Thank the Gods. Are you hurt?"

Ponder was bristling, feathers fluffed and lion's tail swishing in agitation. She screeched again, and Reyna surged forward to silence her. "Dearest, now is *really* not the time—" Her eyes cut to the cave, but no one had surfaced.

That was odd, too. A griffon's screech wasn't exactly *quiet.*

Kianthe strode past Reyna and Ponder, unease spreading in her chest. Overhead, Visk circled, sighting a good spot to land now that the crisis had been averted. And yet, with all of them at this cave's doorstep, no alchemists had surfaced.

Almost like no one was home.

Mountains were calmer than trees, but the ground always knew who walked on it. Kianthe pressed a hand to the face of the mountain, closing her eyes to listen. A beating heart thrummed back at her, so loud she actually winced.

Shit.

"Rain!" Her voice was sharp.

Reyna stepped around Ponder, raising her sword. "What's wrong?"

"The alchemists are gone. But Ponder is right—we may have a problem." And with a flick of her fingers, Kianthe led Reyna up the short path to the cave. It was large, an unnatural divot that had been forcibly carved into the cliffside. Far too messy for an elemental mage, but appropriate for an alchemist attempting elemental magic.

A torch—metal, unlit—decorated the entrance, which quickly narrowed to a passageway of low ceilings and rough walls. Kianthe paused at the entrance, ever aware that a single wrong step could kill them. Her voice was hushed as they faced the darkness of the cavern. "I think the alchemists are gone for a reason. The trees were talking about dragons."

"Well, we *are* near dragon country." Reyna glanced over her shoulder to check on Visk and Ponder—but both griffons had taken to the skies and vanished in the blowing snow. She frowned. "You think there's a bigger problem?"

"I . . . I don't know." Kianthe pressed a hand to the rock again. It was rugged under her touch, sharp and cold. "But there's something inside, and it's loud. Really, really loud."

Reyna readied her blade. "Hopefully it's friendly." Without another word, she gestured ahead, letting Kianthe step in front of her. Normally, Reyna would be leading in this type of situation—but when magic dominated the issue, Kianthe took point.

She summoned an ever-flame, holding the glow closer to her chest. The passageway was narrow, rough, carved with brute magical force. It was mildly comforting to know that no elemental mages were involved in this; they'd never allow something so sloppy. Kianthe kept one hand on the rock, listening, feeling. Caves always felt quiet, almost stale, but this one had a breeze coming from somewhere within, which was strange.

Another hint it was mage-made: the passageway wasn't long. They only followed the twisted path for a few moments, ducking low to avoid hitting the ceiling, when they rounded a corner and emerged into a huge underground cavern.

It was dark. Pitch black, actually. The only reason Kianthe knew it was huge was because the mountain itself told her, its general irritation at being hollowed seeping through the walls. It painted a picture big enough that Kianthe actually tucked her ever-flame under her jacket, casting them in further darkness.

Somewhere, something was breathing.

In.

Out.

Hot air rushed toward them with every exhale.

"A dragon," Reyna murmured, so quietly Kianthe almost missed it. Other than the rhythmic breaths, everything was hushed. The wind of the snowstorm was gone, and the crackle of her ever-flame was piercing in comparison. Kianthe motioned for Reyna to step back into the passageway.

Her wife did so, twisting her sword so it was at her side—still in hand, but not likely to impale anyone. Kianthe followed her back in, deep enough to have a conversation without the dragon overhearing. For added security, she instructed the wind to swallow any words outside their little bubble.

In the ever-flame's flickering light, Reyna's features were sharp and beautiful. "Key. It's *one* dragon."

"Are you sure?" Kianthe frowned.

"Dragon Queen, remember?" Reyna's voice was humorless. Right.

"Can you talk to this one?"

"It's not exactly an open line of communication." Reyna pressed her lips together, clearly puzzling through how to explain it. "They start it. I'm only allowed to converse with them for as long as they allow. *That* dragon's mind is silent."

Kianthe breathed a frustrated sigh. "Okay. Let's cast a bit of light on the situation—but if it's hostile, I want you to run. Through this passage, Rain, and keep going into the forest until Visk and Ponder find you. The dragons near Tawney tolerate us, but I don't trust others to welcome us without a bit of fire."

It was a fitting speech, appropriate for the Arcandor, Mage of Ages, to offer a civilian.

Except Reyna was far from that, and Kianthe rarely managed that tone in their relationship. Even now, Reyna's lips quirked in amusement. "I'm not leaving you to face a dragon alone. If it attacks, we're standing together."

"*I* can manipulate fire. Last I checked, you—"

"I don't think now is the time for this argument, dearest."

Kianthe swallowed a growl of frustration, clenched her eyes shut. When she met her wife's gaze again, Reyna's eyes were bright, almost eager. For all that she loved her quiet comforts, Reyna couldn't turn away from the thrill of adventure . . . or the threat of death.

"What happened to 'whatever you'd like'?" Kianthe whispered, exasperated.

"That was before you pitched sacrificing yourself to a dragon who may be quite friendly, for all we know. And considering *I'm* the one who can speak to them, I believe I'm the asset here, fire manipulation or no." Reyna gestured at the opening. "Shall we?"

Kianthe swallowed a curse. With nothing else to do, she stalked into the cavern, and scattered ever-flame across the cavern's space. The sudden light was off-putting, and when her eyes cleared, Kianthe saw just what they were dealing with.

"Oh, shit," she muttered.

"Shit, indeed," Reyna replied, eyes widening.

15

Reyna

The cavern was a sight. The floor was flat, the high ceiling carved with the same harshness as the passageway here. The entire cavern must have taken up half the mountain, for how deep it was. To their left were tables splayed with parchment, quills, and discarded alchemical circles. Worse, though, was the scent of blood and old flesh; Reyna's eyes roamed over a pile of gnawed bones against the far wall. Clearly, they'd found their missing livestock.

Neither of them looked at that long, though. Not when there was a *dragon* sleeping in the center of the cavern.

They'd expected a dragon, but seeing the reality absolutely broke Reyna's heart. It was young, the same silver-gray as the dragons north of Tawney, and maybe twice the size of Pill Bug and Gold Coin. Big enough that her head would probably reach its belly, small enough that it was obviously a juvenile. It was curled into a tight ball on the cavern floor, deep in slumber, but its body language wasn't at all relaxed.

No, it looked like it was in *pain*. If a creature could exude misery while sleeping, this dragon was doing it. Its tail was tucked protectively under its legs, its wings wrapped around its body like a shield. It had curled its snout under one of its claws, attempting to cover its eyes.

Perhaps it was dreaming that it was far, far from here.

"Oh, Key," Reyna breathed.

"The missing egg," Kianthe whispered, wonder tinging her voice. "It hatched after all."

Reyna had almost forgotten about the third dragon egg, the one they'd tracked to a shoreline north of Lathe . . . and never found. Back then, they'd been distracted by a sea serpent in the Northern Bay, distracted by the drama of Diarn Arlon's horrendous reign. They'd searched the area where Bobbie's mother had placed the egg, but they were about twenty years too late to locate it.

So, they'd given up. They found the eggs that were left: Pill Bug and Gold Coin. After so long, the dragons had been relieved with two of the three. Reyna and Kianthe discussed going after the third egg, but it was brief, mostly academic—without any new leads, it'd be impossible to scour the Realm for it.

Guilt festered in Reyna's chest for a season . . . and then a coup to overthrow Tilaine was presented, and her concern shifted to more *human* matters.

Now, regret slammed into her chest, tightening her breaths. This dragon had hatched all alone, in a wilderness far from others of its kind. And now it was *trapped* here, in this massive cavern, with no access to the sky, completely reliant on livestock handed to it by asshole alchemists.

They shouldn't have given up looking. They should have done something sooner.

Gods, what had she done?

Reyna felt herself trembling. If she squinted, it looked like the dragon was trembling too, curling deeper into itself with every exhale. Her sword was sheathed before she realized she'd moved, her words numb. "We have to help it."

With determination, she moved toward the creature.

Kianthe grabbed her arm with such force, Reyna nearly tossed her wife to the ground on instinct. Only catching the panic and fear in Kianthe's eyes made Reyna pause. "*Key—*"

"*Look* at the ground," Kianthe hissed.

Reyna's eyes dropped to the cavern floor. It took a bit of squinting in the flickering firelight, but then her heart literally skipped a beat. Smudged in dried blood was an alchemical circle maybe double the size of the dragon, encompassing it fully. This creature wasn't just trapped in a cavern. It was trapped with *magic,* confined to a space barely big enough for it to turn around in.

The circle appeared dormant, but clearly it was doing *something,* or the dragon wouldn't have been perfectly inside it. The sudden urge to track down these alchemists and make them intimately familiar with her blade was overwhelming.

It was only years of practice that had her drawing a deep breath instead. She'd slipped up, enraged by this scene, and almost paid a price for it. Lesson one in the Queensguard: *assess* before acting.

She really was getting rusty.

Reyna stepped back. "You're right. My apologies." Kianthe released her, breathing a relieved sigh—although both of them remained tense. They studied the circle for a moment while the dragon slept. It really must just be a baby if it hadn't noticed them yet.

Reyna finally whispered, "Is that—"

"The draining spell. Yeah. Clearly, we're in the right place." Kianthe set her jaw, every bit the Arcandor now. "Let me handle this, okay? Stand back for a minute." Her words were still barely a whisper, the conversation quiet enough not to wake the dragon.

Even a baby dragon could be dangerous if startled.

This time, Reyna didn't argue. She backed along the cavern's edge.

Kianthe raised her arms, clearly pulling magic. This must be a powerful spell, because the air around her sparkled with potential, as if every element around them awaited her command. At first, nothing happened—but then the ground strategically began swallowing the outer edges of the alchemical circle. Bit by bit, holes overturned the ground, trailing around the dragon's form in a methodical display.

It must have been an expert spell. Usually, Kianthe didn't use such finesse—she just ripped things apart and fixed them later if needed. But they both knew this dragon deserved better.

Of course, the dragon wasn't a willing participant in this—and the magic of overturning the ground awoke it.

In an instant, it jolted upright, its dark eyes blazing, wings unfurling in a bold display.

It was still careful to keep the wings *within* the circle's confines, Reyna noted. It must experience physical pain if it stretched too far, and that thought made Reyna's heart ache even more. This poor thing.

For all that she was sympathetic to it, the *dragon* held no love for them. Its dark eyes located Kianthe, still deep in her spell, and it opened its mouth to gather flame. The air scented with a distinct char, like a campfire with an acidic tinge. Considering Gold Coin and Pill Bug hadn't been able to summon flame yet, Reyna wasn't sure what to expect.

But fire definitely flickered in its throat. Even with that, it stepped backward, lowering its head, wings pulled inward a bit, tail lashing. As if it was forced into a bold display of flame and posturing, even when its deepest desire was to be imperceivable.

"Kianthe, it's scared," Reyna said, desperation in her tone.

"I know, Rain. One second." Kianthe grunted past the exertion of this spell, twisting the last bit of the alchemy spell deep into the earth. It was a quiet thing, destroying the magic—something the dragon probably didn't notice.

In a breath, Kianthe shifted her focus to the dragon. "We're here to help, okay?" She infused her words with magic, and even Reyna could tell they held weight. This wasn't her goofy, pun-loving wife—this was the Arcandor, the Mage of Ages, the woman who'd fought an entire dragon horde on the back of a griffon, who cracked jokes and righted worldly wrongs in the same breath.

The fierce determination on her face, the kindness in her voice, was absolutely stunning.

The dragon was still bristling, though.

Kianthe raised her hands, taking a step forward. "You'll be free soon. Put the fire away. We're friends."

It didn't understand. Reyna noticed a second before Kianthe did—the dragon still thought it was trapped, and Kianthe approaching made her a more dangerous threat, especially with her magic. With barely a blink, the dragon roared and spewed fire.

The world *ignited.* Hot, bright flames flowed toward them like a tsunami, washing over them in a swell of heat. Kianthe inhaled sharply, moving her hands fast to twist the flames above their heads. Heat still scorched Reyna's skin, and high above them, rocks of the cavern ceiling melted and dripped like lava.

"Fall back, Rain," Kianthe shouted.

Reyna had never followed an order so fast. She slid into the crevice, protected by cold stone, but the heat still licked at her heels. Through a crack, she watched as the cavern crashed around Kianthe in pools of molten rock.

Some Dragon Queen. She'd never expected how *hot* dragon fire was. Pill Bug and Gold Coin would be a fearsome sight in two decades.

For all its bluster, the flame ended as suddenly as it started. Kianthe cooled down the space with a wave of her hand. "That's it. Flame won't work on me. Okay? Let's try something else." Her voice sounded calm, but considering the cracking of rock cooling rapidly, the shimmer of heat in the air above them, it was as much posturing as the dragon's response.

Beyond Kianthe, the dragon paced inside the remains of the circle, wings spread halfway, talons clawing into stone. It roared, a tiny sound compared to its adult counterparts, and reared for another flame strike.

It was so, so scared. Even as tense with adrenaline as she was, Reyna's heart shattered.

That didn't make it less of a threat. Fire gathered again, although this magic was clearly tiring it out. The dragon hunched, breathing hard, and gulped more air to fuel the flames in its throat.

"Key," Reyna gasped, because even with Kianthe's magic, this was the literal definition of playing with fire. She couldn't bear to see her wife hurt, any more than she could bear to see this creature collapse from exhaustion.

"It's this fucking sigil on my arm," Kianthe grunted, raising a wall of rock this time to shield them. It was a weaker breath this time, significantly less destructive. Heat slid around the edges, and Kianthe spread her arms to counter the flames licking nearby. "I'm not poisoned by dragon magic, but I can't communicate at *all* with them now. Shit. *Shit.*"

Well, then. Reyna's turn.

She closed her eyes, her jaw set. It was hard to concentrate in these conditions, but she could feel the dragon before them. Not its physical body, but its soul—inexplicably linked to hers, the way it *should* be linked to the other dragons. Except this one had grown up alone, isolated, afraid. From the moment it hatched, it had to fight to survive.

And now it was trapped underground, desperate to leave, unable to move, stretch, fly. The only humans it saw were a threat.

Its soul was a flicker, when it should have been a wildfire. Everything about this dragon was anguish and terror . . . but deep inside was a pure, innocent mind waiting to understand safety and security.

Reyna felt that inside her own soul. A link with this dragon didn't exist, but there was some connection here. Likely, it was too young to *allow* conversation—which meant it was also too young to block her from its mind. She pressed her empathy into the link, a gentle moment that translated to: *I'm sorry.*

In an instant, the dragon's barrage ceased. The cavern was dangerously hot, and Kianthe was panting from the effort of keeping their space at an acceptable temperature.

But the dragon wasn't roaring now, or breathing fire. In fact, it had gone quiet.

Listening for her.

"I think I've got it," Reyna said, easing out of the crevice to squeeze Kianthe's arm. "Can you lower the wall?"

Kianthe opened her mouth to protest—then thought better of it. With a sigh, she pulled the wall down, allowing access to the cavern yet again.

Heat rippled. The dragon had lowered its head now, cautious, like a jungle cat ready to pounce. Everything about its body language implied it was curious—but knew that curiosity could hurt. Its wings were pressed tightly against its body, and its dark eyes glimmered as it stared at Reyna.

But they were talking now.

Kianthe sometimes said that elemental magic was bright yellow in color. Well, if that was true, Reyna had no doubt that dragon magic was deep blue, almost purple. The dragon glowed with it now, and its speech was clumsy, like dusting off an old instrument.

Safe?

Oh. Reyna swallowed and stepped closer, raising a hand. *You're safe. I promise.*

Its eyes flicked to her sheathed sword, then to Kianthe. Its talons dug into the ground again, clawing gashes in the stone. *Not safe. Trick.*

This dragon was likely a decade or more old, but that still meant it was barely a child. She carefully untied the sword at her belt, lowering it to the ground. *No trick, love. We're here to take you home.* And in that word, she infused every memory of Tawney she could think of: the warmth, the laughter, the safety.

Home meant a lot of things, and her examples of it would be different from a dragon's, but some definitions transcended species.

The young dragon uncoiled, visibly relaxing. Hope tinged its voice. *Home?*

Now Reyna thought of the dragons, of their expansive mountain range, of their tight-knit hordes. She nodded, reiterating: *Yes. Your home, and ours. You'll be safe there, and loved.*

The dragon keened, soft and low, and tears pricked Reyna's eyes. How long had it been soaring over this landscape, hunting for its family? Reyna wanted to hug it—but of course dragons didn't care about a human's physical touch.

She glanced instead at Kianthe. "We're okay. It's fine. It's trusting us to get it home."

"Damn. That was . . ." Kianthe shook her head. "You're amazing, you know that?"

"I've heard it once or twice," Reyna said, but she couldn't tear her eyes away from the dragon. It didn't seem to know Kianthe had destroyed the alchemy circle, and that made her sad too. She held up her arms, approaching slowly, and was pleased when the dragon didn't back away. She pushed through their link: *You're free. The circle is gone.*

And for emphasis, she stepped into it, scuffing her boot along the upturned earth.

The dragon lowered its head, assessing the circle now. It puffed smoke, but tentatively tested the circle's edge by stretching out one wing. Its eyes clenched shut, as if it was bracing for pain—and then opened into eager pools of black when nothing happened.

Free, the dragon said wonderingly, and leapt out of the circle. It shook its entire body, stretching its wings properly, arching its back like a cat. *Free!*

Reyna laughed delightedly. "I think it's happy you helped."

"No shit." Kianthe snorted, watching it roll around on the ground. Even confined to the cavern, it had more space than it had in . . . who knew how long. Kianthe glanced again at her wrist, at the sigil burned into her skin. "I can't believe Albert gave me a sigil that cut off dragon magic. It helped, but this little guy has the same magical presence as . . . well, Lilac."

"Is that an insult?" Reyna crossed her arms. Her old warhorse was enjoying a well-deserved retirement in a pasture outside the Grand Palace, but she still had to deter Kianthe's disdain for any mount that wasn't a griffon.

Kianthe rolled her eyes. "No, dear. But it *is* unsettling. The dragons always had a magical signature, but I can't feel it at *all* now. Albert had better take this off." She rubbed the sigil on her skin, grimacing.

"Well, it's still better than vomiting if dragons get too close, love." Reyna shook her head.

While they talked, the dragon tackled the bones in the corner of the room. They'd been picked clean—drained of blood for the circle, the remains left as dragon food, no doubt—but the dragon was enjoying gnawing on some of the newer ones. By the size of that pile, it wasn't just livestock from Winterhaven; it was elk and moose from the surrounding area, too.

Reyna seized the distraction to explore the area properly. The alchemical circle was gone, but there were still clues about who'd been here—and why.

Kianthe followed Reyna, keeping one eye on the dragon. Her voice was low. "What's our plan?"

"The alchemists trapped the dragon here. Look around, Key. There's no *exit,* which means they lured it inside and magically erased the door." Irritation surged in Reyna's chest, but she kept herself focused, instead parsing through the parchment on the nearby desk. "They'd clearly bothered enough to feed it recently, so that solves the mystery of the stolen chickens and goats."

Kianthe watched the dragon break off a chunk of bone and chomp it between vicious teeth. She made a face. "Yeah, I suppose it does. So where did the alchemists *go*? And how did they know to clear out right before we got here?"

"Oh, I suspect they've been gone a few days now." Reyna lifted a cloth napkin to reveal a metal plate, sniffing the gristle of meat left behind. She winced at the acrid scent. "This meal is at least that old."

"Cleared out for the Showdown, maybe?"

"Possibly. But it does seem like convenient timing."

Kianthe snorted. "Awfully bold of them to put tables so close to the dragon, considering we almost got scorched, and I'm *the* elemental mage."

"Clearly, they had some protections around it." Reyna pointed to the base of the table, where sigils were etched into the wood. "Perhaps in certain circumstances, alchemy is more powerful than elemental magic."

Kianthe huffed. "Maybe."

Reyna chuckled, sifting through the tables' contents for a few more moments. Nothing of worth. She'd been hoping for something to identify these alchemists, but everything left behind was closer to scratch paper.

Although . . . handwriting was unique. The idea caught like a spark, and Reyna paused at a sheet of parchment with a dozen symbols scribbled on it. Feo had said the draining spell was like no alchemy they'd seen before—as if someone was creating new letters in an established alphabet. That kind of experimentation would require power.

Her eyes slid to the dragon again. It didn't seem magically weak. Physically, it appeared unharmed, albeit maybe too thin compared to Gold Coin and Pill Bug. Its mental state was another story, but it would likely recover with space, time, and other dragons nearby.

And yet, it had been trapped in the center of a draining spell. Why?

"Find anything?" Kianthe asked, raising an eyebrow.

"Nothing of note. Although I do believe we should speak with Feo again." Reyna folded the parchment with the scribbles on it and tucked it into her pocket. "Which bodes well, since we definitely need to get this dragon home."

Kianthe cracked her knuckles. "On it. Prepare the little guy, huh? This might surprise it." And she strolled to the short passageway they'd entered from, grabbing the air as if she were prying open two double doors.

Brace yourself, Reyna told the dragon, stepping well out of Kianthe's way. *We're getting out. Freedom.*

The dragon abandoned the bone pile, prowling back and forth, tail lashing in enthusiasm. Its dark eyes were wide, and it stared at Kianthe as if she were a gift from the heavens themselves.

"Sorry in advance," Kianthe said, but she wasn't talking to

either of them. No, she seemed to be having a conversation with the mountain itself. "This might ache a bit, but you'll feel better when it's done."

Reyna put herself in front of the dragon, arms spread to keep it back. The dragon lowered its head to her height, crouching behind her, its twisting horns almost at her ear. They both held their breath.

With a groan and a grimace, Kianthe wrenched her arms apart. At first, nothing happened—and then a subtle *crack-crack-crack* popped through the space. Time seemed to slow as a fissure splintered from the crevice, spidering to the ceiling, crawling past charred rock and hardened lava. It shook the cavern's ceiling, and boulders slammed around them—but any that got close to her and the dragon were magically diverted.

For its credit, the dragon seemed less terrified, more fascinated by this display. But that wasn't a surprise to Reyna, considering the extensive magic dragons held. This was probably a learning opportunity, rather than a threat.

Kianthe was glowing now, a faint yellow even Reyna could see. The air around them was scented with something odd: it was almost like wildflowers on a spring day. Elemental magic? Reyna hadn't realized it had a smell—although she rarely saw magic of this caliber.

"Almost there," Kianthe gritted out, adjusting her hold.

As soon as she said that, a piercing *BANG* echoed into the night—and the mountain split in half. It happened so fast that Reyna almost missed it. One moment, the cavern was intact, and the next, icy air flooded in, snowdrifts that swelled with the swirling wind. The dust settled, leaving a vivid glimpse of the moon-bathed forest, the dark sky.

Kianthe dropped to her knees, gasping. "One exit, just for you."

Reyna surged forward to help her wife stand, but the dragon didn't care about that. Seeing the night sky so close, it bounded over them, its wings spread wide. With a few powerful beats, it leapt into the air—

—and a griffon landed on its back.

The dragon roared, knocked off-balance, and crashed into the snow at the base of the mountain.

"Oh, shit," Kianthe wheezed. "Ponder, *no!*"

"Get my sword." Reyna hauled her wife to her feet, then sprinted for the opening. The path down the mountain was more treacherous now, splintered from Kianthe's magic. Reyna slid down it, already speaking into her link with the dragon. *It's okay. Friend. That's a friend!*

It was too late. The dragon twisted viciously, forcing Ponder to fly or be squished by its wings. Ponder landed in one of the spruce trees, balancing precariously, her own wings outspread. She chittered curiously, head tilted at the new dragon.

It sighted her, roaring. With a lash of its tail, it splintered the tree she'd landed in, forcing her to take flight again. This time, the dragon followed her into the air, writhing in an attempt to knock her out of the sky. The murderous look in its eyes proved that it wasn't going down without a fight.

And in a fight between a dragon and a griffon, Ponder *would* lose. She just might not know it yet.

Visk landed with a *thump* beside Reyna, and she wasted no time leaping onto his back. "Fair warning. I'm going to kill her," Reyna told him tightly.

Visk screeched, and it almost felt like: *Get in line.*

It was icy, the wind only getting worse as the evening wore on. High above, the night sky was dark, but the wind was kicking snow off the mountains anyway. Reyna had to squint through near-whiteout conditions. It didn't take long to catch sight of both their targets. And as she neared the chaos, it became very, very apparent that Ponder thought she was *playing.*

She'd dip down, nip the dragon's wings or twisting horns, wait until the exact moment the young dragon lashed at her— and then flit away, chittering with laughter. She wove through trees and pivoted off cliffsides as if it were an obstacle course. The snow, the dragon's roar, the occasional burst of fire, it only seemed to spark more happiness in Ponder's soul.

Visk realized it too, and slowed his approach. He hesitantly glanced back at Reyna, as if waiting for a suggestion on how to proceed.

But just as Reyna tried to reach back out to the dragon, its body language changed, too. Instead of sinking into attack mode, it seemed to realize this was a new game. And . . . well, it was still young. Now that it knew Ponder wasn't going to hurt it, the dragon swallowed its fire. A delightful grumble surged from its throat instead, and it beat its wings against a huge snowdrift, sending an avalanche toward Ponder. The griffon dodged it lithely, then landed on the dragon's back, nibbling underneath its left horn—something even Gold Coin and Pill Bug loved.

As Visk and Reyna watched, Ponder made yet another reptilian friend.

"Unbelievable," Reyna sighed, sinking onto Visk's back. "I don't know whether to be impressed or exhausted."

Visk chirped, enacting a slow circle back toward the fractured mountain—and Kianthe. Reyna whistled sharply, glancing over her shoulder to see Ponder leaping back toward them, leading the dragon through yet another round of challenges as they returned to their starting point.

It'd be cute, if Reyna's heart weren't still pounding.

Kianthe was sitting at the mouth of the cave, legs dangling over the ledge, Reyna's sword lying within reach. Behind her, the entire mountain had been stitched back together, smoothed into its former glory. It looked oddly out of place, considering there wasn't snow on it yet, and any trees that had rooted along its surface were regrowing slowly. But in a few days, no one would ever know there'd been an alchemist's experiment here.

Deep bags sat under Kianthe's eyes, and she swallowed a yawn. "Look, I know we're near the Magicary, but that?" She jerked a thumb over her shoulder. "That was a bit more than I wanted tonight. Tell me Ponder didn't get eaten."

"She appears to have made another friend." Reyna slid off Visk's back, strolling to her wife.

Kianthe raised an eyebrow. "Made a friend . . . or enlisted a minion?"

Visk shook his entire body, as if to clear himself of that thought. Kianthe snorted at his reaction.

Reyna offered a hand, pulling Kianthe to her feet. It took a moment for Kianthe to find her balance, which was concerning. Reyna felt her wife's forehead; a bit warmer than she'd like. She sighed. "Magic drain. Was it necessary to fix the mountain tonight?"

"This range is one of the oldest in the Realm." Kianthe draped her arm over Reyna's shoulders, leaning heavily into her side as she swallowed a yawn. "That mountain didn't deserve ants cutting into it, any more than it wanted to trap a dragon. It's not the exact same shape as before, but it said it's close enough."

Reyna helped her onto Visk's back, retrieved her sword, then slid on behind Kianthe. "At least we're not far from the Magicary that you'll recover fast."

"Oh, sure. Ley lines all over this area."

Near the forest below their ledge, Ponder landed heavily in a huge snowdrift. It puffed white powder, and she clawed her way out, covered in snow. Her feathers fluffed, and she shook her whole body.

A breath later, the dragon landed beside her. This time, the snowdrift exploded, scattering snow all over Ponder yet again.

She screeched indignantly.

The dragon roared back, tail swishing in anticipation, glimmering eyes alert.

Ponder leapt into the air, nipped its wing, and slid onto its back. Its long neck twisted to get a better angle—and then it nuzzled her feathers. The grumble coming from its throat sounded almost like a purr.

"Stone be damned." Kianthe sounded half-asleep already. "Maybe we should take notes from Ponder's playbook, huh?"

"Maybe *you* should sleep on the flight home." Reyna nudged Visk into the air, then whistled to get Ponder to follow. Luckily, any thought the dragon had of fleeing had vanished, and it lumbered into the sky after them, dutifully following their procession.

Friend, it said warmly.

Reyna smoothed some hair out of Kianthe's face, resting her chin on her wife's head as they flew back to Winterhaven.

Friends, she affirmed.

16

Kianthe

Kianthe awoke the next morning with a hangover.

Well, she didn't drink, so it wasn't *really* a hangover. But she always imagined this was what a hangover felt like. The Stone of Seeing was feeding her magic, but resituating an entire mountain took a lot of energy, and even the ley lines couldn't replenish magic fast enough to counter the side effects.

Luckily, she had the best wife in the world. A cooling mug of tea sat on the bedside table, and she was bundled in blankets. The curtains were drawn and the room was dark and quiet. Kianthe only vaguely remembered landing in Winterhaven, and she certainly didn't recall reaching the inn—but as always, Reyna had been looking out for her.

Kianthe had just finished reheating the tea with a flame on her fingertip when the door opened and her wife stepped inside. Reyna dusted snow off her jacket and removed her boots, cheeks pink from the cold, eyes bright. "Ah, good, you're awake. Feeling better?"

"If 'better' is more 'walked into a brick wall' and less 'drowning in misery,' then sure." Kianthe snuggled back onto the mattress, hugging her tea close to her chest. It was a careful operation to avoid spilling it, but she managed. Barely. "Where were you?"

"Checking on Spruce."

"Spruce . . . the tree?"

"No, the dragon."

Kianthe raised an eyebrow. "You named the dragon 'Spruce.'"

Reyna hung her cloak by the door, shuddering from the left-over cold. She stepped to the hearth and stoked the dying fire. "Well, it needed a name, and I'm apparently the Dragon Queen. I figured I'd bequeath it one."

"Do dragons *have* names?"

"If they do, they haven't bothered to tell me." Reyna offered a wry smirk. "But it's cute, isn't it? Spruce didn't seem to mind."

"So, Pill Bug, Gold Coin, and Spruce." Kianthe flicked a finger, and the fire inside the hearth swelled proudly. Warmth washed over the room, which gave her the courage to push the blankets to her waist, instead of holding them around her shoulders.

"Well, *Blue* Spruce. Since we found it in a blue spruce forest."

Kianthe snorted. "Fitting."

Reyna slid out of her pants, removed her shirt, and slid into bed. "You seem warm." She was wearing undergarments only, and her skin was ice-cold against Kianthe's. Naturally, she pressed herself against her wife's warm body with merciless insistence. Kianthe inhaled sharply, and Reyna deftly plucked the mug from Kianthe's hands, took a sip. "This is good, isn't it? It's made with—"

It took a moment to recover from the shock of cold skin against her. Kianthe cleared her throat and took back the mug. "Let me guess. Blue Spruce."

Reyna snapped her fingers. "You've got it. Local specialty." She sighed, leaning back against the pillows and Kianthe's shoulder. "Ponder and Visk are watching Spruce, but that dragon's been through a lot. I pieced together some of its history this morning. It hatched on that shoreline, the one north of Lathe. It couldn't make it across the bay, not at that age, so it flew south—but the farther south it went, the weaker the dragon magic got."

Dragon magic was absolutely concentrated near dragon

country. The Stone of Seeing had a solid claim on everything south, which must have confused a baby dragon all to the five hells. And considering the physical positioning of the Magicary within the Vardian Mountains, there really wasn't anywhere for it to go without that elemental influence.

Kianthe's brow furrowed. "So, it got lost."

"Wandered for years. I think at one point, it had a goal to reach its home . . . but as time passed, it forgot why it was bothering." Reyna scrubbed her face, relaxing a bit more. Her head fit perfectly in the curve of Kianthe's neck. "Can you imagine being alone from the time you were born?"

The ache in her voice hurt Kianthe's heart. She smoothed Reyna's hair, gently massaging her scalp. "We'll fix it. It won't be lonely much longer."

Reyna hummed. "Well, Ponder is keeping it company for now. We can take a day and replenish your magic before heading back to Tawney, if you'd like. They've set up toboggan slides along the southern hill after the snow last night. Might be fun."

"Maybe." Kianthe's head thrummed, and it was hard to ignore why they'd been in that cavern at all last night. "The dragon is our top priority, but . . . I might not stay in Tawney long. Albert and I have an overdue meeting." Her eyes dropped to the sigil on her forearm, half-hidden behind Reyna's head.

Reyna twisted out from underneath her arm to see it better. Her gaze darkened, and she ran a gentle finger along the sensitive skin. The burn was raw today, and although Reyna was clearly careful, her touch still had Kianthe wincing. Reyna withdrew immediately, pressing a kiss to Kianthe's palm instead.

"I'll join you for that conversation." For such a kind gesture, Reyna's words were anything but.

Kianthe frowned, running her thumb over Reyna's hand. "It just doesn't make sense. Albert is certainly capable of creating this draining circle, but . . . he's been the Alchemicor for decades. Far longer than I've had my position. He's always been a Magicary favorite."

Reyna's jaw set. "I know. I like him, too. But it is odd that he knew to send us here. I know he got reports of stolen livestock, but this almost seemed too convenient."

"Well, Spruce wasn't hurt. Just trapped and scared." Kianthe finished her tea and extracted herself from bed, waking up enough now. She kissed Reyna's forehead and tugged on her trousers. "You weren't hurt either. Even the Stone of Seeing was only temporarily inconvenienced. If anything, these circles almost seem like—"

"Experimentation," Reyna finished, turning so she was seated on the mattress, feet brushing the wooden floor.

"Yeah." Kianthe tugged her shirt over her head, fluffing her hair as an afterthought. "It's like they're testing various beings of power. You, the queen. The Stone, the epitome of elemental magic in the Realm. And a dragon, with magic all its own."

Reyna was silent for a moment, drumming her fingers on her bare, rather sexy leg. It would be distracting, if the topic were any less serious. Instead, Kianthe turned away, ducking into the washroom to wipe her face with cold water.

Through the open doorway, Reyna sounded contemplative. "Have we considered the thought that these circles don't . . . work?"

"What?" Kianthe stilled, poking her head back into the bedroom. "They clearly work. The Stone of Seeing—"

"Would be affected by any alchemy, I'd imagine." Reyna waited, but when Kianthe didn't argue, she continued. "I felt nothing back in the watchtower. Spruce only experienced pain if it tried to *leave,* so that circle was possibly altered into something meant for containment *and* draining. But Spruce's magic is clearly fine, which implies to me that it's not . . . really working the way it's intended."

"We haven't exactly been copying the new circles down to see any changes," Kianthe admitted. "I've just been destroying them."

"And we know that these circles are attempting to create a new level of alchemy overall." Reyna shrugged. "A true alchemist would likely know how to fix it by this point. So, considering it keeps failing, what if—"

"These circles weren't made by an alchemist at all . . . ?" Kianthe finished, eyes widening.

Reyna shrugged. "It's a possibility."

"Our culprit would still be a mage—or multiple mages. Whoever drew that alchemical circle in the Magicary clearly had free access to the place, and some kind of magic to reach that storage room." Kianthe abandoned her morning routine, pacing the bedroom instead. "But you're right. An elemental mage could have gotten inside there."

"Alchemists are failed elemental mages, correct? Which means any mage can do alchemy, too."

"Any human alive can *technically* do alchemy. We just keep a close hold on the texts for ethical purposes, and without that education, learning it would be nearly impossible. For mages, it *is* possible to be proficient in both. It's just unheard of, because both avenues require a lifetime of study to perfect." Kianthe scrubbed her face, swallowing past a dry throat. "Ugh. But if that's true, that makes this *my* problem after all, not Albert's."

Reyna pushed off the bed, retrieving her own pants. "Well, I thought we could have a lazy day in Winterhaven, but perhaps we shouldn't dally." A pause. "What's the motivation for an elemental mage to try a draining spell on me, or Blue Spruce? Why bother?"

Kianthe's head spun. She'd already started moving around the room, packing their things for the flight home. "I'm not sure. But if we're running through elemental mages as suspects, it'd need to be someone with access to alchemy curriculums *and* years of study behind them already."

". . . Polana?" Reyna hesitated. "You think she's behind this?"

A growl of frustration slipped past Kianthe's lips. "We don't even know what *this* is, but—maybe. Polana leapt to 'exile all alchemists' pretty damn fast. I need to get back to the Magicary, but the dragon has to be handled first."

"I can escort Blue Spruce home," Reyna said firmly.

"No. If a mage attacks you in the air, you won't stand much chance." Kianthe suppressed a shudder, imagining an aerial battle against someone like Polana. She set her jaw. "And Spruce deserves safety before we handle internal affairs. Humans are the reason it grew up alone—so we need to be the ones to help it."

Reyna frowned. "If you're sure . . ."

Kianthe wasn't sure of anything, but this seemed like a logical first step. She could tackle the rest later. "This is conjecture at best. I'm thinking it wouldn't hurt to check with Feo again before leaping into accusations. Fact is, the Stone of Seeing is safe, and this was our last lead. Waiting for their next move might be the smartest play regardless."

"True. I'm sure the tourists will be thrilled to see us again." Reyna's tone was dry, laced with exhaustion.

Kianthe grimaced. "Ah, yeah. That."

Back home, then.

They wove through the Vardian Mountains, maintaining a swift pace—but slow enough that the dragon wouldn't tire. Blue Spruce cut through the clouds, clearly enamored with Ponder's agility and speed. On Visk's back, Reyna heaved a long-suffering sigh. "And here I thought having a griffon mount meant I'd actually get to ride her, sometimes."

"You can," Kianthe said, patting Visk's feathery neck. "But . . . maybe when she doesn't have a baby dragon to entertain."

"I'm beginning to doubt there will be a time when we *aren't* entertaining baby dragons, love."

Kianthe tightened her grip on Reyna's waist, swallowing a laugh. "Fair point."

It was nearing evening when they reached Tawney. The town beckoned, a gleaming beacon amidst vast plains of snow. Dragon country loomed beyond, and Spruce picked up its pace, clearly sensing the magic beyond. Visk kept up easily—on long distances, an adult dragon would outpace a griffon, but Spruce was too young for that. Ponder landed on Spruce's back, chittering in its ear, folding her wings tightly so the wind didn't shove her off. The dragon actually turned its head to listen to her, then rumbled under its breath.

"Nearly there," Kianthe said gratefully. Her reservoirs had replenished over the day, but Tawney had a notoriously terrible ley line. She still wasn't back to full capacity, despite the Stone's best efforts.

All she wanted was their own bed and a nice mug of tea.

"Ah . . ." Reyna peered over Visk's back, squinting against the setting sun. "Dearest, am I hallucinating, or is there a *line* to enter our town?"

"What?" Kianthe followed her gaze. It was tough to see with the forest casting long shadows over the snowy plains, but *yeah.* Tawney only had two roads—one from Shepara, on the western edge, and one into the Queendom from the southeastern side—and both were lined with tents, carts, and people.

Wylan and Feo had mentioned some kind of ticket system to enter the town. Kianthe just hadn't expected them to enact it so soon. What had the townsfolk done? Forcibly expel the tourists, hand out tickets, and ask them to wait their turn for reentry?

Quite possibly.

"I'm glad we weren't around for *that* chaos." Kianthe turned to Visk's other side, shielding her eyes against the setting sun. The sky was deep purple and darkening fast, but while the shadow of the mountains cast the town in darkness, a sliver of sunlight blinded them this high up. Still, Kianthe could see well enough to assess Tawney's situation.

Two checkpoints—one on each road. And even from here, the noise was indisputable—folks arguing for entry into their quiet town. Kianthe couldn't see who was manning the entry points, but she didn't envy that job. It looked like they'd erected a picket fence around the south side of town, just to ensure people followed the rules.

New Leaf Tomes and Tea was one of the places they'd blocked off. Kianthe wasn't sure whether to be annoyed or relieved about that.

"This is a disaster," Reyna muttered. "We need to help solve this."

"We're currently in the middle of our *last* 'we need to help' adventure. Let's focus on Spruce, okay? Tawney clearly has things . . . ah, handled." Kianthe's tone lifted in doubt. "Handled" sounded a bit confident for the bedlam below.

It got worse. The tourists had noticed a dragon cruising overhead, and several shouts of excitement and alarm echoed through the still night air. The noise caught Spruce's attention. The dragon growled low, a warning that even Kianthe heard way back on Visk.

Unlike its siblings, Blue Spruce wouldn't be exploring Tawney anytime soon. It was clearly still skittish around humans.

Ponder wasted no time nipping its horn, then leaping off its back. She flitted in front of it, dancing in the skies, and dragged its attention back to the jagged mountains north of town. With a purposeful screech, she summoned two tiny dragons over the vast plains. They roared welcome.

Pill Bug and Gold Coin.

"Faster, Ponder," Reyna called. "As much distance as you can from Tawney, all right?"

Four more dragons appeared behind the babies. Whatever Ponder had said—or whatever magic they felt off Blue Spruce—the dragon horde had realized something new was approaching. On instinct, Kianthe braced for the nausea, but of course nothing happened.

The creatures approaching them might as well be the spacing between Stars, from Kianthe's magical perspective. They didn't feel like anything at all.

She didn't expect to *miss* dragon magic, but she was facing all kinds of surprises lately.

Reyna, meanwhile, had gone very still. When Kianthe craned around to check on her, her eyes were closed, her face tilted toward the entourage. Must be attuning to the dragons, or something like that.

"I see you watching me," Reyna said, lips upturned in amusement, although she didn't open her eyes.

Kianthe stiffened. "It's *interesting,* okay?"

"Interesting is one word." Reyna was silent a moment more, then smiled. "I've warned them about Blue Spruce. They're thrilled to know the fate of the third egg." And she gestured toward the rugged mountains of dragon country, where at least thirty other dragons had left their caves and perches to meet the child.

Spruce had noticed it, too. It slowed, and no amount of beckoning from Ponder could convince it to progress. With a resolute movement, it landed hard in the snow, folding its wings. Getting small, like an animal facing a threat. They were near the dragons' mountains, but Tawney was closer, a ready escape route.

Blue Spruce must prefer the threat of humans over dozens of fully-grown dragons. That made Kianthe's heart ache.

"Land for us, Visk?" Reyna asked.

Visk obeyed immediately, flitting to the ground. Ponder landed beside him, and as Kianthe helped Reyna off her mount, Visk nibbled Ponder's feathers fondly. Most of the time, he treated her with exasperation, but sometimes true fatherly pride appeared. She'd done a wonderful job getting Blue Spruce this far, after all.

Kianthe shivered in the cold, tightening her cloak as she followed Reyna to Blue Spruce. They had a few moments until the horde would be upon them, and Reyna wasted no time whispering quiet platitudes to the creature.

"They just want to meet you. They're so excited. I know this is scary, but trust me, Spruce. This is where you belong. They'll protect you, and you'll have two younger siblings to play with, and Ponder won't be far." Reyna smiled warmly at the dragon, and to Kianthe's shock, Blue Spruce actually lowered its head, allowing her to stroke its scales. Delight flashed over her features as she felt them. "How interesting. They're harder than Pill Bug and Gold Coin's."

"Dragon scales harden over their lives. They're most vulnerable as babies, but once they reach adulthood, not much can kill them." Kianthe tentatively offered her own hand, and the dragon recoiled. Kianthe frowned, feeling rejected. "Does it think I'm going to hurt it?"

"It thinks the *world* might hurt it, love." Reyna's tone was soothing, but it was unclear if that was for Kianthe's sake or the dragon's. Her eyes locked with Blue Spruce's again, her gaze firm. "Now is the time to be brave, young one. A moment of bravery can offer a lifetime of happiness." And she looped her arm around Kianthe's, resting her head on her wife's shoulder.

Kianthe pulled her closer. "You talking about us?"

"Maybe." Reyna's lips tilted upward.

Dragon roars echoed across the plains, and then one silenced the horde with a burst of fire. The lead dragon—the one who'd locked Kianthe into her bindment spell two years ago, the one they'd created a tentative peace with—landed before them, folding massive wings as it assessed the newcomer.

Blue Spruce trembled, but with Reyna and Ponder at its side, it didn't flee.

Kianthe drew a breath and prayed to the Stone and the Stars that this would go well.

17

Reyna

Welcome back, little queen, the lead dragon intoned.

Reyna didn't know if the dragons had names, at least outside the ones she and Kianthe had sneakily given the babies. So far, none had offered any identifiers, and dragon hierarchy seemed tenuous at best. This dragon appeared to be their designated speaker-to-humans, given its history with Kianthe, although several had allowed communication with Reyna now that she'd assumed the throne.

Reyna swept into a bow, and her skin prickled. Her crisis of faith hadn't been resolved in half a year, but there was absolutely no denying that the dragons were something to be worshiped—or at least respected. "We're sorry to bother you so late. Ah, if—if dragons care about that kind of thing." It was such a human thing to say. With a dragon's immense lifespan, she bet they didn't even notice the time.

Or maybe "time" was an inherently human concept anyway.

At her side, Kianthe snorted. "Never thought I'd see you tongue-tied."

Reyna shot her wife a glare, but it did lighten the tension. Now that she knew people were calling her the Dragon Queen, she couldn't deny the pressure to play this right—to maintain relations with her namesake.

The dragon snorted, smoke trailing from its nostrils. Behind it, dozens of dragons had landed in the snow or were circling overhead. Visk looked on-guard—understandable, given their history with the dragons—but Ponder knew no fear.

Pill Bug and Gold Coin had lunged at her, and the three creatures rolled in the snow. Ponder extracted herself with ease, nipping Gold Coin's nose, brushing Pill Bug with her wings as she leapt into the air. Gold Coin followed, but Pill Bug had noticed the new dragon. It stilled, hiding behind the bulk of one of the adult dragons.

Blue Spruce was trying to watch all of the dragons, and failing miserably. Any earlier ferocity had vanished, and it pulled itself into a tighter ball now. Its tail tucked under its stomach as it lowered itself to the ground.

Reyna placed a comforting hand on its shoulder, which was about as high as she could reach. "As I said, we located the final egg."

We can see. The dragon speaking with her paced closer, wings half-unfurled, tail raised. Blue Spruce was twice the size of the other baby dragons, but less than half as large as a full-grown adult. Reyna took a respectful step back, allowing the dragons space. But as the adult neared and Reyna retreated, Blue Spruce's composure cracked. Facing a giant, it slid into defense, arching like a cat with fire crackling in the back of its throat.

The adult dragon chuckled—or a sound oddly close to it. Although it might have just been in Reyna's mind. It was tough to tell, these days.

Leading with fire. You've had a rough life, young one. With an intentionally slow movement, the adult dragon settled a wing over the child. It draped like a cloak, sheltering Blue Spruce from the world.

Whatever Spruce was expecting, it wasn't that. It froze, fire dying instantly—and when it realized it wouldn't be harmed, its whole body relaxed.

Welcome home, the adult said, nuzzling Spruce with its chin. Their horns knocked briefly, reminiscent of two humans tapping their tankards in cheers. Then the adult stepped back and roared.

All around them, the dragons followed, a deafening cacophony of welcome. Gold Coin and Ponder stopped wrestling, and as an afterthought, Gold Coin joined in. Its roar was higher-pitched, but none less fierce. Pill Bug, getting braver now, stepped out from behind the adult to sniff Blue Spruce.

Ponder inserted herself, making chittering introductions. Spruce's body language had completely changed—gone was the tight fear, replaced with open excitement. It joined the roar, which just incited the other dragons to roar again.

Ponder screeched, and Kianthe covered her ears. "We're going to lose our hearing if this keeps up," she shouted, but she was grinning wide.

Reyna could relate. After all the time they'd spent searching for the missing dragon eggs, this felt like a much-needed victory.

Finally, the dragons fell silent and peeled off, angling back toward the mountains. Blue Spruce hesitated until two other adults nudged it into the air. It grumbled goodbye to the griffons, met Reyna's gaze briefly. *Home,* it said, and the word was so full of warmth that tears pricked Reyna's eyes.

"Visit anytime," she told it, then blew a kiss to Pill Bug and Gold Coin. The babies had realized that it wasn't, in fact, "play with Ponder" time. Clearly disgruntled about it, Gold Coin heaved itself into the air. Pill Bug followed at a more reasonable pace.

The dragons slowly cleared out, until the adult who'd spoken was the only one left. It assessed Kianthe, then Reyna. They'd mounted their respective griffons, but Kianthe paused in urging Visk into the air. A dragon lurking over them was always a reason to pause.

"Uh . . ." Kianthe grimaced. "Is it waiting for something else? I figured Blue Spruce would be enough, but I guess I could grab a souvenir from Tawney. Since we're such a destination, and all."

Reyna snorted, stilling Ponder from taking flight.

The dragon clearly understood human speech, even if it couldn't directly communicate with Kianthe anymore. It tilted its head, glancing at Reyna to translate. *You and the child are tainted with the same magic that the hatchlings were. The mage used to be a different flavor, but now . . .* The dragon leaned lower, sniffing Kianthe. It flinched, sneezed. *Now she is tainted too.*

"Did it just say I smell?" Kianthe inserted indignantly.

"Darling." Reyna silenced Kianthe, fear sliding down her spine. She parsed through her thoughts, then told the dragon, "We're searching for a rogue alchemist." *Probably.* She swallowed that correction. "They used a draining spell on myself, the young dragon, and the Stone of Seeing."

Kianthe realized the topic of this conversation and fell silent, watching the dragon with sharp eyes.

Ah. The power conduit. The dragon contemplated that, eyes tilted to the stars. *This tainted magic should not exist. In the old days, humans were either her flavor . . . or they were not mages at all.*

"It's saying that alchemy was . . . created. By humans. That it's unnatural."

"That's probably true," Kianthe begrudgingly agreed.

Reyna hesitated, then ventured, "Are we in danger from this tainted magic? Is Blue Spruce?"

The dragon snorted at the name, as if amused she'd bothered. *The child will recover. Its magic was probed, nothing more. You are a direct link to us, little queen. Without us, your power is simply human.*

A rush of—what? shock? fear? gratitude?—raced through Reyna's body. She suppressed the urge to bow, to truly worship. As far as she was aware, those gestures meant little to the gods before her. "And the Stone of Seeing?"

The elemental conduit is just that. It could not host another type of magic if it tried.

Reyna read between the lines. "But dragon magic could."

Now the dragon's wings unfurled a bit, and it considered her tone. *Yes,* it said finally, its voice like a murmur in her mind. *The child is young, still developing. But our magic is ancient and strong.* A pause, its posture tensing. *We will watch for your tainted mages.*

"We'll be nearby," Reyna promised. "Please. Let us know if you find them."

The dragon dipped its head, spread its wings, and angled back toward the mountain range. As night fell properly over dragon country, it vanished into a cave in the mountainside, and stillness fell in its wake.

Reyna clicked her tongue. "Come on, Pondie. Back home."

Her griffon leapt into the air, moving slowly—wearily—now that the excitement was done. Visk followed at a steadier pace, aligning with his daughter so Kianthe and Reyna could speak over the wind.

"They're watching for the alchemists?" Kianthe asked, her tone dark.

"Or whoever's behind this." Reyna tugged her fingers from under her cloak, blowing into her hands to warm them. Even with gloves, it was frigid now that night had fallen. "Those circles did something, so I don't think it was a failed experiment after all. I think . . . it was a test. But the dragon confirmed that their magic could be a secondary source. It could power whatever alchemy this mage is trying to create."

Kianthe was silent for a long moment. The griffons soared over the rim, Wylan's manor, the town square, before descending beside New Leaf Tomes and Tea. Kianthe cleared her throat as they touched down on an eerily empty street. "Well. Maybe visiting the Magicary will have to wait."

"Perhaps." Reyna frowned, sliding off Ponder's back. She kissed her griffon and said, "Excellent job, love. But next time, warn me before you attack a dragon, all right?"

Ponder fluffed her feathers, as if to say that she couldn't make promises.

Kianthe offered a similar goodbye to Visk, and once the griffons were flying toward the southwestern forest, Reyna turned her attention to the empty street. Even before visitors flooded Tawney, this road would have *some* folks on it.

New Leaf was dark, empty.

Locked.

Kianthe opened it with a heavy key, stepping inside. "Uh . . . Something tells me they didn't open today."

Everything was still, and it felt unnatural. Kianthe lit a fire in the hearth, which helped brighten the space, since the ever-flames seemed dimmer than usual. "Ah, I don't think that's the case." The bookshop's shelves were rifled, napkins and plates stacked on the counter waiting to be cleaned. Chairs weren't pushed in, and no one had swept or wiped down the tables.

Reyna breathed a sigh, surveying the chaos. "Something tells me Gossley and his girlfriend did not, in fact, have things under control."

"Something tells me *Tawney* doesn't have things under control." Kianthe's voice was tight. She scrubbed her face, glanced back into the empty street. "Should we stop by Hansen's tavern first, or find Wylan and Feo?"

"Tavern." Reyna swept out of their shop as quickly as she'd entered. Whatever happened in the days they were gone, it wasn't good.

They knocked on Sasua's door first, but for once, their next-door neighbor didn't answer the door. Odd, considering it was nearing her son's bedtime; she should be home. With little else to do, they followed the path toward the main road of town—which took them right beside the checkpoint from the Sheparan road.

"—been waiting for days. We traveled all the way from the Roiling Islands," one of the tourists was saying loudly. "Do you know how hard it is to sail around the Southern Seas? You know the Dastardly Pirate Dreggs attacks any ship they find!"

"Well, that's not true." Marlow was apparently guarding the gate, alongside two of the sheriff's newer recruits. The florist's tone was dry, almost amused.

"You're calling me a liar?" the tourist snapped.

Marlow, who was one of the most easygoing people in Tawney, held up their hands. "Of course not. We just—we know
Dreggs—"

"You *know* the infamous pirate captain of the Southern
Seas." If a tone could be drier than a well in the desert, this man
managed it.

Kianthe about-faced from their destination, and Reyna
couldn't even blame her. They detoured to the gate, which was
barely more than a haphazard wooden fence with hastily in-
stalled hinges. The sheriff's recruits had swords out, but looked
highly uncertain—they were young, after all. Up until a season
ago, the sheriff only employed a few others.

"We deserve—"

"What do you deserve?" Kianthe inserted seamlessly, casually stepping between the angry man and Marlow. She crossed
her arms, eyes flashing. "Hi, hello. I'm the Arcandor, the Mage
of Ages, and that's my friend you're yelling at. Think carefully,
sir. What, *exactly,* do you deserve? Unlimited access to our
homes? The ability to voice displeasure at how we're managing
an influx of folks we didn't *ask* for?"

Oh, Gods. Kianthe was sleep deprived, half-hungover—
magically speaking—and facing a far bigger threat than the
traveling public. All that meant her temper hit its limit. Reyna
suddenly felt bad for the tourist.

The man physically stepped back. Behind him, several others
camping nearby perked in interest. They all looked like they'd
been strategically ignoring his rampage, while clearly eaves-
dropping.

"Arcandor," the man swallowed, his earlier candor gone.
"Look—"

"No, *you* look." Kianthe set her jaw, leaning over the fence. It
creaked dangerously with her weight—this fence wouldn't stop
anyone who was truly attempting to enter Tawney. Reyna supposed they should be grateful none had rushed it. "Marlow is a
delightful soul. Everyone in this town is *drowning* because of
you people. Doesn't that make you feel a little bit guilty?"

Silence fell, and the folks behind him turned away. One or two murmured to each other, then began gathering their belongings.

They were leaving.

It didn't feel like the victory it should.

The man inhaled shakily. "My wife is having a baby, and there are complications. We need to be somewhere with well-trained doctors, but—we can't afford the bigger cities." Now he gestured at Tawney, at the meticulous buildings and well-maintained streets. His voice was quiet. "I thought any town that hosts the Arcandor and the queen must have a decent clinic."

Kianthe visibly deflated, glancing at Reyna.

And for once, Reyna didn't know what to say. Behind them, Marlow shifted their weight and said, "We, ah . . . we do have a palace-trained midwife here."

The man slumped, massaging his temples. "I'm sorry for my tone, but I don't know where else to look. If Tawney isn't open for us, where would you recommend, Arcandor?" His voice was pleading now.

Kianthe glanced at Reyna. "I—um . . ."

"We can hardly close off an entire town to folk who want to move here." Reyna patted Kianthe's arm, taking control of this situation. "But we can't make promises about how that process will look—not yet. We need some time."

The man winced, brows knitted together. "Queen Reyna, my wife doesn't *have* time."

"Then get her to the Grand Palace," Reyna replied firmly. With little else to offer, she tugged one of the daggers off her forearm. It had Tilaine's insignia—a relic from her time as a Queensguard. She handed it to him. "Show the Queensguard this. Tell them I sent you, and your wife will be treated with the best midwives the Queendom has to offer. By the time the baby is born, we should have Tawney's expansion plan in place."

"Th-Thank you. *Thank* you, Your Excellency." He clutched the dagger, bowed deeply, then faced Marlow with regret etched on his features. "I'm—I'm so sorry. Thank you all. And . . . good luck. It really does seem like a nice town."

"It is," Kianthe said softly.

Once he departed, another couple surged to the gate—but Marlow hastened Reyna and Kianthe away from the fence. "I'll handle things from here. We all heard the dragons roaring; I'm sure you two have bigger concerns." The florist offered a crooked grin. "Not all of these people are that insistent."

Reyna watched the man hike back to a tiny camping setup and begin packing saddlebags. His pregnant wife was sitting on a bundle of blankets, and she hauled herself up with a grimace, casting a questioning glance toward Marlow. Her expression shifted to shock when her husband presumably relayed the news.

Reyna's mind whirled. "How many visitors have expressed interest in actually moving here?"

"Not many, but some." Marlow shrugged. "Most seem to be here for a glimpse of our local celebrities—you two. Once we implemented the ticketing system, they started coming up with excuses. I figured his was the same story, but . . . well, clearly that wasn't true." Marlow shifted, expression apologetic now.

Kianthe sighed. "Tell me about it. Now I feel like an asshole."

"You're protecting your friends. He could have approached Marlow in a kinder manner." Reyna squeezed Kianthe's arm, although her mind was elsewhere. "Where's the rest of the town? Sasua wasn't home."

"Town meeting at the inn." Marlow rubbed their arm, nodding down the main road. "I don't envy Diarn Feo or Lord Wylan right now. There's a lot of discontent around how to handle this."

Kianthe clapped their shoulder. "Sounds like a fun way to spend the evening. Keep your chin up, Marlow. Let us know if you need help."

"Sure thing." Marlow smiled and waved, strolling back to the makeshift gate.

To the inn, then.

18

Kianthe

Almost two years ago, when Kianthe and Reyna first entered Tawney's inn and tavern, no one glanced their way. They'd found a quiet table beside the hearth, and planned how to renovate the barn that would become New Leaf Tomes and Tea. It was a lovely memory that Kianthe truly cherished.

But times had changed. Today, it felt like the whole town was waiting for them. The moment they pushed open the door, Matild said sharply, "We're closed. Town hall—" Then she realized it was Kianthe and Reyna, and she inhaled sharply. "Oh, thank the Gods. We need your opinions."

"Welcome home," Tarly inserted, offering a pointed look at his wife.

Matild elbowed him, but laughed awkwardly. "Yeah. That too."

At least a quarter of the townsfolk had crammed into the tavern, making the space feel exceptionally small. Reyna noticed a few kids playing together in the front lounge, through an arched doorway that connected the inn to Hansen's tavern. The bartender and his wife, the innkeeper, were draped behind the bar with matching mugs of beer and dark rims under their eyes. Sasua kept glancing at her son, but she seemed tightly furious.

Janice, one of the town bakers, sat beside her, and Sigmund and Nurt capped off their table. Every other chair was occupied.

Feo stood by the hearth, leaning against the heavy stone with their arms crossed. Wylan, oddly, was nowhere to be seen.

Kianthe eased the door closed behind her. "Ah, hello. Sorry we're late."

"Are the dragons attacking again?" the carpenter's wife asked. "We heard them roaring."

It sounded almost . . . hopeful.

Reyna heard it too, raising an eyebrow at Kianthe. There wasn't much room to stand, but Hansen and his wife scooted over and allowed them some space behind the bar. Kianthe leaned against the edge of the counter while Reyna answered: "Not attacking. We found the final missing dragon egg—it hatched on the western edge of the Realm, and traveled through the Vardian Mountains. That roar was one of welcome, not an act of war."

Several people groaned.

"I'm sorry," Kianthe inserted, caught between exasperation and amusement. "Are you *upset* that the dragons aren't torching half the town anymore?"

Feo snorted. "This crowd? Absolutely."

That incited a new round of outrage. Between the two leaders of Tawney, Lord Wylan was more palatable. Townsfolk started defending themselves, shouting over each other, instigating arguments.

"We wouldn't have to hope for that if—"

"—easier when it was just dragon fire—"

"—destroyed my shop, then *left* town. Miscreants!"

And dozens of other conversations Kianthe couldn't even catch. She stared at the bedlam, jaw unhinged. Tawney had never faced this: all their neighbors turning on each other, shouting at their diarn.

It . . . wasn't a great look.

Helplessly, she glanced at Reyna. "Should we say something?"

But Reyna had gone silent, listening to their protests. They'd missed the other town hall meetings, which meant they'd been guessing on public sentiment before. Reyna didn't like guesswork. Her eyes flicked around the room, her jaw tight.

Feo didn't seem bothered by the vitriol directed their way. Instead, their striking blue eyes were locked on Reyna and Kianthe, pinning them from across the tavern. The implication was clear: they'd talked enough, and now it was time for the *other* town leaders to intervene.

Feeling pressured, Kianthe raised her hands. "Okay, okay. Listen up."

Too late. The din was growing in volume, everyone anxious for a piece of the discussion. Anxious to be heard. Anxious to protect their homes, their livelihoods, their safe space. Kianthe clenched her eyes shut, then raised her voice. "Quiet!" A gust of wind swept through the tavern, causing the hearth to flicker, a few sheets of parchment to sweep off the tables.

Everyone turned to her.

"We're scared. Tawney isn't what we remember. I think we all assumed it'd stop with the first good snowstorm, but there are still folks lining up outside." Kianthe straightened, glancing at her wife. Reyna didn't seem inclined to speak; instead, she accepted a pint of beer from Hansen and sipped it, contemplative.

So, Kianthe kept talking. "We, ah . . . we spent the night in Winterhaven, a mountain town west of here. They restructured their entire home to accommodate tourists—they have welcoming committees and themed events and—and a brand. The town is booming as a result." She grimaced. Even saying this aloud made her feel gross, but with no other ideas, she pitched it anyway. "Maybe that's our answer? Embracing this?"

"We don't want to *embrace* anything." Sasua set her jaw, fists clenched on the table. "I've lived in the house beside your barn most of my life, and I can say with confidence that these tourists are *worse* than the bandits. They're camped outside New Leaf all day and half the night. My son's window is right next to the street, and he can barely sleep."

When they first met Sasua, she'd been hard, closed-off. A single mother living beside a crime den. Suspicion and caution had been her shield, at least until Kianthe and Reyna proved they were clearing out the bandits and creating a safe space instead. Over time, she'd loosened, grown warmer and friendly.

Now, that suspicion was back. Her expression was hard, and there wasn't any glimpse of their friend. It was understandable, given that she'd been facing the crowds around their barn first-hand while Kianthe and Reyna flitted about the Realm.

Her tone still hurt.

Hansen's wife inserted her thoughts. "Our inn is booked every night. It's good for business, but we've had to turn folks away because there aren't enough rooms."

"Some of 'em don't leave quietly," Hansen grunted. "I've tossed out more people in the last season than I have my entire career."

"It's like we're a museum of curiosities," Nurt said. He rubbed the back of his neck, glancing at Sigmund for support. "We're getting good gossip, but . . . most of them just want to meet you two. The queen and the Arcandor. And when you two aren't at New Leaf to satisfy . . ."

Sigmund scowled. "It ain't pretty."

Nurt snapped his fingers in agreement.

Guilt coiled in Kianthe's chest. She wanted to sink into a hole and cry. A lump formed in her throat, and she attempted to clear it. "Well . . . if they're here for us, hovering around New Leaf . . . maybe . . ." She trailed off, glancing at Reyna again.

Please, Kianthe almost said. *Tell me you have a new idea. Tell me you aren't drawing the same conclusion I am.*

But the look on Reyna's face was so, so sad.

She squeezed Kianthe's arm and set down the pint, leaning over the bar. "We moved here two years ago because we wanted a fresh life, somewhere remote, away from responsibilities. Instead, we brought our lives to you all—and that isn't fair." Her voice didn't waver, although her eyes shone in the firelight. Probably, no one else noticed, but Kianthe always knew when Reyna was close to tears.

It made it worse that a few people murmured agreement, albeit quietly enough that Kianthe couldn't pinpoint who'd said it.

Reyna heard it too. She drew a slow breath. "The answer is obvious. If they're arriving for a tourist attraction, we *remove* the attraction."

Now Matild recoiled. "What are you saying?"

"Exactly what you're hearing." Reyna's gaze met Kianthe's, and a flash of anguished understanding passed between them. There was no *fix* to this. They couldn't stop people from traveling to a public destination. It was far too late to counter the newspapers, the journals, the word of mouth.

Kianthe intertwined her fingers with her wife's.

But she didn't object when Reyna said it aloud:

"We'll close New Leaf Tomes and Tea."

Shockingly, that incited another round of outrage. Everyone speaking at once, some arguing that it was ridiculous, premature, there had to be another way. But there were others who had fallen silent, grudging respect on their faces. Sasua's eyes dropped to the table, and she didn't speak.

Almost as if she'd been thinking about that solution for a while.

Kianthe drew a shaking breath. "She's right. None of you asked for this. We found something wonderful here, but... things ch-change." That lump in her throat had become suffocating, and she barely finished her sentence. Damn it, she was really going to cry, wasn't she?

The silence in the tavern was somehow louder and scarier than any dragon's roar.

"W-We didn't mean *you* had to change," Matild whispered, anguish in her voice.

"It's the fastest, safest solution, and we all know it. We can't keep those folks outside forever. In half a season, with Tawney's weather, that might be a deadly sentence." Reyna's voice was far calmer than Kianthe's. The mask of her previous career was serving her well, and she had the emotionless demeanor of a Queensguard. "New Leaf has been a beautiful sanctuary, but I'm the queen now. Even with our new parliament, I need to be in the Capital."

She squeezed Kianthe's hand again, a silent plea to be equally strong.

"I've spent too long away from the Magicary," Kianthe admitted. "The Mage of Ages typically keeps residence near the Stone of Seeing, to ensure its magic is healthy. Even recently, I missed something I . . . really should have seen."

Across the room, Feo scoffed, lifting their chin. "This argument feels extreme. I'm a councilmember, but you don't see me moving to Wellia."

"The council is made of diarns—local rulers who converge to discuss business matters in a central location." Reyna offered a sad smile. "It's quite different than our positions."

Feo opened their mouth, closed it, and scowled.

Wow. Kianthe hadn't ever thought she'd see the day *Feo* was rendered speechless.

Reyna seemed to realize Kianthe couldn't talk anymore, not unless she wanted to be a sniveling mess. Her beautiful wife took control once again. "Give us a few days to discuss the logistics. But please start spreading the word that New Leaf is shuttered. Hopefully, that will encourage most of our visitors to go home."

With that done, Reyna started for the door. Kianthe trailed behind her, head down—but neither made it very far before Matild stopped them both. Behind her, Tarly crossed his arms, pointedly reminding them both that he was a burly blacksmith with no intentions of letting them pass.

"Uh-uh. You don't get to leave on that note," Matild said, her voice tight with fury.

Reyna raised one eyebrow. Kianthe laughed, a watery sound.

It only spurred Matild on. "When we fled Queen Tilaine, we settled here knowing her spies might kill us in our sleep. We brought danger to this town." She raised her voice, meeting several townsfolk's gaze. Many looked away, and she scoffed. "But you know what? *We* also mattered. My life, and Tarly's. Our dreams, our hopes for the future . . . they *also mattered*."

"Does anyone here actually want New Leaf to close? Do you really want our friends to leave?" Tarly narrowed his eyes. His jovial nature was gone, and what replaced it was a disapproving scowl.

When it became apparent that no one was willing to respond, Feo pinched their brow, heaving a sigh. "Okay, this might be getting out of hand. Lord Wylan is in the Capital discussing our concerns with Tessalyn and the Queendom's new parliament. He'll return any day now. How about we table discussion of New Leaf closing until then? We can manage a few more days of these visitors, can't we?"

Murmurs of agreement, a few of irritation. Sasua finally said, begrudgingly, "We've managed this long."

Matild put a hand on her hip, waggling a finger at Kianthe and Reyna. "And you won't shutter New Leaf until we've *thoroughly* discussed this, correct? Gossley won't know what to do with himself if that place closes."

"I thought he was apprenticing in the smithy with you, Tarly?" Kianthe forced a smirk. It felt good to talk about something other than shuttering their lifelong dream.

Tarly cleared his throat, and for a breath it felt like old times. "Well, I hardly have the energy for a full-time apprentice."

His lie made Kianthe laugh.

Reyna held up her hands, edging around Matild and Tarly. "You all make good points, and . . . we appreciate it." Her cheeks were pink, and she ducked her head. "However, we *will* need a day to clean the shop—it's in quite a state right now. I'm not certain I want to know how it reached that point."

"The tourists didn't appreciate their eviction," Matild grumbled. She reluctantly stepped aside, allowing access to the tavern's door. "I'll come by tomorrow to help clean. No rash decisions, you two."

Neither of them made promises.

"Meeting adjourned," Feo said, and everyone started filing out.

Locking the door to New Leaf felt like locking their own tomb.

The darkness of the barn appeared even more encompassing now, and Kianthe sank into one of the chairs. She wiped off the leftover crumbs and buried her head in her hands. "I can't believe this."

Reyna's footsteps were nearly inaudible. A *swoosh* as the drapes over the windows closed. A breath of silence. The strike of flint to light the fire beneath her beloved copper kettle. Wooden drawers sliding open, a rustling sound as Reyna sifted through linen bags for her chosen tea.

All without speaking.

That lump was back in her throat again. Kianthe turned her head sideways, watching her wife moving around their home with quiet familiarity. Her face was smooth, neutral, but a storm raged in her stiff movements. She kept her eyes downcast, methodically losing herself in the motion of steeping two mugs of tea.

"Rain?"

Reyna drew a slow breath. "Not yet, Key." Her voice broke on the nickname, and she cleared her throat, her hand briefly tightening on one of the mugs. "Give me a moment to enjoy this."

"Okay," Kianthe murmured. She pushed away from the table, stoking the ever-flame under the hearth with a hand. It flared to life, filling the room with crackling warmth. Another brush of magic, and the ivy snaking through the rafters fluffed, the flowers around the bookcases blooming.

If Reyna wanted a typical New Leaf evening, Kianthe would give it to her. Absently, she began organizing the bookshelves, lining the books just so, correcting any tomes left open or pages bent.

After long moments of silence, a soft sob caught her attention. Kianthe glanced back at her wife. Reyna had lifted the kettle off the tiny flame—then set it on the counter. Tears rimmed her eyes as she stared at the two mugs awaiting water, at the jar of honey she'd tugged out to sweeten their tea. Her shoulders trembled.

"Oh, Reyna," Kianthe breathed, swiftly crossing the space.

"I just—" Reyna pressed her hands to her face. Tears slid down her cheeks. "I *really* thought we could leave the world behind." A choked laugh. "I really thought I'd just be a tea maker, and you'd just be a bookseller, and we'd be happy here forever."

Her voice fractured on the last word. *Forever.*

It broke Kianthe's heart. She pulled Reyna into a fierce, desperate hug. They were about the same height, but Reyna didn't hesitate to bury her nose in the crook of Kianthe's neck, gripping her like a tree in a storm. Her wife's entire body shuddered with silent sobs.

Kianthe tamped down the anguish in her own soul, blinked the tears from her eyes, and rested her chin on Reyna's hair. "*We* will be happy forever, and we'll always be together. This place is just—" The word broke, and she struggled to keep going. "—just a stop on the road."

It didn't feel like a stop on the road. It felt like a physical representation of their relationship. Before this, neither of them really had a home, and they certainly didn't have a future together. Once they agreed to build a bookshop and teahouse, their lives began—and a life with Reyna was something Kianthe could never take for granted.

New Leaf Tomes and Tea wasn't just a building. It wasn't just a shop. It was warmth and family and life and *love.*

Reducing it to anything less was a lie.

"We don't travel by road." Reyna laughed, a despairing sound.

It was a lie Kianthe had to live. When Reyna was down, she picked up the slack—and vice versa. So, Kianthe forced a smile and said, "Semantics." A pause. "Wylan may come up with another solution. And Tessalyn's pretty smart."

"This is the best option, and we both know it. Remove us, and this town is just another remote destination."

Kianthe didn't reply, because Reyna was right. If they left, Tawney would just be a place the Arcandor and queen *used* to live. And that wouldn't be worth the long journey and frigid temperatures . . . not when places like Winterhaven beckoned.

Besides, they had responsibilities elsewhere. It was unfeasible to think the Mage of Ages and her royal wife could pause their duties, abandon their centers of operation, long enough to live fantastically mundane lives on the edge of the world.

The certainty of what they'd proposed settled into Kianthe's bones.

It felt like poison.

She couldn't keep up the lie, it turned out, because tears slid down her own cheeks. A part of her desperately grasped at her fading strength, but it was a futile effort. Unconsciously, she tightened her grip on Reyna. They weren't going to lose much. At the very least, they were married now. Her wife would always be at her side.

Well . . . maybe not always. Most of the time.

Some of the time.

Or *maybe,* Queen Reyna would move back to the Grand Palace, and parliament would fail, and Tessalyn would vanish, and they'd be back to where they were years ago: visiting each other in the dead of night, dating only when schedules allowed, sending lovelorn letters that rarely reached their destinations, tapping code through a spelled set of necklaces. Maybe Kianthe would return to the Magicary and realize she could never leave, and shouldn't have in the first place, and even their marriage would fracture over time.

It was a vicious thought, and it took all of Kianthe's strength to acknowledge it, rather than succumb to it.

"I think I'm spiraling," she whispered, forcing humor into the words even though she felt like dying inside. Around her, the plants sensed her agony and began to wilt.

A year ago, Reyna would have tripped over herself to carry this emotional burden, to reassure Kianthe that they were fine, tabling her own emotions to help Kianthe stabilize.

But now, after everything, Reyna just replied, "Me too."

New Leaf had done that. Those two simple sentences seemed so quiet—but compared to where they'd started, they felt very, very loud to Kianthe. Acknowledging her own anxiety, identifying when the world was falling apart. And Reyna, recognizing that she deserved to fall apart sometimes, too.

They'd found something special in this bookstore. They'd grown into their best selves here. The realization that it was over, that they'd have to leave the shop they'd built from scratch, settled into their souls.

They clutched each other and sank to the dusty wooden floor and cried.

And there was something beautiful in mourning, together.

Eventually, Kianthe couldn't stand it anymore. Her eyes were burning and her nose was dripping and her throat was raw. She pulled away from Reyna, scrubbed her face with her sleeve, and whispered, "Tea? And maybe something chocolate?"

"Yes," Reyna replied, sounding dazed. She took Kianthe's hand, and Kianthe pulled her to her feet. Reyna wiped her own face, blew her nose on a handkerchief from her pocket, and numbly returned to the mugs. "There are some cookies in a tin in the storage room. Left shelf, near the window."

Kianthe seized the opportunity. She ducked into the storage room, closed the door behind her, and stared at the ceiling. More tears streamed down her cheeks, and she muffled her sobs with a hand.

How could she let this place go?

But that wasn't responsible, and their neighbors—their *friends*—deserved better.

Kianthe collected the tin with shaking hands, stepping back into the barn proper. Reyna held two mugs, and her eyes were rimmed with red. She'd composed herself, but only barely. Wordlessly, they convened to the hearth—not on the plush chairs they normally settled into, but rather on the thick rug right beside the fire.

Somehow, sitting on the floor beside her wife again, grieving the house they'd built together, made Kianthe feel better. She pressed her arm against Reyna's, sipped her tea, and mumbled glumly, "Maybe we can open a new shop in the Capital."

Reyna forced a laugh, leaning against Kianthe. "What would that be called? New Leaflette?"

Kianthe laughed, savoring the black tea. Reyna had tossed in a couple cacao nibs, which sweetened it extensively. It was almost like a tiny kiss with every sip. "Stone and Stars. That's a terrible name."

"I gave it my best shot," Reyna agreed, dabbing her eyes. She picked up her mug again, resting her chin on Kianthe's shoulder, watching the flickering fire with a distant stare. "What are we going to do with the back patio? Our engagement tree?"

"We'll replant it. Anywhere you want." Kianthe pressed a kiss to Reyna's temple. "I bet I can live in the Grand Palace, same as I lived here. The Magicary might throw a fit, but with Harold as high-mage . . . well, he's pretty pliable."

Reyna nodded, absently reaching for the tin of cookies. "I r-rather liked the Magicary." She tripped over the word, and it almost started her crying again. "But I like New Leaf more."

"I know," Kianthe said. "I know, Rain. But it's okay. We'll be fine."

They munched cookies, drank tea, and as night progressed, their acute misery lessened into stable sadness. As they trudged to bed, Kianthe couldn't help but think that if this was one of their last nights in New Leaf . . . well, it wasn't a bad way to conclude their time in Tawney.

19

Reyna

The next morning dawned bright, and Reyna's determination dawned with it. She'd endured her moment of sadness, let the homesickness settle—and now it was time to accept all she still had. Her wife, even if their marriage might look different moving forward. Their griffons, the most loyal mounts in the Realm. Her country, and a title she was shaping into a true legacy.

She was lucky, then. Their friends would always be in Tawney, and they could visit anytime—with Ponder and Visk, it was even easier. And in the meantime, she'd excel in her role as queen.

She'd always been a public servant, after all. It just looked different now.

Kianthe stumbled out of their bedroom as Reyna steeped two cups of yerba maté. She paused to kiss Kianthe's cheek. "Good morning, love."

"Somehow, I feel worse today than I did with a magic drain," Kianthe mumbled. "How are you so happy?"

"I grieved, and now it's time to accept our fate. This really is the logical option. It'll cut the tourist traffic instantly, while allowing room for new folk to move here if they really want." Reyna turned her sights on the bookshop, purposefully ignoring the ache in her chest. "I'm already contemplating logistics. The Grand Palace doesn't need more books, and the Magicary hardly does either. But perhaps we can donate these books to Lord Wylan, convince him to open his study to the public."

"A lord's private collection turning into a library?" Kianthe quirked an eyebrow. "What an idea."

Reyna drummed the countertop with a few fingers. There was a pile of unread mail nearby from their recent absence, and she parsed through a few of the letters. "I think he could be convinced. Although, admittedly, his manor isn't exactly welcoming."

"Yeah, he may need to repurpose a building near the town square—something more accessible." Kianthe sat in one of the booths. She hesitated, looking very lonely, and ventured to say, "I know your brain is moving at the speed of a griffon diving for prey, but can you slow down and have tea with me?"

That shook Reyna out of her plans. She tilted her head, abandoning the mail to gather their morning mugs. "Of course, love."

Reyna had baked fresh apple-cinnamon scones this morning, like any normal day of work. Now, she chose two of the best-looking ones and plated them, carrying them to the table. Kianthe was busy running her finger over the polished lacquer, squinting at its surface.

"How long have you been up? It looks like you cleaned half the shop. This table's definitely been wiped."

"I cleaned everything but the floors, actually." Reyna forced a smile. The labor had her blood pulsing, her heart beating. It made her feel good to focus on menial tasks after last night. "The scones took a little while to bake." She tugged her mug closer, took a sip, and added more sugar from a container on the table. "So, love. What's on your agenda—"

"I know what you're doing." Kianthe buried her head in her hands. "Can we just . . . pause for a minute? Like we did last night. This is a *big* decision, Reyna. Closing this shop means ending our livelihood."

Reyna didn't like thinking about that. She'd felt the emotions last night—and asking for more almost felt unfair. She was built for forward motion, and now that they'd decided to close the shop, her next steps were looking ahead at their new life.

But it was obvious Kianthe was suffering, too, so she forced herself to slow down.

"I . . . suppose I figured we'd reached an understanding." Reyna frowned. "Or did I misconstrue?"

"Yes. I mean, no, you didn't misconstrue. Yes, we decided to close New Leaf. But—well, Feo asked for a few more days. I think we should wait that long before doing anything."

Considering that all Reyna had done today was normal, business operations, she was a bit baffled by that. But from her partner's perspective, it must feel like things were careening out of control. Reyna broke a corner off her scone, chewing the crumbling pastry thoughtfully. The cinnamon was a sharp bite to the sweetness of the apple and sugar, but its taste did little to distract her.

She drew a deep breath. "Can you tell me how you're feeling? Because you're right. This is a big decision, and we need to make it together."

Kianthe took a moment to think, then replied, "I have a pounding headache. It feels like my heart has been carved from my chest with a spoon. And I'm scared." She laughed, running a hand through her unruly hair. "Which is to say, I'm feeling *great,* considering the circumstances. But I'm seriously doubting you are."

Defensiveness prickled in her soul like fire, and it took all of her willpower not to snap a retort. That alone shocked her, stilling her words. She hadn't felt the need to argue with Kianthe in ages. Not since the wedding, or maybe before it.

It became apparent Kianthe had nothing left to say. Reyna chose her response carefully, her words heavy with caution. "I . . . I hear what you're saying, and understand your concern. I believe I feel emotions differently than you, and—"

"Reyna," Kianthe snapped.

It broke her control. "What, Key? What would you like me to say?" She pushed the scones away, leaning back in the booth. "I have to move. I *have* to think of the future or I'll be sinking in quicksand. Packing this place will tear me to bits unless I think about how many boxes we'll need, or who's arranging transportation to the Grand Palace." Logistics were safe. Logistics kept her focused. Grief just sucked days and days of her time, and Reyna couldn't spare that. She didn't *want* to, and she channeled that into her next sentence: "New Leaf is closing, and the only way to *not* feel shitty about it is to focus on what's next."

Her anguish from last night had morphed into fury, and it took several moments to realize she'd shouted at her wife.

Stunned into silence, Reyna pushed from the table, pacing to get some distance. Her voice was strangled. "I'm sorry. I—"

"*Thank* you," Kianthe groaned, finally digging into the scones. Despite everything, a smile ghosted along her lips. "That's all I wanted, Rain. Because I was beginning to think last night was a dream, and that *I* was the only one abjectly miserable to be leaving Tawney."

Her voice broke at the end, and she busied herself with chewing a huge chunk of the scone, washing it down with tea.

Reyna pressed her lips together, torn between exasperation and empathy. "There has not been a single moment that I'd *want* to leave Tawney and New Leaf. But even if we make this place private, close it off to the public, they'll still swarm the town. We can't avoid the fact that you're the Arcandor, and I'm somehow royalty now."

"I know." Kianthe swallowed. "I know. The next step is packing."

Reyna was silent. Hearing her admission quelled the fire in Reyna's chest, and she was left feeling hollow and sad. The next step *was* packing. She could lose herself in the details, and that might make her feel better short-term, but it wasn't giving them any space to grieve. It wasn't helping her partner through this.

When this was over, *Kianthe* would be all Reyna had left.

"I'm sorry, dearest." Reyna slid into the booth beside Kianthe, pulling her into a hug. "I didn't mean to lose my temper. This is going to be quite hard, isn't it?"

"Yeah."

Reyna had opened her mouth—for what? more encouragement? it felt silly now—when someone knocked on the front door. She blinked, taken aback, and glanced at the closed drapes. Sunlight was filtering through the windows high in the rafters, but she'd kept everything at street level closed for privacy today.

Apparently, that hadn't stopped the tourists.

Kianthe narrowed her eyes. "Tell them we're busy."

"It's not *their* fault this is happening, love."

"It's a little their fault." Kianthe stubbornly sipped her tea.

Reyna squeezed her wife's shoulder and headed for the door. Of course, she hadn't made it more than a few steps before a glowing red sigil glowed on the wood, and a human-sized hole appeared. The outdoors shone in, revealing the Alchemicor—and behind him, a smaller crowd of curious tourists. Apparently, Marlow had begun admitting people into Tawney today.

Albert stepped through, and the opening vanished behind him. He laughed loudly, dusted his pants, and said, "You've got a crowd out there! Based on their enthusiasm, I'd have thought this was a shop of an *entirely* different nature." He waggled his eyebrows.

Reyna massaged her brow. Well, his arrival saved Kianthe a step, anyway.

Kianthe wrinkled her nose at his implication, hooking one arm over the booth's back. "Stone and Stars. I thought you were finishing up the Alchemical Showdown?"

"Oh, I was. But the turnout this time was rather pathetic. No one truly inspired, nothing that matched my passion for alchemy." Albert swept himself into a powerful pose, then deflated a bit. "Isn't Fylo here? Perhaps I'll challenge them to a duel before I retreat for another half decade."

"They go by *Feo,* now. I told you that." Kianthe sounded mildly annoyed that she had to correct him again.

Granted, Albert was somewhat scatterbrained, and he acknowledged the new name with ease this time. "Duly noted. I remember Feo puzzling through alchemy circles that could bend *time* itself! They'd put a seed in soil and it'd grow in a breath, and not because of elemental magic. They'd literally *speed up time* where the seed was located. Fascinating."

"Sounds dangerous," Kianthe grunted.

"Well, most magic is, Kianthe!" The Alchemicor barked a laugh. "I'm just saying, I'd love a duel. Feo was a rising star in the Magicary, at least before they—" Albert cut off, coughing in embarrassment. "Well, never mind all that."

Reyna was less concerned about Feo's expulsion and more interested in Albert's arrival. She stepped around him, running a hand over their doors. The wood was smooth, unmarred by the magic that had let him enter. She peeked out the window, slightly perturbed. "Did you just sacrifice something on our front lawn?"

"Oh, absolutely not." Albert laughed boldly at the assumption, fishing into his pockets. He produced no fewer than sixteen sheets of parchment, peeling off several to offer Reyna for inspection. "I designed a holding sigil years ago. One day of sacrifice can fuel dozens of these pre-made spells. Slap them on the door, finish the incantation, and *bam*."

"You're hit with a brick," Kianthe guessed, deadpan.

Albert snorted. "Always with the jokes. Anywho, I do hope this isn't a bad time." He bustled farther into the shop, sliding into the booth across from Kianthe. His eyes caught the scones, so pointed that it would be rude to ignore. With a heavy sigh, Kianthe pushed the plate his way.

Reyna followed him, handing back the parchment with sigils. "Ah, Al. I hate to say it, but it is a bad time." She maintained a pleasant air as she slid into the booth beside Kianthe. "We're actually closed today. A much-needed break after freeing that dragon."

She watched his lips, his eyes, his posture. But just like in the Magicary, Albert was a clean slate. If anything, he genuinely appeared surprised. "A *dragon*?"

"North of Winterhaven," Kianthe said tightly. She hadn't

been in a great mood before Albert's arrival, and she didn't seem inclined to warm up now. "No rogue alchemists. Just a baby dragon missing its family."

"What? Oh, *Stars.*" Fury laced Albert's tone—but at himself, not them. He put his scone down, jaw tight. "I'm so sorry, Arcandor. I truly thought they were just stealing livestock. If I'd known they'd captured a *dragon,* I'd have intervened sooner."

Kianthe leaned back in her chair, eyes narrowed. "Sure."

Reyna had her own bone to pick with this man. She steepled her fingers. "I hate to be disrespectful, Alchemicor, but . . . is there any reason you didn't warn Kianthe about the fact that your sigil would burn her flesh and leave a permanent scar?"

She'd spoken mildly, yet chosen her words to have the highest impact. And still, she'd forgotten this was a man who regularly sacrificed in the sake of magic. Albert seemed more confused than embarrassed. "Well, it's a persistent problem, isn't it—accidentally drawing on dragon magic? I made the spell permanent because I figured Kianthe would prefer that the nausea was gone forever." He winced. "Especially considering she's married to you, Dragon Queen."

It made sense. Reyna still didn't like it. "I see. In the future, Albert, I'd prefer you didn't make assumptions about my wife's preferences." Her tone was friendly, but with an underlying edge.

Kianthe crossed her arms. "Yeah. And if you do, some *warning* would be nice. I'd have used that spell on the ground, rather than on the back of my griffon, in the middle of a snowstorm."

Albert glanced between them, eyes wide. "Well, that sounds awful. Deepest apologies, Arcandor. I truly thought you'd surmise its intent, but I should have been more clear. Is it working? I designed that spell myself."

Kianthe begrudgingly ran a finger over the scar on her arm. "Yeah. It's working."

"Excellent!" With that resolved, Albert ate half a scone in a few gulping bites. He swallowed, and happiness seeped into his tone. "This scone is *spectacular,* Reyna. Any chance I can convince you to join me in the Vardian Mountains? My study isn't large, but it's quite peaceful, and I'd make sure you always have sugar for baking."

"Reyna is a *queen,* not your housemaid." Kianthe's tone was scathing.

That stilled Albert. He blinked at both of them, finally noting their pinched expressions, their tense shoulders. Not the most attentive person in the Realm, was he?

Slowly, Albert lowered his scone, pushing away the plate. "Ah. I seem to have misconstrued the situation yet again." Now he chuckled, the sound humorless. "An unfortunate byproduct of spending most of my time in solitude, I'm afraid. Thank you for the scone, dear. It was truly wonderful. I'll . . . ah, come back later."

He scooched out of the booth, stepping toward the door.

Reyna had half a mind to let him leave. Kianthe clearly planned to, based on the way she'd stayed silent and still, glaring at his back.

But the Alchemicor wouldn't have paid a house visit without reason. He could have information on the alchemical sigils and mystery mage. As he reached the door, Reyna pushed out of the booth. "One moment, Albert. Why did you fly all the way to Tawney?"

"I—" Albert hesitated, clearly debating between that and the polite thing to do. He fidgeted with his shirt. "I truly didn't realize my timing was this poor. Next time, I certainly won't—"

"Use alchemy on our front door before we've even had a chance to open it?" Kianthe's tone was dry.

"Yes. That."

He sounded so apologetic, and looked supremely uncomfortable now. Reyna felt a bit bad for their grudging hospitality.

Kianthe sighed and pushed out of the booth too, crossing her arms. "Okay, Al. Something brought you here from the Magicary. What's the problem?" She'd never sounded less enthused to handle an issue.

The Alchemicor's expression firmed. "Ah, there's a problem with the high-mage. Ex-high-mage, rather. Polana."

That caught Kianthe's attention. She scowled. "What? Harold was supposed to send her away."

"He did. Exiled her on your orders. She threw an absolute fit, raving about alchemy discoloring all magic." The Alchemicor's voice hardened, and for the first time Reyna saw a glimpse of anger below his smile. "Polana was an old friend. We schooled together. When I was, ah . . . *advised* to try alchemy, she was my lead support. I'm shocked she feels this way."

Reyna knew the feeling of leaving a career and losing the friends that came with it. There was a reason Venne had been chosen as her lead Queensguard, after all. He was capable, knowledgeable, personable—but he also let her feel like herself. Her old self. Reyna the Queensguard, not Reyna the tea maker, or Reyna the Dragon Queen.

"I'm sorry," she found herself saying.

Albert shook his head, as if he was shaking out of a reverie. "It hardly matters now. I'm highly concerned that Polana is going to attempt something drastic. Last we saw, she was flying east—heading toward the Capital."

"The Capital?" Kianthe set her jaw. "What could she possibly want there?"

Reyna had a theory, but she swallowed it in front of Albert. No matter their kinship, she still wasn't entirely convinced of his motivations. And after decades of respecting people in power, of offering obedience just because of their title, Reyna was finally beginning to question the people everyone seemed to worship.

"I'm not sure. But based on the things she was threatening as she left the Magicary, I doubt it's anything good." Now Albert assessed Reyna, his gaze sharp. "Based on recent history, it's probably a good thing you're here, Your Excellency. If she tried anything, I'm certain you could counter it faster than anyone."

Reyna frowned. "My wife and I can tackle a threat, if there is one. But I'm still confused about why she'd head to a city with no mages, in a country that generally doesn't understand them. What could she gain here that she can't in Shepara?"

Albert winced. "That, I couldn't answer."

Kianthe and Reyna exchanged a glance. Unease prickled in Reyna's chest.

"We'll visit the Capital." Kianthe rolled her shoulders, sounding displeased. "In the meantime, what about the alchemical circle? There was another one up near Winterhaven, in the cave that held the dragon."

Thankfully, she didn't delve into what the dragons had told Reyna. It felt like a blessed secret, and Reyna was pleased to keep it that way—at least until they knew more.

Albert fumbled through his coat for another sheet of parchment, snapping his fingers. "Ah, yes. That's the *second* reason I'm here. There's another piece to this sigil, hidden in the layers of the spell. It is a draining spell—but we're obviously curious where it'd siphon the power."

He showed the circle etched in charcoal, in Reyna's handwriting. The one she'd drawn after being kidnapped, the one they'd handed off to him in the Magicary. He smoothed the parchment, laid it on a table for them both to see.

Kianthe stepped beside Reyna, squinting at the page. "Yeah. Why drain magic if there's nowhere to put it?"

"Exactly." Albert pointed at a tiny letter circled at the base of the sigil. Reyna had seen that letter before, but couldn't quite place where. "This, right here. This tells the magic where to go. I'm not sure what this symbol means, but I suspect if we can identify it, we'll have this alchemist's motive."

"An alchemist? You don't think Polana is behind this?" Reyna frowned.

"Polana is a highly respected elemental mage. Or . . . she was." Albert winced, withdrawing from the table. "It's possible she's explored alchemy, but based on her vitriol before leaving the Magicary, I doubt she'd sully her name with it. Polana in *exile* concerns me because I'm afraid she'll make a rash move, not because she's responsible for these." Albert gestured at the charcoal circle.

"What kind of rash move?" If a hostile mage was moving toward the Capital, Reyna wanted all the information he could give.

Which, apparently, wasn't much. He pursed his lips. "It's impossible to tell."

Hmm.

Kianthe grimaced, scrubbing her face with a hand. "Why can't anything in our lives be simple?"

"I've been asking myself that all season." The Alchemicor heaved an exasperated sigh. "There's a reason I hide in a private study for years on end, Arcandor. Public relations are *your* job, not mine."

"Gee, thanks."

Reyna was still squinting at the symbol. "Albert, are you finished with this? Would you mind if I kept it?"

"Go ahead." Albert turned for the door. "Since I'm here, I'm going to speak with Feo. Perhaps the two of us can puzzle through that symbol. In the meantime, Arcandor, let me know if you need help with Polana. She's an elemental mage, yes, but she's threatening *my* alchemists right now."

Kianthe sighed. "Yeah. We'll head south as soon as we can."

Albert nodded, his expression grim. "Good luck, you two." And he stepped out the door—the normal way, this time. Outside, the crowd of tourists had grown, and some loudly complained about the unfairness of it all—how *that* man got a private tour, but they'd been waiting all morning—

Reyna closed the door on their protests, locking it firmly.

Silence filled his wake.

"Well," Kianthe groused. "I guess we'll meet Wylan at the Capital. Unless he's already heading back this way."

"Mmm." Reyna slid the charcoal circle into her pocket, then flashed a smile. "I think, after all this, I'd like some fresh air. Can you sweep the floors while I'm gone?"

Kianthe quirked an eyebrow, suspicion lacing her tone. "Where are you going?"

"Just . . . out." Reyna winked, feeling a rush of old excitement. "I want to confirm a theory."

"Can I be privy to said theory?"

"Not yet, love." Reyna pressed a kiss to her wife's lips, then strode for the door. "Say hello to Matild for me. Hopefully I didn't leave too much for you two to clean."

Reyna didn't wait for Kianthe's response. She was out the door in moments.

20

Kianthe

With nothing else to do, Kianthe swept, half-heartedly collecting the dust and crumbs in a pan. It was ironic to her that Reyna turned to housework to *clear* her mind—all it did was allow Kianthe undisturbed access to her own thoughts.

And they were a revolving mess of *I don't want toooo.*

She swept the last bit into the dustpan, balancing it as she stepped for the back door. "It doesn't matter," she told herself, cold and tired. A quick breath had her on their back patio, and she dumped the crumbs into the soil surrounding the tiled area. The plants here—several pine trees, a few bushes, and some lovely red flowers—leaned her way, eager for her attention. She sent a subtle wave of magic over them, then collapsed into the wrought iron chairs.

"It doesn't matter, because your neighbors hate you, and your wife has *actual* duties elsewhere." Kianthe stared miserably at their engagement tree, grown from the seed of a pinyon pine where Reyna had first agreed to run away with her. It bloomed white flowers, which wasn't a thing with pinyon pines, but apparently the Arcandor's wedding tree was a special, magical exception.

Now, one broke off the pine, drifting to the ground.

Kianthe glared at it. "That had better not be a sign."

"I have your sign," Matild said, stepping around the trees

and bushes to enter their back patio. She'd clearly cut across the empty lot behind them. Her gaze was disapproving. "*Closing New Leaf?* The absolute *audacity.*"

Kianthe didn't have the energy to debate an already arduous topic with her. "We're waiting on any decisions, just like you asked."

"Liar. You've already made yours. I can see it in your body language." Matild's voice was sharp, but doubt edged in. "You'd give up on Tawney so fast? On all your friends?"

It physically hurt to hear. Kianthe drew a shaking breath, pushing to her feet. "Do you hear them out front? A crowd, even with the ticket system. Waiting to see *us.*" She gestured around the patio. "Where's Gossley? I bet he's still sleeping off his last shift. No one deserves this kind of chaos."

"Gossley is learning blacksmithing from my husband, thank you." Matild waved a hand, stepping back the way she'd come. "Look, you can sit and feel miserable, or you can follow me. Lord Wylan returned from the Capital early, with Tessalyn and James in tow. They want to see you and Reyna."

Huh. Matild's voice was suspiciously devoid of emotion now, and she'd always had a blank face when the time called for it. Kianthe squinted at her for a moment, but decided it really didn't matter what her motives were. At the very least, it couldn't be *worse* news than they'd already had today.

Maybe they'd thought of something better. Maybe she and Reyna wouldn't have to leave Tawney.

It felt like too much to hope for, after last night.

"Reyna's, ah . . . out." Kianthe pushed to her feet, caught between eagerness and resignation. "But, sure. I haven't seen them in a while. It'll be nice to catch up."

Matild shrugged. "Sure. And tomorrow you can open New Leaf like normal, and quell this talk of leaving Tawney for good."

A surge of irritation swept through Kianthe. "Were you not *there* last night? Or did you just ignore what they were saying?" She pointed at their next-door neighbor's house. "Sasua wants us gone. Hansen and his wife can't handle the crowds. We can't lock down Tawney forever. I'm failing to see another option here."

Instead of responding, Matild just beckoned two fingers and stepped back over the bushes.

With little else to do, Kianthe followed. But instead of leading her to Wylan's mansion, Matild cut right, angling straight through the burnt half of town. Kianthe raised an eyebrow, but followed, and as the scenery changed, she examined the buildings around them. They'd housed Dreggs's pirates and some of their wedding guests in the less-dangerous structures, including Kianthe's own parents. But despite that temporary fix, this part of town was far from habitable after years of dragon fire.

And yet, as they entered a second town square, Kianthe was met with . . . construction equipment.

Nothing had started, but stacks of wood, nails, and carpentry tables had been erected. At the base of the old church, Wylan and Tessalyn were in deep discussion. Feo was conferring with the town carpenter, who'd helped them renovate New Leaf in the very beginning. James, Tessalyn's dedicated Queensguard, was sharing a sandwich with his boyfriend, Fauston—who happened to be Kianthe's oldest friend. They waved, even before Matild cleared her throat to announce them.

"One Arcandor, as requested." The midwife crossed her arms. "Reyna wasn't home, but considering Kianthe was griping to her plants, I figured we should inform her before she does anything rash."

"Hey. Acting rashly is her favorite thing." Fauston grinned.

Kianthe flipped him off. "Good to see you too, Fauston. Hope you're enjoying life in the Grand Palace."

"It's not bad. Be better if James had to work less, but . . . eh. I'm flexible." At that, his boyfriend snorted, and Fauston gasped indignantly, slapping James's arm in mock offense. "I *am*."

"Sure," James said.

Kianthe shifted her gaze to Feo. "Did Albert find you yet?"

"The Alchemicor?" Feo quirked an eyebrow, finishing their conversation with the carpenter. "Hardly. I didn't even know he was in town."

"Keep an eye out. I'm sure he'll track you down soon."

Feo smirked. "Considering I just perfected an alchemy circle capable of restoring a house with one goat's sacrifice, I think Albert might need to be careful who he intercepts over the Showdown's timeframe. I won't visit the Magicary, but I have no issue challenging him in my own town."

Kianthe glanced at the carpentry equipment, expression deadpan. "If you made a circle like that, why do we need all these hammers?"

Wylan rolled his eyes. "Because we don't trust alchemy over our own two hands, and that's a lot of goats."

"And I like my job, thanks." The town carpenter shrugged.

"You'll have to take my word for it, Kianthe," Feo said. With a grand gesture at the town square's chaos, they added, "Now, allow me to present Tawney's solution."

She didn't get it. They'd braced the old church with scaffolding, and clearly intended to start extensive renovations, based on all the wood, saws, and nails. "You're . . . repairing this church. I mean, it's not a bad idea. A dedicated space to house the inn's overflow will get those people out of the cold—"

Wylan politely cleared his throat. "Not just the church. We're rebuilding the burnt section of town."

That . . . was a huge undertaking. The dragons attacked Tawney because of the magical signatures below this church—leftover from their three stolen eggs. Unfortunately, the dragons didn't much care where they burned. The whole town would have been demolished, except the citizens gradually moved west and built new homes.

The burnt half was left standing as a warning, but no one bothered with it these days.

Confusion flashed across Kianthe's face, and she rocked back on her heels. "Oookay. That's not going to solve our immediate problem, and it seems like a *lot* of work on the back end."

"Nothing will solve your problem." Tessalyn spoke now. She was wearing work overalls and tied her long hair in a high ponytail—but she still looked startlingly close to her half sister, Tilaine. Although Tilaine wouldn't have been caught dead with a hammer in her hand. Tessalyn slid the handle into a loop on her pants, cocking one hip. "Shock and awe—Tawney isn't the first town to have a major attraction. I called in the cavalry when Reyna told me about your problem."

"And the cavalry are . . . these folk." Kianthe gestured at everyone here.

"No. The *cavalry* are city planners, urban scholars, and national leaders from across the Realm." Tessalyn smirked.

Huh. That shut Kianthe up.

"Your town is inundated because it doesn't have the infrastructure to handle these visitors. We're beyond the point of sending them home—anyone who still hopes that's an option is living in the past." Tessalyn clapped a sympathetic hand on Wylan's shoulder. The lord heaved a sigh, waving a hand for her to continue. She turned again to Kianthe. "Good news is, we can lighten the load. Clear the streets by offering new places to explore. Empty the shops by adding secondary locations."

Exasperation slid through Kianthe's veins. "We pitched that idea last night. The Tawneans don't want it."

"Have you ever attended a town hall meeting?" Feo drawled.

Kianthe quirked an eyebrow, but the answer was a resolute *no*. She always had better things to do. Reyna attended a few that held topics of interest—tax hikes, shop regulation changes, the like—but she never mentioned much except the final verdict.

Feo read her expression. "Thought not. Wylan and I host them regularly, and the one you attended was mild. Mostly, they're just a forum for complaints. People don't attend if they aren't passionate about the subject."

"Meaning," Wylan inserted seamlessly, "that the folks agreeing you should close New Leaf Tomes and Tea are a small minority, and they're only resorting to that because there isn't another plan in place."

His tone was gentle, encouraging, but Kianthe felt vaguely attacked. "We've had this problem for over a season. Why didn't you *present* a plan?"

"We suggested it in fall, but the backlash was resolute. We needed time to experiment with other options, so everyone would know we gave it a fair effort. With my deepest apologies, we needed to resort to something drastic, so *this* seemed reasonable by comparison." Wylan offered a pained smile now, gesturing again at the construction equipment.

Feo inserted bluntly, "We needed you to threaten to close New Leaf."

"What?" Kianthe snapped.

"You two are a pillar of this town, and you created most of the community we *have* by making peace with the dragons. After you left the meeting, seven separate people approached me privately. They all begged to keep you here." Feo examined their nails, then added wryly, "Sasua was first. So, don't think your neighbors actually want you gone."

Kianthe clenched her fists, torn between crippling relief and red-hot irritation. "You couldn't tell us this *last night*? We spent the evening sobbing in our stupid barn."

Now, for the first time, guilt flashed across Feo's face. They coughed, ducking their head. "I told you to wait for Wylan before making any decisions."

"You cornered us into making a decision last night," Kianthe hissed, the air around her sparking. "A heads-up would be nice, next time."

"We'll avoid a 'next time' entirely, shall we?" Wylan seamlessly inserted himself again, tagging into the conversation to placate the very angry elemental mage. Kianthe kept glaring at Feo, but—actual remorse was etched into the downward tilt of Feo's brow.

They were too proud to admit it, but they clearly felt bad.

Kianthe felt bad too, but more over the energy she and her wife apparently *wasted* last night. She ran a hand through her hair, turning away from Feo, back to Tessalyn. "Let's say I'm interested. Let's say we *want* to keep the bookshop open, more than anything. How will expanding Tawney help the tourist problem today? Right now?"

"It won't," James said flatly. "That's why we're here. The Queensguard."

"They're the other cavalry," Tessalyn replied.

Kianthe frowned. "We don't need guards muscling tourists into order." *Again,* based on how their recent eviction from Tawney apparently happened. Still, it was one thing when a town stood up for itself. Another entirely when the queen's private guard seized control.

It felt far too close to Tilaine's reign—and they put an end to that for a reason.

"We're not here to fight anyone." James sounded offended at the implication. "We're here to offer them an option: a travel stipend anywhere but here . . . or a building to claim as their own. They pay for renovation costs, but they get the land for free." He gestured now at the burnt shops and homes around them.

"You're going to use their desire for a quiet life to fix up the town." Kianthe scanned the carpentry supplies with new appreciation, suddenly imagining what the burnt half would look like bustling and beloved.

It was a really nice image.

Lord Wylan chuckled. "Well, it worked with you two. New Leaf Tomes and Tea is the greatest thing to happen to this town since I've been alive. You and Reyna breathed fresh life into a stale place. Even if a bigger town isn't what everyone wants, no one can deny there's a benefit to attracting new residents."

Kianthe was still looking for ways it wouldn't work. Still testing whether her hopes would be dashed a few days from now. "A travel stipend is expensive. I doubt Reyna will approve diving into the Queendom's coffers for one town."

"Luckily, I inherited a rather large sum upon my parents' death." Wylan shrugged. "We've been collecting taxes for generations. It's about damn time it's used to help the townsfolk in a meaningful way. These tourists aren't getting what they hoped for already. I suspect any incentive will steer them back home."

"The Queensguard are just extra bodies," James said. "Officials backed by the queen and local lord to offer added authority. We're spreading the word, nothing more." James polished off his sandwich, licking his fingers. His voice was muffled. "It's a win-win for everyone."

Kianthe looked back at Tessalyn. "Who's going to staff everything? Matild's drowning in work. There's no more space in the inn."

"Shockingly enough, Tawney is an attractive place for skilled workers." Tessalyn's voice was dry. "Weather aside, there's a lot of reasons to move here. I'm working with parliament, the council, and the board to draw up a campaign. We'll have flyers across all three countries to entice the best folk."

"And if we need specific people, specific skillsets, there's a stipend for that, too," Wylan said.

"A couple of my old friends from the Grand Palace already told Wylan they were interested. One's an herbalist, and the other's a doctor." Matild stretched her arms over her head, inordinately pleased. "It'll lighten *my* load, that's certain. I can manage alone until they get here."

Feo seemed to have collected themself. "What do you think, Kianthe? Is this enough to keep New Leaf open, and you two local?" Despite their almost arrogant tone, they still couldn't quite meet her gaze.

It melted the last of Kianthe's anger. She pulled Feo into a hug, crushing their bones. "Yes. Thank you," she breathed, and tears pricked her eyes. "Stone and Stars, we didn't want to leave. We fucking love this place."

"I'm sorry we ever implied you'd have to," Wylan said, rubbing the back of his neck.

Feo pulled away as soon as they were released, smoothing their jacket, face flushed with embarrassment. "Yes, well. It's poor town management if the two best people here are chased out." A pause, and they lowered their voice. "Tawney would be very bland without you both."

Aww, shucks. Kianthe laughed, but the sound caught into a sob. She covered her mouth, choking on the words. "It would, wouldn't it?" Her voice was small. "C-Can I have another hug? With everyone?"

Fauston was the first to stand, towing James over. Tessalyn and Matild weren't far behind. Wylan hesitantly joined the outer conglomeration, and Feo patted Kianthe's shoulder awkwardly, the only part they could reach. Even the carpenter laughed, joining in. "I can't wait for the new business," he said, tossing his arms around the group. "Save our goats, will you?"

"I suppose," Feo grumbled.

Happiness and relief had Kianthe crying all over again. She hugged her friends, her family, and thanked the Stone of Seeing for guiding her here, all those years ago.

Sometimes, the best places were the ones worth fighting for.

21

Reyna

Reyna and Ponder made it almost to the dragons' mountain range without being greeted—a first, for her. Even though Ponder frequently visited the dragons, Reyna herself had never actually flown this far north. There was a hint of luscious pine forests beyond the mountain range, but the rest was hidden by a thick layer of fog.

Ponder landed near the foothills of the dragons' mountain, screeching for emphasis. Reyna winced—the *dragons* wouldn't be why she'd lose hearing—and rubbed her ears. "A bit of warning next time, dear," she whispered to the griffon.

Ponder tilted her head to stare at Reyna, clearly bemused.

"Never mind." Reyna stroked her feathers fondly, then turned her gaze toward the towering mountains. Unlike the ones around Winterhaven, or west of Tawney, which were picturesque and stunning, these screamed *inhospitable*. They were too jagged, almost unnaturally formed. It took a long moment to realize why she felt unsettled: in a landscape of snow and ice, the mountains were bare rock. No snow at all on the mountaintops.

Which must mean they were *incredibly* hot inside.

Made sense, for a dragon lair.

Ponder's pointed request had a few dragons rumbling to each other, perched on ledges near a multitude of caves. A few circled overhead, but they knew Reyna by now. None were hostile, and Ponder kept a careful eye out for her friends.

Pill Bug was the first to emerge, followed by Gold Coin and—to Reyna's delight—Blue Spruce. The three young dragons lurched into the snow, running like jungle cats as they raced each other. Spruce won, skidding to a halt so poorly that Ponder leapt into the air and settled nearby just to avoid being hit. She screeched, feathers fluffing indignantly.

Once she landed again, Reyna loosened her grip, seizing the moment to slide off her back. She trusted Ponder, but getting in the middle of playtime with three dragons wasn't her preferred method of passing time. She patted Ponder's feathery neck. "Okay. Go have fun, but stay close. I doubt this will take long."

Ponder chirped, nuzzled her face briefly, and summoned the young dragons into the air.

Gold Coin was the first to follow, spitting fire at Blue Spruce and Pill Bug when they tried to overtake it. Gold Coin had always been Ponder's favorite, so clearly there was a bit of competition happening now. It was an amusing display, though, considering the youngest dragons didn't have *fire* so much as sparks that fizzled into wet ash.

Blue Spruce, the one who could breathe fire, was clearly using better judgment. It ambled along behind them, as if assessing where it might fit in an established play routine. Reyna watched the three dragons and her griffon for a moment, squinting against the brightness of the winter clouds. She hoped Blue Spruce found a place with its horde and its siblings in time.

Back so soon? a voice said in her mind.

Reyna turned to see the dragon from yesterday stepping lightly through the snow. Its wings were folded, its posture relaxed. If anything, it appeared mildly curious.

Reyna bowed deeply, which still felt awkward. "Yes. Do you have a moment to help me with something?"

The dragon cast a glance to the skies. Pill Bug had regained some confidence and tackled Gold Coin away from Ponder, eager for her attention instead. The adult dragon rumbled, which she was equating to a chuckle these days. *Every time you bring your griffon, they sleep for half the day. You are welcome anytime, little queen.*

For a brief moment, Reyna wondered who had laid those eggs, all those decades ago. Did dragons have dedicated parents? All she'd seen so far was a communal system.

Well, it hardly mattered. Reyna ducked her head in appreciation and fished out the charcoal circle she'd drawn in the watchtower. The sheet of parchment was comically small compared to the size of the dragon, but when she held it up, the dragon peered closer regardless.

Ah, the tainted magic, it mused. *A poor derivative of our own language.*

That made Reyna balk. Her eyebrows shot to her hairline. "You write with these symbols? These, ah, letters?"

We rarely need to write—our histories are passed through stories, spoken from elder to youth. The dragon stepped back, using one claw to draw a new circle in the snow. Reyna craned her neck, peering curiously at the construct. When it was completed, the whole sigil glowed faintly blue.

The dragon lowered its head to Reyna's level, nodding at the circle. *We use this language to channel our magic, same as your tainted mages. But our power comes from the earth at large. It is . . .* The creature paused, contemplating how to explain it. *It is like a blizzard, a perpetual storm we can twist into our desires. But these circles focus that magic. Limit it to gentle snowfall, one with a clear, intentional purpose. They were once very useful in speaking with human mages.*

"So, this was the bindment spell? The one you utilized on Kianthe—ah, the Arcandor—to ensure we found your eggs?"

The dragon puffed smoke. *Not this particular circle, but something similar.* For demonstration, the dragon tapped the circle in the snow with its claw. From it, a tree lurched from the ground, a towering pine that grew in moments.

It was as powerful a demonstration as anything Kianthe could manage, at least this far from the Magicary.

Astonishment smashed into Reyna, and she stepped backward, eyes wide at the pine before her. "Th-That's elemental magic."

The dragon rumbled again, clearly amused. *It is all the same magic, little queen. Our fire comes from somewhere.*

"I—" Reyna felt off-balance. She had to brace herself, lock her knees to keep from dropping. The pine towered over her, matching the height of the adult dragon. What she'd seen was so unnatural, so adverse to everything she knew, that Reyna couldn't look at it. And yet, the wind rustled through its needles all the same.

Kianthe was going to be so confused.

"The Stone of Seeing." Reyna grimaced. "How does it have power, if you're using the same magic? Dragon magic makes her sick. And now you're saying Kianthe is using it anyway?"

The dragon dipped its wings, which almost looked like a shrug. Its tail curled as it straightened. *The stone in the human mage dwelling simplifies our magic. Elements are merely one facet of our power, but it is all that stone is capable of channeling.* Now the dragon paused, tilting its head. *I am not certain how the early mages collected a stone. They are from deep within the earth's core, a space that would melt you, little queen. I do not know that history.*

This was bordering on theological discussion . . . and considering her shift from the Gods, they'd had enough religious crises for the year, thanks.

Besides, this information would be very, very distracting for Kianthe. They had bigger things to focus on, and shattering her wife's worldviews wasn't near the top of Reyna's list.

She drew a slow breath and refocused her attention on the parchment. "That's all right. I'm more concerned with this specific circle—and this symbol here." She pointed to the tiny squiggle the Alchemicor had indicated, the one that directed *where* the magic would be siphoned.

Dragons must have exceedingly good eyesight, because this time, it didn't bend down. It merely lifted its head.

It means "rock."

For a moment, Reyna thought she'd misunderstood. She swallowed a laugh. "Rock? That's it?"

Yes. The dragon didn't seem to understand the humor behind this. It stepped away from the pine tree, drew another circle in the snow. In its center, it added the symbol in question. This time, a tap of its tail was enough to push a huge boulder out of the ground. The dragon nodded at the stone. *Rock.*

Reyna stifled another laugh. She didn't want to be rude, but something about this exchange was hilarious.

"I see. Our alchemist—ah, the leader of the tainted mages—said this circle is designed to drain magic from a source and siphon it into something . . . which I suppose is a rock." As she spoke, her humor faded, and her eyes widened. "A rock. Oh my Gods."

Is something wrong, little queen?

Reyna shook her head, slowly backing up. "No. No, this was exceedingly helpful. Thank you." She pinched her fingers in her mouth and whistled sharply. Far overhead, Ponder screeched back, peeling away from the baby dragons to dive toward her. Reyna didn't waste a breath before leaping onto the griffon's back. "I have to go. I'll send Ponder for more playtime soon."

The adult dragon folded its wings, tail swishing. *We will await her return.*

The young dragons overhead roared, but Ponder had a job to do, and nothing made the griffon more arrogant. She puffed self-importantly, not even saying goodbye as Reyna urged her into the skies. With absolute professionalism, Ponder soared back toward Tawney—but not before double-checking that her dragon friends were watching her leave.

New Leaf was empty when Reyna stepped inside. They'd landed in the lot behind the barn to avoid the crowds out front. Ponder took off immediately, angling back toward dragon country, leaving Reyna to stroll through their patio. The broom and pan were discarded by the back door, so Kianthe must have gotten distracted inside. Reyna paused to caress one of the impossible flowers on their growing pinyon pine, swallowing the sadness that threatened her mood, and stepped into the barn.

It was brighter now, light streaming through the high windows. The place actually did look cleaner . . . but it was empty.

Huh.

"Key?" Reyna called, untying her sword from her belt. She rested it against their bedroom doorframe, then checked the storage room.

Nothing.

Maybe Kianthe had gone to see *Matild,* not the other way around? Or perhaps she was inside her greenhouse across town? Either way, she wasn't home, and this was important. Reyna checked that she had the parchment she needed, then pivoted to leave again. She opened the back door—

—and ran right into Kianthe.

"Stone and Stars," Kianthe yelped, leaping backward. "You're going to give me a heart attack, Rain."

"*Me?*" Reyna crossed her arms. "You startled me first, love."

"You don't startle, and we both know it." Kianthe pressed a hand to her heart, drew a slow breath, and started to laugh. "Either way, *great* timing. Come on. I have to show you something—"

Reyna tugged her inside instead. "I'm afraid mine is more pressing."

The urgency in her voice stopped Kianthe short. She frowned, eyes widening. "What did you find? Your theory panned out?"

"More than that." Reyna locked the door behind them, then led Kianthe farther into the barn. At one of their bigger tables, she tugged the three sheets of parchment from her pocket: the charcoal circle from the watchtower, the scratch paper she'd collected from the cave north of Winterhaven, and . . .

"What is this?" Kianthe squinted at the third sheet of parchment. "This looks like one of Albert's spells."

"It is."

"You stole this."

Reyna shrugged. "He handed several to me. I returned most of them." She considered all three, pressed her lips together, and stepped back to the counter to sift through the mail. As she suspected, one letter stood out—addressed in cursive from a certain ex-high-mage.

> *To the Arcandor, the Mage of Ages.*
> *Urgent Summons. Details inside.*
> *From High-Mage Polana*
> *The Magicary*

Handwritten, which was exactly what Reyna needed. She opened the letter, skimmed its contents—*Stone of Seeing losing power, magic seems unstable, return to the Magicary at once,* et cetera, et cetera—and laid it beside the three pieces of parchment Kianthe was already examining.

Four examples of handwriting. Three iterations of alchemical circles. Two examples of the draining and siphoning spell.

One culprit.

Reyna pointed at the circle from the watchtower. "This is the draining spell in its original form. And *this*"—she tapped the symbol at the base, the mystery letter—"is the piece Albert identified—the one that denotes *where* the magic is being siphoned. I thought it looked familiar once he mentioned it."

"Okay," Kianthe said, eyes skimming over the three pieces of parchment.

Reyna tapped the parchment of scribbled notes. It was scratch paper, where their mystery mage was clearly perfecting the "rock" symbol. The curious thing was that, after experimentation, the scratch paper identified the symbol perfectly—which was *then* added into the circle in Reyna's cell, in the watchtower.

Which meant that Blue Spruce had been captured and experimented on *before* Reyna was kidnapped.

But how long? Reyna racked her brain, thinking back to the cavern. It hadn't been something she'd considered at the time, so set on crisis management. But based on the gnawed bones piled in the corner, the young dragon must have been lured inside weeks earlier.

Kianthe reached the same conclusion. Her tone was dark. "They were practicing. And Spruce was trapped in there the entire time."

"Indeed." Reyna couldn't think about that for long—her heart physically ached to consider it. Spruce was fine now, and would recover in the company of its kind.

And in the meantime, they'd find the person responsible.

She pivoted. "I asked the dragons about it, since it seemed similar to their written language. Turns out it's not *similar*— it's directly copied from dragon magic. Which would explain why Blue Spruce was involved, and why I was kidnapped. If this mage is using dragon symbols, they probably want to tap into dragon magic for some reason."

"What about the Stone of Seeing?" Kianthe sounded frustrated. "Why siphon *that* magic?"

"An experiment, I presume. I think everything we've seen was an experiment. Testing new symbols, variations of the draining spell, attempting to siphon various forms of magic into a vessel."

Kianthe fell silent, narrowing her eyes. "What vessel?"

"I'm getting to that." Reyna set her jaw, tugging out Polana's handwriting. While it wasn't any attempt at alchemical sigils, her cursive held clues. Handwriting was unique, and Reyna had frequently scrutinized letters sent to Tilaine over her rule. Often, they could link potential assassins to threat letters sent months in advance of an attack.

Polana's writing was expansive, tilted slightly left, and spaced appropriately. She had a unique curve to her *S*s that mimicked the "rock" symbol from the dragon language.

And it didn't match at *all* with the watchtower's symbol, or the scratch paper.

"I think Polana is a distraction, nothing more." Reyna's voice was hard, and she showed her evidence to Kianthe. "It seemed odd to me. Albert was so confident she was flying to the Capital, but *why*? We have no mages, and thus no respect in the magical community. If she were truly heading to the Grand Palace, I imagine it'd be for negotiation—offering my citizens space within the Magicary's halls in exchange for exiling all alchemists. But even *that* would be a ridiculous move, considering we're married, and you'd learn of such a deal immediately."

Kianthe dropped into one of the chairs, rolling her eyes. "It was weird to me, too. I honestly just thought Albert was exaggerating—but Polana is powerful enough to be a threat, regardless of whether or not we know her destination or intentions."

"Perhaps. Or maybe she took her exile with more grace, and Albert is lying to us."

"You really don't like him, do you?" Kianthe raised an eyebrow.

Reyna felt vaguely indignant. "I don't like anyone who treats pain so callously. The most dangerous assassins often portrayed themselves as friendly, oblivious folk—they'd infiltrate the court faster than anyone, simply because they appeared pliable and easy to manipulate." That was blood in the water in Queen Tilaine's old court, where cutthroat politics meant everyone clawed their counterparts to get ahead. Reyna set her jaw. "Albert is used to people underestimating him because he seems scatterbrained—but I think he's more cunning than we realize."

For proof, she pulled forward the spell she'd stolen from him earlier that day. It wasn't the same alchemical circle as the draining spell—likely, it was some portal spell instead, like the one he used to get inside New Leaf.

"Albert drew this. Notice any similarities?"

Just like handwriting, even the most meticulous alchemical seals identified the mage who drew it. Kianthe examined the paper, seeing what Reyna had earlier: the specific curve of the bloody script as it wove through foreign sigils. One symbol was nearly identical to the "rock" symbol, with just an added curve at its base.

Which meant it matched the scratch paper, *and* the circle from the watchtower.

"Then Albert is behind it," Kianthe breathed. "Fuck."

Reyna didn't feel any satisfaction. She'd almost been hoping Kianthe would disprove her, but the evidence was laid out before them. And the more she puzzled through it, the more it added up.

"It *was* weird that he flew all the way to Tawney, only to tell us to leave town." Kianthe's voice was tense. "Why not send a hawk telling us to join him in the Capital, if he was so concerned about Polana?"

"My thought exactly." Reyna's fingers ran over the scar on Kianthe's arm, the alchemical circle seared into her skin. "And this? He knew exactly how much pain it would cause. He *chose* not to warn you."

Regardless of its intent, anyone who'd hand off something that dangerous without fully explaining it was a villain in Reyna's mind.

"Stone and Stars," Kianthe cursed. "He's led our alchemists for decades. He's a Stone-damned celebrity, just like me. Proof that alchemists can make a difference in the Realm, even without elemental magic."

That opened up another can of worms, considering what Reyna now knew about dragon magic. She brushed it aside—that would be a much bigger conversation, and it didn't change the fact that Albert was lurking in Tawney, within a stone's throw of the dragons themselves, armed with very dangerous magic.

"You saw the dragons," Kianthe said, distantly. "Did they tell you what that symbol *means*?"

"It means 'rock.' Coupled with the siphoning intent of that circle around the draining spell's base, I think Albert is trying to create a new power conduit. He's stealing magic from various sources, then attempting to push it into a rock."

Kianthe inhaled sharply. Wonder filled her tone. "A Stone of *Sawing*."

Her sudden enthusiasm startled Reyna into a bold laugh. "Excuse me?"

Kianthe feigned offense. "Well, it can't be another Stone of Seeing. The elemental mages already claimed that. But if Albert creates an artificial stone for alchemists to use, he'd have to name it. Ergo, the Stone of Sawing."

"Why—" Reyna barely refrained from rolling her eyes. "My love, why does the rock have to be named?"

"Every magical rock has a name. Anything else is blasphemy," Kianthe replied derisively, but her lips turned upward.

Fondness surged through Reyna, and in that moment, she was immensely grateful that no matter what, she and Kianthe were in this together. She pushed back from the table, clapping her hands together. "I'm not sure what Albert's next move is, but if we're right, I doubt Albert will wait long. Blue Spruce was young, isolated. But the rest of the horde?" Reyna frowned. "They'll have everything he needs."

"Going up against the dragons." Kianthe rolled her shoulders. "What a stupid idea."

"Surely, you don't miss the irony in that statement."

"I was *protecting* you—"

Reyna groaned, turning toward the bedroom for her sword. "Let's not start this again. Come along, dearest. We have to stop your counterpart from draining my gods."

22

Kianthe

They'd barely left New Leaf before running headlong into Venne. He was clad in full Queensguard uniform, complete with the golden epaulets shaped as dragon skulls, and a crimson cloak. Kianthe was honestly surprised Reyna hadn't adjusted that uniform yet—she'd frequently complained at how it was good for appearances and not much else.

"Your Excellency," Venne said, dipping into a bow.

"Venne." Reyna raised an eyebrow. Despite everything they'd done today, it was still only early afternoon. Dark clouds dotted the sky, and one shifted past the sun, forcing her to squint in the sudden brightness. "What are you doing here? I know the procedures, but I hardly need protection in Tawney."

Right. Kianthe had gotten so distracted with Albert's betrayal that she'd completely forgotten to update Reyna on Tawney's situation. She opened her mouth, but Reyna and Venne weren't paying her much mind.

"You ignore our procedures anyway, these days." Venne rolled his eyes, then gestured behind him, where a few of the other Queensguard were speaking privately to the crowd of tourists. There were far fewer people here now, thanks to the ticket system, but it was enough that Kianthe had almost suggested they leave out the back patio. Venne dropped his voice for privacy. "We're rounding up the tourists."

"By force?" Reyna's voice was sharp.

This would spiral, fast. Kianthe hastened to interject. "Rain, they're here on Tessalyn's orders. They're offering the tourists a choice: renovate one of the burnt buildings on the eastern side of town, or a travel stipend back home."

It only took a moment to sink in. Reyna's brow furrowed. "Of course. Renovating the old buildings will expand the town in a healthy manner. It handles the tourists today, and ensures future growth."

"Tessalyn is figuring out the angles. Dedicated stipends for skilled workers, more accommodations, more roadways." Kianthe grinned, bouncing on her toes. "Which means . . ." She trailed off, waiting for Reyna to realize the implications.

Her wife's eyes widened. She faced the barn they'd built together, her voice soft and happy. "New Leaf won't be a burden on our neighbors. We can stay here."

"Yes!" Kianthe pulled her into a hug.

A few of the tourists swooned. One whispered, "Gods, they're even cuter in person," and another shushed her.

Venne pointedly ignored this, clearing his throat. "Parliament gave the order to travel to Tawney and help, but we answer to you, Your Excellency. If you have another idea for our time—"

"No," Reyna cut him off. "This is important. Just remember, these folks could be our future neighbors. Please treat them kindly."

Venne saluted. "Always, Queen Reyna."

He stepped back to the tourists. Reyna watched him leave, cast another glance at New Leaf, and breathed a sigh. Then, just like that, Kianthe watched as her wife compartmentalized the relief for another day. It was honestly incredible, how fast Reyna could switch tasks.

Incredible, and mildly concerning. They'd probably have to talk about that later, too.

"Where's Feo?" Reyna asked. "At their compound, or—"

Well, they did have a job today.

"East side. But Feo said Albert never went to visit them." Kianthe whistled sharply, already walking away from the tourists.

Reyna kept up easily, checking her sword as she scanned the skies. "I suspected as much. Albert's here for one reason, and it isn't to talk with us or Feo."

Overhead, Visk screeched, circling for a spot to land. He must have been nearby, to reach them so fast—but after Reyna's earlier summons of Ponder, perhaps he figured they'd need help. Kianthe and Reyna stepped near another house, and Visk landed hard in the dirt road. He chittered, tilting his head curiously.

"Gotta save the world again, bud." Kianthe leapt onto his back. "Is Ponder coming?"

"She's with the dragons." Reyna slid on behind Kianthe, wrapping her arms around her wife's waist.

Kianthe snorted. "Of course she is. We can find Feo and see if they can help? I'm sure Feo has a locating spell—"

"It might not be necessary. The Alchemicor has a griffon, correct?"

Of course. Kianthe grinned. "Sure does. Hey, Visk. Go find me Albert's griffon, eh?"

Visk chittered darkly, as if he wasn't pleased another griffon had entered Tawney—or maybe not pleased that this *specific* griffon had arrived here. He unfurled his wings and leapt into the air, beating hard to gain some altitude. For a moment, he circled, eagle eyes scanning the surrounding areas. It only took a moment to sight his prey. He angled southwest, toward the pine forest.

As they flew, Kianthe peered at the thinning crowds waiting to enter Tawney. There were far fewer of them today—it was wholly possible that a frigid night outside had them losing determination. Either way, Reyna's Queensguard were moving methodically through the crowds. Word seemed to have spread, because several groups were already packing up campsites.

Marlow was helping supervise the removal of the makeshift gate at the road's entrance.

Relief made Kianthe sigh. "Tawney is getting back to normal."

"It's a wise idea," Reyna said, her arms tightening around Kianthe's waist. "I just wish Tessalyn had informed me that she was working on this project. It would have saved us quite a bit of emotional labor."

"Tell me about it. I already gave Feo hells."

"Lord Wylan will be next." Reyna's voice was far too casual, considering the threat. She buried her chin in Kianthe's unruly hair. "But I am *incredibly* happy. You and I would be fine, but I'd truly miss this place."

Good to know it wasn't entirely compartmentalized. Kianthe quirked a smile. "Me too, Rain."

As they neared the forest, Visk slowed, beating his wings to maintain altitude. He screeched loudly, pointedly. A warning.

An echoing screech resounded, and another huge griffon surfaced from the pines. It was a soft gold color, and wore what appeared to be a bridle and saddle. Visk screeched again, louder, and the other griffon chittered, pivoting south. With a final whistle—one that sounded like the griffon equivalent of *fuck you*—Albert's griffon vanished on the horizon.

"Visk does *not* like Albert's griffon," Kianthe drawled.

"The feeling seems mutual," Reyna replied. "How curious that he's using a saddle. I didn't even know mages made saddles for their griffons."

"It's more common with alchemists. They can't exactly twist the winds to slow their falls, you know? Safer." Now Kianthe craned to look at her wife, her tone teasing. "Unless you're a queen who enjoys tipping off the back of her griffon."

Reyna laughed, lightly shoving Kianthe's shoulder. "Yes, dear. Ponder would never accept a saddle at this point, and you know it." She squinted into the trees as Visk slowly circled, drifting to the ground. "If Albert's griffon just left, where is *he*?"

A good question.

They dismounted, meandering into the forest proper. And as they entered a huge, snowy clearing, they encountered a massive crowd of people. It was like . . . a festival, but an impromptu one haphazardly thrown together. There were banners painted with hasty words like REALM-FAMOUS DRAGON PUPPET SHOW—MIDDAY AND SUNDOWN! and PORTRAITS WITH DENNIS THE DRAGON! A food stand was operated by a man with a wide-brimmed hat lined with fake dragon scales that were, on closer inspection, parchment cutouts secured with pins. He gleefully handed out "dragon jerky" to a gaggle of children and their paying parents.

They stopped at the entrance to the clearing, and a man in a dragon suit bounded up to them. Like the rest, it was hastily made, sewn with what seemed to be tablecloths and drapery. A long, ratted tail trailed behind him, and the wings were constructed with wood that seemed to weigh his entire back.

He opened his arms wide, grunting with the effort of not falling over. "Welcome, weary travelers, to *Dragon Land*!"

Kianthe stared. "What the actual—"

"*Key,*" Reyna interrupted. Kianthe smirked, letting Reyna continue the conversation with a polite "Hello, there. What, exactly, is Dragon Land?"

"Best attraction north of Kyaron," the man boasted.

A child in a headband with carved wooden horns ran past, screeching in happiness. She appeared to be chewing on an icicle, which was abjectly hilarious considering winter in Tawney was *full* of icicles. Kianthe wondered how much her parents had been charged for that.

"I thought Winterhaven was the best attraction north of Kyaron," Reyna said mildly.

Darkness flashed over the man's eyes, briefly. "Buncha prudes—" He seemed to realize they were listening, because he cleared his throat, once again all cheer. Considering that he was entertaining people, his burly beard and dirt-covered skin implied less *businessman* and more *bandit*.

But at least he was getting creative.

"Dragon Land is a recent attraction. You're one of the first to enjoy it—which means *you* get exclusive access to rock-bottom prices." He spun, nearly fell over from the weight of the wings, and staggered back upright. "We got food, shows, and more!"

"Who gave you permission for this?" Kianthe raised an eyebrow.

"Diarn Feo, of course!" The man laughed nervously, which implied Feo had done no such thing. "We have a permit— somewhere."

It was irrelevant, and now that the shock had worn off, Reyna was back to business. "We hate to disrupt this, ah . . . wonderful retreat. Have you seen a taller, older man? He's fairly thin, wears a red cloak, graying hair? He's very enthusiastic; I doubt you'd miss him."

Now the dragon-man paled, the blood draining from his face. "Why? We *told* him not to take that tour group—"

"What tour group?" Kianthe asked sharply.

The man started to curse, saw a child nearby listening in, and beckoned them away from the little festival. In the shadow of several snowy trees, he lowered his voice, false cheer gone. "That asshole came in here claiming to be a 'dragon expert.' Stole half of our crowd before we even knew what happened. Said he was going to give them an *exclusive tour* of dragon country." The man scrubbed his face. "You believe that? Those things breathe *fire*. And he's just gonna gawk at them for a bit."

He would do a lot more than that.

Reyna drew a slow breath through her nose. "Do you know which direction they went?"

"Said he was gonna follow the mountain range over the rim." The man gestured north through the trees. "They're all on horseback, though. You won't catch them."

Kianthe whistled, and a breath later, Visk landed smoothly beside them. She helped Reyna mount, gripping Visk's feathers. "Oh, I wouldn't worry about that." She paused. "Fair warning:

the Queensguard are making their way west, breaking up the tourists. I think they'll want to see that permit."

"Fuck," the dragon-man muttered, signaling the man serving food. His partner hastily slapped a CLOSED sign on the food stand, and began shooing people out of the clearing.

They didn't wait for more. Ensuring Reyna was settled behind her, Kianthe clicked her tongue at Visk, and they flew north.

Problem was, it was tough to see things from overhead. A half day of riding was a long time, and most of this route was covered with a thick pine forest. There wasn't any specific trail to follow, so Visk drifted over the foothills as Kianthe and Reyna squinted through the trees for any sign of the tourists and their horses.

"Well, at least it'll take the dragons a while to notice this group," Kianthe grumbled as the sun began to set. They were a decent distance from Tawney, and had doubled back over the front range three times. There was no way a pack of horses made better time.

And yet, Albert's location was still a mystery.

"Mmm." Reyna's grip tightened on Kianthe's waist. "I'm a bit worried about the implications of this."

"What do you mean?"

Reyna hesitated, voicing the thing Kianthe had been stalwartly ignoring all day. "Alchemy requires sacrifice. Blood. Normally livestock is used, but"—her words were tense— "human sacrifices must create powerful magic."

Kianthe swallowed the urge to gag. "Albert would *never* stoop that low."

"Wouldn't he?" Reyna's voice was cold, calculating, and she didn't wait for an answer. "Has any alchemist tried human sacrifices in the past?"

"Sure. Centuries ago." Kianthe shuddered in the frigid cold, her eyes scanning the darkening landscape. The storm clouds had thickened, but they'd hardly manifested any real snow yet. Still, it was likely they'd awake to fresh powder tomorrow. "The magic was so volatile that it killed the alchemist who attempted it. Everyone learns that when they're children, even elemental mages. Alchemists may be a darker sort, but even within their ranks, it's taboo."

Reyna fell silent, contemplating that.

But the seed of thought had been planted, and unease spread through Kianthe's limbs. Visk circled again, beginning yet another flight north. The mountains to their west cast long shadows over the landscape, and it almost looked like claws raking the snowy plains. "I thought the circle would be for the dragons, not humans."

"I think the circle is meant to *capture* dragons, like it did with Spruce, and drain their magic. But . . ." Reyna leaned farther over Visk, searching the foothills. ". . . even that circle would need a sacrifice to activate, right?"

Kianthe didn't want to admit she had a point. She glanced back toward Tawney. "Maybe we should call in the Queensguard. They could sweep the ground while we search by air. The dragons would probably help, considering the threat."

"That's a wise idea. I only hope it's fast enough."

Kianthe nudged Visk, but the griffon had paused in his flight. He circled tightly, chittering, which meant he'd seen something. "Found something, bud?" Kianthe followed his line of sight. Sure enough, a glimmer of flame peeked through the trees.

A campfire.

"Rain," Kianthe breathed, pointing.

Reyna nodded, her words equally quiet. "We should approach on foot. Those tourists may be hostages now."

Kianthe nodded, checking her magical reservoir for a fight. Tawney's ley line was terrible, but this forest had its own power. She had enough magic for a battle, as long as she didn't try to cut open a mountain or fight a dragon horde.

Visk touched down silently in a nearby clearing. He folded his wings to make it easier for them to dismount, then paused, clearly awaiting orders. Kianthe patted his neck. "Go find Ponder. And alert the Queensguard—lead them here if you can."

Her griffon nibbled her hair affectionately, then took off again.

Reyna unsheathed her sword. "Follow me, and be careful." Then she paused and added, "And also, I love you."

Kianthe laughed nervously. "Ominous."

"No, just true." Reyna gave her a swift kiss, then motioned with two fingers.

Together, they crept through the trees. Reyna always walked far quieter than Kianthe ever managed. But Kianthe's magic told the forest to stifle their approach, which melted the crunching snow and muffled every step with a soft bed of moss.

Reyna realized it and shot her a look that clearly said: *Cheater*.

Kianthe grinned. It wasn't much, but their exchange helped calm her thumping heart.

Kianthe wasn't sure what she expected when they reached the clearing, but they peeked through the foliage to see a dozen weary tourists sharing a hearty meal. And, shockingly, it looked like they were all having a great time. The tourists were laughing and chatting, and Albert stood by the massive pot, doling out bowls to anyone who asked.

It was almost . . . cozy.

Reyna blanched. "Poison?" she breathed.

"Feo told me poisoning the sacrifices taints their magic." Kianthe frowned. They watched a little longer, but the tourists didn't seem to be in danger—at least, not from any active threat. Seven or eight horses were tethered to nearby trees, and overhead, stars glimmered between breaks in the clouds. A few tourists had unrolled sleeping pads. A couple nearby uncorked a bottle of amber liquor.

"Wait here. I'll check for alchemical circles." Reyna spoke so softly Kianthe almost missed it. In a breath, she'd vanished, disappearing between the dark trees.

Kianthe pressed a hand to a nearby tree's trunk, but the forest didn't notice anything amiss. It chattered about the lovely night and not much else. She frowned, squinting at the unsuspecting group of folks—and realized too late that Albert wasn't among them anymore.

Behind her, someone cleared his throat.

"Ah, Arcandor. What a pleasant surprise."

23

Reyna

It was a rare day when Reyna felt like a Queensguard again. Marrying the Realm's most powerful mage meant their conflict was usually head-on, so it was refreshing to fall back into subterfuge, sneaking around the campsite undetected. Her sword felt solid in her hands, a comforting weight, perfectly balanced and sharpened to a deadly point.

She hoped she wouldn't have to use it, but if Albert *did* plan to sacrifice all these innocent people, Reyna wouldn't stay her blade.

Of course, she'd barely rounded the campsite before Albert strolled back into the clearing. "Everyone, an announcement!" He sounded thrilled.

Reyna stilled, her heart in her throat as Kianthe trudged behind him.

How did he find her that fast?

The air flickered around Kianthe, radiating heat, a clear sign that she was ready for battle. Her eyes never left Albert, and her lips were downturned, set in fury.

Albert shared none of that energy. He gestured at her, overly enthused. "The *Mage of Ages* herself decided to join us on this tour. Can you believe it? You all visited Tawney to see her, and she went and found you instead. How wonderful!"

"Yeah. So very wonderful," Kianthe replied tersely.

Reyna ducked behind a dense cluster of trees, watching from the darkness. She stayed clear of the horses—prey animals would always notice someone creeping nearby—but near enough that she could intervene if necessary. While she listened, she scanned their surroundings for any sign of alchemical circles. It seemed impossible that Albert had just *noticed* Kianthe.

Which meant he had a warning system set up.

"As I'm sure most of you know, the Arcandor recently married the Queendom's new sovereign. Did Queen Reyna happen to join you, Kianthe?" Albert peered around her, squinting at the space they'd just vacated.

Reyna's body was tense, her breathing silent, keeping an ironclad grip on her sword.

"She flew back to the Capital. You know. To stop Polana." Kianthe crossed her arms.

"Hmm. Curious that you didn't join her." Albert offered a wry smile. "But no matter. You're right in time for dinner. My tour group was just complaining that they haven't seen any dragons yet—isn't that right? Perhaps with the Arcandor pulsing elemental magic, the dragons will take notice. Maybe we'll get to see a few after all!"

And the tourists—those ridiculous tourists—began murmuring about how *exciting* that would be.

Reyna clenched her teeth, formulating a plan. If Albert was distracted with Kianthe, that gave *her* every opportunity to flank. She could try to knock him out, but with his alchemical ability, she didn't trust such a simple solution. And yet, spilling blood—especially the Alchemicor's blood—might power magic she couldn't even fathom.

Fuck.

Slowly, carefully, Reyna sheathed her sword.

"Huh. It's shocking that you didn't tell them, Albert." Kianthe had her mind on the tourists, the unwitting hostages, although she never turned away from the alchemist.

"Tell them what?" Albert blinked.

Kianthe shrugged. "About the way dragon fire burns flesh and sears bone. Melts folks alive. It's not like real fire, oh no. It's nothing I can manipulate. If a dragon *did* notice us here, we're all toast. Literally."

A few of the tourists shifted nervously. One coughed. Another said, "Um, I was told the dragons wouldn't care about us."

"Yeah, you said they were timid."

"I don't want to be burned alive—"

Reyna began a slow procession through the woods, eyes alert for any alchemical circles. It didn't take long to position herself behind Albert.

The Alchemicor laughed jovially, cutting off their protests. "It's fine! We all know the Arcandor is a bit of a comic."

"Drop the act, Albert. I know everything." Kianthe's voice had turned deadly, and her hands ignited in flame.

A few of the tourists yelped, scrambling away. Of course, the moment they hit the edge of the clearing a flare erupted, bright as a lit fuse. A wall of magic arched to the sky, blocking off any exit. Reyna literally scrambled backward, swallowing a curse as she was cut off from the clearing with magical force.

She didn't see an alchemy circle because the entire *clearing* was an alchemy circle.

And now Kianthe was trapped inside.

For the first time, Reyna didn't have a plan. She was paralyzed, staring at the alchemy circle, imagining a burst of lightning and pain, imagining Kianthe's terrified scream, imagining Ponder's agonizing screech. Imagining the encompassing darkness, and how fast she went from awareness to nothing at all.

Sweat beaded on Reyna's brow, sliding down her spine.

Kianthe, meanwhile, appeared unfazed. "Cute." With a growl, she yanked her hands down. Reyna had seen that trick enough times—she was trying to suck the Alchemicor into the earth itself.

Except nothing happened. Albert merely tilted his head, ignoring the growing screams of panic as the tourists banged against the magical wall. Their pleas drowned as he stepped forward, raising his hand at Kianthe.

She responded again, with louder magic. Fire magic, wind magic, anything she could summon. It raged around her like a tornado—but something was wrong, because it never touched Albert. In fact, the magic was contained to a tight radius around Kianthe. She seemed to realize it, too, because all the other magic died down, and instead wind magic swept around her feet, clearing snow in a breath. Glimmering in the wet dirt was another, smaller alchemy circle. Neither of them had noticed, but she'd stepped right into an alchemical prison.

Albert tapped the air before his face, and a wall of magic rippled under his touch, identical to the one trapping the tourists inside the clearing. "I really didn't think you'd step in that trap, Kianthe. You should know better than to follow an alchemist blindly." He patted the magic like it were a pane of glass, then stepped back toward the tourists.

"Aren't you a tour guide?" one of them gasped, pressing against the edge of the clearing. Behind him, the magic flared transparent red. It might as well be solid brick.

Reyna viciously pinched her arm. She couldn't afford to be swallowed by fear, not when Kianthe was trapped, not when these tourists faced a worse fate. The shock of pain cut through the cloud in her mind, and she turned her gaze to the circle itself, carved into the landscape. Had he done this beforehand, sacrificed something prematurely—or was the sacrifice yet to be paid?

Albert quirked an eyebrow, ignoring the tourist's sad attempt at escape. "It's frankly depressing that no one recognized me. I'm the *Alchemicor*. The Mage of Ages's magical counterpart, leader of all alchemists."

A few choked sobs.

He sighed, scrubbing his face with a hand. "Yes, that's usually how we're treated. It hardly matters. After tonight, alchemists will have everything we need to separate from the Magicary." Now he turned back to Kianthe, his voice hard. "Polana was correct about one thing: elemental mages will never view alchemists as their equals."

Kianthe had twisted the magic to clear the air, seizing a few clean breaths as the dust settled around her and the fire's smoke dissipated. But despite everything, she sank to her knees. Below her, the circle pulsed crimson.

Another draining spell? Reyna had to do something, but what?

Kianthe glared at Albert, coughing. "I don't b-believe that."

"It doesn't matter what you believe. It's a fact. Elemental mages can draw power from the earth itself. But alchemists? We're limited by the blood we're willing to spill." True regret filtered into his voice. "I'm not excited to kill these people, but their sacrifice will allow future alchemy to be completed *without* sacrifice. A few deaths now for thousands spared moving forward. Isn't that a wonderful thing?"

It sent another wave of fear through the tourists. They spun from him, blindly attacking the magical wall with everything from their stew bowls to their knapsacks. Nothing happened. Albert shrugged, turning away from them fully.

Kianthe was his focus right now.

"Some hero," Kianthe wheezed.

That alchemy circle must be attacking her somehow; she was fading too fast. Heart pounding, Reyna paced the outer circle, scouring for a weak spot.

Albert pressed his lips together. "I couldn't care less what my legacy is. But once upon a time, the Stone of Seeing thought *I* was worthy of its power—and then it changed its mind." A flash of anger flitted across his face, replaced immediately with resignation. "Alchemists deserve better. We deserve our own Stone, our own power source."

Kianthe drew a ragged breath and collapsed.

Albert stood over her, drumming his fingers on the circle of magic that trapped her. "How's that draining spell? I was a bit worried it wouldn't contain you, considering it barely inconvenienced the Stone of Seeing. But you're quite far from the Magicary, and the ley line here is rumored to be poor."

"I'm—" Kianthe's breath was barely a whisper. "I'm going to kill you."

"With what, Kianthe? You can't draw on dragon magic anymore; I made sure of that. As far as I can tell, the great Mage of Ages is stuck."

Dragon magic.

It was past time for the element of surprise. Reyna pressed two fingers to her mouth and whistled—piercing, long, insistent.

Albert spun toward her, eyebrows shooting into his hairline. "Your Excellency! Clever girl. Have you been here the whole time?"

Reyna pulled back her shoulders, speaking clearly and carefully. "Hello, Albert. You're going to let everyone go. You'll release my wife, apologize to these nice people, and then *maybe* I won't bury you in a tomb of your own making."

Albert quirked an eyebrow, striding away from Kianthe to rap a knuckle on the magical wall between them. "I hardly think you're in a position to make threats." Farther beyond him, Kianthe was unnaturally still. It made Reyna's heart skip a beat, but she couldn't afford to lose her determination now.

Her training didn't fail her. Everything narrowed to this moment. And she'd remembered something very, very important.

Something that could turn the tides.

"One of the tourists will realize they can attack you," Reyna said, mostly to distract him.

The fact was, the tourists had gone oddly silent, just like Kianthe. They slumped over each other at the edge of the clearing, appearing half-dead already. Albert cast an appraising glance at them, mostly bemused. "My dear, they're already down for the count. Old alchemy trick—an unconscious sacrifice is far less likely to injure the alchemist."

Reyna smirked.

Albert squinted at her. "You're awfully smug for someone trapped outside the action."

"Albert, I'm only smug when I'm about to win." Reyna slid her hand into her pocket, finding the piece she'd almost forgotten: the portal spell she'd stolen from Albert that morning. Pre-powered, he'd said. Ready to go. With her sword in hand, she put that to the test . . . and slammed it on the magical wall.

A flash of crimson light, and a neat hole appeared in the circle, large enough to allow Reyna admittance.

Albert's eyes widened, and he took a nervous step back.

It wouldn't save him.

The portal closed behind Reyna. She narrowed her eyes, swinging her sword into a proper attack stance. The movement was a dance, as easy as breathing, and everything in her body hummed in anticipation of the fight ahead.

"Let's be clear about something. I'm not trapped out there. *You're* trapped in *here*."

24

Kianthe

Everything hurt.

Like, *everything*.

Kianthe sometimes had headaches—migraines, Matild called them—where her eyeballs felt like they were being hollowed out with a spoon. This was exactly like that, except instead of her eyeballs, it was her *entire body*, and instead of a spoon, it was a red-hot fire poker fresh out of the hearth.

Okay, so it wasn't exactly like a migraine, but close enough.

It was shockingly dark, and eventually Kianthe realized it was because her eyes were closed. That was a bad thing, because—well, because of something. She swallowed a groan and pried open an eyelid, squinting at the ground in front of her nose. Dirt, ash, snow, and . . . crimson light, emanating from a circle.

Alchemy.

Fuck.

Somewhere in the distance, she heard a man—Albert?—shout, and the swish of a blade cutting air. Normally, the air would be complaining to her about that, but everything felt still. Her body echoed with the loss of communication, as if the elements couldn't reach her, as if the Stone of Seeing itself had forsaken her.

The world was quiet . . . and it *sucked*.

"Kianthe, you have to get up." Reyna's sharp voice pierced through her haze. She sounded winded, and a clanging of metal echoed. Albert must have found something to protect himself. That nearly made Kianthe laugh, except it turned into a groan that sent pain to her fingertips in radiating waves.

"*Key!*"

"What?" Kianthe tried to cough. Even she could barely hear herself.

Shit. She had to get a grip. If she succumbed to this, Reyna would be fighting alone against the strongest alchemist alive. She was excellent with a sword, but all he'd have to use was a slap of alchemy, and—

Reyna swallowed a cry, and a pathetic mimicry of a fireball crisped the air.

Yeah. That. Kianthe clenched her jaw, forcing herself to focus. Her fingers curled in the dirt, and she fumbled for the edge of the circle. Alchemy couldn't be disrupted without disrupting the circle at large.

In the past, she'd just swallowed the circles whole, sinking them deep into the earth, but Albert had clearly altered this spell into something more dangerous. Like in the Magicary, there didn't seem to be an upper or lower limit to this draining spell. But Kianthe had moved the dust and air inside it just fine, which meant she *did* still have elemental magic—although it was fading fast.

Based on the ringing in her ears, she had one shot at this.

With a pull of magic, she shaped a rock out of the ground. It was barely the size of her fist, cut with jagged edges, but it was something. Lifting her hand felt like a gargantuan effort, but she found the edge of the circle trapping her . . . and began drawing in the dirt.

"I heard you were terrifying with a blade. It's a fascinating reputation for a queen." Albert grunted, and that clang of metal on metal echoed again. A shuffle of footsteps. Kianthe wanted to see if Reyna was okay, but any intense movement would probably render her unconscious at this point.

Pain screamed through her, getting harder to ignore.

Albert chuckled breathily. "Probably shouldn't have picked a fight in here, though. Draining spell is still active."

"Somehow, I'll survive." Reyna's voice was weary, but still fierce.

In the next moment, a wet, squelching sound slid through space. A man's sharp, shaking inhale, followed by the quiet *tip-tip-tip* of blood. Kianthe didn't need to look up to know what had happened. She methodically carved into the dirt, praying to the Stone and the Stars that this would work.

"Now. Free my wife." Reyna's voice was quiet, promising pain far worse than any acts she'd committed.

Albert laughed, a gurgling sound. "L-Lesson two. Never m-make an alchemist bleed."

Around them, the big circle flared crimson. A new wave of pain swelled through Kianthe, cutting off all thoughts, blinding her long enough that she only *barely* heard her wife scream. The ringing in her ears intensified until she was screaming too, and her body acted on instinct.

A squiggly symbol trapped in a circle, up against the circle that trapped her. The rock, nudged into its center, a power conduit to siphon all of her drained magic. Her finger, resting on one sharp corner of the rock.

A final jerk of her hand.

And—a drop of—blood—

Blessed silence.

This was the thing about alchemy. It always originated from existing magic. Siphoning her power into a stone meant channeling it into the earth itself—and that meant all the power that Albert drained from Kianthe went . . . right back *into* Kianthe.

In the span of a few drops of blood, every ache vanished, and bright yellow magic flooded into her. It was warmth and happiness and comfort, and it reinvigorated her with a breath.

Every alchemist was once an elemental mage, after all.

Even more, her alteration of Albert's trapping circle meant its original purpose was moot. When she tested the magical wall, her hand slid right through it. And it *burned* on the other side. She withdrew immediately, eyes widening as she assessed the scene outside her own immediate vicinity.

Alchemy was pulsing, the ground colored crimson with magic and blood. The tourists were writhing in their sleep, and Reyna—*Reyna*—

She had Albert in an iron grip that seemed to be fading fast. Her wife's jaw was clenched, her skin pale, and her sword had fallen to the side. But she seemed determined to hold on to him, even as her eyes flickered to Kianthe.

"S-Smart girl." Albert was on the ground, clutching a wound in his chest, but he still grinned past bloody lips. "Attach to m-me, and avoid their f-fate."

Reyna tightened her grip, fingernails digging into Albert's arm. "You can avoid their fate, too. Stop the spell."

Albert waved a hand. "F-Far too late."

And he went slack.

"Rain," Kianthe gasped, surging forward. "I can—"

"*Don't* move, Key."

Kianthe stopped short, recoiling back into her now-harmless circle. Her finger was the only thing still throbbing, and she pressed the bleeding scrape against her cloak. "The circle—"

"It's going to kill them. Me, too, if we can't get the dragons to disrupt it." Reyna shuddered, clenching her eyes shut. "Kianthe, if I die here—"

"If you finish that sentence, Rain, I might kill you myself." Kianthe whistled sharply, craning toward the sky. Where the *hells* were those dragons? Where were Visk and Ponder?

Reyna swallowed a gasp. "Key, *please*. L-Last time alchemy almost killed me, I didn't get to s-say anything."

A flash of light in Arlon's dim basement. Reyna's body collapsing in a heap.

She hadn't even had time to scream.

"I love you too, okay," Kianthe snapped, anxious energy bringing tears to her eyes. She paced the circle like a caged animal, feeling the ground, running options. Maybe she could drag Reyna into the circle—but it wasn't just *Reyna* who needed saving. Albert was still. Dead? Impossible to say.

Kianthe dug her hands into her hair. "I love you so, so much. I met your gaze in that throne room and I *knew* you were the most spectacular person alive. Everything you do makes me happy. I want to be near you all the time—it doesn't even matter what we're doing. We could be shopping for manure, and it'd be the greatest day I've ever had."

Reyna snorted, fumbling in Al's pockets. Maybe looking for a spell they could use. But Kianthe knew it wouldn't work fast enough. Reyna's voice was faint. "Of course you'd l-love shopping for manure."

"Look, if an elemental mage needs manure, they're a pretty shitty mage."

"Puns? *Now?*"

"I'm not sorry." Kianthe pressed a hand to the ground. They were out of time. The dragons weren't here yet, and the last conversation she'd have with her wife would *not* be about feces. "Brace yourself; I'm going to try something."

Without waiting for a reply, Kianthe shoved elemental magic into the ground. Oddly enough, the stone at her feet pulsed with her . . . almost like a second, smaller Stone of Seeing. Then Albert's spell could work. Ley lines or no, she felt as good as she did inside the Magicary. The new stone collected magic from the very essence of the earth, feeding it into Kianthe until she could move mountains.

So, she did.

Literally.

With a swell of magic, the ground rippled at her feet. The bigger alchemy circle was unpassable, but that only mattered as long as the rest of the ground remained stabilized. She shifted the clearing into a hill, and as the bloodstained rocks tumbled away, the red glow flickered—and vanished.

For good measure, Kianthe wrenched her hands to slice the clearing in half. A jagged crevice groaned into existence, sucking the circle into the earth. Knapsacks and the firepit careened deep underground, but Kianthe twisted the crevice away from any humans or animals. Only once the crimson glow of alchemy faded did Kianthe clap her hands back together, snapping the crevice closed, buttoning up the earth so nothing else could fall in.

The clearing was a disaster now, but everyone was safe. The crackle of alchemy faded, and when Kianthe tested the space outside her circle, it wasn't hot anymore.

Thank the Stone—and the little stone, she supposed. Without wasting time, Kianthe scooped Reyna into her arms. Her wife was already regaining awareness, coughing, her skin clammy and cold.

"Alchemy is the worst," Reyna wheezed.

"Only when it's used like this," Kianthe said, pressing her forehead to her wife's. Safe. She was alive, and safe, and they'd be fine.

Albert might not be. The Alchemicor was still breathing, if shuddering rasps counted as such. For a brief, vindictive moment, Kianthe thought: *Pity.* She tugged from her secondary stone to gather the magic she needed, and encased him in a prison of rock, just as she had with Tilaine over the summer. Then she pulled Reyna a few feet from him, just for good measure.

"You'll be all right?" Kianthe pressed a fast kiss to Reyna's lips, reveling in her strengthening heartbeat, the blush color flooding back into her cheeks.

"Just fine." Reyna pushed herself away from Kianthe, bracing herself on the ground as she coughed. "Check on the tourists, love."

Right. Kianthe jogged over to them, stepping over the mounds of dirt and jagged rocks formed by her magic. The tourists were exactly where they'd collapsed. There were too many of them—eight, at least, maybe ten—to check individually. Instead, Kianthe spread her magic over them, listening for the air moving through their lungs, the blood flowing through their veins.

It took a minute to identify, but every single body had a heartbeat. And the longer she watched, the more they shifted, groaning, collecting themselves from the ordeal. Matild would still have to check them over, but at least they were alive. Thank the Stone itself.

Kianthe stepped back to Reyna, helping her to her feet. Her wife was unsteady, but she still retrieved her bloodied sword, wiping it on her cloak.

"Is it over?" Reyna sounded doubtful, and Kianthe couldn't blame her.

This seemed . . . easy.

"Albert. *Albert.* Is this over?" Kianthe patted the man's cheek. "I know you're breathing. Are you conscious?"

"Dear, I had to stab him—"

"—*mrf*," Albert groaned.

Reyna cleared her throat. "Ah. Never mind."

"Is this over?" Kianthe repeated, irritation seeping into her tone. "We'll get you medical help, but only if you tell us whether there's another circle somewhere waiting to murder people."

Albert took several moments to come to—and when he did, it was in obvious pain. He grimaced, prying open his eyes. His gaze was hazy, distant, and he stared at the storm clouds overhead, at the stars that glimmered through a few sparing breaks. "D-Did they die? Th-Those tourists."

"No. Lucky for you, they'll be fine." Kianthe crossed her arms.

Albert processed that. Frustration and sadness shifted into calm acceptance. When he spoke, it was with a distant, determined tone.

"I c-can still fix it."

Kianthe stared in confusion. At her side, Reyna tensed—but even she couldn't intervene in time. Albert lifted his hand, and Kianthe barely had time to see the alchemical sigil in his palm before he slapped it on his chest. A flash of light burst from the parchment.

His body shuddered, then went eerily still.

He didn't even have time to scream.

"Oh, Gods." Reyna rocked back on her heels, covering her mouth.

Kianthe felt sick. She surged to her feet, stepping several feet away from the body of the Alchemicor. Her eyes scanned the perimeter, mostly because it was easier than looking at Albert's corpse. "His circle was destroyed. *Why* would he still sacrifice—"

She didn't finish it. A griffon's screech echoed through the air.

And around them, the world began to glow crimson.

25

Reyna

He'd killed himself and activated an even larger alchemy circle in the process. Gods, he was serious when he said he didn't care about legacy. Or perhaps he cared *too* much about it—perhaps this was the culmination of his entire life's work.

Even dead, Albert had a ghost of a smile on his lips.

But whatever he'd activated, it was big, dangerous, and expansive. The horses in the edge of the clearing reared—the magic that unsettled them before now had them ready to bolt, and they wrenched against their halters.

The tourists had mostly climbed to their feet, and they stared in horror at the distant crimson glow that seemed to encompass half of dragon country. The draining spell wasn't over them, not quite, but it was close enough that Reyna wasn't willing to test it.

"Get your horses and ride south," she shouted at the tourists. "*Now.*"

They had enough awareness to recognize her tone, to pair it with what just happened. With various screams, they towed whoever was still waking up toward the horses. The animals seemed thrilled to be mounted, stamping their hooves and watching the clearing with wide eyes.

Good. If those horses ran fast and hard, *maybe* those people would survive this.

Kianthe wasn't watching the tourists. Instead, she pulled Reyna back a few feet, allowing space for two griffons to thump beside Albert's body.

Feo barely spared the old Alchemicor a glance. They held out a hand, adjusting their weight so they didn't tip off Visk. "Mount up! We're out of time!"

Reyna had never been so grateful to see another alchemist.

Kianthe also took Feo's presence in stride. She leapt onto Visk behind them, nudging her griffon into the air. "Come on, Rain!"

Reyna slid onto Ponder's back, noting how the young griffon shifted in agitation, eagle eyes wide with panic. It spiked anxiety in Reyna's own chest, even as the creatures took to the sky. *Something* had happened, and she wouldn't know what until they got a better view.

"What are you doing here?" Kianthe asked over the roaring wind. Reyna could barely hear her.

Feo hunkered down, shifting with Visk's powerful wing-beats. The wind was cutting, and overhead the dark clouds had started to snow. Any glimmer of the stars was gone now. "Visk kidnapped me again. But at least this time, it's for good reason. Look."

They had enough altitude now to see what Feo meant. Dragon country spread below them, marred by a glowing crimson circle four times as large as Tawney. If Kianthe's recent prison had been a drop of water in a lake, *this* circle was the ocean. Worse, it was fully active—Albert clearly had intended to sacrifice the tourists and see the result to fruition, but apparently his death held enough power. Sharp crimson threads pulled from his body into the larger circle, fueling it with his intention.

And trapped inside were the three baby dragons: Gold Coin, Pill Bug, and Blue Spruce.

"They were flying to you two when the circle activated. I watched it happen," Feo called over the wind, fury in their tone. "What the hells was Albert trying to do?"

"No time for that. We have to help," Reyna snapped.

Ponder screeched a plea, begging her friends to escape. But

the young dragons had been grounded with invisible ropes, and despite their best efforts, they couldn't seem to take flight. As Reyna watched, two adult dragons plunged into the circle to help—and were instantly sucked inside. They also crashed to the ground, and didn't get back up.

From this high above, she could see the circle's intent: a fully perfected draining spell, with the add-on siphoning symbol near the dragons' mountains. There were a few alterations, such as the tourists' circle, and Kianthe's smaller one inside that.

Feo pointed at a secondary circle rimming the inside of the main one. "He's stacking symbols, which is both stupid and *fucking* brilliant. That interior circle is likely why the dragons are trapped inside. If you look even closer to the baby drag-ons, he used a tethering circle—the kind we usually pull out to wrangle wild griffons at the Magicary. There could be dozens of contingencies in this spell."

Then the draining circle was only the beginning. Reyna shuddered, attributing her sudden chill to the wind and snow. The other dragons seemed to realize rescue was futile, because furious roars echoed across the landscape. They wouldn't at-tempt the same thing twice.

It didn't mean they were happy about it.

"Can we stop it? Disrupt the circle, like you did in the clear-ing?" Reyna's voice was desperate.

Inside the circle, Pill Bug roared feebly, collapsing in a heap over Gold Coin. Blue Spruce seemed to be faring slightly better, and it stood guard over its new siblings—but even its body lan-guage belied its exhaustion.

Kianthe grimaced as Visk banked around the outer edge of the alchemical circle. She sounded devastated. "I don't think I have enough magic. I used up the tiny stone I made disrupt-ing the *last* circle. I'd need the Stone of Seeing itself to cut into something this big."

Reyna wasn't sure what she meant by "tiny stone," but it was a question for another time.

Feo, meanwhile, straightened on Visk's back, shielding their eyes from the onslaught of wind. "It doesn't need to be a big cut, Kianthe. Just enough to disrupt the main circle's connection with its power source."

Albert.

Kianthe didn't look happy about that, but there wasn't an alternative. "Okay. Find something else if this doesn't work, Rain. Feo, you're with me."

"Considering we're sharing a griffon, that's correct," Feo replied sarcastically. Before Kianthe could retort, Visk curved into a graceful dive, falling away from Reyna and Ponder. They disappeared into the snowstorm, angling back toward Albert's body.

Ponder hesitated, clearly torn between following her father and the dragons trapped in the circle. Reyna made the decision for her, urging her higher instead. "We need to reach the other dragons! Find me someone I can talk to, Ponder."

With that mission in mind, Ponder surged upward, beating her wings hard enough that Reyna's stomach flipped. She bent low over her griffon's back as they shot across the sky, skirting the circle to reach the twisting mass of dragons soaring over their mountain range.

Ponder screeched, catching their attention.

One of the dragons roared and peeled away from the horde filling the sky. In a few beats, the dragon drew even with them, its head beside Ponder, its huge wings beating rhythmically behind them.

Little queen, it said, with an urgent tone tinged in fury. *Our youth are injured and fading. We are unfamiliar with this tainted magic. What can we do?*

There was nothing more unnerving than one of her deities asking for advice. Cold determination filled Reyna's soul, and she racked her brain.

Kianthe had been trapped in a similar circle, but managed to escape on her own. From what Reyna had seen, she'd used alchemy to disrupt alchemy—but the dragons said that this was tainted magic. A cheap derivative of their own. If that was true . . .

"Look at the circle. The *language* of it. Are there any weak spots?"

The dragon cast a discerning glance at the circle. Inside, even Blue Spruce had collapsed to the ground, just like the tourists in the smaller clearing. The adults seemed to be faring better, but only slightly. They crawled through the magic as if they were trudging through a swamp, and their roars were swallowed by the circle.

The dragon beat its wings, growling. *It is, regrettably, a fairer imitation than expected.*

If this was Albert's life's work—if he was as much a recluse as everyone said, if he'd been as cunning as Reyna suspected—it was no wonder. He'd likely run every contingency to prepare for this. She'd have to visit the space below Tawney's burnt church again, but she suspected even *that* circle was an early rendition of this final product.

If Albert had been testing draining and siphoning spells for decades, it was obvious who'd hired those bandits to steal eggs from the dragons in the first place. Albert must have been in contact with Arlon decades ago, using his influence and prestige to persuade the diarn into theft.

All for this moment.

Of course, it couldn't be as easy as a misspelled word.

"The circle's purpose is to drain your magic and channel it into a stone. Identical to the one the elemental mages use inside the Magicary." Reyna processed her thoughts aloud, speaking fast. Wind whipped past her hair, and her nose was running from the cold. She scanned the edges of the circle, hunting for the siphoning spell.

And—there. She was right. Albert must have found the stone the dragon had created when Reyna visited that morning. Somehow, he'd drawn a sigil in the snow, carved his mark into the earth around that unnatural, dragon-made boulder.

That stone was huge, meant as more of a demonstration than anything usable. If Kianthe's descriptions were correct, it'd put the Stone of Seeing to shame. But then again, Albert probably hadn't been looking to re-create the Stone of Seeing perfectly.

"There!" She pointed at it. "Their magic is being siphoned into that boulder. If we destroy it—"

The circle remains. This magic cannot be interrupted, and our youth may be permanently harmed. The dragon angled for the stone, and Ponder scrambled to keep pace. The dragon spoke again in Reyna's mind, contemplative now. *But perhaps . . . if we overload it . . .*

Overloading it. Of course! "Even the Stone of Seeing distributes its magic through the ley lines, Kianthe, and the other mages." Reyna's heart pounded, exhilaration sweeping through her soul at a mystery solved. "It never holds all of that magic at once."

Precisely. Magic is every living thing. A rock alone cannot hold the power of our entire horde.

Kianthe had altered her circle somehow, and her magic was powerful enough to eliminate the alchemy. If a bigger circle like this were overloaded with dragon magic, maybe it could be stopped.

But . . .

"That sounds risky. What happens if it doesn't work?" Albert could have planned for that contingency, after all.

The dragon again analyzed the circle, its symbols, its language. *I see nothing that implies it won't. And we cannot slow time around our youth forever.*

Reyna hadn't even realized they were slowing time, but that would explain why the snow seemed to be hovering, rather than pelting. "Be careful." She whispered the words, and wasn't sure the dragon heard.

You as well. The dragon erupted in a fearsome, bone-breaking roar, summoning the horde. As one, all the dragons over the mountains turned toward the alchemy circle, roaring their own approval of whatever plan it had just conveyed. The dragon talking to her paused in its flight, wings beating as it surveyed the crimson circle. *Stay here, little queen. If this does not work, we'll need help.*

Ponder slowed, eyes widening. Reyna carefully gripped her feathers, jaw clenched, shivering in the cold.

With another commanding growl, the dragons began diving into the alchemical circle.

It pulsed, its crimson glow brightening with every dragon that entered. The glow became a flash as dozens, then hundreds, of dragons landed in the circle. The space was mostly large enough to hold them all, but a few crashed into each other, and several surrounded the baby dragons to protect their still forms. As one, all the dragons began emanating a soft blue glow. It deepened until it was almost purple, then brightened until the light was absolutely blinding.

Reyna watched as long as she could, until the intensity of it burned and she had to cover her eyes and Ponder's. When she blinked past tears, the crimson glow was gone. Whatever power had echoed across the landscape cleared the snowstorm, and the clouds thinned to reveal a starry night and bright moon.

By their mountain, the dragon-made stone went dark. Inert. It worked.

Far below, the dragons were recovering. Many of them took to the sky, and a few more approached the baby dragons. Blue Spruce was the first to recover, and it helped Gold Coin stand. Pill Bug shook itself off like a wet dog, wings flapping. None of them appeared harmed now that the alchemy was gone.

Reyna craned her head to find Kianthe in the darkness—but at that moment, a loud *CRACK* cut across the landscape. It sounded like the mountain north of Winterhaven being split apart, but somehow *louder*. Ponder dropped several feet in surprise, making Reyna inhale sharply and grip her tighter. The rest of the dragons took to the air, and three grabbed the baby dragons in case they couldn't fly yet.

"Find out what that was, Ponder," Reyna said, fearing for Kianthe.

Her griffon understood, and dove like a falling arrow, weaving between dragons to reach the western side of the alchemy circle.

And sure enough, there were Kianthe and Feo, standing at the edge of Albert's smaller power circle. Kianthe was perched inside a new alchemy circle, gasping for breath. At her feet, a small rock glowed bright yellow. Blood streamed down Feo's arm. They gripped the wound with their cloak, but laughed in satisfaction.

The ground before them had been split apart, forming a massive crevice that gaped into darkness. It must be deeper than Albert's circle was wide, and it shattered any remains of the draining spell. Albert's body was gone, swallowed by the earth.

Kianthe wasn't done. The circle at her feet shone, bathing her in crimson light, even as she glowed a fierce yellow. She lifted her hands, and as Reyna watched, the earth churned, tracing Albert's circle like a mole tunneling below ground. It swept away from Kianthe in two lines, converging on the far end of the plains, near the dragon-made stone.

When the rumbling ceased, there was no physical sign of Albert's circle at all. No one would ever be able to re-create it—not unless they'd seen it while it was active.

Kianthe dropped her hands as Ponder touched down beside Visk. "Stone and *Stars,* that was awesome." Kianthe stared at the crevice, at her own hands, swaying a bit. The rock at her feet faded into a dull gray from its previous magical yellow. She considered it, then laughed and offered Feo a high five. Feo stared at her raised hand, then lifted their own bloody arm with a deadpan expression.

Kianthe sheepishly tucked her hands in her cloak instead. "Right. Well, nice idea. Never would have thought of a boosting circle for my magic. You might have just solved the ley line issue in Tawney."

"Allow me to contain my enthusiasm," Feo drawled.

Reyna slid off her griffon, running over to Kianthe. Unlike the last alchemy circle she'd been trapped in, her wife stepped out of this one easily. And she didn't seem exhausted. In fact, she appeared invigorated.

"Did you see that, Rain?" she asked, sweeping Reyna into a hug.

Reyna laughed delightedly, then separated to glance at Feo. "How did it work?"

Feo nudged the small rock with their boot, sounding almost proud. "Kianthe created a portable conduit when she was trapped before. The right kind of circle, perfected with language to boost magical impact, allowed her to connect it directly to the Stone of Seeing."

"It worked before, but I used up the energy stopping Albert. Feo's circle . . . renewed it?" Kianthe plucked the stone off the ground, examining it. "We definitely drained it again, though."

"Well, don't look at me. I've donated enough blood today," Feo grumbled, letting Reyna tie a tight bandage around the cut on their arm.

The dragons were starting to clear out overhead, but this reminded Reyna of another problem. The tourists and their horses were gone—hopefully back to Tawney by now—and Albert had vanished into the earth. Reyna mounted Ponder again, gesturing for Kianthe and Feo to follow on Visk.

"That reminds me. There's something you might need to see."

Kianthe slid onto Visk, offering Feo a choice. The alchemist gauged the two of them and reluctantly slid onto Visk's back, likely because the griffon was older and stronger.

"Follow me," Reyna said, and clicked her tongue to get Ponder flying again. The pair of griffons cut across the landscape, and it allowed Reyna to see exactly *how big* that new crevice was. She wondered if Kianthe would repair it eventually, or if it'd be left as a warning—an added barrier to dragon country.

The dragons had mostly cleared out now, returning at their own paces back to their mountain range. The ones who'd plucked the babies off the ground had released them, and Gold Coin and Pill Bug soared over to say hello to Ponder. They seemed wobbly in the air, but grumbled in conversation as they matched Ponder's pace. She chittered with them, clearly pleased that they were all right.

Visk fell back to give them space, which seemed like a huge relief to Feo. Kianthe rolled her eyes and shouted, "We'll catch up, Rain."

It was a welcome reprieve, and for a moment, it seemed like time slowed again. Blue Spruce drew even with Reyna on the opposite side. She glanced at it, brows knitted.

Okay?

The young dragon puffed smoke. *Safe in horde. Home.* And comforting warmth slid between their connection. *Resting now.*

With a roar, it beckoned its siblings. Pill Bug followed first, and Gold Coin circled Ponder in a smooth arc before peeling away too. Any apprehension the youngest dragons still felt for Blue Spruce seemed to have vanished in the alchemy circle, after Spruce had protected them.

Everything was okay.

Ponder chirped goodbye to her dragon friends. Or maybe it was a promise, or an apology. They watched the creatures fly home, and then Ponder refocused on the task at hand, landing lithely beside the massive stone.

Maybe her griffon was growing up after all.

Reyna dismounted, relief settling in her bones, heavy as exhaustion. Today had been so, so very long. Just one more thing to address, and then they could go home and have a cup of tea.

Visk landed nearby, and Reyna wasted no time stepping to him. Feo slid off the griffon, rolling their shoulders. Kianthe swallowed a yawn and didn't dismount, instead leaning her arms on Visk's head. The griffon didn't seem to mind.

"And here I thought you'd avoided a magic drain?" Reyna's words verged on teasing, but her fingers feathered along Kianthe's arm.

"Mostly." Kianthe offered a wry smile. "I'm just tired of standing in snow. My boots are wet enough."

The dragon Reyna usually communicated with landed beside them, tilting its head at Kianthe. Its tone was questioning inside Reyna's mind. *Is the mage suffering again? I can offer some magic.*

"That wasn't the fix you intended, before." Reyna's tone was gentle, almost embarrassed to be clarifying. "Besides, she was seared with alchemy. She can't absorb dragon magic anymore, even if she tried."

Kianthe rested her chin on Visk's head. The griffon seemed to take his position as Kianthe's chair seriously, because he straightened to ensure it was comfortable for her. "Please, Stone and Stars, no more dragon magic. I'm just tired. It's been a *day*."

The dragon's tail swished, its tone almost amused. *Indeed.*

Feo, meanwhile, had stepped to the huge boulder. The earth Kianthe had upturned made the journey to the stone rather treacherous, and it was almost funny to watch Feo climbing the mound of loose dirt. "All of *that* was to make another Stone?" Derision filtered into their tone, but they still squinted at the boulder, as if weighing whether the idea had merit.

"He named it the Stone of Sawing." Kianthe swelled, inordinately pleased.

The look Feo shot her was one of pure exasperation. "Albert would never have called it that."

"No? You don't think that sounds like Al Chemicor, the *Alchemicor*?" Kianthe repeated, a sly grin crossing her features.

Feo rolled their eyes, not deigning to respond.

The dragon, meanwhile, paced around the huge stone. After a few moments, it seemed to have learned what it needed. Its tail swished, and it folded its wings resolutely. *If the tainted mage was attempting to create a conduit to purer magic, it worked.*

Reyna must have misheard. "Excuse me?"

This stone. The dragon tapped it with a claw, and a ripple of purple magic emanated from the point of contact. *It did indeed capture a piece of our magic. Small enough that we will not miss it, but perhaps large enough that your tainted mages can purify themselves.*

Now the dragon's eyes locked on Feo's.

Feo had been stepping down the loose dirt, desperate to put distance between themself and the dragon, but now that they had the creature's attention, they stilled. "Ah, Reyna," Feo said mildly, their tone belying fear. "Why is it looking at me?"

Reyna's heart thumped, and she stared at the diarn too. Her words were breathless. "Try some alchemy, Feo. Draw a circle."

Kianthe perked up. "No fucking way."

Feo, meanwhile, huffed. "I am not some show pony—"

"*Feo,*" Reyna begged.

With a scowl, Feo cautiously moved from the stone, the dragon, the griffons. They moved to untie the bandage around their arm, but Reyna stopped them. "Not with blood. Not with a sacrifice."

"So, you merely wish to see a doodle in the snow." But Feo's interest had been piqued, now, and they cast a glance at the huge boulder nearby. With little fanfare, they bent down and drew a tiny circle in the snow. Barely bigger than Reyna's hand, barely big enough for the dragon to see. Feo analyzed the symbols, sighed, and tapped it with emphasis.

And from their fingers, a flower sprouted from the ground, pushing snow aside and stretching purple petals toward the stars.

Kianthe sucked in air and repeated, "No fucking way."

Satisfaction slid through Reyna's veins. "Albert's sacrifice wasn't in vain after all. It might not have happened the way he hoped, but . . . he got his Stone."

"The Stone of Sawing," Kianthe said in wonder, glancing again at the boulder.

"Absolutely not," Feo replied, but a smile tilted their lips. Like a kid over the Mid-Winter Celebration, they bounced to a clean section of snow and drew another circle, tapping it resolutely. Nothing happened this time.

"One and done?" Reyna asked doubtfully.

"Hardly. I can feel its power now. The language connects to the Stone's core magic, anywhere a circle is drawn. It pairs with my own intention. Flawless." With obvious satisfaction, Feo tossed a handful of snow into the new circle. The moment the snow reached it—it froze in midair, hovering.

No, it wasn't hovering. It *was* moving, albeit very, very slowly. Time magic.

The dragon rumbled again, clearly amused. *Our youth will be learning these spells soon. Your mage is free to join their lessons.*

The implication was clear: Feo's display was child's magic. Reyna swallowed a laugh. "Thank you. We'll remember that."

Feo, meanwhile, had trounced to the Stone again, pressing a hand to its rough surface. On connection, it glowed deep blue, almost purple. They pulled away, almost giddy now, and clapped their hands together.

"Well, that settles it. I will assume the title of Alchemicor."

That redirected Kianthe's attention. She shoved over Visk, causing the griffon to squawk in protest. "*Excuse* you. There was a whole tournament in the Magicary to determine the next Alchemicor."

"And now he's dead, and the tournament is over." Feo lifted their chin.

"You can't just—" Kianthe spluttered. "That title means—"

Feo quirked an eyebrow, patting the new Stone, grinning at every flare of magic. "Your rock chose you. I'm starting to feel a connection with this one." Their tone grew insufferable, even for Reyna. "Or will you, an elemental mage, speak for our Stone? I'm fairly sure that's blasphemous. *Imagine* if an alchemical mage attempted the same for your Stone of Seeing."

Kianthe was left speechless. She gaped at Feo, at the new Stone, then finally at Reyna. "*Do* something."

Reyna heaved a sigh, patting her wife's shoulder. "You said yourself if Feo bothered to attend the Showdown, they'd take the title. And after they helped you channel your magic . . . I think they're free to do what's best for all future alchemists."

Kianthe swallowed her retorts, which only made Feo swell with smug pride.

Reyna turned back to the dragon, who'd watched this entire exchange with curiosity. "Are you positive this won't negatively impact your horde's magical reserves?"

If the elemental mage's conduit didn't interfere, it's doubtful that this one will. The dragon shook out its wings, like a full-bodied sigh of contentment. *Although I'd prefer it does not remain on our—what is the human equivalent . . . ? A front porch?*

Reyna snorted. "We'll move it. But if you can give us some time to decide where, that'd be ideal."

It gestured at the circle with the frozen snow. *As you can see, time means little to us. Take however much you need, little queen. Thank you for your help.* And the dragon spread its massive wings. With a nod at Reyna and barely a glance at the new Stone, it leapt into the skies, following its horde-mates back into the mountains.

26

Kianthe

Eight days later, New Leaf Tomes and Tea hosted an "Oh, Fantastic, We Aren't Closing After All!" party. It was the talk of the town, and so many Tawneans attended that they had to spread into the road to accommodate. The sky was clear and a fresh snowfall glimmered, and three massive bonfires kept folks warm.

"I can't believe you actually called it that," Matild said drily, gesturing with her mug at the linen banner displayed over their barn door. The party's title had been painted in meticulous handwriting, which meant the banner itself was ridiculously long.

Kianthe tossed one arm over Reyna's shoulders. "Well, *I* pitched 'Grand Tea-Opening.'"

The barn was packed, so much that they'd set up multiple tea stations for self-serve. Gossley flitted around checking tea blends and explaining steeping times, handing out sand-filled timers. Several folks perused their newly stocked bookshelves. Warm chatter settled over the barn like a blanket, and every once in a while, a gust of icy wind would slide through the open barn doors.

A smile spread across Kianthe's lips. "Get it? 'Grand Tea-

Opening'?" At Matild's blank stare, Kianthe clarified: "Come on. Like a *re*opening, but better!"

Reyna's cheeks were tinged pink from the wine, and she laughed freely. "I had to remind her that we never *technically* closed, so a reopening—tea or otherwise—is inaccurate."

"Yes. Stone forbid our party banner is inaccurate," Kianthe drawled. When Reyna shoved her shoulder, Kianthe laughed, plucking Reyna's wineglass from her hands and kissing her fiercely. Their eyes met as they pulled apart, and Kianthe was struck with a swell of happiness. Reyna's light brown eyes glimmered, shining from the flickering ever-flame in the rafters above. Gorgeous.

Matild cleared her throat. The pair glanced back at her, and the midwife raised an eyebrow. "I was told there'd be *alcoholic* tea."

That seemed to snap Reyna from her daze. She straightened, clumsily extracting herself from Kianthe's arms. "It's an experiment," she said, trouncing to the counter. Reyna didn't *trounce,* but apparently the wine had hit. "Black tea with lemon, honey, and *rum*." She whispered the last part like a promise.

"Hells yes." Matild grinned, following her.

Kianthe almost followed them, and then . . . didn't.

It was a beautiful disconnect, where she became a mere observer of this perfect moment. Her lovely wife, demonstrating her passion to their best friend. Their neighbors—their family— all around, laughing and drinking and reading and relaxing. Sigmund handed a book to Nurt, tapping the cover resolutely. Ralund and his wife cozied in a corner table, whispering to each other. Patol heaved another jar of honey onto the counter for Reyna. Outside, Hansen was playing the lute, and music wafted through the open door.

This was all Kianthe ever wanted. She leaned against one of the bookcases, imagining what her child self would think if she saw this now. All those years struggling to belong, ghosting through the Magicary's halls without a plan or a friend . . . and then she grew up, and with careful determination and a bit of luck, Kianthe cultivated a gorgeous life.

The Stone of Seeing's magic meant nothing compared to the warmth of love and friendship.

"You're feeling sappy, aren't you?" Fauston stepped up to her, smirking over a mug of cider. Her oldest friend looked fantastic, dressed in Queendom attire—sharp colors, tight fabrics—instead of the farm wear of Jallin.

Kianthe snorted. "I'm an elemental mage. I'm always sappy."

"Cute."

"Thanks." She winked.

Fauston leaned against the wall beside her, surveying the crowd. His eyes landed on James and Tessalyn, and he lowered his mug. "There are days where I miss Jallin. The smell of a fresh harvest, the swell of the waves on a quiet night. I didn't think I'd ever be brave enough to leave home."

She understood that, too. When she left the Magicary, she missed its towering hallways, the plants in every corner, the views out every window. She missed the comfort of her favorite library, that back reading room with the comfy bean sacks. She missed the structure that came from formal education—knowing exactly how her days would progress, even if they were peppered with bullying and magical failure.

There was a comfort in *knowing*. Even if what she knew was mediocre at best, well . . . at least it was predictable.

"Were you scared to leave?" Fauston asked, tilting his head.

"Jallin? Or the Magicary?"

Fauston considered. "Both."

"Yeah." Kianthe lifted the mug of tea from his hands, took a sip. Green tea. A nice, calming option. She handed it back with a shrug. "Leaving what we know is always a risk. But I think we're a lot braver than we know . . . and I think most choices turn out okay, eventually."

"That's a nice thought." Fauston smiled.

They lapsed into silence. Hansen handed off the lute to his

wife, who started a brighter jig. Outside, Tarly swept Matild—alcoholic tea in hand—into a spinning dance that had her laughing. From the armchairs by the fire, Sasua craned over the backrest to watch through the doors. She caught Reyna's eye, and raised her own glass in cheers.

Reyna smiled back, then offered a mug to Venne. The lead Queensguard took a sip, made a face, and handed the mug back. Even across the barn, Kianthe could hear him spluttering that Reyna would dare offer a spiked beverage while he was on duty. She laughed and shoved his arm good-naturedly.

"Do you think you're going to marry James?" Kianthe asked.

"Maybe. Eventually." Fauston laughed slightly. "Our cat would probably be happy. Tough to tell with her, sometimes." A pause, a genuine query: "Do you think you're going to have kids?"

Once upon a time, the idea of kids would have made Kianthe cringe. She hadn't been able to take care of a litter of kittens, much less a child. But now they had a beautiful home and a solid relationship. She and Reyna had tackled sovereigns, pirates, dragons, and everything in between.

A kid might be kind of cute, actually.

"I think so. Reyna will, most likely—or we'll adopt. I doubt a royal bloodline matters much now that Reyna is queen, but we'd have to talk about it." Kianthe slid her hands into the pockets of her cloak, rocking back on her heels. "I feel bad for that kid, though. One mother is the Dragon Queen. The other is the Arcandor."

Fauston snorted, his tone cheerful. "Nothing like setting high expectations."

"Faust!" James called, waving his boyfriend over. At his side, Tessalyn was clearly experimenting with how many chocolates she could fit inside her mouth. She almost seemed ready to quit, but then her eyes caught James's smirk, and she defiantly shoved two more past her lips.

"I better intervene before she makes herself sick. Enjoy the party, Kianthe. You deserve it." Fauston strolled toward them, tossing his hands up in exasperation. "Really, James?"

Kianthe watched him for another moment, but it was getting

warm in here, and the barn was only a quarter of the party. She stepped past the doors, strolling toward one of the nearby bonfires. The icy wind assaulted her immediately, and she absently manipulated it somewhere else. In the resulting calm, someone brushed her jacket.

"I know you don't drink, but I thought I'd offer a sip." Reyna had slipped into her winter cloak, and the fur brushed her chin as she held up a mug. "Rum tea? Venne won't drink it, so I suppose it's mine to finish." She didn't sound particularly upset about that.

"Describe it for me," Kianthe said, squeezing her wife's arm.

"It's bold. The bitterness of the tea is cut with the honey, but the lemon and rum add a punch." Reyna drew a sip, swirling it in her mouth, then swallowed. "It's nice. Rougher than a glass of wine, but feels like something I'd drink if I'm sick."

Kianthe laughed. "Drinking while sick. There's an idea."

"Hey, Matild will tell you. That's an old cure in the Queendom."

"You would know, Your Excellency." Kianthe pressed a kiss to her hair, then pulled her close. They approached the closest bonfire, near enough to feel the heat, but far enough to have privacy. "Are we putting too high of expectations on our kids?"

"Our kids?" Reyna sounded utterly confused. "Who, Gossley? Dear, I know we've joked, but he's hardly—"

Kianthe snorted. "No, no. *Future* children. I assume you'll want some."

Reyna took another sip of her drink, smiling against the rim. "Only when you're ready."

A roar of laughter erupted from the bonfire. Silhouetted by the fire, Gossley tossed up his hands, then turned to his girlfriend and swept her into a dramatic twirl, dipping her low to the ground. She laughed in delight as he kissed her. A few of the adults drank, and several of the teenagers audibly groaned.

Kianthe found herself smiling. "I think I'm ready. Although I probably should find Polana first, just to make sure she isn't spitting mad and plotting something."

"Oh, Locke already did." Reyna chuckled. "For a retired spymaster, he's quick to act. Albert was lying to us—Polana left on your orders, with minimal fuss. Apparently she went to the Capital to find an empty beach and some perspective." Now Reyna tilted her head. "Which is a curious choice. They'll be empty for a reason; our beaches are filled with rocks and icy waters. But I suppose that doesn't mean much for an elemental mage."

"Not really, no." Kianthe sorted through that statement. "Wait a minute. Does Locke have spies *inside the Magicary*?"

Reyna shrugged one shoulder. "Dearest, I would assume Locke has spies everywhere."

"Great," Kianthe muttered. "Well, he'd better put some in Feo's new alchemy school, too. It's only fair."

That was Feo's solution. The new Stone of Sawing—or whatever he was calling it—couldn't exactly be moved to the Magicary, not without rallying dozens of mages. And considering sentiment about alchemy, even Kianthe grudgingly agreed it might be best to let alchemists flourish in a space of their own making.

Hence, a new school. Feo had already chosen the location, deep inside the dense forests between Tawney and the ocean.

A symbol, they'd said. A magic school inside the Queendom. Reyna wouldn't just be the Dragon Queen, now. She'd be the sovereign who ushered in an era of fresh magic for her country.

Reyna smirked now. "Oh, Locke won't need to resort to that. Feo has already opened communications with myself and parliament to secure funding. Venne just told me it was approved."

Huh. Well, Kianthe was staying far, far away from those politics. After all, Feo was right. Elemental mages hadn't exactly been kind to their alchemical counterparts. Whatever happened to the alchemists now, it was their path to decide, not hers.

Although she was a little jealous that the *Magicary* wasn't closer to Tawney.

"Well, good." Kianthe sighed, pulling the next sentence from gritted teeth. "I trust Feo. I guess."

"You do?" Reyna teased.

Kianthe flushed, feeling warm, as if she'd just admitted a devastating secret. She fumbled for clarification. "Most of the time. Except when they use our shop to sway public opinion without *informing us first.*" Now she cast a dark glance around the party—but Feo and Wylan were nowhere to be seen.

Unsurprising, considering them.

"We'll be establishing a proper alliance between alchemy and elemental magic, but things won't change overnight. The point is, I'm not willing to put off our lives." Kianthe leaned a bit heavier against Reyna, kissing her temple. "Anything you want, my love. Children included."

"Well, okay, then," Reyna replied breathlessly. "Maybe we can each have one. Same father, different mothers."

Kianthe wrinkled her nose. "Pregnancy. Ew."

"Or maybe I'll just have one." Reyna laughed.

Overhead, wingbeats caught their attention. Not dragons—a griffon. One, singular, which was odd. Ponder came with her dragon friends, and Visk typically came with Ponder, these days. Kianthe squinted at the dark night sky, tracing the griffon's shape as it approached.

It was wearing a saddle.

Albert's griffon.

Feo was perched in the saddle, with Wylan holding on behind them. Griffons didn't typically change owners, but if one died, it was known to happen. And clearly, Feo had impressed *this* griffon, because the creature fluffed self-importantly as he landed. He had spent decades as the Alchemicor's mount, and he was clearly pleased to continue the tradition.

Kianthe didn't miss how the griffon looked around, his head high, his wings outspread. He wasn't trying to impress the bystanders. Instead, he seemed to be looking for Visk.

Their rivalry continued.

"Visk isn't here," Kianthe told the griffon, rolling her eyes. "He's off with his mate, and he won't be happy you're still lurking."

The griffon squawked, digging his talons into the dirt as if to say, *I'll lurk anyway.*

"Come now, Kianthe. Be nice to my new mount," Feo drawled from the saddle. They dismounted, offering a chivalrous hand to help Wylan. To his credit, the Queendom lord didn't seem fazed by the flight, his movements steady as he accepted Feo's help and hopped to the ground.

"I'm being nice. I'm just stating facts." With his riders dismounted, Kianthe shooed the big griffon. The creature spread his wings and screeched at her. The music faltered, and the group at the nearest bonfire craned to see the commotion.

Kianthe gasped indignantly. "*Don't* you raise that tone with me, sir." Then, to Reyna, "Visk would *never.*"

"This isn't your griffon, love." Reyna stepped closer, offering her hand. The griffon, clearly slighted by Kianthe's attitude, turned up his beak, but when Reyna gently petted his feathers, scratching right where the saddle rested, he relaxed and began nuzzling her hair.

Show-off.

The music resumed, and Wylan cleared his throat. "Apologies for our tardiness, Your Excellency. We meant to be here sooner, but there was a delay at the smithy."

"Namely, the blacksmith left early." Feo cast a surreptitious glance toward New Leaf.

Near the barn's entrance, Tarly and Matild were just stepping away from the dancing circle, gasping and laughing. Matild fanned herself, and Tarly noticed the lords—and the package secured to the griffon's saddle—and abruptly spun on his heel.

"Thanks, Tarly," Feo called.

"I was gonna get to it," Tarly shouted back, then hurried Matild away.

Wylan sighed, untying the package. He patted the griffon's flank, tucking the rectangular package under his arm. "Perhaps we can claim a table near the barn? You'll want some light to see this gift."

"A gift?" Reyna repeated.

Feo released his new griffon, and the creature took to the skies. Unlike Visk, he flew east, toward the forest and new alchemy school. That was probably the only reason Visk hadn't attacked yet. Adult griffons claimed specific airspace, but the distance wouldn't be that wide.

They'd have to just . . . share.

Amicably.

Visk would hate that.

Kianthe crossed her arms. "Well, they'd *better* get us a gift, after making us think we had to close our shop. Really, it's the least they could do."

It was a testament to Reyna's mindset around those circumstances that she lifted her chin, every bit a queen now. "*Quite* right." Despite the effects of the liquor—or perhaps because of them—her eyes flashed threateningly.

"We could still take it back," Feo muttered to Wylan.

Wylan rolled his eyes and started for a vacant table near the barn's entrance. Light spilled from the open doors, and with a wave, Kianthe coaxed a few ever-flames to drift outside for further illumination. Reyna's alcoholic tea must have started to spread, because the attendees in the barn were getting louder, and shouts of amusement echoed through the building.

Kianthe foresaw a menu change in their future.

"As you've surmised, this is an apology," Wylan said, laying the package over the wrought iron table. "And a promise, from Tawney to you both."

Now Kianthe's interest was piqued. She leaned over Reyna's shoulder, bouncing on her toes. "Ooooh. What is it?"

"Open it and see," Feo said, their tone disinterested.

Reyna produced a knife from somewhere—Stone-damned, where did she keep hiding those?—and cut the twine with a practiced motion. Then she paused, offering the package to Kianthe. It was a small thing, but it made Kianthe very pleased. She *loved* opening presents. With vicious glee, Kianthe tore into the parchment.

A formal plaque revealed itself. It was made of polished wood overlaid with metal lettering and a large, bronze picture of their barn. It looked mostly finished, except for the bottom right corner, which clearly could have used more hammering. But Kianthe was more interested in the words:

New Leaf Tomes and Tea

Historical Site

Reyna read the inscription: "'The honored bookshop and teahouse of Her Excellency, Queen Reyna, and Arcandor Kianthe, the Mage of Ages. In a world of duty, they pursued passion.'" Her voice cracked, and she swallowed hard. After a heavy pause, she managed to say, "Passion? That's a bit suggestive."

"Rain." Kianthe laughed out loud. "Have I corrupted you so fully?"

Feo's look could peel paint. "Read the rest."

Kianthe skimmed the inscription at the bottom of the plaque. "'Protected by the Tawney Historical Society.' Does Tawney *have* a historical society?"

"We never bothered before, on account of the dragon fire. Things have changed." Wylan puffed his chest, pride filtering into his voice. "Feo and I were discussing the town's future, and with the interest we received from those tourists, we anticipate Tawney's size will be growing steadily. It's important to identify buildings of note, and take steps to protect them."

"And ours is the first? Surely there are more important buildings in Tawney." Reyna seemed to have composed herself, but her words were still thick with emotion.

Feo sniffed, averting their gaze. "We have a few others in mind as well. But we couldn't think of a better building to receive this honor." They paused, then issued an almost-threat: "Now, you can never close."

"Don't tell me what to do," Kianthe said automatically.

Reyna smacked her arm. "Dearest, please."

"Hey, I'm not the one saying 'passion' is suggestive." Kianthe waggled her eyebrows, and Reyna broke down laughing, her eyes wet with happy tears. As she wiped them, Kianthe glanced at the barn's exterior. "Where do you want to mount it, love?"

"Somewhere for everyone to see. Right by the front door?" Reyna lifted the plaque, running her fingers over the delicate chain Tarly had attached to the top. It was a nice idea, but wholly irrelevant when an elemental mage lived inside.

"Your wish is my command," Kianthe replied. Reyna held it where she wanted it, and with a twist of magic, Kianthe coaxed some thick vines out of the wood exterior. They wound around the plaque, weaving into each other for strength, and secured it properly.

Who needed nails?

"It's perfect," Reyna said, pulling Wylan and Feo into a hug. "Thank you both. We really appreciate it." It lasted only a breath, probably because any more would make Feo uncomfortable.

As they separated, Feo ducked their head. "We *are* sorry."

"We accept your apology," Kianthe said, ruffling their hair affectionately. They slapped her away, and she stuck out her tongue at them.

Tarly and Matild had deemed it safe to approach. Tarly clapped Kianthe's shoulder, grinning as he gestured at the plaque. "Good idea, huh? To be fair, it was *mostly* finished on time." Now he ran a finger along the base of it, where vines hid the bottom corner. "Thanks for hiding that."

"Covering imperfection with plants. My specialty." Kianthe winked.

Matild raised her nearly empty mug of alcoholic tea. "Pillars of our community. Please, never leave."

"I think we're staying for the long haul," Reyna said, admiring the plaque. "But you may rethink that sentiment when we have children."

"Eh." The midwife shrugged. "Kids are my specialty. Just because we're happily childfree doesn't mean *you two* can't enjoy all the sticky, screaming messes."

Kianthe groaned. "Great. Loving this already."

Tarly snorted, but he was still distracted. He cupped his hands over his mouth and bellowed, "Hey, folks! Get out here! New Leaf Tomes and Tea is an official *historical* site. Come see."

At his booming voice, their neighbors strolled out to see the fuss. Kianthe and Reyna stepped back while their friends and neighbors examined the plaque, offered congratulations, shook their hands, nodded approval. Wylan ducked inside New Leaf and resurfaced with two mugs, and when Kianthe cast more ever-flame light in the street, the party effectively moved outside. Feo drew a few alchemical circles in the snow, clearly proud to show off their new abilities by magically warming the street.

No sacrifices needed.

In the din, Reyna stepped closer to her wife, wrapping her arms around Kianthe's waist. Warmth filled Kianthe's entire body, and she draped her arms over Reyna's shoulders, searching her eyes.

"Tell me what you're thinking."

"I'm thinking about the night we took a chance on all this." Reyna drew a slow breath through her nose, swaying as the music shifted into something soft, slow. Her words were low, for Kianthe alone. "Ask me again, Key. Just like before."

Kianthe didn't need prompting. That was a night she'd never, ever forget.

"Hello, Reyna, my wife, my love. You like tea. I like books. Aren't you glad we opened a shop and forgot the world exists?"

The words lingered between them, a whispered promise, a reminder of everything they'd done . . . and everything there was left to do. Kianthe traced her wife's cheek, smoothed back her hair, and held her breath.

And Reyna didn't disappoint.

"I like tea. I like books. But I love you," Reyna breathed, and kissed her again. Against Kianthe's lips, she murmured, "It doesn't matter to me if the world forgets us. As long as we don't forget each other, we'll be okay."

Happiness settled in Kianthe's soul, and she pulled her wife closer. "Always and forever."

"Always and forever," Reyna agreed.

And the night went on.

Reyna

The Arcandor, the Alchemicor, and the queen were taking tea in the atrium when a bell echoed throughout the stone school. It resonated from an alchemy circle drawn above the atrium's doorway, and startled several birds into flight.

Reyna quirked an eyebrow, tracing the rim of her ceramic teacup. It held a vanilla mint blend, a tisane she'd personally crafted from plants in Kianthe's greenhouse. She swallowed, then asked mildly, "Are we under attack?"

It had been quite a while since Reyna had participated in an earnest fight. Her sword was back at New Leaf, but she could find something to use. The stirring spoon, perhaps.

Across the table, Kianthe rolled her eyes. "Why do you sound *excited* about that?"

"Come on, love. You have to admit, it's been a boring few years."

"*Quaint,* not boring," Kianthe drawled. "Sometimes, I think you forget the difference."

Beside Kianthe, Feo pinched their brow. "The alarm," they said, pointedly redirecting the conversation, "is to announce someone at the front gate. A visitor. You know, the *proper* ones who request entrance, rather than landing in our courtyard on a griffon's back."

"Okay, *that's* boring," Kianthe acquiesced, pointing her fork at Feo. Crumbs from her blueberry scone fell to the wooden tabletop, and she wiped them onto the floor for the redspars that lived here.

The glass atrium was a decent intermediary between the heated buildings of the school and the northern Queendom's frigid cold, and Tessalyn had taken pride in stocking it with dozens of tropical plants from Leonol. The result was a humid environment that had both Kianthe's hair and Feo's fluffing from frizz, which meant they looked slightly ridiculous. Reyna hid a smile as Feo inhaled indignantly.

"*Boring?* On the contrary; it's a *brilliant* system. We have alchemy circles above every doorway, but the spellwork can assess the visitor's intentions and translate it accordingly. For example, that bell wouldn't have echoed throughout the school. That'd be distracting for our students. Instead, it rang where I am, which lets me know that the visitor is seeking an audience with *me,* specifically." At that, Feo puffed, swelling like a sparrow in the bath.

Kianthe squinted at them. "How do you know it didn't ring in the classrooms, too? This whole castle is stone. You'd never hear it."

"How dare—"

"Who's the visitor?" Reyna interrupted, spooning a bit more honey into her tea. Patol's bees had really outdone themselves this spring.

Feo rolled their eyes. "How should I know? I'm here, with you." But they pivoted toward the atrium's wooden door, waiting for this visitor to arrive.

Reyna took another sip of her tea. They did afternoon tea on occasion: *a meeting of the minds,* Feo called it, but sometimes Reyna wondered if Feo just missed living near Tawney.

Still, she couldn't argue it was a necessary meeting. The Academy for Alchemical Arts had grown immensely in the decade since its inception. Without the downside of a sacrifice, Feo sorted through hundreds of applications for alchemical mages every season. Many of them were even Queendom citizens, which pleased Reyna more than she expected.

It didn't take long for one such Queendom alchemist—dressed in the crisp blue robes of the Academy—to enter, sweeping into a bow. "Deepest apologies for the interruption, Your Excellency. Arcandor." They pivoted to Feo. "Oh, great Alchemicor. I'm pleased to announce your visitors: Councilmember Serina of Lathe and the Nacean River, and her wife, Diarn Bobbie of the Middle Nacean River."

"And Lathe," Bobbie said, crossing her arms. "Just because I only manage the *middle* Nacean doesn't mean my mother wouldn't kill me for dropping our hometown."

Reyna surged to her feet and ran to the atrium's doorway. "Bobbie! Serina! What a *fantastic* surprise." She laughed, pulling them both into a fierce hug. A few breaths later, Kianthe slammed into them too, and then they were all laughing while the alchemist edged their way out the door.

The quiet *thud* of the wooden double doors closing was their cue to separate.

"How've you two been?" Kianthe asked, scrutinizing them. A grin tilted her lips. "Stars and Stone, I figured those bags under your eyes would fade when the twins grew up."

"'Grew up'? They're seven," Bobbie drawled. "And my bags never go away."

"Mine do. But being a councilmember sucks ass, so I get them back pretty fast." Serina draped over Bobbie's shoulder, quirking an eyebrow. "What are you two doing here? Is Matild babysitting again?"

Kianthe shrugged. "Not today. Quinn is out with Ponder and the dragons, I'd imagine."

Bobbie stared, jaw unhinged. "You don't *know*?"

"She's nine." Kianthe waved a hand, casting an amused glance at Reyna. "When I was nine, I was roaming the Magicary halls catching things on fire."

Reyna smoothly stepped back to the table, carrying two chairs over from a nearby table. Happiness spread through her, a warmth of friendship and good company. It had been over a year since she'd seen Serina and Bobbie—they exchanged letters, but life got busy for everyone recently.

She missed them.

Feo rolled their eyes at Kianthe. "And *that's* why we have a stricter schedule for our students—so they can't inadvertently burn down the school." The Alchemicor offered a hand to shake. "Councilmember. Diarn. Welcome to the Academy for Alchemical Arts. To what do I owe the pleasure?"

"Can't we sit for a cup of tea first?" Reyna settled into her chair. The atrium was large, attached to the western side of the Academy, and sunlight streamed through painted glass windows to their left. A nearby tea cart had been stocked with everything they'd need, and Reyna chose two beautiful cups off its shelves.

"Unfortunately, we've come on business," Bobbie replied, regret tinging her voice.

Reyna quirked an eyebrow. "In a decade of being queen, I haven't encountered business so important it can't be discussed over a cup of tea." She patted the seat next to her, and Kianthe dropped into it. Her wife's finger ignited, reheating the tea in their cups.

No one else moved from the doorway, which sent a prickle up Reyna's spine. Serina, the one person she'd *expected* to prioritize socializing over business, rubbed her arm. "Sorry, Reyna. This might." When Serina turned to Feo, her voice took the low, commanding tone of a councilmember. After Feo stepped down, she'd filled the role seamlessly—which meant she had more time in the job by this point than *they* had. "Alchemicor. When you established the Academy, the council, board, and parliament expressed concerns about alchemy exploding in our cities. Literally."

Ah. One of *those* visits, then.

Feo set their jaw, crossing their arms. "Yes. And as I tested limitations of the Arcanium, we discovered potential options for that."

"Stone of Sawing would have been better," Kianthe muttered with a decade of scorn.

"Arcandor, for the final time, we were never calling it the Stone of Sawing."

Kianthe pouted. Reyna patted her hand in sympathy.

Serina didn't seem amused. She actually looked . . . perturbed. "Yes. The pendants were your preferred solution. A shard of the Arcanium, worn by every alchemist who completed your coursework. Coursework that exemplified respect for a powerful magic, and ensured safety parameters for the general public."

She gestured at Feo's neck, where a single shard of the alchemy Stone had been secured to a golden chain. Much like Kianthe and Reyna's moonstones, this pendant had an alchemical inscription. *Unlike* their moonstones, this inscription glowed purple where the circle had been carved.

"That is correct. Immediate proximity to the Stone allows for sacrifice-free alchemy—but it only works if the students are here, in this forest. Outside of the Academy, they can't pull its power without a shard of their own." Feo sounded irate now, their fingers drifting to their own shard. "If you recall, I proposed eighteen solutions for supervising alchemists in the Realm. These shards were the simplest choice, not the most thorough."

Reyna remembered that meeting. Feo had indeed presented several options, some of which involved *extensive,* ethically dubious oversight by the Alchemicor. In a private meeting after Feo's presentation, the Realm's governing bodies agreed that a shard was the most humane option.

Serina drew a slow breath, casting a glance around the atrium. But they were alone, the entire space cleared out except for flowering plants, towering trees, and a few empty tables. "Well, if you've adhered to it, we have a problem."

"I gathered that, based on your tone." Feo waved a hand for her to get on with it.

Bobbie cut right to the chase. "Someone declared war on the Dastardly Pirate Dreggs and her entire fleet. A new pirate captain, complete with a loyal crew." The diarn finally dropped into the chair beside Reyna, gesturing for a cup of tea.

Reyna raised one eyebrow, pouring her a chai blend. "Dreggs has been fighting insurgents for her title for years. Good luck to whoever thinks they can—"

"Dreggs's flagship was sunk nine days ago." Serina's voice was grave, and she perched in a chair beside her wife.

Silence settled over the atrium. A redspar warbled in one of the trees, and bees buzzed between the flowers, but it all faded. Kianthe sucked in a breath. Reyna gently set her teacup down, eyes sharp. "Did you recover the crew?"

"Their fleet gathered everyone they could find." Serina carefully sat beside Bobbie, drumming her fingers on the table. "Dreggs is missing."

Kianthe stiffened. "D-Dead?"

Reyna held her breath, awaiting the same answer.

"Accounts are uncertain. There was no sign of her after the attack, alive or otherwise." Bobbie pressed her lips together.

Reyna read between those lines. A monument like the Dastardly Pirate Dreggs wouldn't just *drown*. She knew the seas intimately, and was no stranger to staying alive during a vicious attack. More likely, it was a calculated move—Dreggs was exactly the kind to go undercover and weed out insurgents.

Until Reyna saw otherwise, she wouldn't believe Dreggs was truly gone.

"Her pirates are keeping things quiet, just in case." Serina pinched her brow in frustration. "*We* only found out because Pil told me."

One part of Reyna wanted to say that it was natural—that no sovereign, pirate captain or otherwise, was meant to rule forever. Even Reyna had only retained the *title* of queen, not the duties. She was a figurehead; Tessalyn's parliament was a success, and Reyna's public appearances were dwindling these days.

As much as she loved Dreggs, she and Kianthe had to remain impartial in these kinds of power struggles.

But based on the expressions Bobbie and Serina wore, Dreggs wasn't the real problem.

"That news could have been shared with a summons, if you needed our help . . ." Reyna mused, frowning at her friends. She cast a glance at Feo, then back to Serina. "Except you didn't come to New Leaf. You came to the *Academy,* for Feo."

"Which means an alchemist spearheaded that attack." Kianthe set her jaw.

Serina tapped her nose.

"That's impossible," Feo said sharply. "The Arcanium's power is strongest in its vicinity. Even *with* a shard of the Stone, an alchemist in the Southern Seas would be limited. There aren't many alchemists in that region anymore, and I believe Dreggs employs most of them."

"Dreggs's alchemists were accounted for during the attack. Which means our culprit was an unregistered alchemist, without a shard of the Arcanium." Serina leaned back in her chair. "Which *means* this alchemist is using blood sacrifices, just like old times. And based on the destruction of Dreggs's flagship, they're powerful. Dangerously powerful."

"Well, shit." Kianthe stretched her arms over her head, shaking out her wrists. "And here I thought I'd have a nice, relaxing summer."

"Hang on." Feo pushed to their feet, pressing their hands to the table. "This is not *your* problem, Arcandor."

"You're going to need magic that actually works. Alchemists might be weak in the Southern Seas, but the ley lines around the Roiling Islands and the southern Nacean River are strong." Kianthe raised an eyebrow. "I'm also genuinely curious if the Academy can thrive if you're not here, Alchemicor. You haven't exactly set systems in place to keep it running independently. Not like me and High-Mage Harold, my best friend, my buddy, and his ever-so-thrilling assistant, Polana."

Reyna rolled her eyes. After the alchemists relocated here, Polana requested to return to the Magicary. Harold was happy to oblige—provided she took a lower title and did his dirty work. It was a testament to how much Polana missed her old home that she grudgingly agreed.

Feo gritted their teeth. "I can leave my school. For something like this, I will."

"Why should you, when we're ready and able to assist?" Reyna smoothly stood as well, offering a smile as she checked one of the daggers strapped to her forearm. "I've been meaning to check on Tilaine anyway, dear. We'll call it a romantic getaway."

Kianthe bounced. "Can Quinn come? She's getting older now."

"You want our daughter to face off against a dangerous blood alchemist?"

"I want her to get real life experience."

"Perhaps we can enroll her in an apprentice program."

Kianthe groaned. "Dull. Boring. Come on, Rain. When you were Quinn's age, you weren't lighting fires in some Magicary hallway. You were training to kill assassins."

"Well—"

Serina cleared her throat. "Look, I don't care *who* goes. But the council is nervous, and if I can't report that *someone* is intervening, the Academy's future is at risk."

"The Academy is on Queendom land," Feo grumbled.

"And its graduates are settling in every city in the Realm." Serina crossed her arms. "You remember this game, Feo. An example has to be set; we can't have some pirate alchemist on a vendetta against Dreggs's entire fleet. Say what you will about her methods, but Dreggs has kept order in the Southern Seas for decades."

"We'll handle it." Kianthe offered Reyna a hand. Her voice slid lower, amused, and her dark eyes glimmered in the filtered sunshine. "Just like old times, eh, Rain?"

Reyna pulled Kianthe closer and pressed a kiss to her cheek.

"Like old times."

Through the Ringer

"Are you sure this isn't a bit much?" Pil asked, crossing burly arms.

They were standing on the shoreline of the Nacean River, facing a quiet bay hidden by the snarl of islands on the river's northern edge. It was near Arlon's old estate—now Serina's home and Bobbie's place of work—but not so near that they'd be discovered without intention.

Still, Serina nervously checked the woods behind them, rubbing the back of her neck. It was hot today, the summer sunshine cutting through a brisk wind. Or maybe the sweat dripping down her back was just nerves.

"It's not too much. It's perfect!" She forced a laugh, reassessing the bay.

There were no fewer than three ships anchored there, arranged in a semicircle. One was Pil's new schooner, an honest merchant vessel—or so he claimed. One was Rankor and Farley's most recent workplace, a brigantine that hauled wheat, complete with a crew that seemed *very* perplexed about why their navigator had steered then into the bay. The final ship was the *Knot for Sail,* Arlon's old vessel, now the signature ship of Diarn Bobbie of the Middle Nacean River and Lathe.

"It—it is perfect, isn't it?" Doubt filtered into Serina's tone, and she paced on the shoreline. "Stars, you're right. This is ridiculous. It's too much."

Pil grunted, watching his kids—Darlene and Joe—attempt

to toss a huge banner from his schooner to the *Knot for Sail*. On the other deck, Squirrel scrambled to catch it, but the wind whipped it away.

Joe heaved a long-suffering sigh. "Dad, do we *need* the banner?" Their voice sounded tiny from so far away, despite them hitting a growth spurt last year that made them taller and bigger-boned than their father.

Serina buried her hands in her hair and shouted back, "Yes, we need the banner!" Then, quieter, "I *knew* I should have called Kianthe for this."

"A mage would help with the wind," Pil agreed.

"Too late now." Serina laughed loudly. "Stars, what a nightmare. Why does *anyone* propose?"

Her old boatswain quirked a bushy eyebrow. "We were wonderin' that. Considering you and Bobbie are already living together, planning a family—just seems redundant now, four years later."

But it didn't seem redundant to Serina. It seemed . . . like the missing puzzle piece. The one title they could hold up when everything else broke apart, the single thing that assured the world they were a team, even when their personalities clashed or their jobs interfered.

She'd learned a lot about compromise in the years since Reyna's chat in Tawney's inn—but life had thrown more and more shit their way, and sometimes *compromise* didn't feel like enough to keep them afloat.

"I love her," Serina said, and had never meant anything more. She clenched her eyes shut. "I *want* to marry her."

"Why?" Pil's voice was gruff now. "What's a piece of paper going to give you that you two can't give yourself?"

On the schooner, Darlene had scrambled up the mast, making another attempt to toss the banner to Squirrel. The chef lunged for it and nearly toppled off the *Knot for Sail*. She caught herself at the last minute, banner in hand, and laughed triumphantly.

On the brigantine, Rankor clapped. Farley rolled her eyes.

The linen banner had partially unfurled, and the words RRY ME? were visible in bright red paint.

It had to be perfect.

Serina backed up, squinting at the sun. "It'll give us every-thing. Look, I told Bobbie to meet me at the trailhead at sunset, so there's not much time to get it ready. Can you do it?"

"Aye." Pil rolled his eyes. "We'll do it."

"You're the best," Serina said, and pivoted into the forest.

But even as she delved back into the shade, sweat beaded on her brow, and she couldn't shake the feeling that ants had crawled into her boots.

Bobbie was waiting at the trailhead when she clawed her way out of the forest. Her partner hadn't noticed her, instead facing toward the estate. She was dressed in formal attire today, her typical uniform of pressed slacks and a blue jacket with a single golden medal sewn on the shoulder.

Diarns didn't *have* uniforms, but Bobbie had spent years as a proper constable, and now wanted to be a proper diarn. "The uniform helps folk understand who we are," Bobbie had said one night, half-drunk over Kollean wine. "It's ridiculous that diarns don't have one."

Serina had shrugged and said, "Whatever you think, hon. Just don't ask us councilmembers to dress up."

"You should," Bobbie had grumbled, and in the following weeks, she designed one for herself. And true to Bobbie being *Bobbie,* she wore it every day she worked. Even though it was apparently restrictive, scratchy, and hot.

But Stars forbid Serina suggest her partner wear plain clothes for a day.

A teasing smile tugged at Serina's lips, and she crept behind Bobbie. She was trying to be quiet, but the moment she got close, Bobbie pivoted on her heel and pinned Serina's arms be-hind her back.

It was so smooth. Serina smirked, pressing up against her partner to take some of the pressure off her shoulder. "Damn, you've been practicing. Take that to our bedroom, will you?"

In public, Bobbie would have flushed at a statement like that, stammered a response. But here, they were alone. Instead of embarrassment, Bobbie bent forward, pressing a sensuous kiss on Serina's lips.

"I tried. Last time I cuffed you, you couldn't stop laughing."

Even the way Bobbie murmured against her lips *now* was making her laugh. She swallowed it and pulled away, shaking herself out. "It wasn't *that* bad."

"It killed the mood, just a bit." Bobbie snorted, but a smile played on her face too. Her next question lilted into a perplexed inquiry. "Did you already hike without me?"

Bobbie was looking at Serina's hair, which had been cut short in the last few years. Easier upkeep. Upon inspection, she found several leaves and a twig. Stupid trees. Stupid bushes. Give her a clean deck, brisk wind, and the rolling of gentle waves any day.

"I was, um . . . running late. Took a shortcut from the estate."

Bobbie plucked out the leaves, then flicked the twig to the ground. "If you were leaving the estate, why didn't we walk together? All we're doing is examining the bay for a potential shipyard, right?" Suspicion filtered into her tone now.

Did she know?

She couldn't.

Could she?

Serina's heart pounded, and she fumbled with her hands. "Yep. But I didn't know you were at the estate. Anyway, you ready?" Her voice was too high-pitched.

Bobbie, the ex-constable, noticed it. Her brow knitted together. When Serina panic-plowed into the forest, Bobbie kept a close pace.

Bless her, she didn't ask any other questions, which meant the hike was silent. To be fair, Bobbie wasn't much for conversation . . . and Serina wasn't sure she could keep her mouth shut. Every step down the hillside made her more and more anxious—which was why she nearly yelped when Bobbie took her arm.

"What?" She spun on her partner, chest heaving. "What is it?"

"Do you hear that?"

They were almost to the bay. Had the music started too early? Rankor had *assured* her that the brigantine's captain, who moonlighted as a lutist, would be professional and *wait for the cue.*

But Bobbie wasn't looking toward the water. Instead, she was squinting into the forest. "There's something there. It sounds like a kitten."

"A kitten?" Serina repeated.

Of course, that's when a tiny, scared *mew* cried out.

"We have to help," Bobbie said, deviating from the trail to follow the noise.

They did have to help. *And* they were so, so close to the bay—to the proposal—to a brighter future where they could rescue kittens every day as wife and wife. Serina clenched her eyes shut, struggling to sort her thoughts.

"But—"

"Serrie, come on. We have room for another cat. What if it's hurt?"

Shit.

Serina forced a smile. "Okay." She swallowed her next sentence, which would have been a desperate plea to adhere to a plan Bobbie knew nothing about. And if Bobbie suspected Serina was plotting something, it wouldn't be a surprise.

This proposal had to be perfect.

So, she helplessly trudged into the wilderness behind Bobbie. Just a small detour.

Pil, his kids, Farley and Rankor, and Squirrel trudged into the estate's dining room as a bedraggled group. Night had long since fallen, and Serina was draped over the wide table, absently twirling a fork as Bobbie bottle-fed their newest family members. They both glanced up at the entourage of ex-pirates, and Serina paled.

"Ah. *Ah.* W-Welcome, all."

Pil crossed his arms. Beside him, Joe did the same. Darlene looked exasperated, her hair plastered to her face from a long day at sea. Farley seemed vaguely insulted, and Rankor appeared easygoing as always. Squirrel alone didn't seem perturbed, but Squirrel held full-time employment on the *Knot for Sail* and lived in a different wing of the mansion when they weren't sailing.

"This is a surprise," Bobbie said, eyes widening. In her hands, the rescued kitten—one of three—squirmed. It already had a poorly crocheted sweater on, and only tolerated it because that sweater came with milk.

"It *is,* isn't it? I know it's been a while. We probably should have stopped by sooner, but we don't get many vacation days." Farley, their old carpenter, spoke directly to Serina, in a very pointed tone.

Serina winced. "I'm—I'm sure your captain can be persuaded to make an exception, since you've come to visit the diarn, and all." All the while, she held their gazes, begging with her eyes for them to *stay quiet.*

Luckily, that was when Darlene noticed the kittens. "Oh, my Stars. A *kitten*? So *cute!*"

She surged forward, and Bobbie freely handed the kitten off. She gestured at a wooden crate on the table. "We have three. We found them today in the forest, hiking down to the bay."

Understanding flashed on Pil's face, and his irritated posture softened. "Ah. Derailed your day, I imagine."

"A *lot,*" Serina muttered.

Joe had scooped out another kitten, cuddling it to their chest. Rankor plucked out the third, a grin spreading across his face as he handed it to his wife. Farley, previously prickly, deflated instantly when the tiny kitten nuzzled her chin.

"Our captain did say it's good luck to have a cat on board. Maybe this is our excuse," Rankor said cheerfully.

Farley pressed her lips together. "I suppose."

"Always good luck to have a cat aboard," Darlene replied, matter-of-fact. "Dreggs mandates at least three on every ship. Keeps rodents out of the food, and ensures smooth sailing."

Bobbie gestured at the seats around them. The dining room was large, big enough to host parties, and she seemed delighted that company had arrived. "Take a seat, all. I'll get—" She paused, halfway to standing when Squirrel bustled out of the kitchen with plates of food.

Where she'd found those, Serina couldn't fathom, but none of them questioned their local cook.

"—ah, never mind. Squirrel already did," Bobbie finished, amused. She settled back into her chair. "Tell us what you've been up to! Stars, it's been ages since we've all been together."

Serina held her breath, waiting to see if her old pirate crew was still mad. But kittens and food did a lot to mitigate conflict, and everyone pulled out chairs as if they lived here full-time.

Pil subtly patted Serina's hand, and she hoped her eyes said *sorry*. His lips upturned. Then he leaned back in his chair and remarked, "Well, we heard some event was happening up here. But I think we messed up the date."

"Event?" Bobbie raised an eyebrow.

"Unless I'm mistaken—and Serina has something to say?" Pil raised one eyebrow.

Stars, she might kill him.

She forced a laugh, but it sounded more like a choking wheeze. "What makes you think I know why you're all here? I hardly track your comings and goings. I mean, really. Ridiculous." She waved a hand, then bit into a chicken leg with too much fervor.

She couldn't propose here. The ring in her pocket seemed to burn, but she carefully avoided her partner's questioning gaze.

Pil smirked. "Hmm. Well, we'll call this a happy accident, then."

"A happy accident, indeed." Bobbie laughed.

With that settled, their friends plowed into food and drink.

Darlene had set her kitten back on the table, and it prowled around, tail swishing as it stared at the flickering candlelight between them. Joe and Farley were comparing their kittens, cooing over their gorgeous coloring and stripes. Rankor reached for a chicken wing, and Squirrel slapped his hand and pushed a plate of vegetables his way instead.

Bobbie and Serina laughed the night away, chatting about days long past and all the real events coming up.

It was, admittedly, a cozy night.

Of course, even the coziest nights didn't ignore the fact that Serina *still had to propose.*

Half a moon's cycle went by as she feverishly planned her next attempt. The old crew couldn't be pulled into things again—they all had jobs, for one, and facing failure was embarrassing as hells.

It also opened up a new fear: the idea that Bobbie might say no, and Serina would be left disgraced in front of everyone they loved.

She couldn't handle it.

So, the next attempt had to be secretive, private, and uninterruptible. The outdoors offered too many loose ends. She couldn't risk a . . . a bear attack—or *something*—next time.

Serina thought about proposing in the manor, something she could easily control, but Arlon's old estate was . . . well, it wasn't their idea of home. The hallways were too wide, the ceilings were too tall, the décor was too ornate, and there were too many rooms and *servants' quarters* and everything else a huge mansion "needed" to function—"needed" according to their estate manager, whose job appeared to be solely overseeing the intricacies of the mansion and its grounds.

In Serina's opinion, if they needed an estate manager, the estate was too big.

More than once, she'd proposed building a smaller cabin on

the property, and using this place for business operations only. Bobbie always replied that a proper diarn had to live in a house appropriate for diarns.

And then she'd mention that Serina was a *councilmember,* and that should matter more to her, too.

Serina would retort that she'd always been perfectly happy on a hammock in the belly of a ship.

Bobbie would roll her eyes, and they'd stop talking for a bit.

But if Serina proposed in the place where she and Bobbie met, the fields where they became fast friends—maybe Bobbie would remember that titles didn't define them, and they could be whatever they wanted.

Together.

So, Serina tried that.

"A trip to Lathe?" Bobbie asked, banding her poufy hair into sections for the night. She glanced at the bed, where Serina had flopped to the end of the mattress, chin on her palms, feet in the air. Bobbie quirked an eyebrow. "Missing my mother that much?"

"You haven't visited in a while." A strategic pause. "And I'd love to check in on my parents' old farm."

Bobbie tilted her head. "That farm hasn't been in your family since we were kids."

"It's where we met." Serina prickled in defense. That was before Arlon's constables auctioned off the land, and Serina's parents were forced to move to Jallin. But that farm was the start of everything Serina became. It hurt that Bobbie didn't seem to care about it.

Bobbie considered her tone, her words, and spoke carefully. "That's true. We can stop by if you want, but . . ." She paused, drew a slow breath. "I don't know, Serrie. Sometimes I worry you're clinging to the past."

Clinging to the past?

The best time in her life was recently—when she was a recovering pirate, and Bobbie was a constable turned diarn, and they were just beginning this exciting, terrifying thing of *life* together.

It wasn't about the farm. It was about *them,* and what they were.

"When have I clung to the past?" Serina demanded.

"You hate this place." Bobbie gestured around their bedroom.

It was stone accented in wood beams, some of which were carved with intricate designs of farming iconography. There was an entire washroom, a bedroom, and a sitting room dedicated to reading and relaxing after a long day. Overall, it was three times bigger than they needed, and it took years to get used to the way shadows played off the paneled ceiling at night.

Serina puffed indignantly. "Don't *you*? This is Arlon's old room. Of all the rooms in this house, why did we take this one?"

"It's closest to the staircase, which means I can respond to visitors faster." Bobbie shrugged.

So utilitarian, with her.

Serina felt her anger rising—and tried to draw calm breaths the way Reyna said to do. She wouldn't fall back into their old bickering. Instead, she forced her feelings through gritted teeth. "I just feel like a trip to the countryside might be good for us." Then, a sigh. "We don't have to go to the farm. It was just an idea."

A perfect idea.

Bobbie had paused in tying off her hair, staring at Serina curiously. After a long moment, she said, "If it's important to you, we'll go to the farm. I'm sure the new residents will give us a tour, especially if my mother's with us."

"*No,*" Serina yelped.

"You just said we should see my mother."

Serina racked her brain. "I *said* we haven't visited in a while. Can we do the farm trip, just us?"

Bobbie tied off the last of her poufy hair, patting it for bed. She sounded exasperated. "We can do whatever you'd like, Serrie. It was just a suggestion."

Silence.

Bobbie crawled into bed, and Serina flipped around, feeling vaguely miserable. They lay side by side, and after a moment, Bobbie mused, "The leaves will be changing soon. The countryside will be gorgeous, I'm sure."

Her tone was encouraging.

Making amends.

Serina smiled in earnest, nestling against Bobbie's side. "It's a date."

The *Knot for Sail* was all ready for a trip up the river. The ship was docked by the mansion, and its crew scurried around the deck, prepping last-minute accommodations. Squirrel happily strolled by them, and behind her, three of Bobbie's constables carried heavy platters of food for the journey. Two of them yelped when a griffon touched down. The mage they'd contracted to boost wind for the trip dismounted, smirking as he patted his griffon's flank.

"He won't bite," he called to the constables.

A few of them grumbled, but none got closer to test that statement.

Bobbie, still dressed in uniform, surveyed it all from the patio beside the mansion. She had a bag slung over one shoulder, and seemed pleased at the crisp wind in the air. Serina stood in the doorway and watched her for a moment, and was consumed by the thought that no one and nothing could be as beautiful as her partner.

And hopefully soon, her fiancée.

Giddiness and fear swept through Serina again, but she'd battled it so many times this year that she pushed it off.

"You ready to go?" She hefted her own bag for the ship. It was one of the colder days this year, which boded well for the changing leaves as they sailed north. But it did mean she shivered a bit, even dressed in layers.

Bobbie grinned. "Definitely. This will be fun. My mother sent a messenger hawk earlier—she'll be on the lookout for us."

"A meeting of the diarns," Serina said. "And hopefully, a relaxing vacation."

"I could use one of those." Bobbie smiled.

They started down the hillside—and didn't make it more than a few steps before a boy shouted, "Councilmember Serina! Councilmember! Urgent message just arrived for you from Wellia." The boy, a stable hand, lowered his voice. "Delivered by *griffon.* The mage said you can't waste time. He's ready to fly you back."

That stopped them both.

Serina's eyes widened. "What? *Fly* me back to Wellia?" She glanced at the *Knot for Sail,* all ready to go. "Now?"

"He said it's urgent." The boy set his jaw.

Bobbie took the letter in his hands, opening it where Serina could read.

A tropical storm had plowed into Jallin, Mercon, and the western side of Leonol. Relief efforts needed to be coordinated across three countries. The council had declared an urgent meeting to discuss Shepara's contribution.

"This sounds important, Serrie," Bobbie said.

Serina floundered. "I'm on the council. *Everything* is important." She turned to the boy again. "Surely, they can make a decision without my input. We'll enact whatever they need—"

"Not *whatever* they need," Bobbie cut her off. "Winter is approaching and we only have a season to stock our storerooms. We can spare some help, but we'll be the ones needing relief if we offer up too much of our food. You represent the western portion of Shepara in those meetings, Serrie. We need you to stand up for us."

"I—" Serina clenched her eyes shut. "I wanted to go to Lathe."

It was closer to pleading than she'd like.

Bobbie's expression softened, and she pulled Serina into a hug. "I'll visit my mother, and check on your parents' old farm. You're doing important work. We'll survive without you for a bit."

Bobbie didn't understand.

It left Serina feeling hollow inside. She *could* tell Bobbie why this trip was so important. Why their hike had been so important.

But this was supposed to be a surprise—a moment they'd tell their kids about in a decade. A romantic, perfect proposal for a romantic, perfect couple. Even if Serina was feeling farther and farther from that as the seasons passed and their jobs intervened.

Bobbie pressed a kiss to her cheek. "I love you. Go save the Realm, Serrie."

She didn't want to save the Realm. She just wanted to focus on *them* for once.

But the boy had already started jogging back down the path, past the mansion, toward the stables. Bobbie turned away, calling to the crew that they'd be weighing anchor soon. And Serina was left alone, staring blankly at her partner's back, feeling lonelier than ever.

There was no way Serina could have skipped this meeting.

Or rather, *meetings,* because it spread through half a moon's cycle.

The first two meetings were with the council only. On the third day, to Serina's shock, Reyna was seated at the circular table. At her side was Tessalyn—which meant they had the Queendom's sovereign and a parliament representative. There were also a couple of Leonolan board members, and a few folks the board identified as environmental and disaster-relief experts.

They spent three more days analyzing options, weighing food stores and reconstruction efforts. Halfway through the first day, Serina leaned over to Reyna and asked, "Where's your wife?"

Reyna sighed. "A natural disaster decimated a few communities. She flew south the moment we heard. I expect she'll be back in a week, once she's helped clear trees and regrow crops."

"What a good Arcandor," Serina said, only half teasing.

"Indeed. And here we are, in meetings." Reyna didn't sound pleased about it, but she smiled anyway and redirected her attention to the paperwork before them.

Later that night, her friends settled around the fire for drinks. Tessalyn had vanished halfway through the evening to have an animated discussion with the Leonolan board members, and the Queensguard—consisting of Venne and James for this visit—had eventually retired to their rooms.

Serina and Reyna were left.

Reyna took a swig from her mug of ale, leaning back in the lounge chair. The fire was low, a gentle heat rather than roaring flames, and the quiet murmur of conversation filled the tavern. "So." Reyna quirked an eyebrow. "Where's Bobbie? I figured she'd join you for this particular set of meetings."

"Bobbie's in Lathe. We were supposed to have a little vacation, but . . ." Serina trailed off, setting her jaw.

Reyna nodded. "I see."

Her tone made Serina hasten to defend herself. "Don't get me wrong. I'm pleased to help. This *is* important, and being a councilmember is . . . well, it's more prestigious than being a pirate."

"A lot less fun, though." Reyna's knowing tone spoke volumes. A Queensguard turned tea maker turned sovereign. The woman who used to hunt would-be assassins, relegated to days-long meetings about policies and procedures.

Serina could relate.

"Yeah. I don't even mind it, but Bobbie—" Serina cut herself off, clenching her eyes shut.

"Are you two having trouble?" Reyna asked.

It felt embarrassing to admit. Like they'd already figured out one fight, and *should* know better for future ones. After years, Serina expected they'd be stronger than this.

And yet, Bobbie had gone on that vacation, and her engagement ring was still in Serina's pocket.

"I don't know. We love each other, but I just feel . . . like we aren't as solid these days. It's complicated."

Reyna sat with that for a moment, taking another sip of her

ale. She settled into her chair, leaning over one of the armrests, tucking her legs beneath her. "From what I've seen, relationships happen in seasons. We can't be swooning over our partners every day. We'd never get anything done."

That was true. The beginning of her relationship with Bobbie felt like forbidden love—like they'd fought through a war and emerged triumphant, and everything afterward was a genuine gift.

Now, it felt like a constant. Bobbie and Serina, together forever. And neither of them seemed to remember *why*.

Serina's fingers brushed over the small bag in her pocket, the one that held the golden ring she'd commissioned for Bobbie. Here, talking with Reyna, she felt like she could be honest.

"I wanted to propose."

"That's exciting." She didn't sound excited.

Serina deflated. "You think I shouldn't."

"I didn't say that." Reyna paused, as if sorting her thoughts. She traced the rim of her mug thoughtfully. "When Kianthe and I decided to marry, it was a mutual decision. The question wasn't *if,* but *when*. By the time she proposed, I was so excited to move into that next step."

"We're planning a family," Serina muttered. "I know she'll be excited."

Probably.

Hopefully.

"A family isn't the only reason to marry," Reyna said gently.

Serina stared miserably at her own mug. She'd barely touched her golden ale, and now she didn't feel like she wanted to try.

Reyna drew a breath, reaching out to squeeze Serina's forearm. "All I'm saying is that maybe you think about this. Putting pressure on marriage to fix your problems, or because it's the *right* thing to do when you have a family . . . that's not going to help either of you."

"Your reason to marry is love, isn't it?" Serina set her jaw. "I love her. She loves me. Why isn't that enough?"

Reyna smiled. "It is. Or rather, it can be. But if you want my honest opinion, love is the undercurrent, and it rises and fades with our own mindsets. You're perceiving trouble and unrest, so you're already unsettled in your relationship. Love alone won't fix that. Only honest conversation will."

So, she needed to talk with Bobbie.

But the idea of that made Serina squirm. "What if she's feeling this way too?"

"Then you both have a choice to make."

That sounded so final. A lump formed in Serina's throat, and she swallowed hard. "I don't—want to lose her."

Now, Reyna's grin was blinding. "And *there's* your choice. Love is nice, but the thing that ties Kianthe and me together? It's not our marriage, or our feelings. It's the choice. Every single day, we wake up and *decide* to stay together."

Serina wanted to marry Bobbie because, on some level, she figured it would ensure Bobbie would stay with her, always, despite future unrest and indecision. It was security. On the most basic level, if they were married, Bobbie couldn't leave.

And Serina wouldn't be alone.

That realization hit her like a brick.

"I'm . . . not doing this right, am I?" Serina's voice trembled. She always valued freedom—the wind in her sails, the expanse of the river, the ability to choose whether she was heading upstream or down.

Bobbie deserved that.

Reyna shrugged. "Right and wrong are fairly difficult to gauge. Every relationship is different. I know plenty of people who married for love, and plenty more who married for convenience. Most are doing just fine."

But Serina didn't want *just fine*. She wanted amazing, a romance for the ages, a relationship that she could look back on decades from now and feel so, so lucky that she got to experience this life.

She wanted someone who would choose to be with her every day.

Which meant she needed to give Bobbie the freedom to leave—and be prepared for those consequences.

"This helped, Reyna," Serina said, and meant it. "Thank you."

Reyna raised her mug in cheers. "Good luck, Serina. I think you'll both do just fine."

Serina grinned, and tapped her mug to Reyna's.

After the final meeting, Serina trudged back to her suite in the council building—only to find Bobbie perched outside the rooms.

The wooden hallways were lined with statues of plated armor and fancy outfits from centuries past. For a moment, Bobbie looked like one of them, dressed in her handmade diarn uniform. It took a moment for Serina's mind to register that was her *partner,* which was strange in and of itself.

Wellia was nowhere near Lathe, after all.

"Bobbie!" Serina adjusted her grip on the notes from their meetings. She had dozens of summary documents, action plans for food distribution, and even monetary compensation for skilled workers who visited Jallin or Mercon to aid recovery efforts. Her brain was swimming, which meant she had little else to say but "What are you doing here?"

Bobbie hesitated, fidgeting with the hem of her very fancy jacket. "Squirrel told me about your proposal plan. Uh, *plans.*"

All the blood drained from Serina's face. She suddenly felt hot *and* cold, embarrassment and humiliation mingling in a toxic cocktail that emptied her frazzled mind further. "Um— w-what are you talking about?" She laughed, then thought it felt forced and coughed instead.

"Serrie." Bobbie sounded pained.

Why would this cause her pain, unless . . .

She would have refused.

That was the only explanation—Bobbie heard about the proposals and *would have said no.*

Even though Serina wasn't planning on proposing any-more, even though she was just hoping for a nice, pleasant dis-cussion about choices and love, the realization still made her heart sink.

Because if Bobbie would have said no to getting married, she might still say no to staying together.

Serina's earlier determination faded fast. She hadn't really thought Bobbie would leave, given the choice, but . . . maybe that was shortsighted.

This was terrible. If they broke up now, would Serina have to move back onto the *Knot for Sail*? Could she still be a coun-cilmember, having to see her ex for status updates on the middle Nacean?

Who would she rescue kittens with, or kiss at night, or share tea with in silence in the early hours of the morning, when dew covered the grass and fog rolled off the Nacean and the redspars chirped in the distance?

Serina was carrying too many things. They were in a semi-public hallway. She couldn't deal with this right now. "I—I can't talk about this."

She pushed past Bobbie, fumbling to unlock the door, and ac-cidentally dropped a few folders of parchment. Bobbie scooped them up, silent.

Stars, this was the worst.

Serina bustled into the suite, dropping the paperwork on the table.

For a moment, it seemed like Bobbie might leave her alone, but she stepped inside as well and shut the door behind them.

To avoid her, Serina stared glumly out the window. The coun-cil building was one of the taller ones in Wellia, so her view of the rolling countryside beyond the city was extensive. It was late evening, and the sunset colored the sky red. She stepped around the room, lighting candles.

"Did you ride three days just to tell me that?" Serina finally asked.

Bobbie was still standing awkwardly by the door, her folders tucked under one arm. "Um . . . yes? I mean, I guess I felt bad. And sad. And frustrated."

"All wonderful responses to a potential proposal." Serina couldn't quell the sarcasm in her voice.

Bobbie winced.

And then she flipped the script.

"No, not about the proposal. About the fact that I kept *messing up* your proposals."

Wait.

"What do you mean?"

Bobbie ran a hand over her hair. It was tied in a tight ball on the top of her head, and she felt her scalp for wayward hairs. "I didn't *know*. If I had, of course I would have brought those kittens to the bay. You had a banner. You got Farley and Rankor there, and Pil and his kids. That must have taken so much planning!"

Anguish tilted her words.

Serina vaguely wondered how many scarves Bobbie had stress-crocheted on the ride here.

"It—it didn't take a *lot* of planning," Serina lied, sinking into a chair beside the desk.

"It took enough! The gesture was so, so nice. And I ruined it." Bobbie clenched her eyes shut, pacing now.

"You didn't—"

Bobbie cut her off. "I'm not good at recognizing cues, Serrie. I thought you just wanted to hike. I thought it was just a pleasant surprise our old crew came to visit. And then you invited me to Lathe, and the moment work popped up, I just cheerfully sent you on your way. I didn't even *ask* if you wanted to go. I just assumed you would."

"Well, this *was* important." Serina was still bitter about the timing, though.

"Important or not, I should have been more aware. You were going to propose in that field where we met, weren't you?"

Serina swallowed a laugh, ducking her head. "Maybe."

"Stars," Bobbie swore, striding across the room to pull her

into a hug. At this height, Serina was able to rest her head against Bobbie's chest, hear her heartbeat. It was thrumming faster than usual, which meant she was anxious over this.

They both were, clearly.

Best to clear things up while she could.

"If I gave you the choice, would you leave me?" Serina blurted.

Because that was the crux of this, wasn't it?

But instead of nodding along, instead of waving Serina off, her beautiful, stunning, fearsome partner reeled back, eyes widening. "Do you *want* me to?" The fearful tremor of her voice was unmistakable.

Relief slammed into Serina, and she sagged.

"No. Hells no, I don't want you to. But—but Reyna said it's a choice to be together, and I think I was proposing for the wrong reasons, and then I got scared that you might want to leave, and if you did, I'd be *so sad,* Bobbie."

This conversation was a mess. Then again, so were her emotions.

Bobbie massaged her forehead. "Wait. What are the *wrong* reasons for proposing?"

"I wanted to lock you down. Which is pretty ironic, considering if you tried to keep me somewhere I didn't want to be, I'd be very upset."

"Well, you're a retired pirate. Notoriously free-spirited." Bobbie carded her hands through Serina's short hair, still sounding perplexed. "I thought the purpose of marriage *was* to lock down your partner. Make it official?"

"Sure. But if I'm proposing to keep you from leaving me, that's fear-based. Reyna said we should be aiming for love-based."

Bobbie chuckled. "No offense, but we should stop going to Reyna for relationship advice. Our partnership isn't anything like hers and Kianthe's. It's uniquely *us.*" Bobbie paused, sounding embarrassed now. "And . . . I personally love the idea of being locked down."

Serina blinked, pulling back to meet her partner's eyes. "You do?"

"Yeah. It means you're mine, and I'm yours. No matter what, that won't change."

That was what Serina felt too.

She pushed to her feet, pulling her partner into a proper hug, a passionate kiss. When they separated, Serina whispered, "I want that. Lately, I've been feeling like our careers aren't compatible, and it makes me sad. Things are different now than when we were a constable and a pirate."

"More legal, certainly." Bobbie rolled her eyes. "But just because we have other duties and live in a big, fancy house doesn't mean we're not compatible. It doesn't mean we love each other less." She reached for Serina's hand, tracing the finger where a wedding band would be. "Reyna said it's a choice, right?"

"Yeah." Everywhere Bobbie touched felt soothing. Slowly, Serina's muscles untensed.

A smile tilted Bobbie's lips. Her words were contemplative:

"Maybe you propose for the wrong reasons, and I say yes for the wrong reasons—and then we keep making the choice every day to do better with our relationship. I think, eventually, those *wrong* reasons will prove to be right, after all."

That was such a lovely sentiment. Tears welled in Serina's eyes. She'd wanted a proposal to be perfect, but—well, perfect was overrated.

Maybe all they needed was their best.

She stepped back, dropping to one knee. The engagement ring was in her pocket as always, and she tugged it out of its leather satchel. The gold glinted in the setting sunlight, flickering with the candlelight.

Serina held the ring up to Bobbie.

"Since we're such a mess anyway, will you marry me, Diarn Bobbie of the Middle Nacean River and Lathe?"

It felt like the Stars themselves shone in Bobbie's eyes. She laughed, choked on the sound, and whispered, "Yes. Of course. Nothing would make me happier."

Serina wholeheartedly agreed.

She pushed to her feet, fit the ring on Bobbie's finger, and kissed her until they were breathless. Then they dropped to the couch by the suite's fireplace and kissed some more, and then dissolved into whispering about their hopes and dreams and tracing circles on each other's skin—and it was perfect.

Life with her favorite person sounded excellent. Even if it wasn't a fairy-tale romance, it was *theirs*.

Serina would savor every moment of it.

ACKNOWLEDGMENTS

It's the *final boooook,* duh nuh nuh nuh, duh nuh nah nah nuh, danuhanahnuhhhhh—

. . . ahem.

I'm a little shocked I made it to the end of a series. If you've been watching my progress with *This Gilded Abyss,* you'll know that finishing a series isn't my forte. But the Tomes and Tea series was so fun. It was such a delight to revisit Kianthe and Reyna and the world they live in, and watch how it changed through their actions. Every story felt faster than the last.

(I wrote this one in nine days. Did you know that?)

I think I'm still in awe that I'm allowed to write books full time, and it's all thanks to this series. I'm so, so grateful for all of it. Everyone who cheered me on over the decade I wrote before anyone knew me. Everyone who critiqued my writing, educated me on craft, joined me at coffee shops, and insisted that even though there wasn't a paycheck, writing was still a full-time job.

I'm grateful for the moment I finally started making money off this—after participating in an MFA and, by extension, joining TikTok. For the first time in my life, the world shifted around me, and suddenly I felt like I could actually accomplish the things I set out to do.

I'm incredibly grateful for the readers who found me along the way. Especially the ones who knew me from the beginning, and cheered me on the entire time. Without you, this series genuinely wouldn't exist.

And then, for my agent, who introduced me to Tor UK, who introduced me to Bramble, and who (combined) introduced my books back into the world. I've had the greatest experience the last couple years, and can't wait to see where the next few take us!

Thank you all so much for your support, guidance, and inspiration.

The Tomes and Tea series is over, but we're just getting started. Here's to many more stories about badass lesbians, sapphic love, and cozy adventure!

About the Author

REBECCA THORNE is a *USA Today,* Indie, and *Sunday Times* bestselling author, specializing in all things fantasy, sci-fi, and romantic. When she isn't writing (or avoiding writing), she's either working as a flight attendant or hiking with her wife and their dogs.